W9-CBH-698

THE YEAR OF SCIENCE FICTION

Every indication points to 1975 as a year in which science fiction will reach new heights in popularity. In times of transition and uncertainty, it is to science fiction that readers turn for that wide-angle lens that puts our personal problems in galactic perspective.

In presenting herewith our traditional annual selection of the best novelettes and short stories of the year, we find a certain optimism already being reflected.

Here you will find wonders by Isaac Asimov and George R. R. Martin, marvels by Gordon R. Dickson and Sydney Van Scyoc, and other enchantments by the best spinners of logical science fiction projections.

THE 1975 ANNUAL WORLD'S BEST SF is the first and the authentic best.

Available in the same series:

THE 1972 ANNUAL WORLD'S BEST SF
UY1081 $1.25

Featuring Arthur C. Clarke, Larry Niven, Theodore Sturgeon, Poul Anderson, Stephen Tall, and others.
A selection of the Science Fiction Book Club (U.S.A.) and the Literary Guild (Great Britain).

THE 1973 ANNUAL WORLD'S BEST SF
UQ1053   95¢

Featuring Frederik Pohl, Clifford D. Simak, Michael G. Coney, James Tiptree, Jr., and others.
A Selection of the Science Fiction Book Club (U.S.A.) and Victor Gollancz, Ltd. (Great Britain).

THE 1974 ANNUAL WORLD'S BEST SF
UY1109 $1.25

Featuring Harlan Ellison, Gordon Eklund, Robert Sheckley, Norman Spinrad, R. A. Lafferty, and others.
A Selection of the Science Fiction Book Club (U.S.A.) and The Elmfield Press, Ltd. (Great Britain).

THE 1975 ANNUAL WORLD'S BEST SF

Edited by

DONALD A. WOLLHEIM

with Arthur W. Saha

DAW BOOKS, INC.

DONALD A. WOLLHEIM, PUBLISHER

1301 Avenue of the Americas
New York, N. Y.   10019

Copyright ©, 1975, by DONALD A. WOLLHEIM

All Rights Reserved.

Cover art by Jack Gaughan.

DEDICATION

This one is for
TAIMI

FIRST PRINTING, MAY 1975

1 2 3 4 5 6 7 8 9

PRINTED IN U.S.A.

Table of Contents

Copyright © 1974 by Condé Nast Publications, Inc. By permission of the Author.

Copyright © 1974 by UPD Publishing Corp. By permission of the Author.

Copyright © 1974 by UPD Publishing Corp. By permission of the Scott Meredith Literary Agency, Inc.

Copyright © 1974 by Ultimate Publishing Co., Inc. By permission of the Author.

Copyright © 1974 by UPD Publishing Corp. By permission of Robert P. Mills, Ltd., on behalf of the Authors.

INTRODUCTION

Utopia ended two years ago. Unfortunately most of us didn't know we were living through the world's Utopian Age when it was on. For most of the world it did not exist then or now. But for some of the world, a small minority of people living in the United States and Western Europe, it was as near Utopia as human history had ever produced since the dawn of history—and may not produce again for a long, long time.

What we are saying is that the period of the Sixties represented the highest technological level of society ever achieved and the most unlimited expenditure of the planet's resources and energy for the whim and pleasure of those who could afford it. They represented perhaps ten per cent of the inhabitants of the U.S.A. and Canada, and a smaller percentage of people in Britain and the adjoining European areas. As for the rest, the vast majority, they received a few odd drippings from the overflowing table but mainly they had to keep on working to make ends meet and worrying about the same things that people have worried about since the rise of Sumeria.

But for those who had the money, it was a fabulous cornucopia of goodies to be squandered without thought. Even though no one spoke of it as such, future historians may well record the period as the first economic Utopia.

The first indication that the end was near was possibly the decision made by the U.S.A. not to build a supersonic passenger plane of the Concorde type and not to allow others to schedule commercial flights to our shores. It was the first step backward from the irresponsible advance of a luxury-bent and resource-careless society. The reasons given (at least those publicized) were the excessive use of fuel, the excessive pollution of the atmosphere, and the fact that too small a percentage of even the privileged sector would be able to afford it. The last argument was probably the real reason.

But this decision represented the first admission of a limitation on "progress" and thus marked the point at which this highest energy-squandering social order began its slide down-

hill. After that, the knowledge that the world's fuel reserves
were indeed limited began to seep into the public consciousness, along with the general realization that population growth
was reaching a danger level and that food availability was failing to match it. And in 1972 the feast ended. There's a lot of
squandering still going on, but the price is no longer right.

We know now that for the balance of this century we are
going to have to readjust to meet the true situation. We are coming down the slopes of Mount Utopia with increasing rapidity
and we are all busy trying to figure out what is to be done.

For science fiction this came as no surprise. As in the case
of the first men on the moon, science fiction had been there
long before, had discussed all the angles in depth, and gone
on. Future shock has never affected sf writers—it is a matter
only for those unfamiliar with the field of speculative fiction.

That the world was going to have to change its ways to con-
serve its resources; that a quest for new energy sources and
widened food development was on the agenda for this century;
these were all old elements of science fiction. Sf had worried
about everything in advance: safer atomic power, less or more
space flight, limitation of population, economic or military dis-
asters, a new Dark Age, or a new age of controlled stability.

Such things have all been the subjects of novels and short
stories and many and strange have been the accounts. Once
again the science fiction reader is confronted by his fantasies
becoming matter-of-fact daily news and the subject of political
conferences.

Then what are science fiction writers writing about this
year? Reading through the books and magazines of the past
year we have come up with an unexpected answer. They are
talking about Utopias. But not about human ones. They have
gone to the stars and are asking what sort of societies could
achieve harmony and prosperity—and can alien ways have
meaning for the temporarily sidetracked quest for a heaven-
on-Earth?

The best novelettes and short stories of the year, as selected
in this volume, all dwell in one way or another on this topic.
The choice was not deliberate—it worked out that way. Of the
ten tales here, a majority concern themselves with intelligent
species of alien spheres and their varieties of heaven-on-Else-
where.

If science fiction always precedes history by a dozen years,
then what its writers have been thinking about last year

should bode well for this troubled world. There is, they seem to say, light at the end of the tunnel.

At least, that's our interpretation.

—DONALD A. WOLLHEIM

A SONG FOR LYA

George R. R. Martin

The longing for unity and the desire for total understanding are dreams of every human being however much we may suppress them. Perhaps they are also dreams of all sentient beings and perhaps we shall find this to be so some far off day when at last we meet an intelligent species other than our own. But unity and harmony may be achieved in different ways . . . and in this memorable tale a rapidly rising name in sf writing shows us such a way.

The cities of the Shkeen are old, older far than man's, and the great rust-red metropolis that rose from their sacred hill country had proved to be the oldest of them all. The Shkeen city had no name. It needed none. Though they built cities and towns by the hundreds and the thousands, the hill city had no rivals. It was the largest in size and population, and it was alone in the sacred hills. It was their Rome, Mecca, Jerusalem; all in one. It was *the* city, and all Shkeen came to it at last, in the final days before Union.

That city had been ancient in the days before Rome fell, had been huge and sprawling when Babylon was still a dream. But there was no feel of age to it. The human eye saw only miles and miles of low, red-brick domes; small hummocks of dried mud that covered the rolling hills like a rash. Inside they were dim and nearly airless. The rooms were small and the furniture crude.

Yet it was not a grim city. Day after day it squatted in those scrubby hills, broiling under a hot sun that sat in the sky like a weary orange melon; but the city teemed with life: smells of cooking, the sounds of laughter and talk and children running, the bustle and sweat of brickmen repairing the domes, the bells of the Joined ringing in the streets. The Shkeen were a lusty and exuberant people, almost childlike. Certainly there was nothing about them that told of great age or ancient wisdom. This is a young race, said the signs, this is a culture in its infancy.

But that infancy had lasted more than fourteen thousand years.

The human city was the real infant, less than ten Earth years old. It was built on the edge of the hills, between the Shkeen metropolis and the dusty brown plains where the spaceport had gone up. In human terms, it was a beautiful city: open and airy, full of graceful archways and glistening fountains and wide boulevards lined by trees. The buildings were wrought of metal and colored plastic and native woods, and most of them were low in deference to Shkeen architecture. Most of them . . . the Administration Tower was the exception, a polished blue steel needle that split a crystal sky.

You could see it for miles in all directions. Lyanna spied it even before we landed, and we admired it from the air. The gaunt skyscrapers of Old Earth and Baldur were taller, and the fantastic webbed cities of Arachne were far more beautiful—but that slim blue Tower was still imposing enough as it rose unrivaled to its lonely dominance above the sacred hills.

The spaceport was in the shadow of the Tower, easy walking distance. But they met us anyway. A low-slung scarlet aircar sat purring at the base of the ramp as we disembarked, with a driver lounging against the stick. Dino Valcarenghi stood next to it, leaning on the door and talking to an aide.

Valcarenghi was the planetary administrator, the boy wonder of the sector. Young, of course, but I'd known that. Short, and good-looking, in a dark, intense way, with black hair that curled thickly against his head and an easy, genial smile.

He flashed us that smile then, when we stepped off the ramp, and reached to shake hands. "Hi," he began, "I'm glad to see you." There was no nonsense with formal introductions. He knew who we were, and we knew who he was, and Velcarenghi wasn't the kind of man who put much stock in ritual.

Lyanna took his hand lightly in hers, and gave him her vampire look: big, dark eyes opened wide and staring, then mouth lifted in a tiny faint smile. She's a small girl, almost waiflike, with short brown hair and a child's figure. She can look very fragile, very helpless. When she wants to. But she rattles people with that look. If they know Lya's a telepath, they figure she's poking around amid their innermost secrets. Actually she's playing with them. When Lyanna is *really* reading, her whole body goes stiff and you can almost see her tremble. And those big, soul-sucking eyes get narrow and hard and opaque.

But not many people know that, so they squirm under her vampire eyes and look the other way and hurry to release her hand. Not Valcarenghi, though. He just smiled and stared back, then moved on to me.

I *was* reading when I took his hand—my standard operating procedure. Also a bad habit, I guess, since it's put some promising friendships into an early grave. My talent isn't equal to Lya's. But it's not as demanding, either. I read emotions. Valcarenghi's geniality came through strong and genuine. With nothing behind it, or at least nothing that was close enough to the surface for me to catch.

We also shook hands with the aide, a middle-aged blond stork named Nelson Gourlay. Then Valcarenghi ushered everybody into the aircar and we took off. "I imagine you're tired," he said after we were airborne, "so we'll save the tour of the city and head straight for the Tower. Nelse will show you your quarters, then you can join us for a drink, and we'll talk over the problem. You've read the materials I sent?"

"Yes," I said. Lya nodded. "Interesting background, but I'm not sure why we're here."

"We'll get to that soon enough," Valcarenghi replied. "I ought to be letting you enjoy the scenery." He gestured toward the window, smiled, and fell silent.

So Lya and I enjoyed the scenery, or as much as we could enjoy during the five-minute flight from spaceport to tower. The aircar was whisking down the main street at treetop level, stiring up a breeze that whipped the thin branches as we went by. It was cool and dark in the interior of the car, but outside the Shkeen sun was riding toward noon, and you could see the heat waves shimmering from the pavement. The population must have been inside huddled around their air-conditioners, because we saw very little traffic.

We got out near the main entrance to the Tower and walked through a huge, sparkling-clean lobby. Valcarenghi left us then to talk to some underlings. Gourlay led us into one of the tubes and we shot up fifty floors. Then we waltzed past a secretary into another, private tube, and climbed some more.

Our rooms were lovely; carpeted in cool green, and paneled with wood. There was a complete library there, mostly Earth classics bound in synthaleather, with a few novels from Baldur, our home world. Somebody had been researching our tastes. One of the walls of the bedroom was tinted glass, giving a panoramic view of the city far below us, with a control that could darken it for sleeping.

Gourlay showed it to us dutifully, like a dour bellhop. I read him briefly though, and found no resentment. He was nervous, but only slightly. There was honest affection there for someone. Us? Valcarenghi?

Lya sat down on one of the twin beds. "Is someone bringing our luggage?" she asked.

Gourlay nodded. "You'll be well taken care of," he said. "Anything you want, ask."

"Don't worry, we will," I said. I dropped to the second bed, and gestured Gourlay to a chair. "How long you been here?"

"Six years," he said, taking the chair gratefully and sprawling out all over it. "I'm one of the veterans. I've worked under four administrators now. Dino, and Stuart before him, and Gustaffson before *him*. I was even under Rockwood a few months."

Lya perked up, crossing her legs under her and leaning forward. "That was all Rockwood lasted, wasn't it?"

"Right," Gourlay said. "He didn't like the planet, took a quick demotion to assistant administrator someplace else. I didn't care much, to tell the truth. He was the nervous type, always giving orders to prove who was boss."

"And Valcarenghi?" I asked.

Gourlay made a smile look like a yawn. "Dino? Dino's OK, the best of the lot. He's good, knows he's good. He's only been here two months, but he's gotten a lot done, and he's made a lot of friends. He treats the staff like people, calls everybody by his first name, all that stuff. People like that."

I was reading, and I read sincerity. It was Valcarenghi that Gourlay was affectionate toward, then. He believed what he was saying.

I had more questions, but I didn't get to ask them. Gourlay got up suddenly. "I really shouldn't stay," he said. "You want to rest, right? Come up to the top in about two hours and we'll go over things with you. You know where the tube is?"

We nodded, and Gourlay left. I turned to Lyanna. "What do you think?"

She lay back on the bed and considered the ceiling. "I don't know," she said. "I wasn't reading. I wonder why they've had so many administrators. And why they wanted us."

"We're Talented," I said, smiling. With the capital, yes. Lyanna and I have been tested and registered as psi Talents, and we have the licenses to prove it.

"Uh-huh," she said, turning on her side and smiling back at me. Not her vampire half-smile this time. Her sexy little girl smile.

"Valcarenghi wants us to get some rest," I said. "It's probably not a bad idea."

Lya bounced out of bed. "OK," she said, "but these twins
have got to go."

"We could push them together."

She smiled again. We pushed them together.

And we *did* get some sleep. Eventually.

Our luggage was outside the door when we woke. We
changed into fresh clothes, old casual stuff, counting on Valcarenghi's notorious lack of pomp. The tube took us to the top
of the Tower.

The office of the planetary administrator was hardly an office. There was no desk, none of the usual trappings. Just a bar
and lush blue carpets that swallowed us ankle-high, and six or
seven scattered chairs. Plus lots of space and sunlight, with
Shkea laid out at our feet beyond the tinted glass. All four
walls this time.

Valcarenghi and Gourlay were waiting for us, and Valcarenghi did the bartending chores personally. I didn't recognize
the beverage, but it was cool and spicy and aromatic, with a
real sting to it. I sipped it gratefully. For some reason I felt I
needed a lift.

"Shkeen wine," Valcarenghi said, smiling, in answer to an
unasked question. "They've got a name for it, but I can't pronounce it yet. But give me time. I've only been here two
months, and the language is rough."

"You're learning Shkeen?" Lya asked, surprised. I knew
why. Shkeen is rough on human tongues, but the natives
learned Terran with stunning ease. Most people accepted that
happily, and just forgot about the difficulties of cracking the
alien language.

"It gives me an insight into the way they think," Valcarenghi said. "At least that's the theory." He smiled.

I read him again, although it was more difficult. Physical
contact makes things sharper. Again, I got a simple emotion,
close to the surface—pride this time. With pleasure mixed in. I
chalked that up to the wine. Nothing beneath.

"However you pronounce the drink, I like it," I said.

"The Shkeen produce a wide variety of liquors and foodstuffs," Gourlay put in. "We've cleared many for export already, and we're checking others. Market should be good."

"You'll have a chance to sample more of the local produce
this evening," Valcarenghi said. "I've set up a tour of the city,

with a stop or two in Shkeentown. For a settlement of our size, our night life is fairly interesting. I'll be your guide."

"Sounds good," I said. Lya was smiling too. A tour was unusually considerate. Most Normals feel uneasy around Talents, so they rush us in to do whatever they want done, then rush us out again as quickly as possible. They certainly don't socialize with us.

"Now—the problem," Valcarenghi said, lowering his drink and leaning forward in the chair. "You read about the Cult of the Union?"

"A Shkeen religion," Lya said.

"*The* Shkeen religion," corrected Valcarenghi. "Every one of them is a believer. This is a planet without heretics."

"We read the materials you sent on it," Lya said. "Along with everything else."

"What do you think?"

I shrugged. "Grim. Primitive. But no more than any number of others I've read about. The Shkeen aren't very advanced, after all. There were religions on Old Earth that included human sacrifice."

Valcarenghi shook his head, and looked toward Gourlay.

"No, you don't understand," Gourlay started, putting his drink down on the carpet. "I've been studying their religion for six years. It's like no other in history. Nothing on Old Earth like it, no sir. Nor in any other race we've encountered.

"And Union, well, it's wrong to compare it to human sacrifice, just wrong. The Old Earth religions sacrificed one or two unwilling victims to appease their gods. Killed a handful to get mercy for the millions. And the handful generally protested. The Shkeen don't work it that way. The Greeshka takes *everyone*. And they go willingly. Like lemmings they march off to the caves to be eaten alive by those parasites. *Every* Shkeen is Joined at forty, and goes to Final Union before he's fifty."

I was confused. "All right," I said. "I see the distinction, I guess. But so what? Is this the problem? I imagine that Union is rough on the Shkeen, but that's their business. Their religion is no worse than the ritual cannibalism of the Hrangans, is it?"

Valcarenghi finished his drink and got up, heading for the bar. As he poured himself a refill, he said, almost casually, "As far as I know, Hrangan cannibalism has claimed no human converts."

Lya looked startled. I felt startled. I sat up and stared. "What?"

Valcarenghi headed back to his seat, glass in hand. "Human converts have been joining the Cult of the Union. Dozens of them are already Joined. None of them have achieved full Union yet, but that's only a question of time." He sat down, and looked at Gourlay. So did we.

The gangling blond aide picked up the narrative. "The first convert was about seven years ago. Nearly a year before I got here, two and a half after Shkea was discovered and the settlement built. Guy named Magly. Psi-psych, worked closely with the Shkeen. He was it for two years. Then another in '08, more the next year. And the rate's been climbing ever since. There was one big one. Phil Gustaffson."

Lya blinked. "The planetary administrator?"

"The same," said Gourlay. "We've had a lot of administrators. Gustaffson came in after Rockwood couldn't stand it. He was a big, gruff old guy. Everybody loved him. He'd lost his wife and kids on his last assignment, but you'd never have known it. He was always hearty, full of fun. Well, he got interested in the Shkeen religion, started talking to them. Talked to Magly and some of the other converts too. Even went to see a Greeshka. That shook him up real bad for a while. But finally he got over it, went back to his researches. I worked with him, but I never guessed what he had in mind. A little over a year ago, he converted. He's Joined now. Nobody's ever been accepted that fast. I hear talk in Shkeentown that he may even be admitted to Final Union, rushed right in. Well, Phil was administrator here longer than anybody else. People liked him, and when he went over, a lot of his friends followed. The rate's way up now."

"Not quite one percent, and rising," Valcarenghi said. "That seems low, but remember what it means. One percent of the people in my settlement are choosing a religion that includes a very unpleasant form of suicide."

Lya looked from him to Gourlay and back again. "Why hasn't this been reported?"

"It should have been," Valcarenghi said. "But Stuart succeeded Gustaffson, and he was scared stiff of a scandal. There's no law against humans adopting an alien religion, so Stuart defined it as a nonproblem. He reported the conversion rate routinely, and nobody higher up ever bothered to make the correlation and remember just what all these people were converting *to*."

I finished my drink, set it down. "Go on," I said to Valcarenghi.

"I define the situation as a problem," he said. "I don't care how few people are involved, the idea that human beings would allow the Greeshka to consume them alarms me. I've had a team of psychs on it since I took over, but they're getting nowhere. I needed Talent. I want you two to find out *why* these people are converting. Then I'll be able to deal with the situation."

The problem was strange, but the assignment seemed straightforward enough. I read Valcarenghi to be sure. His emotions were a bit more complex this time, but not much. Confidence above all: he was sure we could handle the problem. There was honest concern there, but no fear, and not even a hint of deception. Again, I couldn't catch anything below the surface. Valcarenghi kept his hidden turmoil well hidden, if he had any.

I glanced at Lyanna. She was sitting awkwardly in her chair, and her fingers were wrapped very tightly around her wine glass. Reading. Then she loosened up and looked my way and nodded.

"All right," I said. "I think we can do it."

Valcarenghi smiled. "That I never doubted," he said. "It was only a question of whether you *would*. But enough of business for tonight. I've promised you a night on the town, and I always try to deliver on my promises. I'll meet you downstairs in the lobby in a half-hour."

Lya and I changed into something more formal back in our room. I picked a dark blue tunic, with white slacks and a matching mesh scarf. Not the height of fashion, but I was hoping that Shkea would be several months behind the times. Lya slipped into a silky white skintight with a tracery of thin blue lines that flowed over her in sensuous patterns in response to her body heat. The lines were definitely lecherous, accentuating her thin figure with a singleminded determination. A blue raincape completed the outfit.

"Valcarenghi's funny," she said as she fastened it.

"Oh?" I was struggling with the sealseam on my tunic, which refused to seal. "You catch something when you read him?"

"No," she said. She finished attaching the cape and admired herself in the mirror. Then she spun toward me, the cape swirling behind her. "That's it. He was thinking what he was saying. Oh, variations in the wording, of course, but nothing important. His mind was on what we were discussing, and behind that there was only a wall." She smiled. "Didn't get a single one of his deep dark secrets."

I finally conquered the sealseam. "Tsk," I said. "Well, you get another chance tonight."

That got me a grimace. "The hell I do. I don't read people on offtime. It isn't fair. Besides, it's such a strain. I wish I could catch thoughts as easily as you do feelings."

"The price of Talent," I said. "You're more Talented, your price is higher." I rummaged in our luggage for a raincape, but I didn't find anything that went well, so I decided not to wear one. Capes were out, anyway. "I didn't get much on Valcarenghi either. You could have told as much by watching his face. He must be a very disciplined mind. But I'll forgive him. He serves good wine."

Lya nodded. "Right! That stuff did me good. Got rid of the headache I woke up with."

"The altitude," I suggested. We headed for the door.

The lobby was deserted, but Valcarenghi didn't keep us waiting long. This time he drove his own aircar, a battered black job that had evidently been with him for a while. Gourlay wasn't the sociable type, but Valcarenghi had a woman with him, a stunning auburn-haired vision named Laurie Blackburn. She was even younger than Valcarenghi—mid-twenties, by the look of her.

It was sunset when we took off. The whole far horizon was a gorgeous tapestry in red and orange, and a cool breeze was blowing in from the plains. Valcarenghi left the coolers off and opened the car windows, and we watched the city darken into twilight as we drove.

Dinner was at a plush restaurant with Baldurian decor—to make us feel comfortable, I guessed. The food, however, was very cosmopolitan. The spices, the herbs, the *style* of cooking were all Baldur. The meats and vegetables were native. It made for an interesting combination. Valcarenghi ordered for all four of us, and we wound up sampling about a dozen different dishes. My favorite was a tiny Shkeen bird that they cooked in soustang sauce. There wasn't very much of it, but what there was tasted great. We also polished off three bottles of wine during the meal: more of the Shkeen stuff we'd sampled that afternoon, a flask of chilled Veltaar from Baldur, and some real Old Earth Burgundy.

The talk warmed up quickly; Valcarenghi was a born story-teller and an equally good listener. Eventually, of course, the conversation got around to Shkea and the Shkeen. Laurie led it there. She'd been on Shkea for about six months, working toward an advanced degree in extee anthropology. She was trying to discover why the Shkeen civilization had remained frozen for so many millennia.

"They're older than we are, you know," she told us. "They

had cities before men were using tools. It should have been space-traveling Shkeen that stumbled on primitive men, not the other way around."

"Aren't there theories on that already?" I asked.

"Yes, but none of them are universally accepted," she said. "Cullen cites a lack of heavy metals, for example. A factor, but is it the *whole* answer? Von Hamrin claims the Shkeen didn't get enough competition. No big carnivores on the planet, so there was nothing to breed aggressiveness into the race. But he's come under a lot of fire. Shkea isn't all *that* idyllic; if it were, the Shkeen never would have reached their present level. Besides, what's the Greeshka if not a carnivore? It *eats* them, doesn't it?"

"What do you think?" Lya asked.

"I think it had something to do with the religion, but I haven't worked it all out yet. Dino's helping me talk to people and the Shkeen are open enough, but research isn't easy." She stopped suddenly and looked at Lya hard. "For me, anyway. I imagine it'd be easier for you."

We'd heard that before. Normals often figure that Talents have unfair advantages, which is perfectly understandable. We do. But Laurie wasn't resentful. She delivered her statement in a wistful, speculative tone, instead of etching it in verbal acid.

Valcarenghi leaned over and put an arm around her. "Hey," he said. "Enough shop talk. Robb and Lya shouldn't be worrying about the Shkeen until tomorrow."

Laurie looked at him, and smiled tentatively. "OK," she said lightly. "I get carried away. Sorry."

"That's OK," I told her. "It's an interesting subject. Give us a day and we'll probably be getting enthusiastic too."

Lya nodded agreement, and added that Laurie would be the first to know if our work turned up anything that would support her theory. I was hardly listening. I know it's not polite to read Normals when you're out with them socially, but there are times I can't resist. Valcarenghi had his arm around Laurie and had pulled her toward him gently. I was curious.

So I took a quick, guilty reading. He was very high—slightly drunk, I guess, and feeling very confident and protective. The master of the situation. But Laurie was a jumble—uncertainty, repressed anger, a vague fading hint of fright. And love, confused but very strong. I doubted that it was for me or Lya. She loved Valcarenghi.

I reached under the table, searching for Lya's hand, and found her knee. I squeezed it gently and she looked at me and smiled. She wasn't reading, which was good. It bothered me that Laurie loved Valcarenghi, though I didn't know why, and I was just as glad that Lya didn't see my discontent.

We finished off the last of the wine in short order, and Valcarenghi took care of the whole bill. Then he rose. "Onward!" he announced. "The night is fresh, and we've got visits to make."

So we made visits. No holoshows or anything that drab, although the city had its share of theaters. A casino was next on the list. Gambling was legal on Shkea, of course, and Valcarenghi would have legalized it if it weren't. He supplied the chips and I lost some for him, as did Laurie. Lya was barred from playing; her Talent was too strong. Valcarenghi won big; he was a superb mindspin player, and pretty good at the traditional games too.

Then came a bar. More drinks, plus local entertainment which was better than I would have expected.

It was pitch-black when we got out, and I assumed that the expedition was nearing its end. Valcarenghi surprised us. When we got back to the car, he reached under the controls, pulled out a box of sober-ups, and passed them around.

"Hey," I said. "You're driving. Why do I need this? I just barely got up here."

"I'm about to take you to a genuine Shkeen cultural event, Robb," he said. "I don't want you making rude comments or throwing up on the natives. Take your pill."

I took my pill, and the buzz in my head began to fade. Valcarenghi already had the car airborne. I leaned back and put my arm around Lya, and she rested her head on my shoulder. "Where are we going?" I asked.

"Shkeentown," he replied, never looking back, "to their Great Hall. There's a Gathering tonight, and I figured you'd be interested."

"It will be in Shkeen, of course," Laurie said, "but Dino can translate for you. I know a little of the language too, and I'll fill in whatever he misses."

Lya looked excited. We'd read about Gatherings, of course, but we hardly expected to see one on our first day on Shkea. The Gatherings were a species of religious rite; a mass confessional of sorts for pilgrims who were about to be admitted to the ranks of the Joined. Pilgrims swelled the hill city daily, but Gatherings were conducted only three or four times a year when the numbers of those-about-to-be-Joined climbed high enough.

The aircar streaked almost soundlessly through the brightly-lit settlement, passing huge fountains that danced with a dozen colors and pretty ornamental arches that flowed like liquid fire. A few other cars were airborne, and here and there we flew above pedestrians strolling the city's broad malls. But most people were inside, and light and music flooded from many of the homes we passed.

Then, abruptly, the character of the city began to change. The level ground began to roll and heave, hills rose before us and then behind us, and the lights vanished. Below, the malls gave way to unlit roads of crushed stone and dust, and the domes of glass and metal done in fashionable mock-Shkeen yielded to their older brick brothers. The Shkeen city was quieter than its human counterpart; most of the houses were darkly silent.

Then, ahead of us, a hummock appeared that was larger than the others—almost a hill in itself, with a big arched door and a series of slit-like windows. And light leaked from this one, and noise, and there were Shkeen outside.

I suddenly realized that, although I'd been on Shkea for nearly a day, this was the first sight I'd caught of the Shkeen. Not that I could see them all that clearly from an aircar at night. But I did see them. They were smaller than men—the tallest was around five feet—with big eyes and long arms. That was all I could tell from above.

Valcarenghi put the car down alongside the Great Hall, and we piled out. Shkeen were trickling through the arch from several directions, but most of them were already inside. We joined the trickle, and nobody even looked twice at us, except for one character who hailed Valcarenghi in a thin, squeaky voice and called him Dino. He had friends even here.

The interior was one huge room, with a great crude platform built in the center and an immense crowd of Shkeen circling it. The only light was from torches that were stuck in grooves along the walls, and on high poles surrounding the platform. Soneone was speaking, and every one of those great, bulging eyes was turned his way. We four were the only humans in the Hall.

The speaker, outlined brightly by the torches, was a fat, middle-aged Shkeen who moved his arms slowly, almost hypnotically, as he talked. His speech was a series of whistles, wheezes, and grunts, so I didn't listen very closely. He was much too far away to read. I was reduced to studying his appearance, and that of other Shkeen near me. All of them were hairless, as far as I could see, with softish-looking orange skin that was creased by a thousand tiny wrinkles. They wore simple shifts of crude, multicolored cloth, and I had difficulty telling male from female.

Valcarenghi leaned over toward me and whispered, careful to keep his voice low. "The speaker is a farmer," he said. "He's telling the crowd how far he's come, and some of the hardships of his life."

I looked around. Valcarenghi's whisper was the only sound in the place. Everyone else was dead quiet, eyes riveted on the platform, scarcely breathing. "He's saying that he has four brothers," Valcarenghi told me. "Two have gone on to Final Union, one is among the Joined. The other is younger than himself, and now owns the farm." He frowned. "The speaker will never see his farm again," he said, more loudly, "but he's happy about it."

"Bad crops?" asked Lya, smiling irreverently. She'd been listening to the same whisper. I gave her a stern look.

The Shkeen went on. Valcarenghi stumbled after him. "Now he's telling his crimes, all the things he's done that he's ashamed of, his blackest soul-secrets. He's had a sharp tongue at times, he's vain, once he actually struck his younger brother. Now he speaks of his wife, and the other women he has known. He has betrayed her many times, copulating with others. As a boy, he mated with animals for he feared females. In recent years he has grown incapable, and his brother has serviced his wife."

On and on and on it went, in incredible detail, detail that was both startling and frightening. No intimacy went untold, no secret was left undisturbed. I stood and listened to Valcarenghi's whispers, shocked at first, finally growing bored with the squalor of it all. I began to get restless. I wondered briefly if I knew any human half so well as I now knew this great fat Shkeen. Then I wondered whether Lyanna, with her Talent, knew anyone half so well. It was almost as if the speaker wanted all of us to live through his life right here and now.

His speech lasted for what seemed hours, but finally it began to wind up. "He speaks now of Union," Valcarenghi whispered. "He will be Joined, he is joyful about it, he has craved it for so long. His misery is at an end, his aloneness will cease, soon he shall walk the streets of the sacred city and peal his joy with the bells. And then Final Union, in the years to come. He will be with his brothers in the afterlife."

"No, Dino." This whisper was Laurie. "Quit wrapping human phrases around what he says. He will be his brothers, he says. The phrase also implies they will be him."

Valcarenghi smiled. "OK, Laurie. If you say so . . ."

Suddenly the fat farmer was gone from the platform. The crowd rustled, and another figure took his place: much shorter, wrinkled excessively, one eye a great gaping hole. He began to speak, haltingly at first, then with greater skill.

"This one is a brickman, he has worked many domes, he lives in the sacred city. His eye was lost many years ago, when he fell from a dome and a sharp stick poked into him. The pain was very great, but he returned to work within a year, he did not beg for premature Union, he was very brave, he is proud of his courage. He has a wife, but they have never had offspring, he is sad of that, he cannot talk to his wife easily, they are apart even when together and she weeps at night, he is sad of that too, but he has never hurt her and . . ."

It went on for hours again. My restlessness stirred again, but I cracked down on it—this was too important. I let myself get lost in Valcarenghi's narration, and the story of the one-eyed Shkeen. Before long, I was riveted as closely to the tale as the aliens around me. It was hot and stuffy and all but airless in the dome, and my tunic was getting sooty and soaked by sweat, some of it from the creatures who pressed around me. But I hardly noticed.

The second speaker ended as had the first, with a long praise of the joy of being Joined and the coming of Final Union. Toward the end, I hardly even needed Valcarenghi's translation—I could hear the happiness in the voice of the Shkeen, and see it in his trembling figure. Or maybe I was reading, unconsciously. But I can't read at that distance—unless the target is emoting very hard.

A third speaker ascended the platform, and spoke in a voice louder than the others. Valcarenghi kept pace. "A woman this time," he said. "She has carried eight children for her man, she has four sisters and three brothers, she has farmed all her life, she . . ."

Suddenly her speech seemed to peak, and she ended a long sequence with several sharp, high whistles. Then she fell silent. The crowd, as one, began to respond with whistles of their own. An eerie, echoing music filled the Great Hall, and the Shkeen around us all began to sway and whistle. The woman looked out at the scene from a bent and broken position.

Valcarenghi started to translate, but he stumbled over something. Laurie cut in before he could backtrack. "She has now told them of great tragedy," she whispered. "They whistle to show their grief, their oneness with her pain."

"Sympathy, yes," said Valcarenghi, taking over again. "When she was young, her brother grew ill, and seemed to be dying. Her parents told her to take him to the sacred hills, for they could not leave the younger children. But she shattered a wheel on her cart through careless driving, and her brother died upon the plains. He perished without Union. She blames herself."

The Shkeen had begun again. Laurie began to translate, leaning close to us and using a soft whisper. "Her brother died, she is saying again. She faulted him, denied him Union, now he is sundered and alone and gone without . . . without . . ."

"Afterlife," said Valcarenghi. "Without afterlife."

"I'm not sure that's entirely right," Laurie said. "That concept is . . ."

Valcarenghi waved her silent. "Listen," he said. He continued to translate.

We listened to her story, told in Valcarenghi's increasingly hoarse whisper. She spoke longest of all, and her story was the grimmest of the three. When she finished, she too was replaced. But Valcarenghi put a hand on my shoulder and beckoned toward the exit.

The cool night air hit like ice water, and I suddenly realized that I was drenched with sweat. Valcarenghi walked quickly toward the car. Behind us, the speaking was still in progress, and the Shkeen showed no signs of tiring.

"Gatherings go on for days, sometimes weeks," Laurie told us as we climbed inside the aircar. "The Shkeen listen in shifts, more or less—they try terribly to hear every word, but exhaustion gets to them sooner or later and they retire for brief rests, then return for more. It is a great honor to last through an entire Gathering without sleep."

Valcarenghi shot us aloft. "I'm going to try that someday," he said. "I've never attended for more than a couple of hours, but I think I could make it if I fortified myself with drugs. We'll get more understanding between human and Shkeen if we participate more fully in their rituals."

"Oh," I said. "Maybe Gustaffson felt the same way."

Valcarenghi laughed lightly. "Yes, well, I don't intend to participate *that* fully."

The trip home was a tired silence. I'd lost track of time but my body insisted that it was almost dawn. Lya, curled up under my arm, looked drained and empty and only half-awake. I felt the same way.

We left the aircar in front of the Tower, and took the tubes up. I was past thinking. Sleep came very, very quickly.

I dreamed that night. A good dream, I think, but it faded

with the coming of the light, leaving me empty and feeling cheated. I lay there, after waking, with my arm around Lya and my eyes on the ceiling, trying to recall what the dream had been about. But nothing came.

Instead, I found myself thinking about the Gathering, running it through again in my head. Finally I disentangled myself and climbed out of bed. We'd darkened the glass, so the room was still pitchblack. But I found the controls easily enough, and let through a trickle of late morning light.

Lya mumbled some sort of sleepy protest and rolled over, but made no effort to get up. I left her alone in the bedroom and went out to our library, looking for a book on the Shkeen —something with a little more detail than the material we'd been sent. No luck. The library was meant for recreation, not research.

I found a viewscreen and punched up to Valcarenghi's office. Gourlay answered. "Hello," he said. "Dino figured you'd be calling. He's not here right now. He's out arbitrating a trade contract. What do you need?"

"Books," I said, my voice still a little sleepy. "Something on the Shkeen."

"That I can't do," Gourlay said. "Are none, really. Lots of papers and studies and monographs, but no full-fledged books. I'm going to write one, but I haven't gotten to it yet. Dino figured I could be your resource, I guess."

"Oh."

"Got any questions?"

I searched for a question, found none. "Not really," I said, shrugging. "I just wanted general background, maybe some more information on Gatherings."

"I can talk to you about that later," Gourlay said. "Dino figured you'd want to get to work today. We can bring people to the Tower, if you'd like, or you can get out to them."

"We'll go out," I said quickly. Bringing subjects in for interviews fouls up everything. They get all anxious, and that covers up any emotions I might want to read, and they *think* on different things, too, so Lyanna has trouble.

"Fine," said Gourlay. "Dino put an aircar at your disposal. Pick it up down in the lobby. Also, they'll have some keys for you, so you can come straight up here to the office without bothering with the secretaries and all."

"Thanks," I said. "Talk to you later." I flicked off the viewscreen and walked back to the bedroom.

Lya was sitting up, the covers around her waist. I sat down

next to her and kissed her. She smiled, but didn't respond. "Hey," I said. "What's wrong?"

"Headache," she replied. "I thought sober-ups were supposed to get rid of hangovers."

"That's the theory. Mine worked pretty well." I went to the closet and began looking for something to wear. "We should have headache pills around here someplace. I'm sure Dino wouldn't forget anything that obvious."

"Umpf. Yes. Throw me some clothes."

I grabbed one of her coveralls and tossed it across the room. Lya stood up and slipped into it while I dressed, then went off to the washroom.

"Better," she said. "You're right, he didn't forget medicines."

"He's the thorough sort."

She smiled. "I guess. Laurie knows the language better, though. I read her. Dino made a couple of mistakes in that translation last night."

I'd guessed at something like that. No discredit to Valcarenghi; he was working on a four-month handicap, from what they'd said. I nodded. "Read anything else?"

"No. I tried to get those speakers, but the distance was too much." She came up and took my hand. "Where are we going today?"

"Shkeentown," I said. "Let's try to find some of these Joined. I didn't notice any at the Gathering."

"No. Those things are for Shkeen about-to-be-Joined."

"So I hear. Let's go."

We went. We stopped at the fourth level for a late breakfast in the Tower cafeteria, then got our aircar pointed out to us by a man in the lobby. A sporty green four-seater, very common, very inconspicuous.

I didn't take the aircar all the way into the Shkeen city, figuring we'd get more of the feel of the place if we went through on foot. So I dropped down just beyond the first range of hills, and we walked.

The human city had seemed almost empty, but Shkeentown lived. The crushed-rock streets were full of aliens, hustling back and forth busily, carrying loads of bricks and baskets of fruit and clothing. There were children everywhere, most of them naked; fat balls of orange energy that ran around us in circles, whistling and grunting and grinning, tugging at us every once in a while. The kids looked different from the adults. They had a few patches of reddish hair, for one thing, and their skins were still smooth and unwrinkled. They were the only ones who really paid any attention to us. The adult Shkeen just went about their business, and gave us an occasional friendly smile. Humans were obviously not all that uncommon in the streets of Shkeentown.

Most of the traffic was on foot, but small wooden carts were also common. The Shkeen draft animal looked like a big green dog that was about to be sick. They were strapped to the carts in pairs, and they whined constantly as they pulled. So, naturally, men called them whiners. In addition to whining, they also defecated constantly. That, with odors from the food peddled in baskets and the Shkeen themselves, gave the city a definite pungency.

There was noise too, a constant clamor. Kids whistling. Shkeen talking loudly with grunts and whimpers and squeaks, whiners whining and their carts rattling over the rocks. Lya and I walked through it all silently, hand in hand, watching and listening and smelling and . . . reading.

I was wide open when I entered Shkeentown, letting everything wash over me as I walked, unfocused but receptive. I was the center of a small bubble of emotion—feelings rushed up at me as Shkeen approached, faded as they walked away, circled around and around with the dancing children. I swam in a sea of impressions. And it startled me.

It startled me because it was all so familiar. I'd read aliens before. Sometimes it was difficult, sometimes it was easy, but it was never pleasant. The Hrangans have sour minds, rank with hate and bitterness, and I feel unclean when I come out. The Fyndii feel emotions so palely that I can scarcely read them at all. The Damoosh are . . . *different.* I read them strongly, but I can't find names for the feelings I read.

But the Shkeen—it was like walking down a street on Baldur. No, wait—more like one of the Lost Colonies, when a human settlement has fallen back into barbarism and forgotten its origins. Human emotions rage there, primal and strong and real, but less sophisticated than on Old Earth or Baldur. The Shkeen were like that: primitive, maybe, but very understandable. I read joy and sorrow, envy, anger, whimsy, bitterness, yearning, pain. The same heady mixture that engulfs me everywhere, when I open myself to it.

Lya was reading, too. I felt her hand tense in mine. After a while, it softened again. I turned to her, and she saw the question in my eyes.

"They're people," she said. "They're like us."

I nodded. "Parallel evolution, maybe. Shkea might be an

older Earth, with a few minor differences. But you're right. They're more human than any other race we've encountered in space." I considered that. "Does that answer Dino's question? If they're like us, it follows that their religion would be more appealing than a *really* alien one."

"No, Robb," Lya said. "I don't think so. Just the reverse. If they're like us, it doesn't make sense that *they'd* go off so willingly to die. See?"

She was right, of course. There was nothing suicidal in the emotions I'd read, nothing unstable, nothing really abnormal. Yet every one of the Shkeen went off to Final Union in the end.

"We should focus on somebody," I said. "This blend of thought isn't getting us anywhere." I looked around to find a subject, but just then I heard the bells begin.

They were off to the left somewhere, nearly lost in the city's gentle roar. I tugged Lya by the hand, and we ran down the street to find them, turning left at the first gap in the orderly row of domes.

The bells were still ahead, and we kept running, cutting through what must have been somebody's yard, and climbing over a low bush-fence that bristled with sweethorns. Beyond that was another yard, a dung-pit, more domes, and finally a street. It was there we found the bell-ringers.

There were four of them, all Joined, wearing long gowns of bright red fabric that trailed in the dust, with great bronze bells in either hand. They rang the bells constantly, their long arms swinging back and forth, the sharp, clanging notes filling the street. All four were elderly, as Shkeen go—hairless and pinched up with a million tiny wrinkles. But they smiled very widely, and the younger Shkeen that passed smiled at them.

On their heads rode the Greeshka.

I'd expected to find the sight hideous. I didn't. It was faintly disquieting, but only because I knew what it meant. The parasites were bright blobs of crimson goo, ranging in size from a pulsing wart on the back of one Shkeen skull to a great sheet of dripping, moving red that covered the head and shoulders of the smallest like a living cowl. The Greeshka lived by sharing the nutrients in the Shkeen bloodstream, I knew.

And also by slowly—oh so slowly—consuming its host.

Lya and I stopped a few yards from them, and watched them ring. Her face was solemn, and I think mine was. All of the others were smiling, and the songs that the bells sang were songs of joy. I squeezed Lyanna's hand tightly. "Read," I whispered.

We read.

Me: I read bells. Not the sound of bells, no, no, but the *feel* of bells, the *emotion* of bells, the bright clanging joy, the hooting-shouting-ringing loudness, the song of the Joined, the togetherness and the sharing of it all. I read what the Joined felt as they pealed their bells, their happiness and anticipation, their ecstasy in telling others of their clamorous contentment. And I read love, coming from them in great hot waves, passionate possessive love of a man and woman together, not the weak watery affection of the human who "loves" his brothers. This was real and fervent and it burned almost as it washed over me and surrounded me. They loved themselves, and they loved all Shkeen, and they loved the Greeshka, and they loved each other, and they loved us. They loved us. They loved *me,* as hotly and wildly as Lya loved me. And with love I read belonging, and sharing. They four were all apart, all distinct, but they thought as one almost, and they belonged to each other, and they belonged to the Greeshka, and they were all *together* and linked although each was still himself and none could read the others as I read them.

And Lyanna? I reeled back from them, and shut myself off, and looked at Lya. She was white-faced, but smiling. "They're beautiful," she said, her voice very small and soft and wondering. Drenched in love, I still remembered how much I loved *her,* and how I was a part of her and she of me.

"What—what did you read?" I asked, my voice fighting the continued clangor of the bells.

She shook her head, as if to clear it. "They love us," she said. "You must know that, but oh, I felt it, they *do* love us. And it's so *deep.* Below that love there's more love, and below that more, and on and on forever. Their minds are so deep, so open. I don't think I've ever read a human that deeply. Everything is right at the surface, right there, their whole lives and all their dreams and feelings and memories and oh—I just took it in, swept it up with a reading, a glance. With men, with humans, it's so much work, I have to dig, I have to fight, and even then I don't get down very far. You know, Robb, you know. Oh, *Robb!*" And she came to me and pressed tight against me, and I held her in my arms. The torrent of feeling that had washed over me must have been a tidal wave for her. Her Talent was broader and deeper than mine, and now she was shaken. I read her as she clutched me, and I read love, great love, and wonder and happiness, but also fear, nervous fear swirling through it all.

Around us, the ringing suddenly stopped. The bells, one by one, ceased to swing, and the four Joined stood in silence for a brief second. One of the other Shkeen nearby came up to them with a huge, cloth-covered basket. The smallest of the Joined threw back the cloth, and the aroma of hot meatrolls rose in the street. Each of the Joined took several from the basket, and before long they were all crunching away happily, and the owner of the rolls was grinning at them. Another Shkeen, a small nude girl, ran up and offered them a flask of water, and they passed it around without comment.

"What's going on?" I asked Lya. Then, even before she told me, I remembered. Something from the literature that Valcarenghi had sent. The Joined did no work. Forty Earth-years they lived and toiled, but from First Joining to Final Union there was only joy and music, and they wandered the streets and rang their bells and talked and sang, and other Shkeen gave them food and drink. It was an honor to feed a Joined, and the Shkeen who had given up his meatrolls was radiating pride and pleasure.

"Lya," I whispered, "can you read them now?"

She nodded against my chest and pulled away and stared at the Joined, her eyes going hard and then softening again. She looked back at me. "It's different," she said, curious.

"How?"

She squinted in puzzlement. "I don't know. I mean, they still love us, and all. But now their thoughts are, well, sort of more human. There are levels, you know, and digging isn't easy, and there are hidden things, things they hide even from themselves. It's not all open like it was. They're thinking about the food now and how good it tastes. It's all very vivid. I could taste the rolls myself. But it's not the same."

I had an inspiration. "How many minds are there?"

"Four," she said. "Linked somehow, I think. But not really." She stopped, confused, and shook her head. "I mean, they sort of feel each other's emotions, like you do, I guess. But not thoughts, not the detail. I can read them, but they don't read each other. Each one is distinct. They were closer before, when they were ringing, but they were always individuals."

I was slightly disappointed. "Four minds then, not one?"

"Umpf, yes. Four."

"And the Greeshka?" My other bright idea. If the Greeshka had minds of their own . . .

"Nothing," Lya said. "Like reading a plant, or a piece of clothing. Not even yes-I-live."

That was disturbing. Even lower animals had some vague consciousness of life—the feeling Talents called yes-I-live—usually only a dim spark that it took a major Talent to see. But Lya *was* a major Talent.

"Let's talk to them," I said. She nodded, and we walked up to where the Joined were munching their meatrolls. "Hello," I said awkwardly, wondering how to address them. "Can you speak Terran?"

Three of them looked at me without comprehension. But the fourth one, the little one whose Greeshka was a rippling red cape, bobbed his head up and down. "Yesh," he said, in a piping-thin voice.

I suddenly forgot what I was going to ask, but Lyanna came to my rescue. "Do you know of human Joined?" she said.

He grinned. "All Joined are one," he said.

"Oh," I said. "Well, yes, but do you know any who look like us? Tall, you know, with hair and skin that's pink or brown or something?" I came to another awkward halt, wondering just how *much* Terran the old Shkeen knew, and eyeing his Greeshka a little apprehensively.

His head bobbled from side to side. "Joined are all different, but all are one, all are shame. Shome look ash you. Would you Join?"

"No, thanks," I said. "Where can I find a human Joined?"

He bobbled his head some more. "Joined shing and ring and walk the shacred city."

Lya had been reading. "He doesn't know," she told me. "The Joined just wander and play their bells. There's no pattern to it, nobody keeps track. It's all random. Some travel in groups, some alone, and new groups form every time two bunches meet."

"We'll have to search," I said.

"Eat," the Shkeen told us. He reached into the basket on the ground and his hands came out with two steaming meatrolls. He pressed one into my hand, one in Lya's.

I looked at it dubiously. "Thank you," I told him. I pulled at Lya with my free hand and we walked off together. The Joined grinned at us as we left, and started ringing once more before we were halfway down the street.

The meatroll was still in my hand, its crust burning my fingers. "Should I eat this?" I asked Lya.

She took a bite out of hers. "Why not? We had them last night in the restaurant, right? And I'm sure Valcarenghi would've warned us if the native food was poisonous."

That made sense, so I lifted the roll to my mouth and took a bite as I walked. It was hot, and also *hot,* and it wasn't a bit like the meatrolls we'd sampled the previous night. Those had been golden, flaky things, seasoned gently with orangespice from Baldur. The Shkeen version was crunchy, and the meat inside dripped grease and burned my mouth. But it was good, and I was hungry, and the roll didn't last long.

"Get anything else when you read the small guy?" I asked Lya around a mouthful of hot roll.

She swallowed, and nodded. "Yes, I did. He was happy, even more than the rest. He's older. He's near Final Union, and he's very thrilled about it." She spoke with her old easy manner; the aftereffects of reading the Joined seemed to have faded.

"Why?" I was musing out loud. "He's going to *die.* Why is he so happy about it?"

Lya shrugged. "He wasn't thinking in any great analytical detail, I'm afraid."

I licked my fingers to get rid of the last of the grease. We were at a crossroads, with Shkeen bustling by us in all directions, and now we could hear more bells on the wind. "More Joined," I said. "Want to look them up?"

"What would we find out? That we don't already know? We need a *human* Joined."

"Maybe one of this batch *will* be human."

I got Lya's withering look. "Ha. What are the odds?"

"All right," I conceded. It was now late afternoon. "Maybe we'd better head back. Get an earlier start tomorrow. Besides, Dino is probably expecting us for dinner."

Dinner, this time, was served, in Valcarenghi's office, after a little additional furniture had been dragged in. His quarters, it turned out, were on the level below, but he preferred to entertain upstairs where his guests could enjoy the spectacular Tower view.

There were five of us, all told: me and Lya, Valcarenghi and Laurie, plus Gourlay. Laurie did the cooking, supervised by master chef Valcarenghi. We had beefsteaks, bred on Shkea from Old Earth stock, plus a fascinating blend of vegetables that included mushrooms from Old Earth, groundpips from Baldur, and Shkeen sweethorns. Dino liked to experiment and the dish was one of his inventions.

Lya and I gave a full report on the day's adventures, interrupted only by Valcarenghi's sharp, perceptive questioning.

After dinner, we got rid of tables and dishes and sat around drinking Veltaar and talking. This time Lya and I asked the questions, with Gourlay supplying the biggest chunk of the answers. Valcarenghi listened from a cushion on the floor, one arm around Laurie, the other holding his wine glass. We were not the first Talents to visit Shkea, he told us. Nor the first to claim the Shkeen were manlike.

"Suppose that means something," he said. "But I don't know. They're *not* men, you know. No, sir. They're much more social, for one thing. Great little city builders from way back, always in towns, always surrounding themselves with others. And they're more communal than man, too. Cooperate in all sorts of things, and they're big on sharing. Trade, for instance—they see that as mutual-sharing."

Valcarenghi laughed. "You can say that again. I just spent the whole day trying to work out a trade contract with a group of farmers who hadn't dealt with us before. It's not easy, believe me. They give us as much of their stuff as we ask for, if they don't need it themselves and no one else has asked for it earlier. But then they want to get whatever *they* ask for in the future. They expect it, in fact. So every time we deal we've got a choice; hand them a blank check, or go through an incredible round of talks that ends with them convinced that we're totally selfish."

Lya wasn't satisfied. "What about sex?" she demanded. "From the stuff you were translating last night, I got the impression they're monogamous."

"They're confused about sex relationships," Gourlay said. "It's very strange. Sex is sharing, you see, and it's good to share with everyone. But the sharing has to be real and meaningful. That creates problems."

Laurie sat up, attentive. "I've studied the point," she said quickly. "Shkeen morality insists they love *everybody*. But they can't do it, they're too human, too possessive. They wind up in monogamous relationships, because a really deep sex-sharing with one person is better than a million shallow physical things, in their culture. The ideal Shkeen would sex-share with everyone, with each of the unions being just as deep, but they can't achieve that ideal."

I frowned. "Wasn't somebody guilty last night over betraying his wife?"

Laurie nodded eagerly. "Yes, but the guilt was because his other relationships caused his sharing with his wife to diminish. *That* was the betrayal. If he'd been able to manage it without hurting his older relationship, the sex would have been meaningless. And, if all of the relationships have been real love-sharing, it would have been a plus. His wife would have been proud of him. It's quite an achievement for a Shkeen to be in a multiple union that works."

"And one of the greatest Shkeen crimes is to leave another alone," Gourlay said. "Emotionally alone. Without sharing."

I mulled over that, while Gourlay went on. The Shkeen had little crime, he told us. Especially no violent crime. No murders, no beatings, no prisons, no wars in their long, empty history.

"They're a race without murderers," Valcarenghi said. "Which may explain something. On Old Earth, the same cultures that had the highest suicide rates often had the lowest murder rates, too. And the Shkeen suicide rate is one hundred percent."

"They kill animals," I said.

"Not part of the Union," Gourlay replied. "The Union embraces all that thinks, and its creatures may not be killed. They do not kill Shkeen, or humans, or Greeshka."

Lya looked at me, then at Gourlay. "The Greeshka don't think," she said. "I tried to read them this morning and got nothing but the minds of the Shkeen they rode. Not even a yes-I-live."

"We've known that, but the point's always puzzled me," Valcarenghi said, climbing to his feet. He went to the bar for more wine, brought out a bottle, and filled our glasses. "A truly mindless parasite, but an intelligent race like the Shkeen are enslaved by it. Why?"

The new wine was good and chilled, a cold trail down my throat. I drank it, and nodded, remembering the flood of euphoria that had swept over us earlier that day. "Drugs," I said, speculatively. "The Greeshka must produce an organic pleasure drug. The Shkeen submit to it willingly and die happy. The joy is real, believe me. We felt it."

Lyanna looked doubtful, though, and Gourlay shook his head adamantly. "No, Robb. Not so. We've experimented on the Greeshka, and . . ."

He must have noticed my raised eyebrows. He stopped.

"How did the Shkeen feel about that?" I asked.

"Didn't tell them. They wouldn't have liked it, not at all. Greeshka's just an animal, but it's their God. Don't fool around with God, you know. We refrained for a long time, but when Gustaffson went over, old Stuart had to know. His orders. We didn't get anywhere, though. No extracts that might be a drug, no secretions, nothing. In fact, the Shkeen are the *only* native life that submits so easily. We caught a whiner, you see, and strapped it down, and let a Greeshka link up. Then, couple hours later, we yanked the straps. Damn whiner was furious, screeching and yelping, attacking the thing on its head. Nearly clawed its own skull to ribbons before it got it off."

"Maybe only the Shkeen are susceptible?" I said. A feeble rescue attempt.

"Not quite," said Valcarenghi, with a small, thin smile. "There's us."

Lya was strangely silent in the tube, almost withdrawn. I assumed she was thinking about the conversation. But the door to our suite had barely slid shut behind us when she turned toward me and wrapped her arms around me.

I reached up and stroked her soft brown hair, slightly startled by the hug. "Hey," I muttered, "what's wrong?"

She gave me her vampire look, big-eyed and fragile. "Make love to me, Robb," she said with a soft sudden urgency. "Please. Make love to me now."

I smiled, but it was a puzzled smile, not my usual lecherous bedroom grin. Lya generally comes on impish and wicked when she's horny, but now she was all troubled and vulnerable. I didn't quite get it.

But it wasn't a time for questions, and I didn't ask any. I just pulled her to me wordlessly and kissed her hard, and we walked together to the bedroom.

And we made love, *really* made love, more than poor Normals can do. We joined our bodies as one, and I felt Lya stiffen as her mind reached out to mine. And as we moved together I was opening myself to her, drowning myself in the flood of love and need and fear that was pouring from her.

Then, quickly as it had begun, it ended. Her pleasure washed over me in a raw red wave. And I joined her on the crest, and Lya clutched me tightly, her eyes shrunk up small as she drank it all in.

Afterwards, we lay there in the darkness and let the stars of Shkea pour their radiance through the window. Lya huddled against me, her head on my chest, while I stroked her.

"That was good," I said in a drowsy-dreamy voice, smiling in the star-filled darkness.

"Yes," she replied. Her voice was soft and small, so small I barely heard it. "I love you, Robb," she whispered.

"Uh-huh," I said. "And I love you."

She pulled loose of my arm and rolled over, propping her

head on a hand to stare at me and smile. "You do," she said. "I read it. I know it. And you know how much I love you, too, don't you?"

I nodded, smiling. "Sure."

"We're lucky, you know. The Normals have only words. Poor little Normals. How can they *tell*, with just words? How can they *know*? They're always apart from each other, trying to reach each other and failing. Even when they make love, even when they come, they're always apart. They must be very lonely."

There was something . . . disturbing . . . in that. I looked at Lya, into her bright happy eyes, and thought about it. "Maybe," I said, finally. "But it's not that bad for them. They don't know any other way. And they try, they love too. They bridge the gap sometimes."

"Only a look and a voice, then darkness again and a silence," Lya quoted, her voice sad and tender. "We're luckier, aren't we? We have so much more."

"We're luckier," I echoed. And I reached out to read her too. Her mind was a haze of satisfaction, with a gentle scent of wistful, lonely longing. But there was something else, way down, almost gone now, but still faintly detectable.

I sat up slowly. "Hey," I said. "You're worried about something. And before, when we came in, you were scared. What's the matter?"

"I don't know, really," she said. She sounded puzzled and she *was* puzzled; I read it there. "I *was* scared, but I don't know why. The Joined, I think. I kept thinking about how much they loved me. They didn't even *know* me, but they loved me so much, and they understood—it was almost like what we have. It—I don't know. It bothered me. I mean, I didn't think I could ever be loved that way, except by you. And they were so *close*, so together. I felt kind of lonely, just holding hands and talking. I wanted to be close to *you* that way. After the way they were all sharing and everything, being alone just seemed empty. And frightening. You know?"

"I know," I said, touching her lightly again, with hand and mind. "I understand. We do understand each other. We're together almost as they are, as Normals can't ever be."

Lya nodded, and smiled, and hugged me. We went to sleep in each other's arms.

Dreams again. But again, at dawn, the memory stole away from me. It was all very annoying. The dream had been pleasant, comfortable. I wanted it back, and I couldn't even remember what it was. Our bedroom, washed by harsh daylight, seemed drab compared to the splendors of my lost vision.

Lya woke after me, with another headache. This time she had the pills on hand, by the bedstand. She grimaced and took one.

"It must be the Shkeen wine," I told her. "Something about it takes a dim view of your metabolism."

She pulled on a fresh coverall and scowled at me. "Ha. We were drinking Veltaar last night, remember? My father gave me my first glass of Veltaar when I was nine. It never gave me headaches before."

"A first!" I said, smiling.

"It's not funny," she said. "It hurts."

I quit kidding, and tried to read her. She was right. It *did* hurt. Her whole forehead throbbed with pain. I withdrew quickly before I caught it too.

"All right," I said. "I'm sorry. The pills will take care of it, though. Meanwhile, we've got work to do."

Lya nodded. She'd never let anything interfere with work yet.

The second day was a day of manhunt. We got off to a much earlier start, had a quick breakfast with Gourlay, then picked up our aircar outside the tower. This time we didn't drop down when we hit Shkeentown. We wanted a human Joined, which meant we had to cover a lot of ground. The city was the biggest I'd ever seen, in area at any rate, and the thousand-odd human cultists were lost among millions of Shkeen. And, of those humans, only about half were actually Joined yet.

So we kept the aircar low, and buzzed up and down the dome-dotted hills like a floating roller-coaster, causing quite a stir in the streets below us. The Shkeen had seen aircars before, of course, but it still had some novelty value, particularly to the kids, who tried to run after us whenever we flashed by. We also panicked a whiner, causing him to upset the cart full of fruit he was dragging. I felt guilty about that, so I kept the car higher afterwards.

We spotted Joined all over the city, singing, eating, walking —and ringing those bells, those eternal bronze bells. But for the first three hours, all we found were Shkeen Joined. Lya and I took turns driving and watching. After the excitement of the previous day, the search was tedious and tiring.

Finally, however, we found something: a large group of Joined, ten of them, clustered around a bread cart behind one of the steeper hills. Two were taller than the rest.

We landed on the other side of the hill and walked around to meet them, leaving our aircar surrounded by a crowd of Shkeen children. The Joined were still eating when we arrived. Eight of them were Shkeen of various sizes and hues, Greeshka pulsing atop their skulls. The other two were human.

They wore the same long red gowns as the Shkeen, and they carried the same bells. One of them was a big man, with loose skin that hung in flaps, as if he'd lost a lot of weight recently. His hair was white and curly, his face marked by a broad smile and laugh wrinkles around the eyes. The other was a thin, dark weasel of a man with a big hooked nose.

Both of them had Greeshka sucking at their skulls. The parasite riding the weasel was barely a pimple, but the older man had a lordly specimen that dripped down beyond his shoulders and into the back of the gown.

Somehow, this time, it *did* look hideous.

Lyanna and I walked up to them, trying hard to smile, not reading—at least at first. They smiled at us as we approached. Then they waved.

"Hello," the weasel said cheerily when we got there. "I've never seen you. Are you new on Shkea?"

That took me slightly by surprise. I'd been expecting some sort of garbled mystic greeting, or maybe no greeting at all. I was assuming that somehow the human converts would have abandoned their humanity to become mock-Shkeen. I was wrong.

"More or less," I replied. And I read the weasel. He was genuinely pleased to see us, and just bubbled with contentment and good cheer. "We've been hired to talk to people like you." I'd decided to be honest about it.

The weasel stretched his grin farther than I thought it would go. "I am Joined, and happy," he said. "I'll be glad to talk to you. My name is Lester Kamenz. What do you want to know, brother?"

Lya, next to me, was going tense. I decided I'd let her read in depth while I asked questions. "When did you convert to the Cult?"

"Cult?" Kamenz said.

"The Union."

He nodded, and I was struck by the grotesque similarity of his bobbing head and that of the elderly Shkeen we'd seen yesterday. "I have always been in the Union. You are in the Union. All that thinks is in the Union."

"Some of us weren't told," I said. "How about you? When did you realize you were in the Union?"

"A year ago, Old Earth time. I was admitted to the ranks of the Joined only a few weeks ago. The First Joining is a joyful time. I am joyful. Now I will walk the streets and ring my bells until the Final Union."

"What did you do before?"

"Before?" A short vague look. "I ran machines once. I ran computers, in the Tower. But my life was empty, brother. I did not know I was in the Union, and I was alone. I had only machines, cold machines. Now I am Joined. Now I am"—again he searched—"not alone."

I reached into him, and found the happiness still there, with love. But now there was an ache too, a vague recollection of past pain, the stink of unwelcome memories. Did these fade? Maybe the gift the Greeshka gave its victims was oblivion, sweet mindless rest and end of struggle. Maybe.

I decided to try something. "That thing on your head," I said, sharply. "It's a parasite. It's drinking your blood right now, feeding on it. As it grows, it will take more and more of the things *you* need to live. Finally it will start to eat your tissue. Understand? It will *eat* you. I don't know how painful it will be, but however it feels, at the end you'll be *dead*. Unless you come back to the Tower now, and have the surgeons remove it. Or maybe you could remove it yourself. Why don't you try? Just reach up and pull it off. Go ahead."

I'd expected—what? Rage? Horror? Disgust? I got none of these. Kamenz just stuffed bread in his mouth and smiled at me, and all I read was his love and joy and a little pity.

"The Greeshka does not kill," he said finally. "The Greeshka gives joy and happy Union. Only those who have no Greeshka die. They are . . . alone. Oh, forever alone." Something in his mind trembled with sudden fear, but it faded quickly.

I glanced at Lya. She was stiff and hard-eyed, still reading. I looked back and began to phrase another question. But suddenly the Joined began to ring. One of the Shkeen started it off, swinging his bell up and down to produce a single sharp clang. Then his other hand swung, then the first again, then the second, then another Joined began to ring, then still another, and then they were all swinging and clanging and the noise of their bells was smashing against my ears as the joy and the love and the feel of the bells assaulted my mind once again.

I lingered to savor it. The love there was breathtaking, awesome, almost frightening in its heat and intensity, and there was-so much sharing to frolic in and wonder at, such a soothing-calming-exhilarating tapestry of good feeling. Something happened to the Joined when they rang, something touched them and lifted them and gave them a glow, something strange and glorious that mere Normals could not hear in their harsh clanging music. I was no Normal, though. I could hear it.

I withdraw reluctantly, slowly. Kamenz and the other human were both ringing vigorously now, with broad smiles and glowing twinkling eyes that transfigured their faces. Lyanna was still tense, still reading. Her mouth was slightly open, and she trembled where she stood.

I put an arm around her and waited, listening to the music, patient. Lya continued to read. Finally, after minutes, I shook her gently. She turned and studied me with hard, distant eyes. Then blinked. And her eyes widened and she came back, shaking her head and frowning.

Puzzled, I looked into her head. Strange and stranger. It was a swirling fog of emotion, a dense moving blend of more feelings than I'd care to put a name to. No sooner had I entered than I was lost, lost and uneasy. Somewhere in the fog there was a bottomless abyss lurking to engulf me. At least it felt that way.

"Lya," I said. "What's wrong?"

She shook her head again, and looked at the Joined with a look that was equal parts fear and longing. I repeated my question.

"I—I don't know," she said. "Robb, let's not talk now. Let's go. I want time to think."

"OK," I said. What was going on here? I took her hand and we walked slowly around the hill to the slope where we'd left the car. Shkeen kids were climbing all over it. I chased them, laughing. Lya just stood there, her eyes gone all faraway on me. I wanted to read her again, but somehow I felt it would be an invasion of privacy.

Airborne, we streaked back toward the Tower, riding higher and faster this time. I drove, while Lya sat beside me and stared out into the distance.

"Did you get anything useful?" I asked her, trying to get her mind back on the assignment.

"Yes. No. Maybe." Her voice sounded distracted, as if only part of her was talking to me. "I read their lives, both of them. Kamenz was a computer programmer, as he said. But he wasn't very good. An ugly little man with an ugly little personality, no friends, no sex, no nothing. Lived by himself, avoided the Shkeen, didn't like them at all. Didn't even like people, really. But Gustaffson got through to him, somehow. He ignored Kamenz' coldness, his bitter little cuts, his cruel jokes.

He didn't retaliate, you know? After a while, Kamenz came to like Gustaffson, to admire him. They were never really friends in any normal sense, but still Gustaffson was the nearest thing to a friend that Kamenz had."

She stopped suddenly. "So he went over with Gustaffson?" I prompted, glancing at her quickly. Her eyes still wandered.

"No, not at first. He was still afraid, still scared of the Shkeen and terrified of the Greeshka. But later, with Gustaffson gone, he began to realize how empty his life was. He worked all day with people who despised him and machines that didn't care, then sat alone at night reading and watching holoshows. Not life, really. He hardly touched the people around him. Finally he went to find Gustaffson, and wound up converted. Now . . ."

"Now . . .?"

She hesitated. "He's happy, Robb," she said. "He really is. For the first time in his life, he's happy. He'd never known love before. Now it fills him."

"You got a lot," I said.

"Yes." Still the distracted voice, the lost eyes. "He was open, sort of. There were levels, but digging wasn't as hard as it usually is—as if his barriers were weakening, coming down almost . . ."

"How about the other guy?"

She stroked the instrument panel, staring only at her hand. "Him? That was Gustaffson . . ."

And that, suddenly, seemed to wake her, to restore her to the Lya I knew and loved. She shook her head and looked at me, and the aimless voice became an animated torrent of words. "Robb, listen, that was *Gustaffson*, he's been Joined over a year now, and he's going on to Final Union within a week. The Greeshka has accepted him, and he wants it, you know? He really does, and—and—oh Robb, he's *dying!*"

"Within a week, according to what you just said."

"No. I mean yes, but that's not what I mean. Final Union isn't death, to him. He believes it, all of it, the whole religion. The Greeshka is his god, and he's going to join it. But before, and now, he was dying. He's got the Slow Plague, Robb. A terminal case. It's been eating at him from inside for over fifteen years now. He got it back on Nightmare, in the swamps, when his family died. That's no world for people, but he was there, the administrator over a research base, a short-term thing. They lived on Thor; it was only a visit, but the ship crashed. Gustaffson got all wild and tried to reach them before the end, but he grabbed a faulty pair of skinthins, and the spores got through. And they were all dead when he got there. He had an awful lot of pain, Robb. From the Slow Plague, but more from the loss. He really loved them, and it was never the same after. They gave him Shkea as a reward, kind of, to take his mind off the crash, but he still thought of it all the time. I could see the picture, Robb. It was vivid. He couldn't forget it. The kids were inside the ship, safe behind the walls, but the life system failed and choked them to death. But his wife—oh, Robb—she took some skinthins and tried to go for help, and outside those *things*, those big wrigglers they have on Nightmare—?"

I swallowed hard, feeling a little sick. "The eater-worms," I said, dully. I'd read about them, and seen holos. I could imagine the picture that Lya'd seen in Gustaffson's memory, and it wasn't at all pretty. I was glad I didn't have her Talent.

"They were still—still—when Gustaffson got there. You know. He killed them all with a screechgun."

I shook my head. "I didn't think things like that really went on."

"No," Lya said. "Neither did Gustaffson. They'd been so—so *happy* before that, before the thing on Nightmare. He loved her, and they were really close, and his career had been almost charmed. He didn't have to go to Nightmare, you know. He took it because it was a challenge, because nobody else could handle it. That gnaws at him, too. And he remembers all the time. He—they—" Her voice faltered. "They thought they were *lucky*," she said, before falling into silence.

There was nothing to say to that. I just kept quiet and drove, thinking, feeling a blurred, watered-down version of what Gustaffson's pain must have been like. After a while, Lya began to speak again.

"It was all there, Robb," she said, her voice softer and slower and more thoughtful once again. "But he was at peace. He still remembered it all, and the way it had hurt, but it didn't bother him as it had. Only now he was sorry they weren't with him. He was sorry that they died without Final Union. Almost like the Shkeen woman, remember? The one at the Gathering? With her brother?"

"I remember," I said.

"Like that. And his mind was open, too. More than Kamenz, much more. When he rang, the levels all vanished, and everything was right at the surface, all the love and pain and everything. His whole life, Robb. I shared his whole life with him, in an instant. And all his thoughts, too . . . he's seen the

caves of Union . . . he went down once, before he converted.
I . . . "

More silence, settling over us and darkening the car. We
were close to the end of Shkeentown. The Tower slashed the
sky ahead of us, shining in the sun. And the lower domes and
archways of the glitting human city were coming into view.

"Robb," Lya said. "Land here. I have to think a while, you
know? Go back without me. I want to walk among the Shkeen
a little."

I glanced at her, frowning. "Walk? It's a long way back to
the Tower, Lya."

"I'll be all right. Please. Just let me think a bit."

I read her. The thought fog had returned, denser than ever,
laced through with the colors of fear. "Are you sure?" I said.
"You're scared, Lyanna. Why? What's wrong? The eater-
worms are a long way off."

She just looked at me, troubled. "Please, Robb," she repeated.

I didn't know what else to do, so I landed.

And I, too, thought, as I guided the aircar home. Of what
Lyanna had said, and read—of Kamenz and Gustaffson. I
kept my mind on the problem we'd been assigned to crack. I
tried to keep it off Lya, and whatever was bothering her. That
would solve itself, I thought.

Back at the Tower, I wasted no time. I went straight up to
Valcarenghi's office. He was there, alone, dictating into a machine. He shut it off when I entered.

"Hi, Robb," he began. "Where's Lya?"

"Out walking. She wanted to think. I've been thinking, too.
And I believe I've got your answer."

He raised his eyebrows, waiting.

I sat down. "We found Gustaffson this afternoon, and Lya
read him. I think it's clear why he went over. He was a broken
man, inside, however much he smiled. The Greeshka have him
an end to his pain. And there was another convert with him, a
Lester Kamenz. He'd been miserable, too, a pathetic lonely
man with nothing to live for. Why *shouldn't* he convert?
Check out the other converts, and I bet you'll find a pattern.
The most lost and vulnerable, the failures, the isolated—those
will be the ones that turned to Union."

Valcarenghi nodded. "OK, I'll buy that," he said. "But our
psychs guessed that long ago, Robb. Only it's no answer, not
really. Sure, the converts on the whole have been a messed-up
crew, I won't dispute that. But why turn to the Cult of the Un-

ion? The psychs can't answer that. Take Gustaffson now. He was a strong man, believe me. I never knew him personally, but I knew his career. He took some rough assignments, generally for the hell of it, and beat them. He could have had the cushy jobs, but he wasn't interested. I've heard about the incident on Nightmare. It's famous, in a warped sort of way. But Phil Gustaffson wasn't the sort of man to be beaten, even by something like that. He snapped out of it very quickly, from what Nelse tells me. He came to Shkea and really set the place in order, cleaning up the mess that Rockwood had left. He pushed through the first real trade contract we ever got, *and* he made the Shkeen understand what it meant, which isn't easy.

"So here he is, this competent, talented man, who's made a career of beating tough jobs and handling men. He's gone through a personal nightmare, but it hasn't destroyed him. He's as tough as ever. And suddenly he turns to the Cult of the Union, signs up for a grotesque suicide. Why? For an end to his pain, you say? An interesting theory, but there are other ways to end pain. Gustaffson had years between Nightmare and the Greeshka. He never ran away from pain then. He didn't turn to drink, or drugs, or any of the usual outs. He didn't head back to Old Earth to have a psi-psych clean up his memories—and believe me, he could've gotten it paid for, if he'd wanted it. The colonial office would have done anything for him, after Nightmare. He went on, swallowed his pain, rebuilt. Until suddenly he converts.

"His pain made him more vulnerable, yes, no doubt of it. But something else brought him over—something that Union offered, something he couldn't get from wine or memory wipe. The same's true of Kamenz, and the others. They had other outs, other ways to vote no on life. They passed them up. But they chose Union. You see what I'm getting at?"

I did, of course. My answer was no answer at all, and I realized it. But Valcarenghi was wrong too, in parts.

"Yes," I said. "I guess we've still got some reading to do." I smiled wanly. "One thing, though. Gustaffson hadn't really beaten his pain, not ever. Lya was very clear on that. It was inside him all the time, tormenting him. He just never let it come out."

"That's victory, isn't it?" Valcarenghi said. "If you bury your hurts so deep that no one can tell you have them?"

"I don't know. I don't think so. But . . . anyway, there was more. Gustaffson has the Slow Plague. He's dying. He's been dying for years."

Valcarenghi's expression flickered briefly. "That I didn't know, but it just bolsters my point. I've read that some eighty percent of Slow Plague victims opt for euthanasia, if they happen to be on a planet where it's legal. Gustaffson was a planetary administrator. He could have *made* it legal. If he passed up suicide for all those years, why choose it now?"

I didn't have an answer for that. Lyanna hadn't given me one, if she had one. I didn't know where we could find one, either, unless . . .

"The caves," I said suddenly. "The caves of Union. We've got to witness a Final Union. There must be something about it, something that accounts for the conversions. Give us a chance to find out what it is."

Valcarenghi smiled. "All right," he said. "I can arrange it. I expected it would come to that. It's not pleasant, though, I'll warn you. I've gone down myself, so I know what I'm talking about."

"That's OK," I told him. "If you think reading Gustaffson was any fun, you should have seen Lya when she was through. She's out now trying to walk it off." That, I'd decided, must have been what was bothering her. "Final Union won't be any worse than those memories of Nightmare, I'm sure."

"Fine, then. I'll set it up for tomorrow. I'm going with you, of course. I don't want to take any chances on anything happening to you."

I nodded. Valcarenghi rose. "Good enough," he said. "Meanwhile, let's think about more interesting things. You have any plans for dinner?"

We wound up eating at a mock-Shkeen restaurant run by humans, in the company of Gourlay and Laurie Blackburn. The talk was mostly social noises—sports, politics, art, old jokes, that sort of thing. I don't think there was a mention of the Shkeen or the Greeshka all evening.

Afterwards, when I got back to our suite, I found Lyanna waiting for me. She was in bed, reading one of the handsome volumes from our library, a book of Old Earth poetry. She looked up when I entered.

"Hi," I said. "How was your walk?"

"Long." A smile creased her pale, small face, then faded. "But I had time to think. About this afternoon, and yesterday, and about the Joined. And us."

"Us?"

"Robb, do you love me?" The question was delivered almost matter-of-factly, in a voice full of question. As if she didn't know.

I sat down on the bed and took her hand and tried to smile.
"Sure," I said. "You know that, Lya."

"I did. I do. You love me, Robb, really you do. As much as
a human can love. But . . ." She stopped. She shook her head
and closed her book and sighed. "But we're still apart, Robb.
We're still apart."

"What *are* you talking about?"

"This afternoon. I was so confused afterwards, and scared. I
wasn't sure why, but I've thought about it. When I was reading, Robb—I was in there, with the Joined, sharing them and
their love. I really was. And I didn't want to come out. I didn't
want to leave them, Robb. When I did, I felt so isolated, so cut
off."

"That's your fault," I said. "I tried to talk to you. You were
too busy thinking."

"Talking? What good is talking? It's communication, I
guess, but is it *really?* I used to think so, before they trained
my Talent. After that, reading seemed to be the real communication, the real way to reach somebody else, somebody like
you. But now I don't know. The Joined—when they ring—
they're so *together*, Robb. All linked. Like us when we make
love, almost. And they love each other, too. And they love us,
so intensely. I felt—I don't know. But Gustaffson loves me as
much as you do. No. He loves me more."

Her face was white as she said that, her eyes wide, lost,
lonely. And me, I felt a sudden chill, like a cold wind blowing
through my soul. I didn't say anything. I only looked at her,
and wet my lips. And bled.

She saw the hurt in my eyes, I guess. Or read it. Her hand
pulled at mine, caressed it. "Oh, Robb. Please. I don't mean to
hurt you. It's not you. It's all of us. What do *we* have, compared to *them?*"

"I don't know what you're talking about, Lya." Half of me
suddenly wanted to cry. The other half wanted to shout. I sti-
fled both halves, and kept my voice steady. But inside I wasn't
steady, I wasn't steady at all.

"Do you love me, Robb?" Again. Wondering.

"Yes!" Fiercely. A challenge.

"What does that mean?" she said.

"You know what it means," I said. "Dammit, Lya, *think!*
Remember all we've had, all we've shared together. *That's*
love, Lya. It is. We're the lucky ones, remember? You said
that yourself. The Normals have only a touch and a voice,
then back to their darkness. They can barely find each other.
They're alone. Always. Groping. Trying, over and over, to

climb out of their isolation booths, and failing, over and over. But not us, we found the way, we know each other as much as any human beings ever can. There's nothing I wouldn't tell you, or share with you. I've said that before, and you know it's true, you can read it in me. *That's* love, dammit. *Isn't it?*"

"I don't know," she said, in a voice so sadly baffled. Soundlessly, without even a sob, she began to cry. And while the tears ran in lonely paths down her cheeks, she talked. "Maybe that's love. I always thought it was. But now I don't know. If what we have is love, what was it I felt this afternoon, what was it I touched and shared in? Oh, Robb. I love you too. You know that. I try to share with you. I want to share what I read, what it was like. But I can't. We're cut off. I can't make you understand. I'm here and you're there and we can touch and make love and talk, but we're still apart. You see? You see? I'm alone. And this afternoon, I *wasn't*."

"You're not alone, dammit," I said suddenly. "I'm here." I clutched her hand tightly. "Feel? Hear? You're not alone!"

She shook her head, and the tears flowed on. "You don't understand, see? And there's no way I can make you. You said we know each other as much as any human beings ever can. You're right. But how much can human beings know each other? Aren't all of them cut off, really? Each alone in a big dark empty universe? We only trick ourselves when we think that someone else is there. In the end, in the cold lonely end, it's only us, by ourselves, in the blackness. Are you there, Robb? How do I know? Will you die with me, Robb? Will we be together then? Are we together *now*? You say we're luckier than the Normals. I've said it too. They have only a touch and voice, right? How many times have I quoted that? But what do *we* have? A touch and two voices, maybe. It's not enough anymore. I'm scared. Suddenly I'm scared."

She began to sob. Instinctively I reached out to her, wrapped her in my arms, stroked her. We lay back together, and she wept against my chest. I read her, briefly, and I read her pain, her sudden loneliness, her hunger, all aswirl in a darkening mindstorm of fear. And, though I touched her and caressed her and whispered—over and over—that it would be all right, that I was here, that she wasn't alone, I knew that it would not be enough. Suddenly there was a gulf between us, a great dark yawning thing that grew and grew, and I didn't know how to bridge it. And Lya, my Lya, was crying, and she needed me. And I needed her, but I couldn't get to her.

Then I realized that I was crying too.

We held each other, in silent tears, for what must have been an hour. But finally the tears ran out. Lya clutched her body to me so tightly I could hardly breathe, and I held her just as tightly.

"Robb," she whispered. "You said—you said we really know each other. All those times you've said it. And you say, sometimes, that I'm *right* for you, that I'm perfect."

I nodded, wanting to believe. "Yes. You are."

"No," she said, choking out the word, forcing it into the air, fighting herself to say it. "It's not *so*. I read you, yes. I can hear the words rattling around in your head as you fit a sentence together before saying it. And I listen to you scold yourself when you've done something stupid. And I see memories, some memories, and live through them with you. But it's all on the surface, Robb, all on the top. Below it, there's more, more of *you*. Drifting half-thoughts I don't quite catch. Feelings I can't put a name to. Passions you suppress, and memories even you don't know you have. Sometimes I can get to that level. Sometimes. If I really fight, if I drain myself to exhaustion. But when I get there, I know—I *know*—that there's another level below *that*. And more and more, on and on, down and down. I can't reach them, Robb, though they're part of you. I don't know you, I can't know you. You don't even know yourself, see? And me, do you know me? No. Even less. You know what I tell you, and I tell you the truth, but maybe not all. And you read my feelings, my surface feelings—the pain of a stubbed toe, a quick flash of annoyance, the pleasure I get when you're in me. Does that mean you know me? What of *my* levels, and levels? What about the things I don't know myself? Do *you* know them? How, Robb, how?"

She shook her head again, with that funny little gesture she had whenever she was confused. "And you say I'm perfect, and that you love me. I'm so right for you. But *am* I? Robb, *I read your thoughts*. I know when you want me to be sexy, so I'm sexy. I see what turns you on, so I do it. I know when you want me to be serious, and when you want me to joke. I know what kind of jokes to tell, too. Never the cutting kind, you don't like that, to hurt or see people hurt. You laugh *with* people not *at* them, and I laugh with you, and love you for your tastes. I know when you want me to talk, and when to keep quiet. I know when you want me to be your proud tigress, your tawny telepath, and when you want a little girl to shelter in your arms. And I *am* those things, Robb, because you want me to be, because I love you, because I can feel the joy in your mind at every *right* thing that I do. I never set out to do it that way, but it happened. I didn't mind. I don't mind. Most of the time it wasn't even conscious. You do the same thing, too. I read it in you. You can't read as I do, so sometimes you guess wrong—you come on witty when I want silent understanding, or you act the strong man when I need a boy to mother. But you get it right sometimes, too. And you *try*, you always try.

"But is it really *you*? Is it really *me*? What if I wasn't perfect, you see, if I was just myself, with all my faults and the things you don't like out in the open? Would you love me *then*? I don't know. But Gustaffson would, and Kamenz. I know that, Robb. I saw it. I know *them*. Their levels . . . vanished. I *KNOW* them, and if I went back I could share with them, more than with you. And they know me, the real me, all of me, I think. And they love me. You see? *You see?*"

Did I see? I don't know. I was confused. Would I love Lya if she was "herself"? But what was "herself"? How was it different from the Lya I knew? I thought I loved Lya and would always love Lya—but what if the real Lya wasn't like my Lya? *What* did I love? The strange abstract concept of a human being, or the flesh and voice and personality that I thought of as Lya? I didn't know. I didn't know who Lya was, or who I was, or what the hell it all meant. And I was scared. Maybe I couldn't feel what she had felt that afternoon. But I knew what she was feeling then. I was alone, and I needed someone.

"Lya," I called. "Lya, let's try. We don't have to give up. We can reach each other. There's a way, our way. We've done it before. Come, Lya, come with me, come to me."

As I spoke, I undressed her, and she responded and her hands joined mine. When we were nude, I began to stroke her, slowly, and she me. Our minds reached out to each other. Reached and probed as never before. I could feel her, inside my head, digging. Deeper and deeper. Down. And I opened myself to her, I surrendered, all the petty little secrets I had kept even from her, or tried to, now I yielded up to her, everything I could remember, my triumphs and shames, the good moments and the pain, the times I'd hurt someone, the times I'd been hurt, the long crying sessions by myself, the fears I wouldn't admit, the prejudices I fought, the vanities I battled when the time struck, the silly boyish sins. All. Everything. I buried nothing. I hid nothing. I gave myself to her, to Lya, to *my* Lya. She had to know me.

And so too she yielded. Her mind was a forest through which I roamed, hunting down wisps of emotion, the fear and the need and the love at the top, the fainter things beneath, the half-formed whims and passions still deeper into the woods. I don't have Lya's Talent, I read only feelings, never thoughts. But I read thoughts then, for the first and only time, thoughts she threw at me because I'd never seen them before. I couldn't read much, but some I got.

And as her mind opened to mine, so did her body. I entered her, and we moved together, bodies one, minds entwined, as close as human beings can join. I felt pleasure washing over me in great glorious waves, my pleasure, her pleasure, both together building on each other, and I rode the crest for an eternity as it approached a far distant shore. And finally as it smashed into that beach, we came together, and for a second —for a tiny, fleeting second—I could not tell which orgasm was mine, and which was hers.

But then it passed. We lay, bodies locked together, on the bed. In the starlight. But it was not a bed. It was the beach, the flat black beach, and there were no stars above. A thought touched me, a vagrant thought that was not mine. Lya's thought. We were on a plain, she was thinking, and I saw that she was right. The waters that had carried us here were gone, receded. There was only a vast flat blackness stretching away in all directions, with dim ominous shapes moving on either horizon. *We are here as on a darkling plain,* Lya thought. And suddenly I knew what those shapes were, and what poem she had been reading.

We slept.

I woke, alone.

The room was dark. Lya lay on the other side of the bed, curled up, still asleep. It was late, near dawn I thought. But I wasn't sure. I was restless.

I got up and dressed in silence. I needed to walk somewhere, to think, to work things out. Where, though?

There was a key in my pocket. I touched it when I pulled on my tunic, and remembered. Valcarenghi's office. It would be locked and deserted at this time of night. And the view might help me think.

I left, found the tubes, and shot up, up, up to the apex of the Tower, the top of man's steel challenge to the Shkeen. The office was unlit, the furniture dark shapes in the shadows. There was only the starlight. Shkea is closer to the galactic center than Old Earth, or Baldur. The stars are a fiery canopy across the night sky. Some of them are very close, and they burn like red and blue-white fires in the awesome blackness above. In Valcarenghi's office, all the walls are glass, I went to one, and looked out. I wasn't thinking. Just feeling. And I felt cold and lost and little.

Then there was a soft voice behind me saying hello. I barely heard it.

I turned away from the window, but other stars leaped at me from the far walls. Laurie Blackburn sat in one of the low chairs, concealed by the darkness.

"Hello," I said. "I didn't mean to intrude. I thought no one would be here."

She smiled. A radiant smile in a radiant face, but there was no humor in it. Her hair fell in sweeping auburn waves past her shoulders, and she was dressed in something long and gauzy. I could see her gentle curves through its folds, and she made no effort to hide herself.

"I come up here a lot," she said. "At night, usually. When Dino's asleep. It's a good place to think."

"Yes," I said, smiling. "My thoughts, too."

"The stars are pretty, aren't they?"

"Yes."

"I think so. I—" Hesitation. Then she rose and came to me. "Do you love Lya?" she said.

A hammer of a question. Timed terribly. But I handled it well, I think. My mind was still on my talk with Lya. "Yes," I said. "Very much. Why?"

She was standing close to me, looking at my face, and past me, out to the stars. "I don't know. I wonder about love, sometimes. I love Dino, you know. He came here two months ago, so we haven't known each other long. But I love him already. I've never known anybody like him. He's kind, and considerate, and he does everything well. I've never seen him fail at anything he tried. Yet he doesn't seem driven, like some men. He wins so easily. He believes in himself a lot, and that's attractive. He's given me anything I could ask for, everything."

I read her, caught her love and worry, and guessed. "Except himself," I said.

She looked at me, startled. Then she smiled. "I forgot. You're a Talent. Of course you know. You're right. I don't know what I worry about, but I do worry. Dino is so perfect, you know. I've told him—well, everything. All about me and my life. And he listens and understands. He's always receptive, he's there when I need him. But—"

"It's all one way," I said. It was a statement. I knew.

She nodded. "It's not that he keeps secrets. He doesn't. He'll answer any question I ask. But the answers mean nothing. I ask him what he fears, and he says nothing, and makes me believe it. He's very rational, very calm. He never gets angry, he never has. I asked him. He doesn't hate people, he thinks hate is bad. He's never felt pain, either, or he *says* he hasn't. Emotional pain, I mean. Yet he understands me when I talk about my life. Once he said his biggest fault was laziness. But he's not lazy at all, I know that. Is he really that perfect? He tells me he's always sure of himself, because he *knows* he's good, but he smiles when he says it, so I can't even accuse him of being vain. He says he believes in God, but he never talks about it. If you try to talk seriously, he'll listen patiently, or joke with you, or lead the conversation away. He says he loves me, but—"

I nodded. I knew what was coming.

It came. She looked up at me, eyes begging. "You're a Talent," she said. "You've read him, haven't you? You know him? Tell me. Please tell me."

I was reading her. I could see how much she needed to know, how much she worried and feared, how much she loved. I couldn't lie to her. Yet it was hard to give her the answer I had to.

"I've read him," I said. Slowly. Carefully. Measuring out my words like precious fluids. "And you, you too. I saw your love, on that first night, when we ate together."

"And Dino?"

My words caught in my throat. "He's—funny, Lya said once. I can read his surface emotions easily enough. Below that, nothing. He's very self-contained, walled off. Almost as if his only emotions are the ones he—*allows* himself to feel. I've felt his confidence, his pleasure. I've felt worry too, but never real fear. He's very affectionate toward you, very protective. He enjoys feeling protective."

"Is that all?" So hopeful. It hurt.

"I'm afraid it is. He's walled off, Laurie. He needs himself, only himself. If there's love in him, it's behind that wall, hidden. I can't read it. He thinks a lot of you, Laurie. But love—well, it's different. It's stronger and more unreasoning and it comes in crashing floods. And Dino's not like that, at least not out where I can read."

"Closed," she said. "He's closed to me. I opened myself to him, totally. But he didn't. I was always afraid—even when he was with me, I felt sometimes that he wasn't there at all—"

She sighed. I read her despair, her welling loneliness. I didn't know what to do. "Cry if you like," I told her, inanely. "Sometimes it helps. I know. I've cried enough in my time."

She didn't cry. She looked up, and laughed lightly. "No," she said. "I can't. Dino taught me never to cry. He said tears never solve anything."

A sad philosophy. Tears don't solve anything, maybe, but they're part of being human. I wanted to tell her so, but instead I just smiled at her.

She smiled back, and cocked her head. "You cry," she said suddenly, in a voice strangely delighted. "That's funny. That's more of an admission than I ever heard from Dino, in a way. Thank you, Robb. Thank you."

And Laurie stood on her toes and looked up, expectant. And I could read what she expected. So I took her and kissed her, and she pressed her body hard against mine. And all the while I thought of Lya, telling myself that she wouldn't mind, that she'd be proud of me, that she'd understand.

Afterwards, I stayed up in the office alone to watch the dawn come up. I was drained, but somehow content. The light that crept over the horizon was chasing the shadows before it, and suddenly all the fears that had seemed so threatening in the night were silly, unreasoning. We'd bridged it, I thought—Lya and I. Whatever it was, we'd handled it, and today we'd handle the Greeshka with the same ease, together.

When I got back to our room, Lya was gone.

"We found the aircar in the middle of Shkeentown," Valcarenghi was saying. He was cool, precise, reassuring. His voice told me, without words, that there was nothing to worry about. "I've got men out looking for her. But Shkeentown's a big place. Do you have any idea where she might have gone?"

"No," I said, dully. "Not really. Maybe to see some more Joined. She seemed—well, almost obsessed by them. I don't know."

"Well, we've got a good police force. We'll find her, I'm certain of that. But it may take a while. Did you two have a fight?"

"Yes. No. Sort of, but it wasn't a real fight. It was strange."

"I see," he said. But he didn't. "Laurie tells me you came up here last night, alone."

"Yes. I needed to think."

"All right," said Valcarenghi. "So let's say Lya woke up, decided she wanted to think too. You came up here. She took a ride. Maybe she just wants a day off to wander around Shkeentown. She did something like that yesterday, didn't she?"

"Yes."

"So she's doing it again. No problem. She'll probably be back well before dinner." He smiled.

"Why did she go without telling me, then? Or leaving a note, or *something?*"

"I don't know. It's not important."

Wasn't it, though? *Wasn't it?* I sat in the chair, head in my hands and a scowl on my face, and I was sweating. Suddenly I was very much afraid, of what I didn't know. I should never have left her alone, I was telling myself. While I was up here with Laurie, Lyanna woke alone in a darkened room, and—and—and *what?* And left.

"Meanwhile, though," Valcarenghi said, "we've got work to do. The trip to the caves is all set."

I looked up, disbelieving. "The caves? I can't go there, not now, not alone."

He gave a sigh of exasperation, exaggerated for effect. "Oh, come now, Robb. It's not the end of the world. Lya will be all right. She seemed to be a perfectly sensible girl, and I'm sure she can take care of herself. Right?"

I nodded.

"Meanwhile, we'll cover the caves. I still want to get to the bottom of this."

"It won't do any good," I protested. "Not without Lya. She's the major Talent. I—I just read emotions. I can't get down deep, as she can. I won't solve anything for you."

He shrugged. "Maybe not. But the trip is on, and we've got nothing to lose. We can always make a second run after Lya comes back. Besides, this should do you good, get your mind off this other business. There's nothing you can do for Lya now. I've got every available man out searching for her, and if they don't find her you certainly won't. So there's no sense dwelling on it. Just get back into action, keep busy." He turned, headed for the tube. "Come. There's an aircar waiting for us. Nelse will go too."

Reluctantly, I stood. I was in no mood to consider the problems of the Shkeen, but Valcarenghi's arguments made a certain amount of sense. Besides which, he'd hired Lyanna and me, and we still had obligations to him. I could try anyway, I thought.

On the ride out, Valcarenghi sat in the front with the driver, a hulking police sergeant with a face chiseled out of granite. He'd selected a police car this time so we could keep posted on the search for Lya. Gourlay and I were in the back seat together. Gourlay had covered our laps with a big map, and he was telling me about the caves of Final Union.

"Theory is the caves are the original home of the Greesh-ka," he said. "Probably true, makes sense. Greeshka are a lot bigger there. You'll see. The caves are all through the hills, away from our part of Shkeentown, where the country gets wilder. A regular little honeycomb. Greeshka in every one, too. Or so I've heard. Been in a few myself, Greeshka in all of *them*. So I believe what they say about the rest. The city, the sacred city, well, it was probably built *because* of the caves. Shkeen come here from all over the continent, you know, for Final Union. Here, this is the cave region." He took out a pen, and made a big circle in red near the center of the map. It was meaningless to me. The map was getting me down. I hadn't re-alized that the Shkeen city was so *huge*. How the hell could they find anyone who didn't want to be found?

Valcarenghi looked back from the front seat. "The cave we're going to is a big one, as these places go. I've been there before. There's no formality about Final Union, you under-stand. The Shkeen just pick a cave, and walk in, and lie down on top of the Greeshka. They'll use whatever entrance is most convenient. Some of them are no bigger than sewer pipes, but if you went in far enough, theory says you'd run into a Greeshka, sitting back in the dark and pulsing away. The big-gest caves are lighted with torches, like the Great Hall, but that's just a frill. It doesn't play any real part in the Union."

"I take it we're going to one of them?" I said.

Valcarenghi nodded. "Right. I figured you'd want to see what a mature Greeshka is like. It's not pretty, but it's educa-tional. So we need lighting."

Gourlay resumed his narrative then, but I tuned him out. I felt I knew quite enough about the Shkeen and the Greeshka, and I was still worried about Lyanna. After a while he wound down, and the rest of the trip was in silence. We covered more ground than we ever had before. Even the Tower—our shining steel landmark—had been swallowed by the hills behind us.

The terrain got rougher, rockier, and more overgrown, and the hills rose higher and wilder. But the domes went on and on and on, and there were Shkeen everywhere. Lya could be down there, I thought, lost among those teeming millions. Looking for what? Thinking what?

Finally we landed, in a wooded valley between two massive, rock studded hills. Even here there were Shkeen, the red-brick domes rising from the undergrowth among the stubby trees. I had no trouble spotting the cave. It was halfway up one of the slopes, a dark yawn in the rock face, with a dusty road wind-ing up to it.

We set down in the valley and climbed that road. Gourlay ate up the distance with long, gawky strides, while Valcarenghi moved with an easy, untiring grace, and the policeman plodded on stolidly. I was the straggler. I dragged myself up, and I was half-winded by the time we got to the cave mouth.

If I'd expected cave paintings, or an altar, or some kind of nature-temple, I was sadly disappointed. It was an ordinary cave, with damp stone walls and low ceilings and cold, wet air. Cooler than most of Shkea, and less dusty, but that was about it. There was one long, winding passage through the rock, wide enough for the four of us to walk abreast yet low enough so Gourlay had to stoop. Torches were set along the walls at regular intervals, but only every fourth one or so was lit. They burned with an oily smoke that seemed to cling to the top of the cave and drift down into the depths before us. I wondered what was sucking it in.

After about ten minutes of walking, most of it down a barely perceptible incline, the passage led us out into a high, brightly-lit room, with a vaulting stone roof that was stained sooty by torch smoke. In the room, the Greeshka.

Its color was a dull brownish-red, like old blood, not the bright near translucent crimson of the small creatures that clung to the skulls of the Joined. There were spots of black, too, like burns or soot stains on the vast body. I could barely see the far side of the cave; the Greeshka was too huge, it towered above us so that there was only a thin crack between it and the roof. But it sloped down abruptly halfway across the chamber, like an immense jellied hill, and ended a good twenty feet from where we stood. Between us and the great bulk of the Greeshka was a forest of hanging, dangling red strands, a living cobweb of Greeshka tissue that came almost to our faces.

And it pulsed. As one organism. Even the strands kept time, widening and then contracting again, moving to a silent beat that was one with the great Greeshka behind them.

My stomach churned, but my companions seemed unmoved. They'd seen this before. "Come," Valcarenghi said, switching on a flashlight he'd brought to augment the torchlight. The light, twisting around the pulsing web, gave the illusion of some weird haunted forest. Valcarenghi stepped into that forest. Lightly. Swinging the light and brushing aside the Greeshka.

Gourlay followed him, but I recoiled. Valcarenghi looked back and smiled. "Don't worry," he said. "The Greeshka takes hours to attach itself, and it's easily removed. It won't grab you if you stumble against it."

I screwed up my courage, reached out, and touched one of the living strands. It was soft and wet, and there was a slimy feel to it. But that was all. It broke easily enough. I walked through it, reaching before me and bending and breaking the web to clear my path. The policeman walked silently behind me.

Then we stood on the far side of the web, at the foot of the great Greeshka. Valcarenghi studied it for a second, then pointed with his flashlight. "Look," he said. "Final Union."

I looked. His beam had thrown a pool of light around one of the dark spots, a blemish on the reddish hulk. I looked closer. There was a head in the blemish. Centered in the dark spot, with just the face showing, and even that covered by a thin reddish film. But the features were unmistakable. An elderly Shkeen, wrinkled and big-eyed, his eyes closed now. But smiling. Smiling.

I moved closer. A little lower and to the right, a few fingertips hung out of the mass. But that was all. Most of the body was already gone, sunken into the Greeshka, dissolved or dissolving. The old Shkeen was dead, and the parasite was digesting his corpse.

"Every one of the dark spots is a recent Union," Valcarenghi was saying, moving his light around like a pointer. "The spots fade in time, of course. The Greeshka is growing steadily. In another hundred years it will fill this chamber, and start up the passageway."

Then there was a rustle of movement behind us. I looked back. Someone else was coming through the web.

She reached us soon, and smiled. A Shkeen woman, old, naked, breasts hanging past her waist. Joined, of course. Her Greeshka covered most of her head and hung lower than her breasts. It was still bright and translucent from its time in the sun. You could see through it, to where it was eating the skin off her back.

"A candidate for Final Union," Gourlay said.

"This is a popular cave," Valcarenghi added in a low, sardonic voice.

The woman did not speak to us, nor we to her. Smiling, she walked past us. And lay down on the Greeshka.

The little Greeshka, the one that rode her back, seemed almost to dissolve on contact, melting away into the great cave creature, so the Shkeen woman and the great Greeshka were

joined as one. After that, nothing. She just closed her eyes,
and lay peacefully, seemingly asleep.

"What's happening?" I asked.

"Union," said Valcarenghi. "It'll be an hour before you'd
notice anything, but the Greeshka is closing over her even
now, swallowing her. A response to her body heat, I'm told. In
a day she'll be buried in it. In two, like him—". The flash
found the half-dissolved face above us.

"Can you read her?" Gourlay suggested. "Maybe that'd tell
us something."

"All right," I said, repelled but curious. I opened myself.
And the mindstorm hit.

But it's wrong to call it a mindstorm. It was immense and
awesome and intense, searing and blinding and choking. But it
was peaceful too, and gentle with a gentleness that was more
violent than human hate. It shrieked soft shrieks and siren
calls and pulled at me seductively, and it washed over me in
crimson waves of passion, and drew me to it. It filled me and
emptied me all at once. And I heard the bells somewhere,
clanging a harsh bronze song, a song of love and surrender
and togetherness, of joining and union and never being alone.

Storm, mindstorm, yes, it was that. But it was to an ordinary mindstorm as a supernova is to a hurricane, and its violence was the violence of love. It loved me, that mindstorm,
and it wanted me, and its bells called to me, and sang its love,
and I reached to it and touched, wanting to be with it, wanting
to link, wanting never to be alone again. And suddenly I was on
the crest of a great wave once again, a wave of fire that washed
across the stars forever, and this time I knew the wave would
never end, this time I would not be alone afterwards upon my
darkling plain.

But with that phrase I thought of Lya.

And suddenly I was struggling, fighting it, battling back
against the sea of sucking love. I ran, ran, *ran, RAN* . . . and
closed my minddoor and hammered shut the latch and let the
storm flail and howl against it while I held it with all my
strength, resisting. Yet the door began to buckle and crack.

I screamed. The door smashed open, and the storm whipped
in and clutched at me, whirled me out and around and around.
I sailed up to the cold stars but they were cold no longer, and
I grew bigger and bigger until I *was* the stars and they were
me, and I was Union, and for a single solitary glittering instant
I was the universe.

Then nothing.

I woke up back in my room, with a headache that was trying to tear my skull apart. Gourlay was sitting on a chair reading one of our books. He looked up when I groaned.

Lya's headache pills were still on the bedstand. I took one hastily, then struggled to sit up in bed.

"You all right?" Gourlay asked.

"Headache," I said, rubbing my forehead. It *throbbed*, as if it was about to burst. Worse than the time I'd peered into Lya's pain. "What happened?"

He stood up. "You scared the hell out of us. After you began to read, all of a sudden you started trembling. Then you walked right into the goddamn Greeshka. And you screamed. Dino and the sergeant had to drag you out. You were stepping right in the thing, and it was up to your knees. Twitching, too. Weird. Dino hit you, knocked you out."

He shook his head, started for the door. "Where are you going?" I said.

"To sleep," he said. "You've been out for eight hours or so. Dino asked me to watch you till you came to. OK, you came to. Now get some rest, and I will too. We'll talk about it tomorrow."

"I want to talk about it now."

"It's late," he said, as he losed the bedroom door. I listened to his footsteps on the way out. And I'm sure I heard the outer door lock. Somebody was clearly afraid of Talents who steal away into the night. I wasn't going anywhere.

I got up and went out for a drink. There was Veltaar chilling. I put away a couple of glasses quick, and ate a light snack. The headache began to fade. Then I went back to the bedroom, turned off the light and cleared the glass, so the stars would all shine through. Then back to sleep.

But I didn't sleep, not right away. Too much had happened. I had to think about it. The headache first, the incredible headache that ripped at my skull. Like Lya's. But Lya hadn't been through what I had. Or had she? Lya was a major Talent, much more sensitive than I was, with a greater range. Could that mindstorm have reached *this* far, over miles and miles? Late at night, when humans and Shkeen were sleeping and their thoughts dim? Maybe. And maybe my half-remembered dreams were pale reflections of whatever she had felt the same nights. But my dreams had been pleasant. It was waking that bothered me, waking and not remembering.

But again, had I had this headache when I slept? Or when I woke?

What the hell had happened? What was that thing, that reached me there in the cave, and pulled me to it? The Greeshka? It had to be. I hadn't even time to focus on the Shkeen woman, it *had* to be the Greeshka. But Lyanna had said that Greeshka had no minds, not even a yes-I-live . . .

It all swirled around me, questions on questions on questions, and I had no answers. I began to think of Lya then, to wonder where she was and why she'd left me. Was this what she had been going through? Why hadn't I understood? I missed her then. I needed her beside me, and she wasn't there. I was alone, and very aware of it.

I slept.

Long darkness then, but finally a dream, and finally I remembered. I was back on the plain again, the infinite darkling plain with its starless sky and black shapes in the distance, the plain Lya had spoken of so often. It was from one of her favorite poems. I was alone, forever alone, and I knew it. That was the nature of things. I was the only reality in the universe, and I was cold and hungry and frightened, and the shapes were moving toward me, inhuman and inexorable. And there was no one to call to, no one to turn to, no one to hear my cries. There never had been anyone. There never would be anyone.

Then Lya came to me.

She floated down from the starless sky, pale and thin and fragile, and stood beside me on the plain. She brushed her hair back with her hand, and looked at me with glowing wide eyes, and smiled. And I knew it was no dream. She was with me, somehow. We talked.

Hi, Robb.

Lya? Hi, Lya. Where are you? You left me.

I'm sorry. I had to. You understand, Robb. You have to. I didn't want to be here anymore, ever, in this place, this awful place. I would have been, Robb. Men are always here, but for brief moments.

A touch and a voice?

Yes, Robb. Then darkness again, and a silence. And the darkling plain.

You're mixing two poems, Lya. But it's OK. You know them better than I do. But aren't you leaving out something? The earlier part, "Ah love, let us be true . . ."

Oh, Robb.

Where are you?

I'm—everywhere. But mostly in a cave. I was ready, Robb. I was already more open than the rest. I could skip the Gath-

ering, and the Joining. My Talent made me used to sharing. It took me.

Final Union?

Yes.

Oh, Lya.

Robb. Please. Join us, join me. It's happiness, you know? Forever and forever, and belonging and sharing and being together. I'm in love, Robb, I'm in love with a billion billion people, and I know all of them better than I ever knew you, and they know me, all of me, and they love me. And it will last forever. Me. Us. The Union. I'm still me, but I'm them too, you see? And they're me. The Joined, the reading, opened me, and the Union called to me every night, because it loved me, you see? Oh, Robb, join us, join us. I love you.

The Union. The Greeshka, you mean. I love you, Lya. Please come back. It can't have absorbed you already. Tell me where you are. I'll come to you.

Yes, come to me. Come anywhere, Robb. The Greeshka is all one, the caves all connect under the hills, the little Greeshka are all part of the Union. Come to me and join me. Love me as you said you did. Join me. You're so far away, I can hardly reach you, even with the Union. Come and be one with us.

No. I will not be eaten. Please, Lya, tell me where you are.

Poor Robb. Don't worry, love. The body isn't important. The Greeshka needs it for nourishment, and we need the Greeshka. But, oh Robb, the Union isn't just the Greeshka, you see? The Greeshka isn't important, it doesn't even have a mind, it's just the link, the medium, the Union is the Shkeen. A million billion billion Shkeen, all the Shkeen that have lived and Joined in fourteen thousand years, all together and loving and belonging, immortal. It's beautiful, Robb, it's more than we had, much more, and we were the lucky ones, remember? We were! But this is better.

Lya. My Lya. I loved you. This isn't for you, this isn't for humans. Come back to me.

This isn't for humans? Oh, it IS! It's what humans have always been looking for, searching for, crying for on lonely nights. It's love, Robb, real love, and human love is only a pale imitation. You see?

No.

Come, Robb. Join. Or you'll be alone forever, alone on the plain, with only a voice and a touch to keep you going. And in the end when your body dies, you won't even have that. Just an eternity of empty blackness. The plain, Robb, forever and ever. And I won't be able to reach you, not ever. But it doesn't have to be . . .

No.

Oh, Robb. I'm fading. Please come.

No. Lya, don't go. I love you, Lya. Don't leave me.

I love you, Robb. I did. I really did . . .

And then she was gone. I was alone on the plain again. A wind was blowing from somewhere, and it whipped her fading words away from me, out into the cold vastness of infinity.

In the cheerless morning, the outer door was unlocked. I ascended the tower and found Valcarenghi alone in his office. "Do you believe in God?" I asked him.

He looked up, smiled. "Sure." Said lightly. I was reading him. It was a subject he'd never thought about.

"I don't," I said. "Neither did Lya. Most Talents are atheists, you know. There was an experiment tried back on Old Earth fifty years ago. It was organized by a major Talent named Linnel, who was also devoutly religious. He thought that by using drugs, and linking together the minds of the world's most potent Talents, he could reach something he called the Universal Yes-I-Live. Also known as God. The experiment was a dismal failure, but *something* happened. Linnel went mad, and the others came away with only a vision of a vast, dark, uncaring nothingness, a void without reason or form or meaning. Other Talents have felt the same way, and Normals too. Centuries ago there was a poet named Arnold, who wrote of a darkling plain. The poem's in one of the old languages, but it's worth reading. It shows—fear, I think. Something basic in man, some dread of being alone in the cosmos. Maybe it's just fear of death, maybe it's more. I don't know. But it's primal. All men are forever alone, but they don't want to be. They're always searching, trying to make contact, trying to reach others across the void. Some people never succeed, some break through occasionally. Lya and I were lucky. But it's never permanent. In the end you're alone again, back on the darkling plain. You see, Dino? *Do you see?*"

He smiled an amused little smile. Not derisive—that wasn't his style—just surprised and disbelieving. "No," he said.

"Look again, then. Always people are reaching for something, for someone, searching. Talk, Talent, love, sex, it's all part of the same thing, the same search. And gods, too. Man invents gods because he's afraid of being alone, scared of an empty universe, scared of the darkling plain. That's why your men are converting, Dino, that's why people are going over.

They've found God, or as much of a God as they're ever likely to find. The Union is a mass-mind, an immortal mass-mind, many in one, all love. The Shkeen don't die, dammit. No wonder they don't have the concept of an afterlife. They *know* there's a God. Maybe it didn't create the universe, but it's love, pure love, and they say that God is love, don't they? Or maybe what we call love is a tiny piece of God. I don't care, whatever it is, the Union is it. The end of the search for the Shkeen, and for Man too. We're alike after all, we're so alike it hurts."

Valcarenghi gave his exaggerated sigh. "Robb, you're overwrought. You sound like one of the Joined."

"Maybe that's just what I should be. Lya is. She's part of the Union now."

He blinked. "How do you know that?"

"She came to me last night, in a dream."

"Oh. A dream."

"It was *true*, dammit. It's all true."

Valcarenghi stood, and smiled. "I believe you," he said. "That is, I believe that the Greeshka uses a psi-lure, a love lure if you will, to draw in its prey, something so powerful that it convinces men—even you—that it's God. Dangerous, of course. I'll have to think about this before taking action. We could guard the caves to keep humans out, but there are too many caves. And sealing off the Greeshka wouldn't help our relations with the Shkeen. But now it's my problem. You've done your job."

I waited until he was through. "You're wrong, Dino. This is real, no trick, no illusion. I *felt* it, and Lya too. The Greeshka hasn't even a yes-I-live, let alone a psi-lure strong enough to bring in Shkeen and men."

"You expect me to believe that God is an animal who lives in the caves of Shkea?"

"Yes."

"Robb, that's absurd, and you know it. You think the Shkeen have found the answer to the mysteries of creation. But look at them. The oldest civilized race in known space, but they've been stuck in the Bronze Age for fourteen thousand years. We came to *them*. Where are their spaceships? Where are their towers?"

"Where are our bells?" I said. "And our joy? They're happy, Dino. Are we? Maybe they've found what we're still looking for. Why the hell is man so driven, anyway? Why is he out to conquer the galaxy, the universe, whatever? Looking for God, maybe . . .? Maybe. He can't find him anywhere, though, so on he goes, on and on, always looking. But always back to the same darkling plain in the end."

"Compare the accomplishments. I'll take humanity's record."

"Is it worth it?"

"I think so." He went to the window, and looked out. "We've got the only Tower on their world," he said, smiling, as he looked down through the clouds.

"They've got the only God in our universe," I told him. But he only smiled.

"All right, Robb," he said, when he finally turned from the window. "I'll keep all this in mind. And we'll find Lyanna for you."

My voice softened. "Lya is lost," I said. "I know that now. I will be too, if I wait. I'm leaving tonight. I'll book passage on the first ship out to Baldur."

He nodded. "If you like. I'll have your money ready." He grinned. "And we'll send Lya after you, when we find her. I imagine she'll be a little miffed, but that's your worry."

I didn't answer. Instead I shrugged, and headed for the tube. I was almost there when he stopped me.

"Wait," he said. "How about dinner tonight? You've done a good job for us. We're having a farewell party, anyway, Laurie and me. She's leaving too."

"I'm sorry," I said.

His turn to shrug. "What for? Laurie's a beautiful person, and I'll miss her. But it's no tragedy. There are other beautiful people. I think she was getting restless with Shkea, anyway."

I'd almost forgotten my Talent, in my heat and the pain of my loss. I remembered it now. I read him. There was no sorrow, no pain, just a vague disappointment. And below that, his wall. Always the wall, keeping him apart, this man who was a first-name friend to everyone and an intimate to none. And on it, it was almost as if there were a sign that read, THIS FAR YOU GO, AND NO FARTHER.

"Come up," he said. "It should be fun." I nodded.

I asked myself, when my ship lifted off, why I was leaving. Maybe to return home. We have a house on Baldur, away from the cities, on one of the undeveloped continents with only wilderness for a neighbor. It stands on a cliff, above a high waterfall that tumbles endlessly down into a shaded green pool. Lya and I swam there often, in the sunlit days between assignments. And afterwards we'd lie down nude in the shade of the orangespice trees, and make love on a carpet of silver moss. Maybe I'm returning to that. But it won't be the same without Lya, lost Lya . . .

Lya whom I still could have. Whom I could have now. It would be easy, so easy. A slow stroll into a darkened cave, a short sleep. Then Lya with me for eternity, in me, sharing me, being me, and I her. Loving and knowing more of each other than men can ever do. Union and joy, and no darkness again, ever. God. If I believed that, what I told Valcarenghi, then why did I tell Lya no?

Maybe because I'm not sure. Maybe I still hope, for something still greater and more loving than the Union, for the God they told me of so long ago. Maybe I'm taking a risk, because part of me still believes. But if I'm wrong . . . then the darkness, and the plain . . .

But maybe it's something else, something I saw in Valcarenghi, something that made me doubt what I had said. For man is more than Shkeen, somehow; there are men like Dino and Gourlay as well as Lya and Gustaffson, men who fear love and Union as much as they crave it. A dichotomy, then. Man has two primal urges, and the Shkeen only one? If so, perhaps there is a human answer, to reach and join and not be alone, and yet to still be men.

I do not envy Valcarenghi. He cries behind his wall, I think, and no one knows, not even he. And no one will ever know, and in the end he'll always be alone in smiling pain. No, I do not envy Dino.

Yet there is something of him in me, Lya, as well as much of you. And that is why I ran, though I loved you.

Laurie Blackburn was on the ship with me. I ate with her after liftoff, and we spent the evening talking over wine. Not a happy conversation, maybe, but a human one. Both of us needed someone, and we reached out.

Afterwards, I took her back to my cabin, and made love to her as fiercely as I could. Then, the darkness softened, we held each other and talked away the night.

DEATHSONG

Sydney J. Van Scyoc

The longing for immortality appears to be as old as human intelligence and manifests itself in the innumerable religious faiths that have been with us since the first sub-man looked at the stars. Here is a story of how one intelligent race sought to achieve immortality—real functioning immortality—at the expense of others. In some ways it is curiously complementary to the preceding novelette; in other ways it is a rather different side of the coin.

I

Late afternoon hung sodden and unfragrant beneath the musty leaf canopy that sheltered the sediment-choked stream. At ground level vegetation was a competitive tangle of green, scarlet and black. Verrons leaned from the hover-scooter. A kilometer downstream he had spotted footprints in the mud that aproned the stream. Now they led him to five gaunt humanoids sprawled naked on the streambank. He approached slowly, assessing sleep-slack faces. Bifurcate nostrils bracketed round oral orifices. Curtains of crepelike violet tissue flowed from the lower arc of the mouth. Two of the five slept curled around partly devoured branches of yellow berries. None stirred as Verrons hovered over.

They appeared as brute dumb as the survey crew had reported. He set the scooter to ground and circled back afoot, stunner in hand. Still the aborigines did not stir. A year ago the survey crew had counted a dozen of them in the temple vicinity, none elsewhere. Now Verrons could find only these five. From their starveling appearance they wouldn't survive another year.

He shrugged. Unfit races died. Satisfied that they offered no threat to his own party, Verrons reboarded. Lofting, he caught a blaze of color from above. The temple complex sat high upon a steep mesa, its stone columns and arcades architectural poetry—out of time, out of place—an anomaly on this deserted jungle world. It splintered late afternoon sunlight to pink fire.

Again Verrons shrugged. Heller was already inflamed with cosmic probabilities. The lean professor functioned from an intellectual matrix of galaxy-wide evolutionary thrusts and manipulative cosmic consciousnesses. Fortunately Verrons' only obligation was to see that the two professors and their assistants survived the year.

Verrons rode the dusk to camp. He was dishing his evening meal when the two professors approached. Balsky, chubby, balding, regarded him from cover of an anxious frown. Heller was a different breed, stringy and thrusting.

"I assume we can schedule initial survey of the temples tomorrow," he demanded.

Verrons bristled. "I don't see the need to push, Professor. We have a year."

"Barely a moment in the overall scale. You were gone for two hours. Did you locate the aborigines?"

Verrons' jaw knotted stubbornly. "I found five of them sleeping upstream." He hoisted a belaying palm. "No, I didn't attempt communication. And now I'm taking supper. Thereafter I draw rest. We'll schedule tomorrow tomorrow. At my pace."

Argument ensued. Verrons remained obdurate. Finally Heller lunged away in defeat, Balsky in his wake.

When dark fell Verrons prowled the perimeters of camp. He found no sign of the single form reported dangerous to man, a fierce mock-monkey that rode the bending stalks of the jungle. Returning to his tent, he stretched on his cot and stared up into darkness, victim of the tension that always marked his first days on a new world.

He was falling asleep when sound brought him upright: a distant sounding of notes, random, plaintive. Verrons plunged from the tent. Who was playing flute on this forsaken world?

Heller and Balsky emerged from their own tents. Assistants gathered. "The aborigines?"

"The sound emanates from the mesa," Heller said assertively. "And those aren't wood or reed recorders. Those are metal instruments."

"In the hands of primitives?"

"I refer to tonal quality. Did the aborigines carry instruments when you sighted them?"

"The abos I spotted didn't carry anything." Verrons dodged

back to his tent and holstered his stunner. "I'm going for a look. No one leaves camp before I return."

Heller called after him but Verrons did not alter trajectory. Afoot, he moved quickly in the direction of the stream. Double moons—brilliant, white—rode the sky. The mud wallow where he had located the aborigines earlier was deserted. Fresh tracks led upstream. Half a kilometer later, the tracks disappeared up a steep gully. Verrons peered up the mesa wall. The sound of flutes was discordant above. Locating a series of eroded footholds, he mounted the gully.

Reaching the mesa top, he peered across a shimmering stone plaza toward a long colonnade, imposing by moonlight. Verrons slipped across the plaza silently, stunner in hand. The sound of flutes came from a high-walled courtyard near plaza's edge. He started toward it.

And halted, suddenly aware of a soft corona that graced the air above the enclosed area, faint, blue-white—totally unexpected. And possibly revealing. He dove to cover in the shadow of the courtyard wall. Glancing up, he found misty blue radiance surging faintly in the air beyond the wall. Flutes sounded spiritlessly.

Verrons edged the length of the wall, slipped around a corner and located the courtyard entry. Unfortunately it was blocked by a solidly hung stone sheet door.

Verrons considered alternatives, then scampered to conceal himself behind a stone column. The survey crew had found the temple complex totally barren of activity and artifact. Yet now he encountered metal flutes and unaccountable illumination. Verrons pondered possibilities, none particularly credible, his feet slipping into hibernation. The glow above the courtyard remained faint, the sound of flutes tuneless.

An hour later he stood and stamped life back into numb toes, unwilling to spend his first night planetside crouched and cramping. He crossed the shimmering plaza, thumped down the gully and returned to camp.

The sound of flutes continued to lace the night. Verrons stared up at darkened tent panels, considering. This was a world that apparently had washed its face of two races—the aborigines, for all practical purposes extinct, and the race that had created the temple complex. According to the survey report, centuries-old craters dotted this world, presumably the nuclear deathpocks of advanced civilization. It was logical to assume that the race that had created that civilization had also created the temple complex, simply neglecting to destroy it in the apocalyptic conflict. But would it be equally logical to assume that the abos were the degenerate tailings of that same race, breeding messily downhill into delayed extinction?

When Verrons emerged from his tent next morning Heller was upon him, ready to scrap. Briefly Verrons communicated what he had observed, both streamside in the afternoon and mesa top by night. "The survey boys do some night study, but it's entirely possible to miss highly localized nocturnal phenomena. So it's landed on our platter, whatever it is."

"Well, it's obvious we must establish communication with the aborigines. They apparently have access to artifact stores the survey party missed. And as you have pointed out, they're a highly perishable resource."

The aborigines were. "Pick a party, Professor, and we'll have a try at parley."

A half-hour later they waded sucking mud toward the aborigines' wallow. The sound of their approach stimulated random muscular twitches in the sleeping humanoids. When Heller cleared his throat a single humanoid rolled over and opened dull eyes, lip veil trembling weakly. The eyes closed before Heller could complete his introductory homily. When Young Nevins squatted and uttered the humanoid universals he had learned in the American University system the response was further repose on the part of the aborigines.

"Are they trying to discompose us?" Heller demanded, bristling.

"This is the same reaction the survey team drew. Which is to say—none. They may be more responsive after dark." Verrons doubted it. He could read nothing but fatal lethargy in the emaciated bodies.

"Well, it's obvious they're starving. But why? Don't you see berries and fruit freely available? Don't you see—"

"What I don't see are metal flutes."

Heller fanned restive eyes over the area. There was no sign the aborigines claimed anything beyond their own muddy pelts. "Yet it was their footprints that led you to the mesa top last night, Commander. We'll detail a pair of assistants to search the area immediately."

Verrons squelched him promptly. "No one pokes around outside camp today unless he's under my direct supervision." Neither aborigines nor immediate terrain appeared dangerous. But it was too early to trust appearances—or the judgment of professor or assistants. "So you have a choice. I stay here and tag a single searcher. Or I loft you and Balsky to the mesa for initial survey."

A little later Verrons and the professors lofted. The temple complex was sunwashed against the clear late-morning sky, columns and arches graceful. At Heller's direction, Verrons circuited the complex. They hovered over plazas, arcades and courtyards that joined a succession of progressively more imposing temples. The climax of the complex was an elevated domed temple that seemed to join the sky in the light grace of its structure. The centuries had inflicted minimal damage.

"Which structure did you track the flutes to last night, Commander?"

Quickly Verrons swung the scooter. They settled in the plaza.

By daylight the rectangular courtyard was totally barren. Heller inspected it with sharp dissatisfaction. "There's certainly no sign of any light fixture here."

"There's no sign of anything here," Verrons agreed. There was only dust and a half-open stone sheet door.

Nor was there sign of anything in the remainder of the complex. The three men took it afoot, boot heels clattering. They were small beneath soaring pink arches, solitary on glazed stone walks, silent beneath the brilliantly patterned dome of the grand temple. They emerged and stood with the complex at their feet. Beyond the mesa lay jungle, a mist-veiled tangle of scarlet and green. On the western horizon a single crater was dimly visible.

Verrons surveyed the expanse of barren pink stone with dissatisfaction. The survey report had prepared him for the lack of structural damage, for the emptiness. But he had not anticipated the hollow sense of stones that had never been walked, of walls that had never housed activity. "I don't think this place was ever used."

"Exactly," Heller declared incisively, his heightening agitation coming to full focus. "This complex is exactly what I suspected when the survey photographs were released: a statement." He arced a gesture at sunlight stone. "Think about it, Commander—the prominent elevation, the exquisite symmetry and proportion, the fact that all extraneous matter has been systematically destroyed—"

"You mean the artifacts we should have found here?"

"I mean every population center on this planet was deliberately obliterated so we would not be distracted from what we are intended to learn from this set of structures."

Verrons recoiled from Heller's visionary vehemence and paced down stone steps.

Balsky shared his unease. "Isn't it possible the complex was never furnished or used due to the outbreak of hostilities?"

"Possible." Any number of things were. "Meanwhile we have a handful of aborigines with metal—we think—flutes and a lot of empty stone."

"Sufficient," Heller pronounced crisply, hoisting chin. "We will return tonight to observe the group during its waking period. You will accompany us, of course, Commander."

Verrons gnawed lip. "We'll come." He led way back to the courtyard and studied it. There was no cover. Nor was there any overlooking structure. "We could simply establish ourselves here before dark and wait. There's a chance the abos will consider that aggressive and retaliate."

"Hardly a serious threat. We saw no weapons in their sleeping grounds."

"And no flutes either."

"We have stunners," Heller declared staunchly.

The three men reboarded the hoverscooter and lofted off the mesa. They were briefly suspended in late afternoon sunlight. Upon the mesa, the temple complex floated, glistening, enigmatic.

II

Near dusk they ascended a gully that mouthed near the encampment. When dark came they huddled in a corner of the courtyard, stunners at hand. Balsky's breath rasped. Heller's was a dry whisper. Neither moon had risen.

They heard bare feet on stone. The first humanoid appeared. He paused at the courtyard door, gaunt, hunched. Dull eyes found the human intruders. Lip-veils quivered weakly. Warily he sidled into the yard and hunkered opposite them. Gaze fixed, he raised a forked hand.

The flute he held was gracefully formed, its metal barrel ornate and untarnished. The aborigine's nostrils flared. Lip tissues rippled as he mouthed the instrument. The flute yielded a tuneless sigh.

Others followed. Finally all five hunched, dull eyes fixed on the humans. They mouthed flutes tunelessly, dark spittle stringing down through fluttering lip veils. But by that time Verrons was little aware of the unprepossessing mien of the players. Because as flutes sounded another presence was in the courtyard.

It came as a cloud of light that gradually brightened until it filled the yard with soft, shadowless radiance. As it brightened, metal flutes glowed. Verrons watched bony fingers grope aimlessly up and down luminous instruments. There was neither order nor beauty in the sounds produced.

Yet those sounds somehow caused the cloud of light to birth a single tenuous light-presence. It darkened slowly from the heart of the cloud, taller than human or aborigine but similar to both in form and proportion. The presence glimmered across the courtyard, radiantly blue, its natal cloud luminous about it. It bowed before the huddle of aborigines, extruding long arms of blue light that it slowly wound and wove about itself and reincorporated. Then long arms rippled free again. The apparition arched into the air, threw itself backward and cartwheeled about the yard, passing easily through humans and aborigines, light-limbs flickering.

Flutes continued to sound. The apparition flung itself erect at the center of the yard, light-limbs spiraling around its body. Helplessly Verrons was drawn into the vortex, his consciousness absorbed and irradiated. Then the first moon appeared above the courtyard wall, a flat white disk. The apparition at the center of the yard brightened visibly, changing form.

The guise it assumed was flame—licking arms, surging head, consuming maw. Initially it was an intense blue flame that seemed to flare from a rupture in some other dimension. Then it spread, brightening fiercely. Verrons groaned as fiery arms licked him. Desperately he tried to gain his feet, a silent scream filling his mind. Balsky grunted in agony beside him.

An eternity later, when both moons hung halfway up the sky, flame drew back and began to spin, drawing fiery arms after it until it was a brilliant wheel that spun around the yard. And as it whirled, fiery red became orange, orange yellow.

Reaching the end of the visible spectrum, the progression of color was reversed. Verrons tongued dry lips. With effort he extracted one corner of consciousness from the dazzle of light. "Balsky."

Balsky did not respond but Heller retained articulacy. "Verrons—what is it?"

"It's—" Verrons had no answer. It was a wheel of light. It was turning, drawing his awareness back.

Reclaiming it.

And then the wheel began to fade. Verrons shuddered, the ragged sound of flutes swimming back into his ken. He peered around, eyes burning. Only a diffuse cloud of light remained in the yard.

The tallest aborigine sprawled forward, head touching pavement, flute still clutched in his forked hand. His fellows stared at him, their own fading instruments forgotten. One reached forward and jammed the flute between his quivering lips.

Play! The word was a silent scream in Verrons' mind. His mates battered the exhausted flutist with brutal hands. But he did not respond. Flutes lay silent on stone. Light died.

Verrons shuddered to full consciousness and gained his feet. Heller followed suit, springing away. Verrons slapped Balsky urgently, maneuvered him up and steered him around the cluster of aborigines and into the plaza. Overhead the moons were haughty white twins. By the time the three reached the gully, Balsky moved under his own power. The gully was steep, shadow-choked. "Can you make it?"

Balsky's bald scalp flashed affirmative. They bumped down the ravine. Heller emerged last, springing up in battle stance. "Commander—"

Verrons shook his head. "Keep your stunner ready, Professor." He sought bending stalks for threat.

They reached camp without incident. Pole lamps glowed, competing with moonlight. Their own brand of reality was reassuring, tent panels rustling, young voices in conference from a nearby tent. From above the sound of flutes resumed, thin and disorganized. "My tent," Verrons said brusquely, leading way.

Verrons kept a small flask in his case, one he had filled two years ago near the center of the galaxy. Now he decanted three drops of pale liquid into the lid of the flask and inhaled. The liquid evaporated instantly, creating a brief pungency in Verrons' nostrils. He proffered the flask. *"Didion?"*

Balsky accepted and followed Verrons' example. Heller was dubious. "What is the effect?"

"It smells good. Sometimes it brings on the smarts."

"An intelligence booster?"

"A temporary stimulant." Unfortunately Verrons' system rejected the effect tonight.

And Heller declined frostily. "I don't see the need."

Verrons returned the flask to his case, shrugging. But Balsky seemed brightened. His bare pate crawled. "If you will reconstruct the interior of the grand temple, you'll remember that we saw the wheel of light motif there this afternoon. It was a prominent theme in the geometric pattern that covered the interior surface of the dome. So if the wheels of light appear on the dome, couldn't we anticipate seeing other components of the dome pattern played out in light, too? If we were rash enough to return to the courtyard?"

"You feel that would be rash?"

"I'd be very reluctant to re-expose myself to the experience without understanding it. I'd want to know if what we saw exists in an electro-physical sense or if it was purely an event of the nervous system. And there are a dozen other possibilities I'd want to explore." Balsky raised plump shoulders apologetically. "But we're not likely to learn much without going back for an encore. Have you encountered anything like this before, Commander?"

"I'm afraid my circuit runs to hungry vines and Class Nine ruins, the kind you approach with a tender touch and a lot of imagination." Verrons paced the small area. He had, in fact, warped here equipped with a standardized set of responses. Now he would have to retool.

Heller's lean body flexed aggressively. "Well, I will tell you this, Verrons. We may have been the subjects of brain center stimulation or we may have witnessed an actual event. In either case, it will be necessary to confront the event again. And when we do, I want those flutes in our hands."

Verrons' brows went north. "You want us to blow the flutes?"

"Do I have to say it twice? Did you relish being manipulated by savages?"

"I had the impression they were as much in the grip of the thing as we were. And I certainly don't want anyone putting lip to flute before I—"

Heller's stringy forearms bunched. "Verrons, I didn't travel this far to be balked in my purpose."

Verrons bristled. "Oh? And what is your purpose?"

Heller's gesture was slashing, all inclusive. "To add to our race's knowledge of other races and other times, to participate in the revelation of the evolutionary plan that does exist and does encompass us all. To—"

Verrons shook his head. "Professor, no privately funded study party is allowed access to any peripheral world without escort of a Surface Commander commissioned by Service Central. In this case, me. While I have no authority in the area of your researchers per se, I carry full authority in matters related to survival. If you contravene my orders you can be convicted of mutiny when you warp downline to Earth."

"I doubt that!" Heller whipped around and plunged from the tent.

Verrons turned back to Balsky, bemused. The plump professor's face had grown crazed with fatigue. "Another jolt, Professor?"

"Not tonight, Commander." His voice was faint.

The next morning Verrons led the entire group to the mesa top. Heller flared a taut gaze over sunwashed stone. "Commander, I would like to examine the courtyard again."

Verrons remanded the party to Balsky's custody and accompanied Heller. In the small courtyard they found waiting stone, nothing more. Heller scanned the yard fiercely, then stalked away.

Verrons followed. Heller strode the plaza to the arcade where Balsky had gathered the party. By the time Verrons caught up, the professors had already conducted the group into the first of the series of ascending temples. It was not until Verrons passed under the portico that he realized an event was in progress.

Within the temple, the party was frozen. Verrons' gaze darted to the point of their converging gaze. From the polished stone floor, a substantial rectangular block rose. It elevated until it stood somewhat higher than human eye level. A diagonal grain marked its lateral surfaces.

Verrons' reaction was swift. His stunner came to hand. "I don't want anyone to touch that stone."

Heller's eyes darted to his, hawkish. "You—"

"No one!"

Slowly the end portion of the block slid inward. From the interior of the block, a dark rectangular object slid gently to the floor. Verrons lunged to squat over the object. His fingers tasted smooth surfaces. The object appeared to be a case.

The stone block withdrew into the floor, Verrons hefted the case.

It was moderately heavy. "I'm going to take this to the plaza to open it."

No one objected. Outside he kneeled in sheeting sunlight, the case shaded—and shielded from the party under the portico. He pried at its seams. It opened easily and he stared down at a double rank of ornate metal flutes—fourteen altogether.

And fourteen people waited under the portico. Verrons rose slowly, shaken. Sunlight fingered the flutes and splintered brilliantly.

"Well?"

Verrons gestured them near. "This is what we draw. And I still don't want anyone to touch."

The party encircled the case. Heller counted and bared challenging teeth. "Well, Commander, it appears we've each been allotted a flute—except you. Is that some indication of your status with the local powers?"

"It's more an indication of the fact that I wasn't within the structure when the mechanism initiated its cycle, Professor."

Heller's brow arched. "Then you do concede that it is not pure coincidence that there are exactly fourteen flutes here."

"I don't concede anything. We're not staging a debate." Verrons snapped the case shut. He catalogued the party. Yesterday he, Heller and Balsky had received no such thoughtful offering. "Winchell, Olsen, Gomes—come with me. The rest of you wait here." Taking the case, he led the three back into the temple.

Inside they waited expectantly. The temple made them no offering. Verrons grunted. "Olsen, go fetch one more."

She pattered away and returned with Arguilar. The four regarded Verrons alertly. Still the temple did not yield. "Another."

Four assistants later they were still unrewarded. Verrons paced off the section of flooring that had risen before. The seam was barely perceptible. "I could have sworn we had a pressure sensitive floor here, one discriminating enough not to respond to individuals or very small groups. Now how much does it want before it produces?"

"Commander, maybe it knows we're carrying flutes already." Olsen indicated the case in his hand.

"Ah. Let's check. Take this case to Balsky and come back."

She obeyed. And the stone block rose from the temple floor again. Grained lateral surfaces shone richly. Slowly the end panel slid up. The block birthed a second rectangular case, smaller than the first.

Verrons opened it quickly, grimly. There were nine flutes, one for each person in the temple.

"Now that's a pretty intelligent mechanism," Winchell commented, squatting beside Verrons.

Verrons met clear green eyes set in a solid face. "Very." He chewed cheek, debating. He did not want anyone setting lip to flute before he did. Neither did he care to spend the day encumbered with superfluous cases. Quickly he instructed Olsen again. She took the second flute case and withdrew to the portico. A moment later she reentered, hands empty.

When the stone block began to rise, she retrieved the second flute case. The end of the block slid open and Verrons was ready. Before the mechanism could disgorge a third case, Verrons jammed the second back into its maw.

He half-expected the effort to fail. But the block accepted the case, reconsuming it along with the case it had intended to deliver, and withdrew into the floor. Relieved, Verrons shooed everyone from the structure.

Heller's thin mouth twisted. "Now presumably we can see what other structures have to offer."

"I'm hardly finished here." Verrons selected assistants again. "I'm going to step back into the temple. Follow one at a time, at sixty second intervals, until we see how many of us it requires to trigger the dispensing mechanism."

Seven minutes later he had his answer. It required six persons. He retested, selecting and sequencing to obtain a lighter mix. Again the temple responded when six members of the party had gathered. "So it's not sensitive to weight, but to the number of individuals. Now we'll have a look uphill."

The second, third and fourth temples proffered flutes. Verrons refused delivery. "Obviously they were meant to be played. But whether the race that built the complex intended them for its own use, for the aborigines' use—"

"I don't see how you can suggest they were intended for savages," Heller argued immediately.

"They have oral cavities, don't they? They can direct an air stream through the barrel of the instrument. They may even be descendants of the race that built the complex."

"I certainly don't conceive of the degenerated aboriginal specimens we saw last night as either the authors or the intended clientele of this establishment."

"Then what *is* your interpretation of the situation?"

"First I suggest that an establishment of this complexity was not erected here by chance. There is purpose—beyond the merely local. And since we are the ones who have arrived, I suggest that the establishment was placed here for reasons related to our coming, to convey a central truth to us."

"Oh? To all of us—or to you in particular?"

"To whichever of us is ready to recognize the truth."

"I see. But if each recognizes a different truth?"

"Then most are misled by inadequate powers of comprehension."

Verrons studied the lean face. Could his own inability to patter through such airy intellectual constructs be construed as a deficiency? Or a saving sanity? He shrugged. "Let's move."

The next two temples offered flutes on the same terms as before. When they reached the third, the central block did not rise from the temple floor. Instead it slowly recessed and moved aside, revealing a square opening.

"Back." Verrons approached cautiously. Light glowed alive below. He looked down a metal ladder into a narrow corridor. He bent. Corridor walls were polished metal, the floor glazed stone. Both were otherwise featureless. He stood and stepped away, face grim.

"Look."

Heller kneeled and peered into the opening. When he stood his hazel eyes were inflamed with portent. "Obviously there is an extensive substructure here, Commander."

"Obviously."

"And just as obviously you do not intend to permit anyone to descend."

"You're so right—not today. If there is a grand plan we'll fulfill it soon enough."

"You know, the entire mesa may be hollow," Balsky suggested.

"It could even be an artificial land feature," Winchell speculated, "specifically constructed to house storage."

And to elevate the temple complex into greater prominence, like a piece of bait? The entire establishment, exquisite, empty, began to feel to Verrons like a mousetrap. He turned to confront questioning eyes. "I want to make myself clear. I'm not being obstructive when I refuse to allow anyone down that ladder today. I have to do some hard thinking. Because when we do go, we go to learn more about this specific situation, not to expose ourselves to the revelation of any great truth, human, alien—or universal."

Heller's lips whitened.

The party proceeded. Successive temples opened to further stretches of underground corridor. In the grand temple, beneath the complexly patterned surface of the interior dome, a broad stone staircase with carved railings led down. Verrons eyed the stairs stonily. He did not appreciate structures that snatched the initiative from the explorer.

"Commander, do you still want sketches of the interior dome surface?"

Verrons stepped back. His eyes panned across the dome. "And photographs."

Waller and Gomes unpacked paraphernalia and undertook to oblige him.

III

The party returned to camp in late afternoon. Verrons did not stay to sample the postprandial analysis of events. He snatched a quick meal, reiterated instructions that no one was to leave camp and moved through the jungle, flute case under arm, toward the aborigines' wallow.

When he did not locate them there he tracked them downstream and into the jungle. They fed noisily in the shaded dusk, tearing down branches of fruit and berries, stuffing horn-lined mouths with brute concentration, grunting and mumbling. Juice, yellow, scarlet, strung through violet lip veils and puddled on gaunt chests.

They fed until their lean bellies bulged tumorously. Then they hiked upstream, shadowy faces stuporous. Near the mouth of the gully, two kneeled and rooted at the base of a husky brown stalk. They unearthed a case similar to the one Verrons carried. When the case was reburied, the group stumbled into the gully, flutes in hand.

Verrons waited before following. When he reached the plaza, flutes already sounded across the complex. Verrons strode away from the sound. Night lay bright across shimmering stone. Twin moons hung over the resplendent pink shoulder of the grand temple.

Within the grand temple, the stone floor glistened palely. Overhead the interior reaches of the dome were shadowshrouded. Verrons' footsteps echoed as he moved along the wall and sat. Bracing himself against cold stone, he opened the flute case and selected an instrument. It was little more than an ornate barrel with fingerholes, a mouthpiece at one end, a flaring belled extrusion at the other. The metal barrel was cool. Experimentally Verrons touched lip to the instrument and blew.

The air clouded brilliantly before him. Verrons raised his head. The figures on the dome surface took fire and began to move, wheels of light rotating, geometric forms changing, color and line merging and flowing with hypnotic sinuosity. Staring up, Verrons was barely aware of the instrument in his hands or of the breath he nurtured it with. He was aware only of the writhing ceiling and of the slow resolution of cloudbrightness into light-being.

This was not the featureless blue being of the night before. This was a golden creature who draped herself in the remnants of her natal cloud with a graceful sweep of long-fingered hands. She moved across the floor on long muscular toes that splayed from the tapered ends of her bare legs. Her drapery of light concealed nothing, but her body, a sweetly modeled sheath for her being, was in turn marked by no suggestion of profane function. Her face—vertical eyes, arching mouth— was a compelling composition of golden light. A separate cloud of light enveloped her head, iridescing faintly.

Verrons continued to flute. Overhead the inner surface of

the dome had become as broad as the sky, as deep—and suddenly as dark. Light wheels spun from the dome surface and arched down through forever, fusing the air. Luminescent geometric figures flowed after, cascading in brilliant confusion.

Chaos engulfed Verrons. His flute glowed with colors he had never seen before, colors he did not see now but felt in his burning fingertips. From the depths of confusion, Verrons' golden creature arched and sprang upward. She arrowed sleekly through an eternity of dark space, flexed her body and flattened herself across the distant black surface of the dome, arms and legs elongating. She hung there, dimming, becoming tenuous. Then she resorbed her fading limbs and contracted until she was a gaudy yellow sun in a black sky, burning. Suddenly her limbs exploded outward again. Rippling, she launched herself downward, swimming air to where Verrons cowered.

He was overwhelmed by darting light figures. The golden creature swooped to penetrate Verrons' chest and disappeared into the temple wall behind him. Swiftly she emerged meters away. She swooped up again, threading the living forms upon her arms, ordering and taming them. With them she created a pyramid in the air. Then, with a sweeping motion, she directed them back through the air. They flattened against the surface of the dome, surrendering motion.

She flowed near. Her words were blown into Verrons' mind. *I live again in the precincts of your power.* Muscular toes arched and curled. Fingers rippled air.

Verrons struggled to form words of his own. Instead the sound of his flute increased in volume.

She brightened, her features becoming distinct. *I waited in the matrix of light. I waited to live in your power. Now it moves me.* Eagerly she arched backward.

Unexpectedly a second cloud appeared. Surging brightness condensed into a second being, dark, violent, his body powerful. He moved on long, thick toes, gathering the remnants of his cloud around him. Then, flexing, he cast himself straight into the air, spinning swiftly.

Verrons heard a gasp. Winchell crouched over the flute case, glowing instrument pressed to his lips. Verrons stared at the young assistant helplessly, unable to move.

A faint remonstrance. *I waited.*

Distracted, he had let the flute slip from his lips. His golden dancer dispersed into mist. Verrons jammed the instrument between his teeth and exhaled with will. She flared bright, her

eyes suddenly glowing green. Exultant, she sprang again, tossing herself up—

—and into the spokes of the violet wheel that flashed across
the temple dome. Quickly she arched her body to form a second wheel. Together they spun through the air, feature and
limb obscured by the fiery speed of motion.

As the two wheeled through the reaches of the dome, Verrons became aware of a third light entity, the blue being of the
night before. It precipitated from the air, flared brilliantly and
flung itself into union with the other two.

Verrons pulled his glance aside. The five aborigines
crouched two meters away. The tallest blew his instrument in-
tently. The others cradled theirs. Light—golden, violet, blue
—reflected across the surfaces of their eyes.

After a time the three entities separated. Verrons' resumed
original form and swooped through the stone above his head,
to reappear from the opposite wall of the temple moments later. She glided to a halt before him. *When I had flesh, I ran the
stones on toes that flexed like springs. I flew with sparks in my
hair and between my eyes I wore a jewel that caught sunlight
and made it a cleaving sword.*

Verrons' mind was lanced with intense light. Into his consciousness flashed a vision that raced stone pavement, a crackling mane sparking behind her. She tossed back a glance and
he knew the line of mouth and eyes. But now she wore flesh
instead of light, her body supple and brown. When she turned
again, her eyes were as green as the flashing jewel recessed
into the flesh between them.

With a leap she soared into the air. They rode above a city
of glassy structures set in aprons of stone plaza. At the edges
of the plaza, jungle crawled dense and wet. *I flew. But my
powers were unmatured. I sank down again, unsatisfied.*

They did sink. Muscular toes touched stone. *But I knew my
power would strengthen, because my line is strong. My male
parent crossed the tangles and the deserts many times and returned with fire still flashing in his jewel. My female parent
rode the high strata, a flesh-deity, until the day she was caught
by storm and torn to her death. I knew it was in my line to
soar the sky.*

I flew. Again she launched herself. This time their journey
was longer. They darted on invisible currents, her sensitive fingers tasting air, her hair crackling as she swung it around her
shoulders. They soared across the city, reached the jungle's
edge and swooped high. Trees grew small below. Suddenly,
fiercely, she arched her back and dove.

They accelerated crazily at the treetops. Verrons' flute uttered a harsh note. She swooped up again and arched through a puffy white cloud. Then she dove again, this time carrying them to rest at the edge of the city.

I flew. But I walked too. My feet carried me a seeking course. I tasted, I smelled, I looked, I touched. My hair caught current from the air and transformed it to fire and my powers grew. I was a force in my time.

Verrons was drawn into a whirl of activity as she flung through the city, testing and examining, trying and discarding. In her eagerness, she seemed to bounce off her world, leaping from situation to situation. Verrons saw color, saw patterns, saw objects and structures, saw others of her kind. But she moved too swiftly for him to resolve anything into detail.

I was, she echoed in his mind. *And now I am again. I take life from your power. I leap, I fly.*

She leapt. She was briefly suspended against a background of brilliant light. Then she began to recede until Verrons held her at a distance, an apron of darkness wide around her. She stood, hair crackling, her arms thrown back to embrace a giant crystal. Throwing her head back, she faded against the crystal, dissolving into it until she was no more than a golden gleam somewhere deep beneath its flashing faces.

Then she emerged again. But somewhere within the crystal she had shed flesh for light. Her hair was a cloud of radiance. *I am!*

She was. She arched about the dome, flashing through darkness like a manic sun. Then she swooped back. *When I had flesh . . .*

Verrons followed her back through the crystal into flesh again. He lived with her her urgent search for a mate, her frantic sorting and testing of males, her ultimate selection. Then two brown bodies arched the skies, darting and racing, green jewel and red flashing. Wind-torn deities, they mingled crackling manes and joined arching bodies. Then they parted, returning to their separate lives.

Verrons lived with her the months she carried the products of conception. Then he fled with her to the stone cavern where she ripped her four young from her own dilating cervix and hissed first life into their gaping mouths. He emerged with her when all four breathed and whisked with her to find an underling to suckle and tend them.

They grew. First hair appeared, but only one of the four sprouted a crackling little mane of power. The others grew hair silky and limp. She flashed the clouds, venting her fury upon the air. Then she tore to a dark quarter where she abandoned her ungifted three. She darted away without looking back. *Let whatever scuttling little person wants them claim them. Let them be reared to sweep and clean, serve and tend. With their dead hair and their powerless minds—they are none of mine.*

She bore her remaining daughter into the clouds. Child in arms, she cometed the sky. When they returned her daughter's eyes glowed red. That was the color of the jewel that was recessed into infant flesh upon the anniversary of the birth. *And I bore my daughter up and taught her. And power flashed between us, an enduring umbilical . . .*

Verrons followed her through subsequent years, through the quests and victories of her ever-developing power. He conquered with her that portion of her world she claimed as her own. Scuttling little people, brows bare of jewels, hair lifeless, swept and cleaned and tended and served—and when she flashed green fire into their weak eyes, they cried and begged to serve some more.

When I had flesh . . .

As she flung through the years, Verrons' strength waned. The sound of his flute grew ragged—his body became numb. But there was no way to communicate his exhaustion to her. Finally she lived in a single dim chamber of his mind, flying, commanding, reigning, surging, a force in her time. Doggedly Verrons supplied the flute with breath.

Finally even that last lighted chamber of his mind darkened. His limbs laxed. The flute fell to the stone floor with a clatter. Verrons slumped unconscious.

Time was a well—deep, black, inescapable. He struggled mindlessly against its dark walls. Much later he returned from a distance, Winchell's voice urgent. "Commander! It's light. We have to get back to camp."

Verrons opened unfocused eyes. He lay on his side on cold stone, muscles unresponsive. With Winchell's help he sat. His flute lay near. Possessively he closed fingers around its cool barrel. "How long was I out?"

"I don't know. I—the aborigines took four of our flutes. Out of our case."

Verrons groped across the floor to the open case. The aborigines had abandoned their own instruments nearby.

"I didn't try to stop them. I—I wasn't much better off than you, except I had my eyes open. They had to carry their lead man away, the big one who was blowing the—the blue."

Verrons nodded numbly. "Same one fainted first night." He

crawled across the floor and examined the abandoned instruments. His muddled mind produced one coherent thought. "Dead."

"What?"

"The abos left them—because they're dead. The flutes, I mean—worn out. Lost their charge. Whatever. That's why—" His voice dribbled away.

"That's why there was only your golden dancer, my violet one and the blue," Winchell said, green eyes sparking with comprehension. "And with only five in their party they couldn't key the mechanism to issue new flutes."

Verrons nodded. Slowly he came to his feet. "We'd better get downhill before they send searchers."

Winchell's features were suddenly anxious. "Commander, when I came up last night I only intended to observe. I didn't— "

"Forget it." When they reached the plaza, Verrons stared toward the single crater on the horizon. Perhaps it marked the city from whose stone pavement they had soared into the air. Perhaps those distant trees were descendants of the ones they had almost intersected in flight. Certainly this sun, rising . . .

His hand tightened on the flute. He had walked half a hundred worlds in the course of his career. He had never before risen and looked over one as alive as this one today.

Even with its former inhabitants dead.

Dead?

"Commander?"

Verrons made the long journey back to the present and accompanied Winchell to the gully. "A few days sleep—"

"We might grab a few hours if we slide in before anyone wakes."

They succeeded and Verrons fell across his cot. He slept dreamlessly, unresponsive to the wakening sounds of camp.

A few hours later he was roused by a more urgent stimulus. He staggered up and plunged out, gripped by an agony of hunger. Rubber legs carried him to the dining area, where one of the cook shift made advance preparations for the noon meal. Verrons communicated his need and the assistant raided a storage box for him. When Verrons had eaten, sending back twice for refills, he slumped across the table.

He was next brought to by an aggressive throat-clearing. Heller. Commander, it was my understanding that anyone who disregarded your orders about remaining in camp last night would be charged with mutinous conduct."

Verrons' tongue responded thickly. "I've appointed Winchell my special assistant. For the duration."

"Oh? I'm surprised you didn't tell me before now."

"So'm I," Verrons responded obdurately.

Heller's hazel eyes narrowed. "Well, I assume you have had time for whatever thinking you consider necessary before permitting us to enter the underground facility."

Blackmail. Verrons sighed. "We'll go after lunch. I'll take Winchell below as my special assistant. You can choose one of your people." His chrono communicated a welcome fact. He had an hour and a half to sleep before he mounted the gully again.

He woke only when Olsen assaulted him with a wet towel. "Commander, Professor Heller is very agitated. You're half an hour late."

Verrons sat up dizzily, his head refusing to clear. Before he was made sufficiently alert with a chemical boost from the med kit, he was later still for his appointment.

Heller greeted him sternly. They ascended, the gully seeming to loom into Verrons' consciousness from another dimension, neither quite real nor illusion. His feet suffered the same malady.

He steadied when faced with the staircase that led to the corridor beneath the grand temple. Moments later he stood below with Winchell, Heller and Nevins. Before them stretched glazed stone floor. At first glance the corridor appeared to lead only to a blank wall. But before they had taken five steps, paneled walls glided aside and they stood in a chamber of the same proportions as the temple above. The ceiling was low, illuminated by glowing panels.

Verrons' head snapped around. His gaze traveled sixty degrees and was captured by a life-size figure of stone. Long and brown she stood, head raised, blue eyes cast up. A blue jewel was recessed into the flesh of her brow. Her long arms were flung backward around an oblong multi-faceted crystal as tall as she. She grasped the stone floor with muscular toes, ready to spring. Verrons was drawn. He stared up into her stone face. The questing spirit captured there was familiar. The individual features were not.

"Commander—around here."

She reappeared on the opposite face of the crystal, this time vividly blue, her body subtly contoured to suggest energy flow. Her arms reached upward. The air around her head was softly illuminated. Verrons gazed into her transformed face, mouth drying. Winchell—last night, did you see anything like this?"

There was brief reticence in Winchell's clear eyes. "You

mean passage through the crystal from—from one state of being to another?"

"Passages from states of being?"

Heller's ears fanned from his skull as he descended upon them. "Just what *did* you learn last night?"

Reluctantly Verrons related his evening's experience, watching it filter through Heller's charged brain and emerged transmogrified. When he had finished, fiery eyes flashed to Winchell.

Winchell related his own experience. "I think the crystal passages were symbolic, Commander, a stylistic device for leading our awareness into the past and back again. I never saw the giant crystal except at those transitions and evidently neither did you. But later—after you passed out, I guess—when I followed my being all the way to the end of his life, I saw him take a small crystal identical to this large one into his hand. He had gone to what he called the dying house and the crystal was brought to him. It was about half the size of the first segment of my little finger. He held it in his hand and—he died. The attendants returned then and opened his hand and the crystal had changed. There was a violet spot at its center—that hadn't been there before."

"And you don't consider *that* symbolic, a stylistic device?" Heller demanded.

Winchell's green eyes were troubled. "I don't know. He—he didn't explain fully what was happening. Maybe the crystal was just a device for registering death. Or it could have been a communicator to summon the attendant. Or it could be that when he died, something—some electro-physical expression of his personality—passed into the crystal. A—a soulprint, you might call it. That's what I think happened."

Heller's eyes flashed to Verrons, incandescent. "Commander? How do *you* interpret what Winchell witnessed?"

Verrons shook his head. He wasn't venturing interpretations until he had taken the journey into her life again, until he had followed her down the passage to her own death . . .

. . . *tonight? Did he want to live her death tonight?*

But it would not be final death, not while he held her flute in hand, her Lazarus-factor.

"Surely you have formulated an interpretation, even if you don't care to share it?"

"I suppose you have, too, Heller." *From your complete dearth of knowledge . . .*

"I most certainly have. The race that created this complex

was obviously in possession of very unusual powers—powers we humans have dreamed of for centuries."

"Provided last night wasn't just flute fantasy."

"Neither of you has presented it as such. These people were able to draw the sun's energy through crystal forms implanted in their flesh. They were able to levitate and to fly for considerable distances. In their later lives they exercised control over inert objects and over the ungifted members of their own race. And now you understand why we have been brought here, don't you, Commander?"

Verrons glummed at the floor. "The grand design?"

"Exactly! We were summoned to become the next race to gain the powers these people held. We have been chosen, of all the races in the galaxy, to take the next step up the evolutionary ladder."

"Then where do the aborigines fit? Don't you grant them any credibility as descendants of the race that constructed the complex?"

"How could they be? Do you see any physical resemblance —beyond the fact that they're humanoid?"

"Mutation. The globe is dotted with nuclear craters." The argument was unsound, he knew. The craters were scarcely old enough to have permitted mutation through the inevitable period of genetic chaos and then reconsolidation into a single homegeneous race. He swung on Heller aggressively. "Then if you're determined they're of different stock, why isn't it their destiny to be the next superrace, Professor?"

"Obviously they're too primitive to make the leap. There is too much developmental ground to be covered. They can't even be classified as stone age—we've seen no sign of tools or weapons. Although, I suppose, if the superrace were physically present to guide them—"

"The abos come up here and toot flute every night."

"That obviously isn't sufficient. They don't have the intelligence to question, to seek and probe."

Verrons abandoned argument. Glancing up, he caught a ring of intent faces at the head of the stairs. "If we're going to seek and probe, we'd better move."

IV

Two additional stone and crystal tableaux occupied the large chamber. The party examined them cursorily while Verrons paced the walls of the chamber. He had covered barely a quarter of his route when panels slid and he looked down a gently sloping corridor.

The others joined him. "Before we go I want to locate all the exits from this chamber and sketch them for reference."

They found three additional exit corridors. They entered the last and the wall behind them closed. Simultaneously walls either side of them folded away. They stood on a ramp in a second large chamber. Verrons scanned their new surroundings. The chamber floor was set with compartmentalized display cases. Within each sealed compartment reposed a single glistening object.

Professor and students launched themselves with glad cries. Only Verrons reacted with choler. For seventeen years study parties under his guidance had chipped and prayed after their precious finds. Here everything was considerately presented in glass-sided cases. The analogy of the interstellar rodent trap twittered to mind. Verrons wriggled his nose suspiciously. His littermates scuttled for the cheese.

Succulent cheese it was. They were offered a well-arranged collection of art objects, fragile bowls and vessels, containers intricately wrought, delicate implements, objects woven of gleaming wire, jewelry massive and grand.

And this chamber was antechamber to still another elaborate display room. Which in turn gave way to another and another.

But the collection, exquisite, extensive, quickly proved finite. Two hours later they found themselves in a chamber that connected only to the one from which they had entered. That chamber in turn connected only to two other cul-de-sac rooms and to the larger chamber from which they had entered it.

When they had exhausted all possibilities Heller flashed hawkish eyes over Verrons' sketch pad. He compared it with the companion map Verrons had rendered of the surface features of the complex. "If you have proportioned these maps correctly, there is an entire underground area we are unable to reach, Commander."

"Where else do you think they put the flute dispensing mechanism and related storage?"

"Ah—of course. But presumably there is entry to those chambers, though apparently we won't discover it here." His eyes flashed over their surroundings. "What do you think of all this, Commander?"

"Very pretty."

"And totally useless. There is nothing of practical usage here and nothing suggesting or depicting day-to-day life. Nothing to tell us more than that the people who assembled this collection included some very gifted artists and craftsmen. Have you any idea why the collection should be so limited?"

"I haven't given it thought."

"It is limited, obviously, because it is only intended as a brief concrete sampling of their abilities. The rest we are intended to learn through the flutes."

Verrons shrugged. "Granted."

"Then you don't intend to obstruct us from coming to the complex as a group tonight? The experience obviously did you and Winchell no harm."

Shrugging again Verrons abdicated sole proprietorship of flutes.

"And now that you've inspected this area, you won't object to my sending a party down tomorrow to photograph and catalogue."

"Not if we make it out in good shape."

"As we shall."

Ladders were strategically placed. When they set foot to rung, the ceiling produced passage. They mounted and emerged.

It was dark when Verrons woke again, anticipation a heady surge in his blood. Sitting, he uncased his flute and stroked its cool barrel, briefly victim of temptation to breathe life to it here and now.

But this was not the place.

Nor, he decided when the party reached the mesa top, was the grand temple. Not tonight. The remainder of the party trekked there, footsteps hushed on shimmering stone. They single-filed into the structure, spread along the walls and sat, silent, hesitant. Flutes were distributed from cases—they had drawn a second case to replace the flutes taken by the aborigines—and came self-consciously to pale lips.

And Verrons didn't want to share light with them. He slipped from the temple as the first tentative notes sounded. Quickly he loped down stone steps. He took her to a small temple that bore twin moons in its arched window. Hands quivering, he brought flute to lips. He tongued the mouthpiece, drew breath and blew.

And nothing happened, nothing beyond a faint haze that draped dolorously in the air. Disconcerted, Verrons blew again, his fingers picking out a simple tune no one had ever heard before.

No one heard it now. No one but Verrons squatting alone in

the chill temple, his lips suddenly cold, twin moons gliding icily across his glazed retinas.

Did she demand the company of her kind? Verrons thought not. But when the hands of his chrono measured a leaden quarter hour and his breath produced nothing but mist, he creaked to his feet and measured tread to the grand temple.

On another night the hypnotic tumult of light might have claimed his awareness. Around the walls of the temple humans and aborigines squatted will-less, glazed eyes reflecting radiant chaos. But Verrons was not dazzled. Stiffly he sat. Muscles clenched in anticipatory agony, he placed his own flute to lips and blew.

She did not materialize. There was only the limp curtain of light he had blown in the lesser temple, forlorn, barren.

Later he barely remembered his staggering journey back across the complex, his perilous descent of the gully. In his own tent, by lamplight, he found the flute's seams.

A complexity of miniature elements occupied the metal barrel: ceramic units, gleaming wires—and a single white crystal, half as large as the first segment of his little finger, at its depths, a golden speck. *His dancer*. But the crystal was shot with fracture lines. When he probed it splintered.

Shattered. Verrons shook bright shards into his palm, loss claiming him. A soulprint etched in crystal—an electrophysical expression of the personality, captured at the moment of death and preserved—but in a medium fatally fragile. He had resurrected her to dance a single night. Exhausted, he had dropped her to the pavement. The clatter of flute on stone echoed in his mind.

He closed his hand around sharp fragments. Verrons left his tent and slipped into the night jungle. The sound of flutes from the mesa laced the night. He emerged at streamside, the smell of mud thick in his nostrils.

I flew with sparks in my hair and between my eyes I wore a jewel that caught sunlight and made it a cleaving sword. Now she cried to light the upper atmosphere with a final crystalline surge. It was gross injustice to lay her to rest in the jungle.

Then he saw the shimmer of twin moons on the surface of the stream. His body tightened. With a flick of his wrist, he committed her to rest. She broke silvered water lightly. Twin disks rippled briefly and she was gone.

Gone from the night, gone from the world. Verrons moved through an empty jungle to a barren tent. He lay staring at an inner play of light, his hands clenched tightly on nothing.

It was dawn when sounds wakened him. He hurried to the

dining area. The party had returned. With single-minded vo-
racity they attacked the food supplies, pulling out bags of concentrate, scooping up powder and pellets with bare hands. Balsky had hauled a bag of carbo-powder to the shadow of the
supply tent and was systematically packing his mouth.

Verrons located Heller at the other side of the tent,
crouched with the five aborigines, spilling hi-pro pellets into
mess bowls.

"You're feeding them?"

Heller's head bobbed up, features haggard. "They're starving, Commander. Feeding them could stimulate them to communicate."

"Then I hope you're prepared to communicate fast, Professor. You're probably poisoning them."

Heller's glance flickered across the aborigines in quick
alarm. "I—" he jabbed at his hairline distractedly. "I hadn't
thought of that. Their metabolisms may not be comparable to
ours at all. I—" His hand quivered. "I saw opportunity. I—"

"Well, don't stop now. This may be your last chance."

Heller bobbed up nervously. "Nevins is my communications
major. Nevins—" His gaze jerked back to the aborigines. They
by-passed the mess bowls and upended the bag of pellets on
the ground. Greedily forked hands scooped. The largest aborigine launched himself face first at the pile of pellets, lip veil
switching.

Verrons yelped for Nevins. Heller and Nevins initiated a
valiant effort involving the humanoid universals, hand language, body language and finally slashing in the moist soil with
finger and pointed stick. "Paper would only confuse them,"
Nevins informed Verrons hastily. "Never employ a medium
more sophisticated then the cultural level of the subject."

"In this case, language," Verrons suggested dryly. The response to Nevins' effort was encouraging. The aborigines continued to feed, scrabbling after elusive pellets, then upending
mess bowls over horn-lined mouths.

By the time bowls were empty the effort had attracted an audience. "Commander, what about the substance we used night
before last?" Balsky suggested.

"Didion? Want to test another brand of poison, Heller?"
Heller acceded immediately.

"Then don't dole out more calories. If the didion takes, let's
establish the condition that food is contingent upon communication. That will give us a lever."

The aborigines accepted the pale liquid readily, sniffing in turn from the vaporizing lid. Dull eyes took gleam almost immediately.

"It's working," Heller crowed. "Their brain tissues—"

"—are still computing food," Verrons snapped as the first aborigine barreled past him, lunging for the supply tent. He fielded the attempt and found himself wrestling a bony fury. The aborigine grunted fiercely, joints flexing in unanticipated directions. Fingers grappled for Verrons' windpipe. A horn-lined mouth affixed itself to Verrons' left cheek. "Stun him!" Verrons bellowed.

The other aborigines had broken the line of startled humans and tore into the supply tent. Their performance commanded more attention than Verrons' plight. "Drop him!"

Winchell seized the weapon from Heller's belt and fired around the frozen professor. The aborigine yelped and slackened. Tearing one arm free, Verrons pulled his own stunner and rendered the abo limp. Hand on bloodied cheek, he bounded to the supply tent to drop the remaining four.

"There is intelligence there," Heller insisted, eyes blazing, as Verrons ordered the five lax bodies dragged beyond camp.

"There's hunger there. Even a dog can find food if he's hungry enough."

"But a dog doesn't bear humanoid form! A dog—"

It was not the moment to explore cosmic implications. "If you want to try again when they unnumb, fetch a bag of pellets—one. And I want stunners at hand. These pretties have just popped up the scale from presumed harmless to potentially deadly. I don't want to drop the 'potentially.' "

The aborigines tossed off the stunner effect quickly. Nevins labored earnestly to convey the connection between the single bag of pellets and the humans' desire for communication. The aborigines responded by launching attack, battering the young assistant savagely.

When they were felled again, Verrons regarded the five lax bodies grimly. "I think we start from the top again, Heller, first getting across the connection between their aggressive tactics and all-all-down. Then we move on to food-communication."

Heller nodded haggardly. "Perhaps the *didion* stimulated aggressive instincts rather than true intelligence," he admitted.

"And maybe when you're starving, aggression is the intelligent response."

But when the aborigines revived, the effects of *didion* had visibly ebbed. They huddled, gazes moving sullenly from stunners to pellets, lip veils fluttering. The largest took his feet, head lowered. Verrons' hand tightened on his stunner. But instead of lunging, the abo turned. His group followed him into the jungle, stalks crackling underfoot.

Heller was crestfallen. Verrons holstered his stunner. "They'll be back. So I'll keep guard over the supplies while the rest of you sleep off the big night." Turning, Verrons noted for the first time the exhaustion of professors and students alike.

His sympathy evaporated when he confronted the mess he was committed to guarding. Boxes and bags had been torn open, powders, pellets, wafers and grains scattered across every surface, including the ground. Grimly Verrons policed the area, salvaging what he could. When the place was tidied he settled in for a long dull day, stunner at hand. Shadows moved silently, stalks bending in the light breeze, green and scarlet leaves rippling. The aborigines did not return.

Not until dusk, when Arguilar summoned Verrons to the edge of camp. The aborigines emerged from the jungle in a group, lip veils switching. The tallest thrust his hands at Verrons.

Verrons stared at the object foisted upon him. It was a small study metal barrel, both ends open, its interior surface set with lightweight metal paddles. Suspended at its center was a round instrument face marked with needled dials. The metal of the barrels was lightly pitted, the clear face of the instrument pack completely unmarked.

The aborigine gestured at the object and grunted.

"Trade?" Verrons guessed, startled. He jabbed at his mouth. The aborigine did likewise, lip veil wagging sharply.

"Fetch a bag of hi-pro pellets," Verrons ordered Arguilar quickly. "Snack wafers too. And Heller if he's close."

Arguilar returned with all three. "They brought this? What is it?" Heller demanded.

Verrons thrust it at him. "Your guess. Ari, keep my stunner ready." He tossed the weapon to the assistant and breached the bag of pellets.

The aborigines dined with gusto, pouring out the pellets in a heap and scooping them up. They sampled the wafers and dispatched them enthusiastically.

"Off hand, I believe it's a weather instrument, Commander. An anenometer." Heller held it up. Dial hands moved as the paddles caught the breeze and rotated within the barrel.

"Sophisticated offering from this crew. And in excellent condition."

"Exactly. It's apparent from this that there are stores of artifacts we know nothing of, items that have been in sheltered storage since the holocaust."

V

Verrons nodded abstractedly. The survey crew had reported total destruction of population centers. Not even minimal debris remained. They had not, however, combed dense jungle over the entire face of the planet. Verrons glanced up at the darkening sky. "You're planning to take the party to the complex tonight?"

"Assuredly. While we all underwent vivid experiences last night, we learned absolutely nothing of the technology, nothing of how these people achieved their effects."

"I don't think it *was* technology. The power was inborn."

"But the crystal set between the eyes was not. Nor the ones like you tell me you found in your flute. And if we can simply learn to record the personality for future reference, it will be a tremendous step forward. Can you imagine being able to walk with Socrates? To follow Newton and Einstein, Leakey and Pardini through their life's work? Can you imagine looking over Shakespeare's shoulder as he—"

"Shakespeare is already dead. But I see your point. So uphill we go and tomorrow I'll try to persuade our friends to fetch more trade booty. But this time I'll follow them."

That night, when the party emerged from the gully, Olsen drew him aside. She pressed her flute into his hand. "I'm not going to use this again. But I think—I think you should, Commander."

Before he could question her she darted ahead like a person who has fulfilled a distasteful duty. Puzzled, Verrons examined the flute.

Winchell fell into step beside him. He indicated the clutch of aborigines trailing the party. "Commander, I've queried the entire party this afternoon. No one caught sight of their race in the visions last night."

"Oh?"

"In fact, I've quizzed almost everyone on their experiences. You know, the people who were born with the power certainly don't seem to have developed scruples to match. There were some instances of really sophisticated brutality and a lot of the other—callousness, unconscious brutality. Evidently they didn't consider the ones who were born without power as truly —human?"

"Little people who scuttled and served?" Verrons frowned. Certainly the quality of mercy had not been strained in his own golden dancer. She had exhibited little empathy for her inferiors. "Well, mark it one sign of intelligence then that the abos avoided contact."

Winchell nodded. "I guess so. You know, the abos might even have developed into an intelligent race. If they'd lasted long enough."

Verrons' sympathies were not engaged. "If the spark had been there they would have hung on."

"But the others didn't, the lightdancers and their underpeople."

Verrons grunted. "And no one caught a hint of what happened to them?"

Winchell's clear eyes flickered away. "I—I'm not sure. Olsen wouldn't talk to me. But none of the others caught anything."

"Well, we'll see."

He said that without suspecting he shortly would see, when he braced himself against the temple wall, put Olsen's flute to mouth and breathed a burning red being into life. For with that fiery vision he breathed more than another surging lightdancer. He breathed another time, another circumstance, when the scuttling little people had become the preponderant mass of the population, when the sparking manes of power had grown few.

Too few. *And in our sparse numbers, we maintained our rule. The weak, the powerless, still they cringed before our swords of light. But we saw that in too few generations we would be not just extinct but dishonored. We saw that when the last of us died the underpeople would cease to give our ancestors life-of-sight with their breath. Instead they would viciously destroy the flutes that are our immortality. We would perish in our crystalline shells, victims of the genetic whimsy that has rendered our offspring too few to continue our kind.*

We would be lost to the universe—the universe that is ours!

But the remaining elite knew they were not alone in that universe. They looked up and they speculated. Somewhere was other life, life similar to their own. For—arrogantly—wasn't the human form the most efficient possible, the most logical? And some day that life, venturing, would inevitably find their planet.

When it did, they would be waiting. Waiting to dance and fly, to flash and spiral. Waiting to relive their entire history, each of them preserved, every line represented, first to last.

And there would be nothing to distract the comers from the waiting flutes. Nor would there be mutinous underpeople to destroy those fragile and precious instruments.

There would be no underpeople at all.

Verrons lived the first steps of temple construction. A site far from any population center was selected and the mesa raised. A storage vault to house the entire collection of flutes —the revered ancestors—was constructed, carefully buffered and shielded. On its inner walls the history of the powered race was inscribed, victory by victory, glory by glory. There were no defeats. Nor would there be.

Verrons was spared the final holocaust only by the death of his escort. In the interval between that deathhouse passage into crystal and the reappearance of the fiery wheel of light, Verrons forcibly extracted his consciousness from the vision world. He jerked the flute from his lips, fingers cramping.

They had destroyed the underpeople to insure their own precarious immortality. First they had erected the temple complex—star bait—and then they had systematically blasted and exterminated. Verrons didn't have to see to know. In a reflex gesture, he hurled the flute. *Die!* It clattered against stone floor.

But disgust was not sufficient to rout him from the temple while other wheels of light flashed. Nor did destruction of the fiery entity cleanse him of ugliness. And at dawn he tore through the food stores with the others, scattering and wasting. Human and aborigine fed side by side, forked hand and fingered pawing greedily.

Verrons was half asleep on his cot when Olsen loomed above him, hesitant. "Commander—"

"You didn't flute." The words were thick.

"No, I—"

"Good. You guard the food. From the abs. Get me if y'have trouble."

"With the aborigines? You want me to—"

"Take m'stunner. Come get me if they go 'way." He lapsed into semi-consciousness.

Sometime later she reappeared. "Commander, the aborigines—I didn't let them at the food stocks. I stunned them. Now they've gone into the jungle."

Verrons sat and peered muzzily at the dial of his chrono. Midday. "Going for trade goods?"

"I don't know. I—do you want me to follow them and find out? By myself?"

Verrons managed to wag an emphatic negative. "Med kit,"

he demanded gruffly. The inside of his head had congealed.

Ten minutes later, stimulants at work, he stepped from the tent and swayed lightly in the noonday breeze. Olsen led him into the jungle. "They have a quarter-hour start now."

"They travel like turtles." And a little like elephants too. Fortunately his mind cleared and his legs steadied. Verrons found the aborigines' trail quickly, followed it easily, Olsen in his wake.

"Commander—"

"We can't gab and sneak simultaneously."

"Oh." Evidently what she had meant to say was not urgent.

Neither was the aborigines' pace through the jungle. They crossed the stream and led Verrons and Olsen away from the temple complex. Soon the two humans drew near enough to hear the tread of feet. "We'd better stay well behind," Verrons whispered hoarsely.

"Commander, the flute I gave you—"

Verrons' jaw tightened. "I destroyed it." The answering flicker in Olsen's pale eyes told him the impulse had touched her, too. He glanced at his chrono, rubbing his stomach. "We should have packed lunch."

"Because the flutes make us hungry," she hissed.

"They—" Verrons halted. He stared at her, his stomach convulsing in fresh hunger.

"All that light and motion—it's *our* energy that powers it," she said vehemently. "Those crystals draw directly from *us*."

Verrons pulled himself very straight, digesting her words. The stumbling fatigue, the voracious hunger, the dizzy faintness—none were simply the result of late nights and irregular hours. He suffered all the symptoms of an exhausted power cell. "Olsen, how do you always hit just the right nail?"

"By being fairly bright," she shot back with asperity. "And by knowing when I'm being used."

As he should have known himself. As he would have known, given a few more days, a few more fainting spells. But the aborigines were moving ahead. "We'll talk about this when we get back to camp. At length."

She nodded grim satisfaction. They moved forward.

As they moved into dense vegetation beyond the stream the aborigines' pace quickened. They stopped twice to feed, pulling down branches heavy with yellow berries and gorging. Verrons and Olsen watched from cover of damp foliage, Verrons' stomach clenching enviously. "If we dared touch native vegetation—"

Olsen glanced at him sharply.

"If we dared," he concluded, settling back.

When they continued, he traveled with stunner at hand, seeking bending stalks and swaying shadows alertly. Underfoot the soil was damp and black, rich with decay.

It was late afternoon when the jungle march halted. Ahead, the aborigines' heavy tread was silenced. Verrons and Olsen waited, then moved forward vigilantly.

Ahead a small dome sat on the jungle floor, partly overgrown with vine. Its door stood open. From its interior Verrons heard the unmistakable grunts of their humanoid guides. And beyond the first dome were others of similar size and construction, lower panels translucent brown, upper panels transparent green.

Cautiously Verrons edged past the first dome and around the first of the second rank. He tapped translucent paneling lightly. It was a plastic material, virtually untouched by deterioration. He pressed his forehead to transparent paneling. Within the dome he could see only dim immobile shapes.

Olsen's features were as bemused as his own. Then, glancing away, she touched Verrons' arm and pointed. Through dense vegetation, he spotted a second cluster of domes. He flared a look back at the structure the aborigines had entered. Quickly he slipped the stunner from Olsen's belt and popped it into her hands. "Keep an eye on them. If they head back toward camp, join me." A motion of his hand indicated the dome cluster ahead. He dodged away.

The second cluster was more extensive than the first and more varied. It included a single longhouse, several small domes and a half-dozen larger ones. Again the exterior paneling, although assaulted by vine, was unmarked by deterioration. Verrons pushed through a hinged door into the longhouse.

The interior held deserted stillness—and chaos. And even by the limited light that filtered through transparent green paneling, Verrons recognized the nature of this particular chaos. Containers large and small were littered and strewn, the floor and every surface of the structure were stained and caked with dried smears. Verrons forded the length of the structure, recognizing other things too—tables, chairs, cook units, water tanks—all of alien design, but recognizable in their function, granted a humanoid context. He had found a cookshack—a devastated one.

Devastated like the supply tent he had policed yesterday morning, devastated by a raging localized storm of hunger.

Pulling at a cabinet door, he found stacked plastic mess trays. Their fastidious arrangement was ironic counterpoint to the unmannered chaos around him.

Disturbed, he emerged at the far end of the cookshack and entered one of the larger circular domes. Again light was dim but contents were recognizable: cots, tables, chairs, chests, miscellany. But this time everything was in fair order.

He was sifting miscellany when Olsen found him. "They've headed back toward camp."

His head snapped up. "Taking what?"

"Another weather instrument, I think. I examined the structure they emerged from before coming for you. It's evidently a storage shed for weather instruments and meteorological supplies. None of them are exactly like anything I handled when I took Instruments, but they're close enough. And there are logs, too. Not very extensive—lots of empty pages. I couldn't read the script, of course, or the numbering system—"

"Just as I can't read this," Verrons interrupted. The item he thrust at her consisted of long limp plastic pages bound with adhesive. They were covered with an incomprehensible interlacing of line and curve. "As bad as my own handwriting."

Her eyes flickered down the limp page. "Meaning we're dealing with someone who has hands? Like our aborigines?"

He nodded. He indicated the furnishings of the dome. "And someone who has arms and legs and torsos and probably heads —like our aborigines. Or some other humanoid race."

"There were only two humanoid races on this world," she reminded him, "unless you want to sub-classify the underpeople as a separate race."

"But they've been dead for several centuries. Totally dead. And this cluster of domes hasn't been here more than a few years."

"The aborigines then?"

The suggestion was ludicrous.

"I'm not too surprised the survey boys missed this. It's well camouflaged, green and brown sunk in jungle growth. And it's far enough from the temple complex that the area wasn't intensively surveyed beyond overflight with animal-life sensors. After all, the survey crew had less than a month to spend on the entire globe.

"But our light-dancers ruled—and flew—this world for centuries. If the abos were coming up the evolutionary scale anywhere near creating this sophisticated a layout, they would have known about it. Yet we didn't sight the abos through any of the fourteen or so flutes we sampled. The one you and I shared was the most recent and he certainly had no knowledge of a second intelligent race sharing this world."

She nodded thoughtfully. "Then there is one other possibility."

"Right. The race that created this outpost came from offworld, as we did."

"So this has to be just that—an outpost."

"And I suggest we paw around some more before we carry speculation farther."

She agreed. They tackled miscellany together.

Five minutes later they had their key. Verrons spread it on a table and they bent over it together. Heavy silence stretched between them.

"A photo album," Olsen said finally, softly.

"Of the folks back home." The faces that looked up at him from printed plastic pages were familiar: bifurcate nostrils, round oral orifices, fleshy violet veils cascading from the lower lip arcs. The forked hands were familiar too. The physiques might have been, starved of fat and muscle tissue, bared of gowns, robes, trousers and brilliant swathings, the flesh smeared instead with mud. Verrons flicked quickly through the volume. Their 'aborigines' appeared against the technological background of some unidentifiable other world, patron-masters of science and the machine. Even though they could not decipher the script that covered the page backs, Verrons and Olsen read substantially from the photo presentation.

When they had reached the last page, they slapped the album shut and gazed at each other. "They were either surveying this place or actually settling it," Verrons said finally. "A quick look around should tell us. And a bedcount should tell us how many of them there were originally."

Olsen nodded somberly.

The original party had consisted, they soon determined, of better than four dozen members. And they had come equipped to farm. Verrons even located their seed storage. Bags and cartons had been untidily opened and thrown about. "Presumably the seed was never planted," he said, prying a single flat green seed from a crevice in the flooring. "Probably just devoured when the kitchen stocks ran out."

"Surely they brought some surplus food supplies," Olsen said. "Enough to carry them a season or two if their first crops didn't do well."

"But flutes make hungry. And that's not all. Flutes make sleepy, dizzy, dull—"

"Dead," Olsen finished tersely. "Especially since they were

finally left to live off the land. Which obviously supplies them nothing like a balanced or adequate diet for their species. Do you think—if our supplies will stretch to feed them—they have any chance of recovery? Of actually going ahead with their settlement?"

Verrons shrugged. "Who knows? *If* there's been no substantial brain damage, *if* both sexes are represented, provided that's necessary, *if* we could find a few more stray seed—if, if, if." He glanced up. Dusk eased across the face of the jungle. "Are you game to trek back by moonlight?"

Olsen was game. Rolling the photo album and tucking it into a pocket, Verrons led way, stunner in hand, eyes watchful.

"The light-dancers used them like disposable power packs. That's how they used their underpeople and that's how they're using us too, Commander," Olsen said grimly. "We'll exhaust our supplies prematurely and we certainly won't do the work we came to do. You can see disorganization creeping in already."

"I can—now. But you and I know something the other members of our party don't."

"Oh? We'll tell them, won't we? When we get back?"

"No, I mean something else. We know a lot about the structure of the underground flute storage chambers. We know, for instance, that the substructure area was carefully engineered so the flutes would not be endangered when the population centers were bombed."

She stared at him blankly.

"That means—conversely—that if we deliver an explosive to the storage area the force of the explosion will be absorbed there without seriously damaging the terrain around camp—or even, probably, the mesa and the temple complex."

Olsen brightened. She flicked back pale hair. "We have explosives, Commander."

"We sure do." He stared down at his hand. Two nights ago it had cradled his golden dancer's accidentally shattered crystal. Last night it had deliberately terminated the fiery dancer's immortality. Now, he vowed, that hand would operate on a grander scale.

When they reached camp, pole lamps glowed spottily, a few lighted, most dark. The supply tent was in a state of devastation. From the mesa flutes sounded, melody of night, drunken, disorganized.

Dying.

"We'll have to wait till light," Verrons reminded Olsen.

"Can't take the chance of collapsing the grand temple on Heller's head. Think you can slip uphill and snatch a couple of flute cases without disturbing our dreamers? And without falling under the spell yourself?" His mood was suddenly euphoric.

"Why do you keep asking if I can deliver?" she jibed, disappearing into darkness.

Why indeed? By the time he had extracted the explosive from storage, studied the use manual, calculated and measured, she had returned with two empty flute cases. He glanced up sharply, almost expecting to see the dazzle of light reflected in her eyes.

Instead he saw purpose. "What are we going to do about the flutes they have with them, Commander?"

"You're ready to launch a real vendetta, aren't you?"

She bared small white teeth. "I'll settle for total destruction."

He nodded. They had shared more than one tempering experience in the past two days. "You don't think we should leave Heller one or two flutes? For research purposes?"

There was no ambivalence in her expression. "No, I don't. Why should we be any more compassionate than they were?"

But Olsen had never entertained a golden dancer. She had never mated in the clouds, even if only vicariously. Her red dancer had been too busy with weighty affairs to skim the morning sky, to dance the rainbow. He had shown her only the coldly brutal side of his race.

Verrons' golden dancer had shown him more. His hands quivered as he packed the two flute cases and fused the contents. "Now. Think you can sleep?"

She wagged her head emphatically. "No."

He didn't think he could either. But neither of them kept death watch that night. Within the hour both were flung across cots—she brought hers from her tent—asleep.

Tent panels lightened with dawn. Verrons awoke. He sat stiffly and gazed down at his partner in destruction. She was less fearsome in sleep. She looked, in fact, as if she could be disregarded if he changed his mind and returned the explosive to its container, the flute cases to Heller. She looked less compelling than a vision that brandished green light like a sword.

Until she opened her eyes. "They're back." A quick motion brought her to her feet, flute case in hand.

Supply tent revels rang from the opposite end of camp as they slipped into the dawn jungle. Fortunately they met no stragglers. They fleeted dense shadow and mounted the gully.

At the top, when they stepped to glistening pink stone, even Olsen softened. "Just in case, I want to have a last look at the grand dome."

"You don't trust our red man to have engineered the sub-structure adequately?"

She tossed off a wry gesture. "I've been dreaming explosions. So—just in case, I'm going to have a look."

Just in case, he accompanied her.

Their attention was distracted from architecture by the single lax body that sprawled on the stone floor beneath the grand dome. Verrons bent quickly. It was Heller, his flute still clutched tight in protective fingers. Verrons placed ear to chest. "He's alive—just unconscious."

"And they were too brute-dumb-hungry to revive him and get him back to camp," Olsen said indignantly. "Now we'll have to do it. We'll have to drag him down the gully with us after we—"

But her indignation buzzed in Verrons' ears like the diatribe of a bee, furious, futile. His knees buckled and he sat on the cold stone floor, suddenly shaking with hysterical glee. Some mad-dog bomb squad they made, the grizzled Service veteran and the freckle-faced coed. He laughed gustily, tears coming to his eyes. When he regained control, he demanded hoarsely, "What are we going to use for bodies, killer?"

Olsen didn't see cause for risibility. "Bodies?" Coldly.

"We're going to drop our explosives down the dispensing blocks, aren't we? And make boom?"

"We are."

"Well, it takes six bodies to persuade the stone to open its mouth, Olsen. I count three here, one we'll have to drag, the other two sound enough physically but a little mush-headed. Don't you think?"

Slowly Olsen sat, her mouth sagging. "I forgot. All our plans, so much happening—" She shook her head. But her demoralization was brief. Her slight features cleared and she jumped up again, jabbing a forefinger at the unconscious professor. "He stumbled and broke his ankle, Commander, coming out of the grand temple. We'll need help to get him down the gully to camp."

Verrons' brows flickered up in admiration. "You're right. We'll need at least three strong young bodies. Winchell for starts. The other two I'll leave to your discretion."

She was off again. Verrons stood, prying the flute from Heller's clenched fingers. He examined the instrument, then zippered it into a tool pocket. The professor he dragged toward the temple where Olsen had agreed to bring her party.

As they crossed the plaza, early sunlight touched Heller's eyes. They opened and stared, unfocused. "Professor? Feel like walking?" Verrons probed gently.

"Ngwf."

By the time they reached the small temple, Heller was able to focus his eyes, somewhat. Life returned to his limbs. They moved, if uncoordinatedly. His response to Verrons' cautiously phrased queries were more forceful. Verrons squatted, forcing himself to watch Heller's weak struggles with a clinical eye. Over a period of two years, three, four at most, the flutes had transformed a party of fifty-two vigorous and enterprising settlers into a clutch of five naked starving brutes. Verrons juggled fancy terminology: tissue starvation, brain damage, terminal malnutrition.

The flutes would wreak the same damage to the human party if unchecked. The light-dancers had destroyed their own mother race and they would destroy any other humanoid race that walked into their glistening trap. Because their own flashy survival was all they had considered of significance, Verrons stroked explosive flute cases.

Then he heard human voices echoing across the stone plaza. When they drew near, he activated the fuse timers and jumped up, both cases in hand.

Olsen led Winchell, Waller and Balsky into the temple. "The professor insisted on coming." She indicated the bag on her back. "And I picked up the rest of the flutes lying around the supply and dining area." Her jaw squared vengefully. "No one thought to ask about stretcher or splints."

That Verrons could believe. It was a rumpled and stuporous crew she had assembled, heads listing, shoulders sagging, eyes vacant.

But this wasn't the occasion for parade call. Their presence had already been noted. From the center of the temple floor the stone block rose, slowly, with inevitable majesty.

With less majesty, Verrons darted forward. A rectangular case appeared from the maw of the mechanism. He jammed it back into the hold and shoved a second case after it.

The end of the block closed. Slowly stone reunited with floor. Olsen's pale eyes flashed wildly. She visibly restrained herself from crowing.

"Come on," Verrons snapped, grabbing at Heller's armpit. "I gave us fifteen minutes to lob in two booms and get down the gully."

They wrestled the lean professor across the plaza to the next temple, their three cohorts zombieing behind, eyes glazed. There, again, stone rose.

"My turn," Olsen insisted.

And a nice job she did, Verrons acknowledged later. A nice job they both did, herding their stuporous colleagues across the plaza and into the mouth of the gully. Pausing at the edge of stone, Olsen wriggled the bag of flutes off her back. With a gesture exultant, she flung it over the side of the mesa.

By the time they reached the bottom of the gully themselves, Heller was live with protest, all limbs indignant, eyes blazing. "Commander, I can travel under my own power. I'm no invalid. I—"

"Then run!" Verrons seized the professor's arm and propelled him toward the jungle. Glancing back, he saw that Olsen urged the other three into motion.

A sharp crump halted the entire party. Briefly frozen, all stared back at the mesa. A second crump moved its rocky sides and lifted the hat briefly off the single temple visible above. Slowly stone settled back into place. The temple quivered but held.

Heller's lean throat writhed and gave birth. "Commander, what—"

"We've killed the flutes!" Olsen said.

No one believed her. All eyes swung to Verrons for contradiction. Even Winchell. Waller and Balsky achieved fleeting alertness.

Verrons nodded. "We slung explosive into the flute crypts. The rest of the temple complex should be intact—more or less —for future researchers. You can draw historical data from the interior wall of the crypts—they're inscribed with a detailed history of the race—if you can piece them back together and decipher them. You might even pin down the technology there—to whatever extent it ever existed. But you can forget the flutes."

Heller gobbled. "You've casually, unilaterally, shattered the instruments of the evolutionary plan? You've—"

"The plan is survival, Heller. Nothing esoteric about that. It's the same on every world. Who can survive does. Who can't —doesn't."

Heller didn't see it that way. Frothing, gesticulating, he launched verbal attack. "You cannot subvert the plan and live, Verrons. The plan has existed since time began. Not just Earth time—total time, consciousness time. The plan—"

"Then look at it this way, Heller. If there is a plan I'm a part of it, too. And I've just fulfilled my function." Turning, Verrons waded away through jungle growth, abandoning them. He had only done what he had to.

He had, in fact, done what he had to in more ways than one. His step quickened as he touched Heller's flute, still zippered securely into his pocket. He felt confident it was alive. When he reached camp, he would hide it in his case and no one would know it had survived. But one night soon Verrons would make his way from camp to some deserted spot far away and he would soar the clouds again. Patting the metal barrel, he sprinted toward camp.

A FULL MEMBER
OF THE CLUB

Bob Shaw

Take a knowledge of the British club system, add the evidence of social castes in modern society, and a perceptive author recently transplanted from embattled Belfast to England, an you come up with a realistic evaluation of how an alien civilization might conduct profitably its contacts with our not-too-civilized world.

It was a trivial thing—a cigarette lighter—which finally wrecked Philip Connor's peace of mind.

Angela and he had been sitting at the edge of her pool for more than an hour. She had said very little duriing that time, but every word, every impatient gesture of her slim hands, had conveyed the message that it was all over between them.

Connor was sitting upright on a canvas chair, manifestly ill at ease, trying to understand what had brought about the change in their relationship. He studied Angela carefully, but her face was rendered inscrutable, inhuman, by the huge insect eyes of her sunglasses. His gaze strayed to a lone white butterfly as it made a hazardous flight across the pool and passed, twinkling like a star, into the shade of the birches.

He touched his forehead and found it buttery with sweat. "This heat is murderous."

"It suits me," Angela said, another reminder that they were no longer as one. She moved slightly on the lounger, altering the brown curvatures of her semi-nakedness.

Connor stared nostalgically at the miniature landscape of flesh, the territory from which he was being evicted, and reviewed the situation. The death of an uncle had made Angela rich, *very* rich, but he was unable to accept that as sufficient reason for her change in attitude. His own business interests brought him more than two-hundred thousand a year, so she knew he wasn't a fortune hunter.

"I have an appointment in a little while," Angela said with a patently insincere little smile.

Connor decided to try making her feel guilty. "You want me to leave?"

He was rewarded by a look of concern, but it was quickly gone, leaving the beautiful face as calm and immobile as before.

Angela sat up, took a cigarette from a pack on the low table, opened her purse and brought out the gold cigarette lighter. It slipped from her fingers, whirred across the tiles and went into the shallow end of the pool. With a little cry of concern she reached down into the water and retrieved the lighter, wetting her face and tawny hair in the process. She clicked the dripping lighter once and it lit. Angela gave Connor a strangely wary glance, dropped the lighter back into her purse and stood up.

"I'm sorry, Phil," she said. "I have to go now."

It was an abrupt dismissal but Connor, emotionally bruised as he was, scarcely noticed. He was a gypsy entrepreneur, a wheeler-dealer, one of the very best—and his professional instincts were aroused. The lighter had ignited first time while soaking wet, which meant it was the best he had ever seen, and yet its superb styling was unfamiliar to him. This fact bothered Connor. It was his business to know all there was to know about the world's supply of sleek, shiny, expensive goodies, and obviously he had let something important slip through his net.

"All right, Angie." He got to his feet. "That's a nice lighter —mind if I have a look?"

She clutched her purse as though he had moved to snatch it. "Why don't you leave me alone? Go away, Phil." She turned and strode off toward the house.

"I'll stop by for a while tomorrow."

"Do that," she called without looking back. "I won't be here."

Connor walked back to his Lincoln, lowered himself gingerly onto the baking upholstery and drove into Long Beach. It was late in the afternoon but he went back to his office and began telephoning various trade contacts, making sure they too were unaware of something new and radical in cigarette lighters. Both his secretary and telephonist were on vacation so he did all the work himself. The activity helped to ease the throbbing hurt of having lost Angela, and—in a way he was unable to explain—gave him a comforting sense that he was doing something toward getting her back or at least finding out what had gone wrong between them.

He had an illogical conviction that the little gold artifact was somehow connected with their breaking up. The idea was utterly ridiculous, of course, but in thinking back over the interlude by the pool with Angela it struck him that, amazingly for her, she had gone without smoking. Although it probably meant she was cutting down, another possibility was that she had not wanted to produce the lighter in his presence.

Realizing his inquiries were getting him nowhere, he closed up the office and drove across town to his apartment. The evening was well advanced yet seemingly hotter than ever—the sun had descended to a vantage point from which it could attack more efficiently, slanting its rays through the car windows. He let himself into his apartment, showered, changed his clothes and prowled unhappily through the spacious rooms wishing Angela was with him. A lack of appetite robbed him of even the solace of food. At midnight he brewed coffee with his most expensive Kenyan blend, deriving a spare satisfaction from the aroma, but took only a few disappointed sips. *If only*, he thought for the thousandth time, *they could make it taste the way it smells*.

He went to bed, consciously lonely, yearned for Angela until he fell asleep.

Next morning Connor awoke feeling hungry and, while eating a substantial breakfast, was relieved to find he had regained his usual bouyant outlook on life. It was perfectly natural for Angela to be affected by the sudden change in her circumstances, but when the novelty of being rich, instead of merely well off, had faded he would win her back. And in the meanwhile he—the man who had been first in the country with Japanese liquid display watches—was not going to give up on a simple thing like a new type of cigarette lighter.

Deciding against going to his office, he got on the phone and set up further chains of business inquiries, spreading his net as far as Europe and the Far East. By midmorning the urge to

see Angela again had become very strong. He ordered his car
to be brought round to the main entrance of the building and
he drove south on the coast road to Asbury Park. It looked
like being another day of unrelieved sunshine, but a fresh
breeze from the Atlantic was fluttering in the car windows and
further elevating his spirits.

When he got to Angela's house there was an unfamiliar car
in the U-shaped driveway. A middle-aged man wearing a tan
suit and steel-rimmed glasses was on the steps, ostentatiously
locking the front door. Connor parked close to the steps and
got out.

The stranger turned to face him, jingling a set of keys. "Can
I help you?"

"I don't think so," Connor said, resenting the unexpected
presence. "I called to see Miss Lomond."

"Was it a business matter? I'm Millett of Millett and Fies-
ler."

"No—I'm a friend." Connor moved impatiently toward the
doorbell.

"Then you should know Miss Lomond doesn't live here any
more. The house is going up for sale."

Connor froze, remembering Angela had said she wouldn't
be around, and shocked that she had not told him about selling
out. "She did tell me, but I hadn't realized she was leaving so
soon," he improvised. "When's her furniture being collected?"

"It isn't. The property is being sold fully furnished."

"She's taking nothing?"

"Not a stick. I guess Miss Lomond can afford new furniture
without too much difficulty," Millett said drily, walking toward
his car. "Good morning."

"Wait a minute." Connor ran down the steps. "Where can I
get in touch with Angela?"

Millett ran a speculative eye over Connor's car and clothing
before he answered. "Miss Lomond has bought Avalon—but I
don't know if she has moved in yet."

"Avalon? You mean . . . ?" Lost for words, Connor pointed south in the direction of Point Pleasant.

"That's right." Millett nodded and drove away. Connor got
into his own car, lit his pipe and tried to enjoy a smoke while
he absorbed the impact of what he had heard. Angela and he
had never discussed finance—she simply had no interest in the
subject—and it was only through oblique references that he
guesstimated the size of her inheritance as in the region of a
million, perhaps two. But Avalon was a rich man's folly in the
old Randolph Hearst tradition. Surrounded by a dozen square

miles of the choicest land in Philadelphia, it was the nearest thing to a royal palace that existed outside Europe.

Real estate was not one of Connor's specialties, but he knew that anybody buying Avalon would have had to open the bidding at ten million or more. In other words, Angela was not merely rich—she had graduated into the millionaires' super-league, and it was hardly surprising that her emotional life had been affected.

Connor was puzzled, nevertheless, over the fact that she was selling all her furniture. There was among several cherished pieces, a Gaudreau writing desk for which she had always shown an exaggerated possessiveness. Suddenly aware that he could neither taste nor smell the imported tobacco which had seemed so good in his pouch, Connor extinguished his pipe and drove out onto the highway.

He had traveled south for some five miles before admitting to himself that he was going to Avalon.

The house itself was invisible, screened from the road by a high redbrick wall. Age had mellowed the brickwork, but the coping stones on top had a fresh appearance and were surmounted by a climb-proof wire fence. Connor drove along beside the wall until it curved inwards to a set of massive gates which were closed. At the sound of his horn a thickset man with a gun on his hip, wearing a uniform of *cafe-au-lait* gabardine, emerged from a lodge. He looked out through the gate without speaking.

Connor lowered a car window and put his head out. "Is Miss Lomond at home?"

"What's your name?" the guard said.

"I'm Philip Connor."

"Your name isn't on my list."

"Look, I only asked if Miss Lomond was at home."

"I don't give out information."

"But I'm a personal friend. You're obliged to tell me whether she's at home or not."

"Is that a fact?" The guard turned and sauntered back into the lodge, ignoring Connor's shouts and repeated blasts on the horn. Angered by the incident, Connor decided not to slink away. He began sounding the car horn in a steady bludgeoning rhythm—five seconds on, five seconds off. The guard did not reappear. Five minutes later a police cruiser pulled alongside with two state troopers in it and Connor was moved on with an injunction to calm down.

For lack of anything better to do he went to his office.

A week went by, during which time Connor drew a complete blank on the cigarette lighter and was almost forced to the conclusion that it had been custom-built by a modern Faberge. He spent hours trying to get a telephone number for Angela, without success. Sleep began to elude him, and he felt himself nearing the boundary separating rationality from obsession. Finally, he saw a society column picture of Angela in a New York nightspot with Bobby Janke, playboy son of an oil billionaire. Apart from making Connor feel ill with jealousy the newspaper item provided him with the information that Angela was taking up residence at her newly acquired home sometime the following weekend.

Who cares? he demanded of his shaving mirror. *Who cares?*

He began drinking vodka tonics at lunchtime on Saturday, veered onto white rum during the afternoon, and by nightfall was suffused with a kind of alcoholic dharma which told him that he was entitled to see Angela and to employ any means necessary to achieve that end. There was the problem of the high brick wall but, with a flash of enlightenment, Connor realized that walls are mainly psychological barriers. To a person who understood their nature as well as he did, walls became doorways. Taking a mouthful of neat rum to strengthen his sense of purpose, Connor sent for his car.

Avalon's main entrance, scene of earlier defeat, was in darkness when he reached it, but lights were showing in the gate lodge. Connor drove on by, following the line of the wall, parked on a deserted stretch of second-class road. He switched off all lights, opened the trunk, took out a heavy hammer and chisel, crossed the verge and—without any preliminaries—attacked the wall. Ten minutes later, although the mortar was soft with age, he had not succeeded in removing one brick and was beginning to experience doubts. Then a brick came free and another virtually tumbled out after it. He enlarged the hole to an appropriate size and crawled through onto dry turf.

A dwarfish half-moon was perched near zenith, casting a wan radiance on the turrets and gables of a mansion which sat on the crest of a gentle rise. The building was dark and forbidding, and as he looked at it Connor felt the warm glow in his stomach fade away. He hesitated, swore at himself and set off up the slope, leaving his hammer and chisel behind. By bearing to the left he brought the front elevation of the building into view and was encouraged to see one illuminated window on the first floor. He reached a paved approach road, followed it to the Gothic-style front entrance and rang for admission. A full minute later the door was opened by an archetypal and startled-looking butler, and Connor sensed immediately that Angela was not at home.

He cleared his throat. "Miss Lomond . . ."

"Miss Lomond is not expected until mid . . ."

"Midnight," Connor put in, expertly taking his cue. "I know that—I was with her this afternoon in New York. We arranged that I would stop by for a late drink."

"I'm sorry, sir, but Miss Lomond didn't tell me to expect visitors."

Connor looked surprised. "She didn't? Well, the main thing is she remembered to let them know at the gate lodge." He squeezed the butler's arm democratically. "You know, you couldn't get through that gate in a Sherman tank if your name wasn't on the list."

The butler looked relieved. "One can't be too careful these days, sir."

"Quite right. I'm Mr. Connor, by the way—here's my card. Now show me where I can wait for Miss Lomond. And, if it isn't imposing too much, I'd like a Daiquiri. Just one to toy with while I'm waiting."

"Of course, Mr. Connor."

Exhilarated by his success, Connor was installed in an enormous green-and-silver room and supplied with a frosty glass. He sat in a very comfortable armchair and sipped his Daiquiri. It was the best he had ever tasted.

The sense of relaxation prompted him to reach for his pipe but he discovered it must have been left at home. He prowled around the room, found a box of cigars on a sideboard and took one from it. He then glanced around for a lighter. His gaze fell on a transparent ruby-colored ovoid sitting upright on an occasional table. In no way did it resemble any table lighter he had ever seen, but he had become morbidly sensitive on the subject, and the ovoid was positioned where he would have expected a lighter to be.

Connor picked it up, held it to the light and found it was perfectly clear, without visible works. That meant it could not be a lighter. As he was setting it down, he allowed his thumb to slide into a seductively shaped depression on the side.

A pea-sized ball of radiance—like a bead fashioned from sunlight—appeared at the top of the egg. It shone with absolute steadiness until he removed his thumb from the dimple.

Fascinated by his find, he made the tiny globe of brilliance appear and disappear over and over again, proved its hotness with a fingertip. He took out the pocket magnifier he always carried for evaluating trinkets and examined the tip of the egg.

The glass revealed a minute silver plug set flush with the surface, but nothing more. Following a hunch, Connor carefully guided one drop of liquid from his drink onto the egg and made sure it was covering the nearly invisible plug. When he operated the lighter it worked perfectly, the golden bead burning without wavering until the liquid had boiled off into the air.

He set the lighter down and noticed yet another strange property—the ruby egg was smoothly rounded at the bottom yet it sat upright, with no tendency to topple over. His magnifier showed an ornate letter P engraved in the base, but provided no clue as to how the balancing act was achieved.

Connor gulped the remainder of his drink and, with eyes suddenly sober and watchful, took a fresh look around the room. He discovered a beautiful clock, apparently carved from solid onyx. As he had half-expected there was no way to open it and the same elaborate P was engraved on the underside.

There was also a television set which had a superficial resemblance to an expensive commercial model but which bore no maker's name plaque. He checked it over and found the now-familiar P inscribed on one side where it would never be noticed except by a person making a purposeful search. When he switched the set on the image of a newscaster which appeared was so perfect that he might have been looking through a plate glass window into the man's face. Connor studied the picture from a distance of only a few inches and could not resolve it into lines or dots. His magnifier achieved no better results.

He switched the television off and returned to the armchair, filled with a strange and powerful emotion. Although it was in his nature to be sharp and acquisitive—those were attributes without which he could never had entered his chosen profession—it had always remained uppermost in his mind that the world's supply of money was unlimited, whereas his own allocation of years was hopelessly inadequate. He could have trebled his income by working longer and pushing harder, but had always chosen another course simply because his desire for possessions had never taken control.

That, however, had been before he discovered the sort of possessions real money could buy. He knew he was particularly susceptible to gadgets and toys, but the knowledge did nothing to lessen the harsh raw hunger he now felt.

There was no way that anybody was going to stop him from joining the ranks of those who could afford future-technology artifacts. He would prefer to do it by marrying Angela, because he loved her and would enjoy sharing the experiences, but if she refused to have him back he would do it by making the necessary millions himself.

A phrase which had been part of his train of thought isolated itself in his mind. *Future technology*.. He weighed the implications for a moment then shrugged them off—he had lost enough mental equilibrium without entertaining fantasies about time travel.

The idea, though, was an intriguing one. And it answered certain questions. The lighters he coveted, partly for their perfection and partly because they could earn him a fortune, were technically far in advance of anything on the world's markets, yet it was within the realms of possibility that a furtive genius was producing them in a back room somewhere. But that impossibly good television set could not have been manufactured without the R&D facilities of a powerful electronics concern. The notion that they were being made in the future and shipped back in time was only slightly less ridiculous than the idea of a secret industry catering exclusively for the superrich . . .

Connor picked up the cigar and lit it, childishly pleased at having a reason to put the ruby egg to work. His first draw on the cool smoke gave him the feeling that he had been searching for something all his life and suddenly had found it. Cautiously at first and then with intense pleasure he filled his lungs with the unexpected fragrance.

He luxuriated. This was smoking as protrayed by tobacco company commercials—not the shallow disappointing experience commonly known to smokers everywhere. He had often wondered why the leaf which smelled so beguiling before it was lit, or when someone nearby was smoking, promising sensual delights and heart's ease, never yielded anything more than virtually tasteless smoke.

They promise you 'a long cool smoke to soothe a troubled world', Connor thought, *and this is it*. He took the cigar from his mouth and examined the band. It was of unembellished gold and bore a single ornate P.

"I might have known," he announced to the empty room. He looked around through a filigree of smoke, wondering if everything in the room was different from the norm, superior, better than the best. Perhaps the ultra-rich scorned to use *any-thing* that was available to the man-in-the-street or advertised on television or . . .

"Philip!" Angela stood in the doorway, pale of face, shocked and angry. "What are you doing here?"

"Enjoying the best cigar I've ever had." Connor got to his feet, smiling. "I presume you keep them for the benefit of guests—I mean, a cigar is hardly your style."

"Where's Gilbert?" she snapped. "You're leaving right now."

"Not a chance."

"That's what you think." Angela turned with an angry flail of blonde hair and cerise skirts.

Connor realized he had to find inspiration and get in fast. "It's too late, Angela. I've smoked your cigar, I lit it with your lighter, I have checked the time with your clock, and I've watched your television."

He had been hoping for a noticeable reaction and was not disappointed—Angela burst into tears. "You bastard! You had no *right!*"

She ran to the table, picked up the lighter and tried to make it work. Nothing happened. She went to the clock, which had stopped; and to the television set, which remained lifeless when she switched it on. Connor followed her circuit of the room, feeling guilty and baffled. Angela dropped into a chair and sat with her face in her hands, huddled and trembling like a sick bird. The sight of her distress produced a painful churning in his chest. He knelt in front of Angela.

"Listen, Angie," he said. "Don't cry like that. I only wanted to see you again—I haven't done anything."

"You touched my stuff and made it change. They told me it would change if anybody but a client used it . . . and it has."

"This doesn't make sense. Who said what would change?"

"The suppliers." She looked at him with tear-brimmed eyes and all at once he became aware of a perfume so exquisite that he wanted to fall toward its source like a suffocating man striving toward air.

"What did you . . . ? I don't . . ."

"They said it would all be spoiled."

Connor tried to fight off the effects of the witch-magic he had breathed. "Nothing has been spoiled, Angie. There's been a power failure . . . or something . . ." His words trailed away uncertainly. The clock and the television set were cordless. He took a nervous drag on the half-smoked cigar and almost gagged on the flat acrid taste of it. The sharp sense of loss he experienced while stubbing it out seemed to obliterate all traces of his scepticism.

He returned to Angela's chair and knelt again. "They said this stuff would stop working if anybody but you touched it?"

"Yes."

"But how could that be arranged?"

She dabbed her eyes with a handkerchief. "How would I know? When Mr. Smith came over from Trenton he said something about all his goods having an . . . essence field, and he said I had a molecular thumbprint. Does that make sense?"

"It almost does," Connor whispered. "A perfect security system. Even if you lost your lighter at the theatre, when somebody else picked it up it would cease to be what it was."

"Or when somebody breaks into your home."

"Believe me, it was only because I had to see you again, Angie. You know that I love you."

"Do you, Philip?"

"Yes, darling." He was thrilled to hear the special softness return to her voice. "Look, you have to let me pay for a new lighter and television and . . ."

Angela was shaking her head. "You couldn't do it, Philip."

"Why not?" He took her hand and was further encouraged when she allowed it to remain in his.

She gave him a tremulous smile. "You just couldn't. The installments are too high."

"Installments? For God's sake, Angie, *you* don't buy stuff on time."

"You can't buy these things—you pay for a service. I pay in installments of eight hundred and sixty-four thousand dollars."

"A year?"

"Once every forty-three days. I shouldn't be telling you all this, but . . ."

Connor gave an incredulous laugh. "That comes to about six million a year—nobody would pay that much!"

"Some people would. If you even have to think about the cost Mr. Smith doesn't do business with you."

"But . . ." Connor incautiously leaned within range of Angela's perfume and it took his mind. "You realize," he said in a weak voice, "that all your new toys come from the future? There's something fantastically wrong about the whole set-up."

"I've missed you, Philip."

"That perfume you're wearing—did it come from Mr. Smith, too?"

"I tried not to miss you, but I did." Angela pressed her face against his and he felt the coolness of tears on her cheek. He kissed her hungrily as she moved down from the chair to kneel against him. Connor spun towards the center of a whirlpool of ecstasy.

"Life's going to be so good when we're married," he heard

himself saying after a time. "Better than we could ever have dreamed. There's not much for us to share and . . ."

Angela's body stiffened and she thrust herself away from him. "You'd better go now, Philip."

"What is it? What did I say?"

"You gave yourself away, that's all."

Connor thought back. "Was it what I said about sharing? I didn't mean your money—I was talking about life . . . the years . . . the experiences."

"Did you?"

"I loved you before you even knew you would inherit a cent."

"You never mentioned marriage before."

"I thought that was understood," he said desperately. "I thought you . . ." He stopped speaking as he saw the look in Angela's eyes. Cool, suspicious, disdainful. The look that the very rich had always given to outsiders who tried to get into their club without the vital qualification of wealth.

She touched a bellpush and continued standing with her back to him until he was shown out of the room.

The ensuing days were bad ones for Connor. He drank a lot, realized that alcohol was no answer, and went on drinking. For a while he tried getting in touch with Angela and once even drove down to Avalon. The brickwork had been repaired at the point where he had made his entry, and a close inspection revealed that the entire wall was now covered with a fine mesh. He had no doubt that tampering with it in any way would trigger off an alarm system.

When he awoke during the night he was kept awake by hammering questions. What was it all about? Why did Angela have to make such odd payments, and at such odd intervals? What would men from the future want with Twentieth Century currency?

On several occasions the thought occurred that, instead of concentrating on Angela, he would do better to find the mysterious Mr. Smith of Trenton. The flicker of optimism the idea produced was quenched almost immediately by the realization that he simply did not have enough information to provide a lead. It was a certainty that the man was not even known as Smith to anybody but his clients. If only Angela had revealed something more—like Smith's business address . . .

Connor returned each time to brooding and drinking, aware but uncaring that his behavior was becoming completely obsessive. Then he awoke one morning to the discovery that he already knew Smith's business address, had known it for a long time, almost from childhood.

Undecided as to whether his intake of white rum had hastened or delayed the revelation, he breakfasted on strong coffee and was too busy with his thoughts to fret about the black liquid being more tasteless than ever. He formulated a plan of action during the next hour, twice lighting his pipe—out of sheer habit—before remembering he was finished with ordinary tobacco forever. As a first step in the plan he went out, bought a five-inch cube of ruby-colored plastic and paid the owner of a jobbing shop an exorbitant sum to have the block machined down to a polished ovoid. It was late in the afternoon before the work was finished, but the end product sufficiently resembled a P-brand table lighter to fool anyone who was not looking too closely at it.

Pleased with his progress thus far, Connor went back to his apartment and dug out the .38 pistol he had bought a few years earlier following an attempted burglary. Common sense told him it was rather late to leave for Trenton and that he would be better waiting until morning, but he was in a warmly reckless mood. With the plastic egg bumping on one hip and the gun on the other, he drove westward out of town.

Connor reached the center of Trenton just as the stores were showing signs of closing for the day. His sudden fear of being too late and of having to wait another day after all was strengthened by the discovery that he was no longer so certain about locating Mr. Smith.

In the freshness of the morning, with an alcoholic incense lingering in his head, it had all seemed simple and straightforward. For much of his life he had been peripherally aware that in almost every big city there are stores which have no right to be in existence. They were always small and discreet, positioned some way off the main shopping thoroughfares, and their signs usually bore legends—like "Johnston Bros" or "H&L"—which seemed designed to convey a minimum of information. If they had a window display at all it tended to be nothing more than an undistinguished and slightly out-of-style sport jacket priced three times above what it had any chance of fetching. Connor knew the stores were not viable propositions in the ordinary way because, not surprisingly, nobody ever went into them. Yet in his mind they were in some indefinable way associated with money.

Setting out for Trenton he had been quite sure of the city block he wanted—now at least three locations and images of three unremarkable store fronts were merging and blurring in his memory. *That's how they avoid attention,* he thought, refusing to be disheartened, and began cruising the general area he had selected. The rush of home-going traffic hampered every movement and finally he decided he would do better on foot. He parked in a sidestreet and began hurrying from corner to corner, each time convincing himself he was about to look along a remembered block and see the place he so desperately wanted to find, each time being disappointed. Virtually all the stores were closed by now, the crowds had thinned away, and the reddish evening sunlight made the quiet dusty facades look unreal. Connor ran out of steam, physical and mental.

He swore dejectedly, shrugged and started limping back to his car, choosing—as a token act of defiance—a route which took him a block further south than he had originally intended going. His feet were hot and so painful that he was unable to think of anything but his own discomfort. Consequently he did a genuine double-take when he reached an intersection, glanced sideways and saw a half-familiar half-forgotten vista of commonplace stores, wholesalers' depots and anonymous doorways. His heart began a slow pounding as he picked out, midway on the block, a plain store front whose complete lack of character would have rendered it invisible to eyes other than his own.

He walked towards it, suddenly nervous, until he could read the sign which said GENERAL AGENCIES in tarnished gold lettering. The window contained three pieces of glazed earthernware sewer pipe, beyond which were screens to prevent anyone seeing the store's interior. Connor expected to find the door locked, but it opened at his touch and he was inside without even having had time to prepare himself. He blinked at a tall gaunt man who was standing motionless behind a counter. The man had a down-curving mouth, ice-smooth gray hair, and something about him gave Connor the impression that he had been standing there, unmoving, for hours. He was dressed in funeral director black, with a silver tie, and the collar of his white shirt was perfect as the petals of a newly-opened flower.

The man leaned forward slightly and said, "Was there something, sir?"

Connor was taken aback by the quaintness of the greeting but he strode to the counter, brought the ruby egg from his pocket and banged it down.

"Tell Mr. Smith I'm not satisfied with this thing," he said in an angry voice. "And tell him I demand a repayment."

The tall man's composure seemed to shatter. He picked up

the egg, half-turned toward an inner door, then paused and examined the egg more closely.

"Just a minute," he said. "This isn't . . ."

"Isn't what?"

The man looked accusingly at Connor. "I've no idea what this object is, and we haven't got a Mr. Smith."

"Know what *this* object is?" Connor produced his revolver. He had seen and heard enough.

"You wouldn't dare."

"No?" Connor aimed the revolver at the other man's face and aware that the safety catch was on, gave the tigger an obvious squeeze. The tall man shrank against the wall. Connor muttered furiously, clicked the safety off, and raised the gun again.

"Don't!" The man shook his head. "I beseech you."

Connor had never been beseeched in his life but he did not allow the curious turn of speech to distract him. He said, "I want to see Mr. Smith."

"I'll take you to him. If you will follow me . . ."

They went through to the rear of the premises and down a flight of stairs which had inconveniently high risers and narrow treads. Noting that his guide was descending with ease, Connor glanced down and saw that the tall man had abnormally small feet. There was another peculiarity about his gait but it was not until they had reached the basement floor and were moving along a corridor that Connor realized what it was. Within the chalk-stripe trousers, the tall man's knees appeared to be a good two-thirds of the way down his legs. Cool fingers of unease touched Connor's brow.

"Here we are, sir." The black-clad figure before him pushed open a door.

Beyond it was a large brightly-lit room and at one side was another tall cadaverous man dressed like a funeral director. He too had ice-smooth gray hair and he was carefully putting an antique oil painting into the dark rectangular opening of a wall safe.

Without turning his head, he said, "What is it, Toynbee?"

Connor slammed the door shut behind himself. "I want to talk to you, Smith."

Smith gave a violent start, but continued gently sliding the gold-framed painting into the wall. When it had disappeared he turned to face Connor. He had a down-curved mouth and —even more disturbingly—his knees, also, seemed to be in the wrong place. *If these people come from the future,* Connor thought, *why are they made differently from us?* His mind shied away from the new thought and plunged into irrelevant speculations about the kind of chairs Smith and Toynbee must use . . . if any. He realized he had seen no seats or stools about the place. With a growing coldness in his veins, Connor recalled his earlier impression that Toynbee had been standing behind the counter for hours, without moving.

". . . welcome to what money we have," Smith was saying, "but there's nothing else here worth taking."

"I don't think he's a thief." Toynbee went and stood beside him.

"Not a thief! Then what does he want? What is . . . ?

"Just for starters," Connor put in, "I want an explanation."

"Of what?"

"Of your entire operation here."

Smith looked mildly exasperated. He gestured at the wooden crates which filled much of the room. "It's a perfectly normal agency set-up handling various industrial products on a . . ."

"I mean the operation whereby you supply rich people with cigarette lighters that nobody on this Earth could manufacture."

"Cigarette lighters—"

"The red egg-shaped ones which have no works but light when they're wet and stand upright without support."

Smith shook his head. "I wish I *could* get into something like that."

"And the television sets which are too good. And the clocks and cigars and all the other things which are so perfect that people who can afford it are willing to pay eight hundred sixty-four thousand dollars every forty-three days for them— even though the goodies are charged with an essence field which fades out and converts them to junk if they fall into the hands of anybody who isn't in the club."

"I don't understand a word of this."

"It's no use, Mr. Smith," Toynbee said. "Somebody has talked."

Smith gave him a venomous stare. "*You* just did, you fool!" In his anger Smith moved closer to Toynbee, so that his body was no longer shielding the wall safe. Connor noticed for the first time that it was exceptionally large, and it occurred to him that a basement storeroom was an odd place for that particular type of safe. He looked at it more closely. The darkness of the interior revealed no trace of the oil painting he had just seen loaded into it. And, far into the tunnel-like blackness, a bright green star was throwing off expanding rings of light, rings which faded as they grew.

Connor made a new effort to retain his grasp of the situation. He pointed to the safe and said, casually, "I assume that's a two-way transporter."

Smith was visibly shaken. "All right," he said, after a tense silence, "who talked to you?"

"Nobody." Connor felt he could get Angela into trouble of some kind by mentioning her name.

Toynbee cleared his throat. "I'll bet it was that Miss Lomond. I've always said you can't trust the *nouveau riche*—the proper instincts aren't sufficiently ingrained."

Smith nodded agreement. "You are right. She got a replacement table lighter, television and clock—the things this . . . person has just mentioned. She said they had been detuned by someone who broke into her house."

"She must have told him everything she knew."

"And broken her contract—make a note of that, Mr. Toynbee."

"Hold on a minute," Connor said loudly, brandishing the revolver to remind them he was in control. "Nobody's going to make a note of anything till I get the answers I want. These products you deal in—do they come from the future or—somewhere?"

"From somewhere," Smith told him. "Actually, they come from a short distance in the future as well, but—as far as you are concerned—the important thing is that they are transported over many light years. The time difference is incidental, and quite difficult to prove."

"They're from another planet?"

"Yes."

"You, too?"

"Of course."

"You bring advanced products to Earth in secret and sell or rent them to rich people?"

"Yes. Only smaller stuff comes here, of course—larger items, like the television sets, come in at main receivers in other cities. The details of the operation may be surprising, but surely the general principles of commerce are well known to you."

"That's exactly what's bothering me," Connor said. "I don't give a damn about other worlds and matter transmitters, but I can't see why you go to all this trouble. Earth currency would be of no value on . . . wherever you come from. You're ahead on technology, so there is nothing . . ." Connor stopped talking as he remembered what Smith had been feeding into the black rectangle. An old oil painting.

Smith nodded, looking more relaxed. "You are right about your currency being useless on another world. We spend it here. Humanity is primitive in many respects, but the race's artistic genius is quite remarkable. Our organization makes a good trading surplus by exporting paintings and sculptures. You see the goods we import are comparatively worthless."

"They seem valuable to me."

"They *would* seem that way to you—that's the whole point. We don't bother bringing in the things that Earth can produce reasonably well. Your wines and other drinks aren't too bad, so we don't touch them. But your coffee!" Smith's mouth curved even further downward.

"That means you're spending millions. Somebody should have noticed one outfit buying up so much stuff."

"Not really. We do quite a bit of direct buying at auctions and galleries, but often our clients buy on our behalf and we credit their accounts."

"Oh, no," Connor breathed as the ramifications of what Smith was saying unfolded new vistas in his mind. Was this why millionaires, even the most unlikely types of men, so often became art collectors? Was this the *raison d'etre* for that curious phenomenon, the private collection? In a society where the rich derived so much pleasure from showing off their possessions, why did so many art treasures disappear from the public view? Was it because their owners were trading them in against P-brand products? If that was the case the organization concerned must be huge and it must have been around for a long time. Connor's legs suddenly felt tired.

He said, "Let's sit down and talk about this."

Smith looked slightly uncomfortable. "We don't sit. Why don't you use one of those crates if you aren't feeling well?"

"There's nothing wrong with me, so don't try anything," Connor said sharply, but he sat on the edge of a box while his brain worked to assimilate shocking new concepts. "What does the P stand for on your products?"

"Can't you guess?"

"Perfect?"

"That is correct."

The readiness with which Smith was now giving information made Connor a little wary, but he pressed on with other questions which had been gnawing at him. "Miss Lomond told me her installments were eight hundred and sixty-four thousand dollars—why that particular figure? Why not a million?"

"That *is* a million—in our money. A rough equivalent, of course."

"I see. And the forty-three days."

"One revolution of our primary moon. It's a natural accounting period."

Connor almost began to wish the flow of information would slow down. "I still don't see the need for all this secrecy. Why not come out in the open, reduce your unit prices and multiply the volume? You could make a hundred times as much."

"We have to work underground for a number of reasons. In all probability the various Earth governments would object to the loss of art treasures, and there are certain difficulties at the other end."

"Such as?"

"There's a law against influencing events on worlds which are at a sensitive stage of their development. This limits our supply of trade goods very sharply."

"In other words, you are crooks on your own world and crooks on this one."

"I don't agree. What harm do we do on Earth?"

"You've already named it—you are depriving the people of this planet of . . ."

"Of their artistic heritage?" Smith gave a thin sneer. "How many people do you know who would give up a Perfect television set to keep a da Vinci cartoon in a public art gallery five or ten thousand miles away?"

"You've got a point there," Connor admitted. "What have you got up your sleeve, Smith?"

"I don't understand."

"Don't play innocent. You would not have talked so freely unless you were certain I wouldn't get out of here with the information. What are you planning to do about me?"

Smith glanced at Toynbee and sighed. "I keep forgetting how parochial the natives of a single-planet culture can be. You have been told that we are from another world, and yet to you we are just slightly unusual Earth people. I don't suppose it has occurred to you that other races could have a stronger instinct toward honesty, that deviousness and lies would come less easily to them than to humans?"

"That's where we are most vulnerable," Toynbee put in. "I see now that I was too inexperienced to be up front."

"All right, then—be honest with me," Connor said. "You are planning to keep me quiet, aren't you?"

"As a matter of fact, we do have a little device . . ."

"You don't need it," Connor said. He thought back careful-

ly over all he had been told, then stood up and handed his revolver to Smith.

The good life was all that he had expected it to be, and—as
he drove south to Avalon—Connor could feel it getting better
by the minute.

His business sense had always been sharp, but whereas he
had once reckoned a month's profits in thousands, he now
thought in terms of six figures. Introductions, opportunities
and deals came thick and fast, and always it was the P-brand
artifacts which magically paved the way. During important
first contacts he had only to use his gold lighter to ignite a
pipeful of P-brand tobacco—the incredible leaf which fulfilled
all the promise of its "nose", or glance at his P-brand watch,
or write with the pen which produced any color at the touch
of a spectrum ring, and all doors were opened wide. The various beautiful trinkets were individually styled, but he quickly
learned to recognize them when they were displayed by others,
and to make the appropriate responses.

Within a few weeks, although he was scarcely aware of it,
his outlook on life had undergone a profound change. At first
he was merely uneasy or suspicious when approached by people who failed to show the talisman. Then he became hostile,
preferring to associate only with those who could prove they
were safe.

Satisfying though his new life was, Connor had decided it
would not be perfect until Angela and he were reunited. It was
through her that he had achieved awareness and only through
her would he achieve completeness. He would have made the
journey to Avalon much sooner but for the fact that there had
been certain initial difficulties with Smith and Toynbee. Handing over the revolver had been a dangerous gambit which had
almost resulted in his being bundled through their matter
transmitter to an unknown fate on another world. Luckily,
however, it had also convinced them that he had something
important to say.

He had talked quickly and well that evening in the basement
of the undistinguished little store. Smith, who was the senior
of the pair, had been hard to convince; but his interest had
quickened as Connor enumerated all the weaknesses in the organization's procurement methods. And it had grown feverish
when he heard how Connor's worldly knowhow would eliminate much of the wasteful financial competition of auctions,
would streamline the system of purchasing through rich
clients, would institute foolproof controls and effective new
techniques for diverting art treasures into the organization's

hands. It had been the best improvisation of his life, sketchy in places because of his unfamiliarity with the art world, but filled with an inspired professionalism which carried his audience along with it.

Early results had been so good that Smith had become possessive, voicing objections to Connor's profitable side dealings. Connor smoothed things over by going on to a seven-day work schedule in which he also worked most evenings. This had made it difficult to find the time to visit Angela, but finally his need to see her had become so great that he had pushed everything else aside and made the time . . .

The guard at the gate lodge was the same man as before, but he gave no sign of remembering his earlier brush with Connor. He waved the car on through with a minimum of delay, and a few minutes later Connor was walking up the broad front steps of the house. The place looked much less awesome to Connor but while ringing for admission he decided that he and Angela would probably keep it, for sentimental reasons as much as anything else. The butler who answered the door was a new man, who looked rather like a retired seaman, and there was a certain lack of smoothness in his manner as he showed Connor to the large room where Angela was waiting. She was standing at the fireplace with her back to the door, just as he had last seen her.

"Angie," he said, "it's good to see you again."

She turned and ran to him. "I've missed you so much, Phil."

As they clung together in the center of the green-and-silver room Connor experienced a moment of exquisite happiness. He buried his face in her hair and began whispering the things he had been unable to say for what seemed a long, long time. Angela answered him feverishly all the while he spoke, responding to the emotion rather than the words.

It was during the first kiss that he became aware of a disturbing fact. She was wearing expensive yet ordinary perfume —not one of the P-brand distillations of magic to which he had become accustomed on the golden creatures he had dated casually during the past few weeks. Still holding Angela close to him he glanced around the big room. A leaden coldness began to spread through his body. Everything in the room was, like her perfume, excellent—but not Perfect.

"Angela," he said quietly, "why did you ask me to come here?"

"What kind of a question is that, darling?"

"It's a perfectly normal question." Connor disengaged from

her and stepped back suspiciously. "I merely asked what your motives were."

"*Motives!*" Angela stared at him, color fleeing from her cheeks, then her gaze darted to his wristwatch. "My God, Philip, you're *in!* You made it, just like you said you would."

"I don't know what you mean."

"Don't try that with me—remember I was the one who told it all to you."

"You should have learned not to talk by this time."

"I know I should, but I didn't." Angela advanced on him. "I'm out now. I'm on the outside."

"It isn't all that bad, is it? Where's Bobby Janke and the rest of his crowd?"

"None of them come near me now. And you know why."

"At least you're not broke." Small solace.

She shook her head. "I've got plenty of money, but what good is it when I can't buy the things I want? I'm shut out, and it's all because I couldn't keep myself from blabbing to you, and because I didn't report the way you were getting on to them. But you didn't mind informing on me, did you?"

Connor opened his mouth to protest his innocence, then realized it would make no difference. "It's been nice seeing you again, Angela," he said. "I'm sorry I can't stay longer but things are stacking up on me back at the office. You know how it is."

"I know exactly how it is. Go on, Philip—get out of here."

Connor crossed to the door, but hesitated as Angela made a faint sound.

She said, "Stay with me, Phil. Please stay."

He stood with his back to her, experiencing a pain which slowly faded, then he walked out.

Late that afternoon Connor was sitting in his new office when his secretary put through a call. It was Smith, anxious to discuss the acquisition of a collection of antique silver.

"I called you earlier but your girl told me you were out," he said, with a hint of reproach.

"It's true," Connor assured him. "I was out of town—Angela Lomond asked me down to her place."

"Oh?"

"You didn't tell me she was no longer a client."

"You should have known without being told." Smith was silent for a few seconds. "Is she going to try making trouble?"

"No."

"What did she want?"

Connor leaned back in his chair and gazed out through the window, toward the Atlantic. "Who knows? I didn't stay long enough to find out."

"Very wise," Smith said complacently.

When the call had ended, Connor brewed some P-brand coffee, using the supply he kept locked in the drinks cabinet. The Perfection of it soothed from his mind the last lingering traces of remorse.

How on Earth, he wondered idly, *do they manage to make it taste exactly the way it smells?*

THE SUN'S TEARS

Brian M. Stableford

Taking his usual wholly different approach, the author of such variegated epics as the Dies Irae *novels and the* Star-Pilot Grainger *novels approaches the questions of unity, paradise and immortality from a space flight basis . . . and does so with the talent that has caused Stableford to be considered one of the best new writers in the field.*

You think that if you're twenty years an Earthman, you'll be an Earthman forever. But it isn't so. After a lousy twenty years you've finished growing. You have all the brain cells you're ever going to have, and from then on it's downhill all the way. What you are is the sum total of all your experiences pinned, painted and plastered on to the framework you were born with. What you're born with is all Earthman, and all your developing life you're Earthman. But what you *are* is only a small part of what you *might be,* and what you've seen and done is a pitifully tiny fraction of all there is to see and do when the whole universe is available to you.

That's why starmen aren't Earthmen any more. That's why starmen forget their homes and cast off their humanity. No matter what sort of man it is that takes a ship out to the stars, the stars will seduce him, imprison him, claim him for their own. There's no power on Earth that can resist.

Colfax, of course, thought that it could never happen to him. In a way, he was right, because Colfax had little enough humanity to lose. He was a mechanical man, was Colfax—a man whose emotions obeyed orders, and who never remembered his dreams when he woke up in the morning.

He first set out from his home world when he was twenty years old, crewman on the starliner *Leda*. He returned seven times, twice with the *Leda* and then with other ships. The eighth time he lifted, it was in his own ship, the *Grey Bitch*. He never returned.

A dozen years and a little more he gave to wandering, to doing what he could wherever he could, and all the while imagining himself to be a part of the great universal entity, a particle of true existence, possessing nothing save freedom, unencumbered by the limitations of principles, philosophies, perspectives, ideas and laws. But in time the boundless impartiality of space robbed him of even that illusion, and he embarked in the end (as do they all) upon the Starman's Quest, the search for his own, personal perfect world; his Spiritual Home, his Heaven.

This story is about Colfax and not someone else because he (unlike the others) reached his Heaven. He found his perfect world. You may think of it as luck if you wish. Every starman believes that somewhere in the universe there is a world shaped for his needs, and that only luck decides whether he finds it or not. Conversely, you may believe that there was something in Colfax that was not in other men, something which allowed him to find what other men died looking for.

It happened like this.

On Marsyad, there was a girl.

The law of poetic justice (in conjunction with the laws of chance and assisted by the vagaries of wishful thinking) gives rise to the illusion that on *every* world there is a girl. It is an exaggeration, but it isn't so far from the truth as cynicism might lead one to suspect. Girls (human, pseudohuman and humanoid) come in all shapes and sizes and all the colours of the rainbow. When one descends to fundamentals, there is only one indispensable qualification, and that isn't particularly complicated. Given that, only a narrow mind can stand between a starman and a girl in every port. The finding of beauty is, after all, only a matter of an educated eye.

And so there was a girl on Marsyad. Colfax, naturally enough, wasn't fool enough to believe that paradise could be found purely and simply in a girl. However, like most people, he believed that a girl was indispensible for the purposes of enjoying paradise once he found it.

The girl, Siorane, was the daughter of a shopkeeper whose

most noticeable and distinctive characteristic was his xenophobia. This applied particularly to out-worlders, most particularly to Earthmen, and most particularly of all to Colfax. The shopkeeper's name was Orgoglio. He reminded Colfax of a vulture, because of his naked, wrinkled head, his bluish skin, his big-boned nose and his wicked little eyes. To be fair, most of these were racial characteristics and in no way correlated with his evil disposition towards others. Siorane too had many of these characteristics, but in her they combined to give a totally different overall impression. If Orgoglio was like a vulture, then Siorane was a falcon, black plumed, sleek and graceful.

When Colfax first saw the girl (at a distance) he said to himself: "That's the one I want." There was no nonsense in his head about love, nor even about beauty. Colfax was no romantic—he thought in terms of acquisition and possession. He had seen marsyades before, on other worlds, and knew that they could be bought and sold with reasonable ease, provided that one had the price. The marsyads regarded their women as little more than chattels (considerably less than chattels in some ways) and they were natural-born horse traders. Usury and extortion were national sports on Marsyad, and milking outworlders the most popular pastime.

It took Colfax a day or two to locate the girl, and he permitted himself a day or two more to study the case in depth. He decided that his initial judgment had in no way played him false, and that this was indeed the precise augmentation required by his as-yet-unfound perfect world. He also came to the conclusion that some sort of deal could be made. He knew the way things worked on Marsyad, and he reckoned that he could work the system and not come out of it too badly. He reckoned, however, without the inate ugliness of Orgoglio's soul.

It might be in order here to point out that a certain amount of Colfax's troubles can be laid at his own door. Had he not been such a cold, calculating individual—had he had the ordinary human failing of romantic foolishness—he might have bypassed Orgoglio and the customs of Marsyad and employed the time-honoured Earth strategy of enticement, seduction and elopement. It might not have worked, but on the other hand, planets where women are treated like dirt are custom-made for the success of such earthly courtesies. But Colfax was Colfax, and he thought commerce was commerce, so he went to see Orgoglio, and never so much as spoke to Siorane herself.

Orgoglio took one look at Colfax and decided to get rid of

him. This was in no way concerned with paternal affection, and the indigestion from which he was suffering at the time probably played the largest part in deciding his attitude. Indigestion is one of those nagging afflictions which takes away even a con man's pleasure in cheating people.

"You like my daughter, hey?" said Orgoglio, sounding remarkably like Shylock. Colfax expressed a certain superficial interest which might wane within the minute unless Orgoglio made a quick and reasonable offer.

"Well," Orgoglio retorted, "I'm not selling her to *you*."

At this, Colfax was surprised, disconcerted and not a little offended. It was no way to run a business.

He persisted.

Orgoglio remained firm.

Siorane listened.

Now Siorane was no fool. She wasn't fond of her father, and she wasn't enamoured of Marsyad either. Of course, she'd never been anywhere else, and thus wasn't in a position to make comparisons, nor was she foolish enough to believe travellers' tales. But merely to know that there *were* other worlds was enough. Siorane had never been happy in the whole of her short life.

She saw in Colfax a chance to get away. She also saw in Colfax a strong, cruel, empty man who was almost as bad as her father. The decision was agonizing. In the end she decided that the best way out of the dilemma (all this assuming, of course, that she could contrive to influence the bargain) was to set a price on herself that the Earthman would find extremely difficult to pay, thus assuring her value in his eyes. She was clever enough to guess that the more Colfax had to pay for her, the higher would be the regard in which he held her.

She therefore went to her father and whispered in his ear that the quickest way to get rid of the Earthman and make a fool of him at the same time was to demand of him that he should pay as a price for her one of the sun's tears.

Orgoglio laughed, causing himself sharp pains in the gut. The "tears of the sun" were gems highly prized on Marsyad. They were impossible to steal, almost impossible to buy, and damnably difficult to find. Yet the task was safely within the bounds of credibility. It sounded like a pleasant joke.

"You can have her," said Orgoglio, rolling his eyes with the histrionic dismay of a trader pretending that he has been beaten down below his profit margin, "in exchange for one of the sun's tears."

Colfax thought it over.

"What the hell are the sun's tears?" he asked cautiously.

"That," said Orgoglio, "is for you to find out."

"And where shall I find out?"

Orgoglio shrugged.

Having arrived at a price, Colfax was reluctant to let go. Not only had he formed an uncommonly strong desire to buy the girl, but his pride had been offended by the manner of Orgoglio's bargaining. He struggled with his reason for a moment or two, and then agreed. To you, it may perhaps seem a ridiculous bargain to have made, but Colfax was a starman, a questor, and when a man is consumed by a quest which has no clear destination, he is very willing to accept commissions which lend some kind of substance to his searching. Colfax had, indeed, promised a very high price for a marsyade girl. But it was not too high a price to pay for a purpose to his life. That is a paradox of the Starman's Quest: it is probably only a search for something to search for.

Colfax returned to the *Grey Bitch*. Sitting beneath the ship was a man—an Earthman. He was old and thin and much marked by scars and space and alien air. He was one who had taken the Quest and failed. He'd lost his money and his ship, having given away his humanity and his identity. He was nothing now but a beggar on a lonely, hostile world.

"I greet you, brother," said the old man.

Colfax dug his hand into his pocket, and fetched out all the coins therefrom. None of them was Marsyad, but all of them were good and would buy food and clothing, if little else. Without pause, Colfax handed them over. It was not generosity, not charity. It told nothing about Colfax's character. It was convention—necessary custom. Starmen had to look after their own, because they had no one else to look after *them*. "I greet you, brother" meant exactly what it said.

"Tell me, brother," asked Colfax, kneeling to help the old man to his feet, "what would I mean if I talked about the sun's tears?"

"If you were to speak literally," replied the old one, "shining gems found only in the deepest mines of a few hot-cored worlds, Marsyad being one. If you were to say it, though, in conversation, you would mean it to convey the almost impossible."

Colfax and the old man shook hands. "I thank you, brother," said Colfax. The other smiled but offered no thanks. Colfax expected none. It was the old one who had rendered a service, not he.

The starman ate aboard his ship, then packed himself a bag

containing clothes, currency, and all that was saleable, locked
the door of the *Grey Bitch*, paid the port authority for her ac-
comodation and set off in search of the sun's tears. He headed,
not for the mines where the sun's tears might occasionally be
unearthed, but for the oldest city on the world, the city of Anses Almagel. He did not need to ask to know that that was the
place, on Marsyad, where the impossible was most likely to
happen. It was the last remaining city (on this world, at least)
of the Galacella.

Marsyad had, since the days of the first spaceship, been conquered three times. One conquest the marsyads had reversed,
two they had absorbed. There was no trace of any conqueror
on Marsyad now. But in their day, the conquerors had brought
in, amongst their accoutrements and retinues, members of other conquered races. Most of these had been absorbed along
with the conquerors, into the local cultures and the local races.
But the Galacella had refused to be treated thus. Because they
had no quarrel with the marsyads (no quarrel with anyone, in
fact), they had been allowed to stay whilst their erstwhile
slave masters had not. T' home world of the Galacella had
never been identified. They existed only as the jetsam of em-
pires, in ones and twos and tiny towns, scattered all over the
universe. No one paid them much heed, and they had little to
say to other people, but there was no Earthman who ever lived
who did not find a use for the Galacella at least once in his
life. Earthmen are the most curious people in the universe because they know so little, while the Galacella are the least curious of all peoples because they know so much. That, in fact,
is not the only remarkable difference. Earthmen are the most
consistent, consummate and accomplished liars in the universe,
while the Galacella always tell the truth, the whole truth and
nothing but the truth, as they see it. You can see, therefore,
why there is a natural affinity between Earthmen and the Galacella and why Colfax, faced with a difficulty, went looking
for them.

The journey to Anses Almagel took some time, but all that
occurred thereon was commonplace in nature, and there is no
point in boring you with a blow by blow account of it. Suffice
it to say that he got there and nothing relevant to the story
happened in the meantime.

Once there, he simply stopped the first Gallacellone that he
passed in the street, and said: "Where can I obtain one of the
sun's tears?"

The Gallacellone looked him over with a ruminative expression in his big, baby-blue eyes, and thought it over for a cou-

ple of minutes. Then he said: "If you are ever to possess one of the sun's tears, then it will be a gift from the Avageyn, which is a female creature inhabiting a planetoid called Exar in the system of the star Callia."

Then he smiled, gave Colfax a friendly nod, and went about his business.

Colfax began the long walk back.

You may think that Colfax had come a long way for very little, and that there were a lot of other things he could have asked the Galacella while they were available. But Colfax was a clever man, and he'd had dealings with the Galacella before. Also, he'd been warned. You don't mess about with oracles. Curiosity killed the cat, and cats have nine lives, which adds up to pretty convincing evidence that curiosity is one of the most lethal things you can fall prey to. Colfax knew better than to follow up his question with some idiotic comment like "How do you know?" Because the Gallacellone would simply have smiled, and said nothing. That was the whole and absolute truth. There was no way he *could* know. He just did.

Nor was there any point in querying the fact that the Gallacellone had said "if". *All* truth is conditional, even the whole truth—*especially* the whole truth—though it takes a clever man to see it, let alone to understand why.

On the way back, Colfax's feet began to hurt. That may seem irrelevant to you, but in defining Colfax's destiny, it was important. Colfax was a Questor, and the one thing which a Questor always needs is a destination—however temporary. When you have a destination then you can simply head towards it and forget everything else. Having a destination is enough in itself to give one a sense of purpose. You don't ask questions, you don't worry. You just go. And so Colfax never questioned what he was doing while he was simply going from point A to point B.

Until, that is, his feet started hurting. There is nothing like blisters for making a man stop in his tracks and say to himself "Why the hell am I doing this?"

And Colfax did. He had second thoughts. He knew that the girl wasn't really worth all this effort. After all, the law of Stereotypic existence clearly stated that there was a girl on every world. So why flog himself to death over this one?

Then he got round to thinking about how much one of the sun's tears was worth, and how it might not be a bad idea to fly out to Callia anyway, just in case, to see if the Avageyn thought it was his birthday.

This is probably the branching point of the story. Had Colfax, like any normal moron, gone running off to Callia in single-minded search of the price of the girl he loved, he might indeed have enjoyed the favour of the cosmic whim, got hold of the gem, got the girl and turned the whole story into a meaningless farce. Contrary to popular opinion, that is no way to reach paradise. Instead, because his feet hurt, Colfax flew to Callia with mixed motives (which, being versatile, are usually useful motives to carry around) and what happened was quite different.

The Avageyn was huge. She lay in the dust of her airless abode looking for all the world as if she were made of black rock. Her face reminded one of a giant, wide-mouthed, bug-eyed lizard. Her eyes never shifted from her contemplation of the silent stars. She never blinked, or smiled, or sneezed, or slept.

Colfax landed the *Grey Bitch* between two of her sixteen tentacles, orientated so that the cleanest of the portholes gave him a clear view of her austere visage. Then he waited.

Waiting was one of the few things within the scope of mankind that Colfax was not very good at. He fretted, he fidgeted and he worried. The Avageyn simply ignored him.

How big, wondered Colfax, was the Gallacellone's "if"?

A long time passed. Day by day (Exar turned on its axis about once an hour) and night by night Colfax watched the sunlight wander across the Avageyn's unwavering eyes, and then leave her to deepest shadow again.

Eventually, he tired of sitting and doing nothing. It was obvious that if things remained as they were, then the incredible beast would never even deign to notice him. Therefore, he put on his spacesuit and left the ship. He walked along one of the tentacles until he stood beneath the colossal face, looking up into the vast lenticular eyes.

They gave no sign that his presence was known to the Avageyn. She was as impassive as the legendary Sphinx. Colfax felt a twinge of irritation as he wondered what to do next. He felt like a fool, standing so close to such a creature. She seemed as unsympathetic to his cause as did the cold silver light of the multimillion stars.

His mind formed the word "Please" and he radiated the thought with all his might. There was no response. He felt helpless. After a few more minutes of silent confrontation, he turned away. And as he turned, the Avageyn pounced. Her great wide mouth split and gaped and her tongue lapped him up as if he were an ant. The lips slapped shut as he was drawn into the cavernous maw, and he was sealed in darkness.

Colfax never had time to be frightened, or even to know that something had happened. As the stars were switched off, so was his mind. There was no sensation of time passing. He had turned away from the face of the alien leviathan, and then he was naked, breathing, keen, lilac-scented air.

He stood on a silver beach, a narrow strip of lustrous sand which separated a cerulean ocean from a high forest of pale trees. Flower petals drifting on the wind fell about him like roseate rain and brushed his skin with spidery lightness.

Between the trees were houses built on tall stilts, their walls woven into the canopy of the forest. There were people too, crouching among the branches and watching him. Most of them were children.

Three men, tall and silver haired, came from the trees to greet him. They appeared to have expected his coming, because there was warmth in their voices, and no surprise. Colfax could not understand what they said, but the way in which they spoke was welcome enough.

They gave him food and wine, and talked to him continually in their unfamiliar but appealing language. The flow of meaningless sound had a mesmeric effect upon him, and the sweetness of the air was narcotic . . .

The bloom fell from the trees, and in time, the fruit ripened. The air was always alive with scent and sunlight. Colfax walked on air, his very breathing a delight. The time slid past him and around him at colossal speed. The days were born and the days died just as if he was on any ordinary world of the known universe, and yet each day and each night contained fifteen hours and more. His mind was clear like the night skies, which in this place had no stars. His thoughts were liquid and his feelings glowed and sparkled within his body.

Beneath his lofty hut were the woven branches of a great tree, and between the roots of the tree were small pools in which swam tiny silver fish. He fed upon the fruit as it matured on the branches and on the bread which the villagers gave him, which they made from corn which grew in fields beyond the forest to the east. On three days out of five he would join them in the fields, or in the mill or at any other place where they chose to labour. He loved the work and he loved the people, although he never learned a word of their language —not even their names. They still talked to him as though he was one of their own, and because it did not matter to them that he could not understand, it did not matter to him either.

And still the days and the nights hurried by and their number mounted and grew. And still he breathed the sweetness and the heaviness of the air, which trapped him—unknowing and uncaring—within the confines of his dream.

Three hundred days passed, and each day longer than the days by which he had counted his life, before that day came when the leaves began to fall from the trees and the last of the fruit had been eaten and the air lapsed into staleness and life-lessness.

He awoke on that morning and looked at his hands and found calluses worn into the palms as testimony to the labour which had been his share of the life of the village. He stared at the lemon-yellow sun as it rose behind a veil of thin mist. He knew that it was a real star and that he was in a real place. But he also knew that this was no place that the *Grey Bitch* could bring him to.

That day was the first day he spent with his eyes fully open and his mind unclouded. He found the people as pleasant and as friendly as they had always been. He found the forest as beautiful, the sand as silver and the sea as blue. But he no longer looked at them with the same eyes. The air was cool and empty and *dead*. And when he went to his bed that night, he wanted to dream of the *Grey Bitch*, and of bright stars, even though he would not remember his dreams when another morning came.

And when he awoke into that morning, he was in his bunk aboard the *Grey Bitch* and clutched within the fist of his right hand was one of the sun's tears.

It was coloured like fire and it was warm. It glowed and the sparks within its surface were in continuous chaotic movement. Colfax looked at it and he laughed. It was power, it was wealth. The cosmic whim had shown him one of its rare kindnesses—so he thought—and he had paid such a small price in that year he had spent on the world where the Avageyn had sent him.

He returned to Marsyad, and he sought out Orgoglio the shopkeeper.

Orgoglio took one look at the sun's tear, and he also laughed. There were mixed emotions in Orgoglio's laugh. For one thing, it was a fine joke to have played upon an Earthman to command him to find one of the sun's tears and have the command carried out to the letter. For another, he thought that this priceless gem might actually become *his* in return for his almost-worthless daughter. Let it not be imagined that Orgoglio liked Colfax better now than he had a year previously. But his eyes were now fixed upon the fire-stone, and he never saw Colfax at all.

Colfax laughed too, because he had caught sight of the girl, in the back of the shop. She was radiating happiness. Her most romantic of childish daydreams seemed to be coming true. The Earthman had managed to find one of the sun's tears, as she had hoped he might. (She had had no real conception of the difficulties which could be involved when she had suggested the task.) Now he had come back to claim her, or so she thought.

But Colfax's laughter signified anything but that. He was laughing at himself, and the crazy notions which sometimes entered his head. Siorane was still beautiful, but she was not unusual. The spark of infatuation was dead inside him. She had been worth the price that was asked of him—but only when that price was asked. Now that he could afford to pay the price, she was not worth one thousandth of it.

Colfax laughed long, and Orgoglio's laughter faded away.

Then Colfax laughed even harder, and Siorane saw the truth, but stoically refused to weep. She knew her own foolishness and absorbed its pain very rapidly. That is a useful talent which marsyades need and therefore possess.

The gem made Colfax very rich. He sold it on Pelera for a small fortune. He sold the *Grey Bitch* and bought a far finer ship called the *Rainbow*. And he set off once again on his Quest.

It took him ten years and more to realize that he had found his paradise and forsaken it. It took him ten years to remember the scents of that alien summer, and how they had made him feel, and what they had made him *into*.

That it took so long is one of the innumerable corollaries to the Law of Poetic Justice. A man at a different age is a different man. The goal of Colfax's Quest changed as he changed, and by the time he grew to know his destination, he grew to know that he had abandoned it a good many years before.

He went back to Exar in the system of Callia, and found the Avageyn just as he had left her, immutable and untiring. He left his space ship and went to stand within the shadow of her face, and there he found his old spacesuit, which had stood there during all of the ten years, and the year which he had spent elsewhere, as though it was waiting.

He took it back to the *Rainbow*, and got into it as he had done before, and went back to the Avageyn exactly as he had on the previous occasion. His mind formed the word "Please", and he radiated it with all his might. There was no response. He felt helpless. There was a different man inside the suit, with different thoughts and dreams and needs. He waited for a long time, but he waited in vain. The Avageyn had no more gifts for him.

A good deal later, on Stagirite, he met a Gallacellone, and took upon himself the tremendous responsibility of asking:

"Where is the world where I once spent a summer, which has no stars in its skies?"

"If it exists," said the Gallacellone, "then it is beyond your power to find it again."

And that, of course, was a virtual sentence of death upon poor Colfax. He didn't go away and commit suicide, nor did he waste away and die. That wasn't his way at all. But after that encounter with the truth, he was an empty man even by his own empty standards.

A thousand other men searched like Colfax for their own version of heaven, and never even caught a glimpse. Colfax lived in his paradise for a long, long summer. That is probably more luck than any starman is entitled to. After all, the Cosmic Whim isn't exactly fond of starmen. It lends its greatest favours to those men who *know* who and what they are, who do not need the Quest, and who *understand* when other men speak to them in friendship.

THE GIFT OF GARIGOLLI

Frederik Pohl & C. M. Kornbluth

It would appear that Frederik Pohl, Kornbluth's collaborator, turned up some fragments which he completed with the usual success that had marked the amalgam of two cleverly different minds. It's interesting to speculate on the elements here. We think that Garigolli's style is that of Kornbluth, but the plot twist with its very modern premise is surely Pohl's.

Garigolli

To Home Base

Greeting, Chief,

I'm glad you're pleased with the demographics and cognitics studies. You don't mention the orbital mapping, but I suppose that's all complete and satisfactory.

Now will you please tell me how we're going to get off this lousy planet?

Keep firmly in mind, Chief, that we're not complainers. You don't have a better crew anywhere in the Galaxy and you know it. We've complied with the Triple Directive, every time, on every planet we've explored. Remember Arcturus XII? But this time we're having trouble. After all, look at the disproportion in mass. And take a look at the reports we've sent in. These are pretty miserable sentients, Chief.

So will you let us know, please, if there has ever been an authorized exception to Directive Two? I don't mean we aren't going to bust a link to comply—if we can—but frankly, at this moment, I don't see how.

And we need to get out of here fast.

Garigolli.

Although it was a pretty morning in June, with the blossoms dropping off the catalpa trees and the algae blooming in the 12-foot plastic pool, I was not enjoying either my breakfast or the morning mail.

The letter from the lawyer started, the way letters from lawyers do, with

Re: GUDSELL VS. DUPOIR

and went on to advise Dupoir (that's me, plus my wife and our two-year-old son Butchie) that unless a certified check arrived in Undersigned's office before close of business June 11th (that was tomorrow) in the amount of $14,752.03, Undersigned would be compelled to institute Proceedings at once.

I showed it to my wife, Shirl, for lack of anything better to do.

She read it and nodded intelligently. "He's really been very patient with us, considering," she said. "I suppose this is just some more lawyer-talk?"

It had occurred to me, for a wild moment, that maybe she had $14,752.03 in the old sugar bowl as a surprise for me, but I could see she didn't. I shook my head. "This means they take the house," I said. "I'm not mad any more. But you won't sign anything for your brother after this, will you?"

"Certainly not," she said, shocked. "Shall I put that letter in the paper-recycling bin?"

"Not just yet," I said, taking off my glasses and hearing aid. Shirl knows perfectly well that I can't hear her when my glasses are off, but she kept on talking anyway as she wiped the apricot puree off Butchie's chin, rescued the milk glass, rinsed the plastic infant-food jar and dropped it in the "plastics" carton, rinsed the lid and put it in the "metals" box and poured my coffee. We are a very ecological household. It astonishes me how good Shirl is at things like that, considering.

I waved fruit flies away from the general direction of my orange juice and put my glasses back on in time to catch her asking, wonderingly, "What would they do with our house? I mean, I'm not a demon decorator like Ginevra Freedman. I just like it comfortable and neat."

"They don't exactly want the house," I explained. "They just want the money they'll get after they sell it to somebody else." Her expression cleared at once. Shirl always likes to understand things.

I sipped my coffee, fending off Butchie's attempt to grab the cup, and folded the letter and laid it across my knees like an unsheathed scimitar, ready to taste the blood of the *giaour*, which it kind of was. Butchie indicated that he would like to eat it, but I didn't see that that would solve the problem. Although I didn't have any better way of solving it, at that.

I finished the orange juice, patted Butchie's head and, against my better judgment, gave Shirl the routine kiss on the nose.

"Well," she said, "I'm glad that's settled. Isn't it nice the way the mail comes first thing in the morning now?"

I said it was very nice and left for the bus but, really, I could have been just as happy if Undersigned's letter had come any old time. The fruit flies were pursuing me all the way down the street. They seemed to think they could get nourishment out of me, which suggested that fruit flies were about equal in intelligence to brothers-in-law. It was not a surprising thought. I had thought it before.

Garigolli

To Home Base
Chief,

The mobility of this Host is a constant pain in the spermatophore. Now he's gone off on the day-cycle early, and half the crew are still stuck in his domicile. Ultimate Matrix knows how they'll handle it if we don't get back before they run out of group empathy.

You've got no reason to take that tone, Chief. We're doing a good job and you know it. "Directive One: To remain undetected by sentients on planet being explored." A hundred and forty-four p.g., right? They don't have a clue we're here, although I concede that that part is fairly easy, since they are so much bigger than we are. "Directive Three: Subject to Directives One and Two, to make a complete study of geographic, demographic, ecological and cognitic factors and to transmit same to Home Base." You actually complimented us on those! It's only Directive Two that's giving us trouble.

We're still trying, but did it ever occur to you that maybe these people don't *deserve* Directive Two?

Garigolli

I loped along the jungle trail to the bus stop, calculating with my razor-sharp mind that the distance from the house was almost exactly 14,752.04 centimeters. As centimeters it didn't sound bad at all. As money, $14,752.03 was the kind of sum I hadn't written down since Commercial Arithmetic in P.S. 98.

I fell in with Barney Freedman, insurance underwriter and husband of Ginevra, the Demon Decorator. "Whatever became of Commercial Arithmetic?" I asked him. "Like ninety-day notes for fourteen thousand seven hundred and fifty-two dollars and three cents at six per cent simple interest? Although why anybody would be dumb enough to lend anybody money for ninety days beats me. If he doesn't have it now, he won't have it in ninety days."

"You're in some kind of trouble."

"Shrewd guess."

"So what did Shirl do now?"

"She co-signed a note for her brother," I said. "When he went into the drying-out sanitarium for the gold treatment. They wouldn't take him on his own credit, for some reason. They must have gold-plated him. He said the note was just a formality, so Shirl didn't bother me with it."

We turned the corner. Barney said, "Ginevra didn't bother me once when the telephone company—"

"So when Shirl's brother got undrunk," I said, "he told her not to worry about it and went to California. He thought he might catch on with the movies."

"Did he?"

"He didn't even catch cold with the movies. Then they sent us the bill. Fourteen thou—well, they had it all itemized. Three nurses. Medication. Suite. Occupational Therapy. Professional services. Hydrotherapy. Group counseling. One-to-one counseling. Limousine. Chauffeur for limousine. Chauffeur's helper for limousine. Chauffeur's helper's hard-boiled eggs for lunch. Salt for chauffeur's helper's hard-boiled—"

"You're getting hysterical," Barney said. "You mean he just skipped?" We were at the bus stop, with a gaggle of other prosperous young suburbanites.

I said, "Like a flat rock on a pond. So we wrote him, and of course the letters came back. They didn't fool around, the 'Institute for Psychosomatic Adjustment' didn't."

"That's a pretty name."

"I telephoned a man up there to explain, when we got the first letter. He didn't sound pretty. Just tired. He said my wife shouldn't sign things without reading them. And he said if his house was—something about joint tenancy in fee simple, he would break his wife's arm if she was the type that signed things without reading them, and keep on rebreaking it until she stopped. Meanwhile they had laid out a lot of goods and services in good faith, and what was I going to do about it?"

The bus appeared on the horizon, emitting jet trails of Diesel smog. We knotted up by the sign. "So I told him I didn't know," I said, "but I know now. I'll get sued, that's what I'll do. The Dupoirs always have an answer to every problem."

Conversation was suspended for fifteen seconds of scrimmage while we entered the bus. Barney and I were lucky. We wound up with our heads jammed affectionately together, not too far from a window that sucked in Diesel fumes and fanned them at us. I could see the fruit flies gamely trying to get back to my ear, but they were losing the battle.

Barney said, "Hey. Couldn't you sell your house to somebody you trusted for a dollar, and then they couldn't—"

"Yes, they could. And then we'd both go to jail. I asked a guy in our legal department."

"Huh." The bus roared on, past knots of other prosperous young suburbanites who waved their fists at us as we passed. "How about this. I hope you won't take this the wrong way. But couldn't there be some angle about Shirl being, uh, not exactly *competent* to sign any kind of—"

"I asked about that too, Barney. No hope. Shirl's never been hospitalized, she's never been to a shrink, she runs a house and a husband and a small boy just fine. Maybe she's a little impulsive. But a lot of people are impulsive, the man said."

Garigolli

To Home Base
Chief,

I think we've got it. These people use a medium of exchange, remember? And the Host doesn't have enough of it! What could be simpler?

With a little modification there are a couple of local organisms that should be able to concentrate the stuff out of the ambient environment, and then—

And then we're off the impaling spike!

Garigolli.

The bus jerked to a stop at the railroad station and we boiled out on successive rollers of humanity which beached us at separate parts of the platform.

The 8:07 slid in at 8:19 sharp and I swung aboard, my mighty thews rippling like those of the giant anthropoids among whom I had been raised. With stealthy tread and every jungle-trained sense alert I stalked a vacant seat halfway down the aisle on the left, my fangs and molars bared, my liana-bound, flint-tipped *Times* poised for the thrust of death. It wasn't my morning. Ug-Fwa the Hyena, scavenger of the mighty Limpopo, bounded from the far vestibule giving voice to his mad cackle and slipped into the vacant seat. I and the rest of the giant anthropoids glared, unfolded our newspapers and pretended to read.

The headlines were very interesting that morning. PRES ASKS $14,752.03 FOR MISSILE DEFENSE. "SLICK" DUPOIR SOUGHT IN DEFAULT CASE. RUMOR RED PURGE OF BROTHER IN LAW. QUAKE DEATH TOLL SET AT 14,752.03. BODY OF SKID ROW CHARACTER IDENTIFIED AS FORMER PROSPEROUS YOUNG SUBURBANITE; BROTHER IN LAW FLIES FROM COAST, WEEPS "WHY DIDN'T HE ASK ME FOR HELP?" FOSTER PARENTS OF "BUTCHIE" DUPOIR OPEN LEGAL FIGHT AGAINST DESTITUTE MA AND PA, SAY "IF THEY LOVE HIM WHY DON'T THEY SUPPORT HIM?" GLIDER SOARS 14,752.03 MILES. DUPOIR OFF 147.52 —no, that was a fly speck, not a decimal point—OFF 14,752.03 FOR NEW LOW, RAILS AND BROTHERS AND LAW MIXED IN ACTIVE TRADING. I always feel you're more efficient if you start the day with the gist of the news straight in your mind.

I arrived at the office punctually at 9:07, late enough to show that I was an executive, but not so late that Mr. Horgan would notice it. The frowning brow of my cave opened under the grim rock front that bore the legend "International Plastics Co." and I walked in, nodding good morning to several persons from the Fourteenth Floor, but being nodded to myself only by Hermie, who ran the cigar stand. Hermie cultivated my company because I was good for a dollar on the numbers two or three times a week. Little did he know that it would be many a long day before he saw a dollar of mine, perhaps as many as 14,752.03 of them.

Garigolli

To Home Base

Further to my last communication, Chief,

We ran into a kind of a setback. We found a suitable organic substrate and implanted a colony of modified organisms which extracted gold from environmental sources, and they were performing beautifully, depositing a film of pure metal on the substrate, which the Host was carrying with him.

Then he folded it up and threw it in a waste receptacle.

We're still working on it, but I don't know, Chief, I don't know.

Garigolli.

I find it a little difficult to explain to people what I do for a living. It has something to do with making the country plastics-conscious. I make the country plastics-conscious by writing newspaper stories about plastics which only seem to get printed in neighborhood shopping guides in Sioux Falls, Idaho. And by scripting talk features about plastics which get run from 11:55 PM to 12:00 midnight on radio stations the rest of whose progamtime is devoted to public-service items like late jockey changes at Wheeling Downs. And by scripting television features which do not seem ever to be run on any station. And by handling the annual Miss Plastics contest, at least up to the point where actual contestants appear, when it is taken over by the people from the Fourteenth Floor. And by writing the monthly page of Plastics Briefs which goes out, already matted, to 2,000 papers in North America. Plastics Briefs is our best bet because each Brief is illustrated by a line drawing of a girl doing something with, to or about plastics, and her costume is always brief. As I said, all this is not easy to explain, so when people ask me what I do I usually say, "Whatever Mr. Horgan tells me to."

This morning Mr. Horgan called me away from a conference with Jack Denny, our Briefs artist, and said: "Dupoir, that Century of Plastics Anniversary Dinner idea of yours is out. The Fourteenth Floor says it lacks thematic juice. Think of something else for a winter promotion, and think big!" He banged a plastic block on his desk with a little plastic hammer.

I said, "Mr. Horgan, how about this? Are we getting the break in the high-school chemistry textbooks we should? Are we getting the message of polythene to every boy, girl, brother in law—"

He shook his head. "That's small," he said, and went on to explain: "By which I mean it isn't big. Also there is the flak we are getting from the nature nuts, which the Fourteenth Floor does not think you are dealing with in a creative way."

"I've ordered five thousand pop-up recycling bins for the test, Mr. Horgan. They're not only plastic, they're *recycled* plastic. We use them in my own home, and I am confident—"

"Confidence," he said, "is when you've got your eyes so firmly fixed on the goal that you trip on a dog-doodie and fall in the crap."

I regrouped. "I think we can convert the present opposition from the ecology movement to—"

"The ecology movement," he said, "is people who love buzzards better than babies and catfish better than cars."

I fell back on my last line of defense. "Yes, Mr. Hogan," I said.

"Personally," Mr. Horgan said, "I *like* seeing plastic bottles bobbing in the surf. It makes me feel, I don't know, like part of something that is going to last forever. I want you to communicate that feeling, Dupoir. Now go get your Briefs out."

I thought of asking for a salary advance of $14,752.03, but hesitated.

"Is there something else?"

"No, Mr. Horgan. Thank you." I left quietly.

Jack Denny was still waiting in my office, doodling still-life studies of cornucopias with fruits and nuts spilling out of them. "Look," he said, "how about this for a change? Something symbolic of the season, like 'the rich harvest of Plastics to make life more gracious,' like?"

I said kindly, "You don't understand copy, Jack. Do you remember what we did for last September?"

He scowled. "A girl in halter and shorts, very brief and tight, putting up plastic storm windows."

"That's right. Well, I've got an idea for something kind of novel this year. A little two-act drama. Act One: She's wearing halter and shorts and she's taking down the plastic screens. Act Two: She's wearing a dress and putting up the plastic storm windows. And this is important. In Act Two there's wind, and autumn leaves blowing, and the dress is kind of wind-blown tight against her. Do you know what I mean, Jack?"

He said evenly, "I was the youngest child and only boy in a family of eight. If I didn't know what you meant by now I would deserve to be put away. Sometimes I think I *will* be put away. Do you know what seven older sisters can do to the psychology of a sensitive young boy?" He began to shake.

"Draw, Jack," I told him hastily. To give him a chance to recover himself I picked up his cornucopias. "Very nice," I said, turning them over. "Beautiful modeling. I guess you spilled some paint on this one?"

He snatched it out of my hand. "Where? That? That's gilt. I don't even have any gilt."

"No offense, Jack. I just thought it looked kind of nice." It didn't, particularly, it was just a shiny yellow smear in a corner of the drawing.

"Nice! Sure, if you'd let me use metallic inks. If you'd go to highgloss paper. If you'd *spend* a few bucks—"

"Maybe, Jack," I said, "It'd be better, at that, if you took these back to your office. You can concentrate better there, maybe."

He went out, shaking.

I stayed in and thought about my house and brother in law and the Gudsell Medical Credit Bureau and after a while I began to shake too. Shaking, I phoned a Mr. Klaw, whom I had come to think of as my "account executive" at Gudsell.

Mr. Klaw was glad to hear from me. "You got our lawyer's note? Good, good. And exactly what arrangements are you suggesting, Mr. Dupoir?"

"I don't know," I said openly. "It catches me at a bad time. If we could have an extension—"

"Extensions we haven't got," he said regretfully. "We had one month of extensions, and we gave you the month, and now we're fresh out. I'm really sorry, Dupoir."

"With some time I could get a second mortgage, Mr. Klaw."

"You could at that, but not for $14,752.03."

"Do you want to put me and my family on the street?"

"Goodness, no, Mr. Dupoir! What we want is the sanitarium's money, including our commission. And maybe we want a *little* bit to make people think before they sign things, and maybe that people who should go to the county hospital *go* to the county hospital instead of a frankly de luxe rest home."

"I'll call you later," I said.

"Please do," said Mr. Klaw sincerely.

Tendons slack as the limp lianas, I leafed listlessly through the *dhowani-bark* jujus on my desk, studying Jack Denny's draftsmanship with cornucopias. The yellow stain, I noted, seemed to be spreading, even as a brother in law's blood might spread on the sands of the doom-pit when the cobras hissed the hour of judgment.

Mr. Horgan rapped perfunctorily on the doorframe and came in. "I had the impression, Dupoir, that you had something further to ask me at our conference this morning. I've learned to back those judgments, Dupoir."

"Well, sir—" I began.

"Had that feeling about poor old Globus," he went on. "You remember Miss Globus? Crying in the file room one day. Seems she'd signed up for some kind of charm school. Couldn't pay, didn't like it, tried to back out. They wanted their money. Attached her wages. Well. Naturally, we couldn't have that sort of financial irresponsibility. I understand she's a PFC in the WAC now. What was it you wanted, Dupoir?"

"Me, Mr. Horgan? Wanted? No. Nothing at all."

"Glad we cleared that up," he grunted. "Can't do your best work for the firm if your mind's taken up with personal problems. Remember, Dupoir. We want the country plastics conscious, and forget about those ecology freaks."

"Yes, Mr. Horgan."

"And big. Not small."

"Big it is, Mr. Horgan," I said. I rolled up Jack Denny's sketches into a thick wad and threw them at him in the door, but not before he had closed it behind him.

Garigolli

To Home Base

Listen Chief,

I appreciate your trying to work out a solution for us, but you're not doing well as we're doing, even. Not that that's much.

We tried again to meet that constant aura of medium-of-exchange need from the Host, but he destroyed the whole lash-up again. Maybe we're misunderstanding him?

Artifacts are out. He's too big to see anything we make. Energy sources don't look promising. Oh, sure, we could elaborate lesser breeds that would selectively concentrate, for instance, plutonium or one of the uraniums. I don't think this particular Host would know the difference unless the scale was very large, and then, blooie, critical mass.

Meanwhile morale is becoming troublesome. We're holding together, but I wouldn't describe the condition as *good*. Vellitot has been wooing Dinnoliss in spite of the secondary directives against breeding while on exploration missions. I've cautioned them both, but they don't seem to stop. The funny thing is they're both in the male phase.

Garigolli.

Between Jack Denny and myself we got about half of the month's Plastics Briefs before quitting time. Maybe they weren't big, but they were real wind-blown. All factors considered, I don't think it is very much to my discredit that two hours later I was moodily drinking my seventh beer in a dark place near the railroad station.

The bartender respected my mood, the TV was off, the juke box had nothing but blues on it and there was only one fly in my lugubrious ointment, a little man who kept trying to be friendly. From time to time I gave him a scowl I had copied from Mr. Horgan. Then he would edge down the bar for a few minutes before edging back. Eventually he got up courage enough to talk, and I got too gloomy to crush him with my mighty thews, corded like the jungle-vines that looped from the towering *nganga*-palms.

He was some kind of hotel-keeper, it appeared. "My young friend, you may think you have problems, but there's no business like my business. Mortgage, insurance, state supervision, building and grounds maintenance, kitchen personnel and purchasing, linen, uniforms, the station wagon and the driver, carpet repairs—oh, God, carpet repairs! No matter how many ash trays you put around, you know what they do? They steal the ashtrays. Then they stamp out cigarettes on the carpets." He began to weep.

I told the bartender to give him another. How could I lose? If he passed out I'd be rid of him. If he recovered I would have his undying, doglike affection for several minutes, and what kind of shape was I in to sneer at that?

Besides, I had worked out some pretty interesting figures. "Did you know," I told him, "that if you spend $1.46 a day on cigarettes, you can save $14,752.03 by giving up smoking for 10,104 and a quarter days?"

He wasn't listening, but he wasn't weeping any more either. He was just looking lovingly at his vodka libre, or whatever it was. I tried a different tack. "When you see discarded plastic bottles bobbing in the surf," I asked, "does it make you feel like part of something grand and timeless that will go on forever?"

He glanced at me with distaste, then went back to adoring his drink. "Or do you like buzzards beter than babies?" I asked.

"They're all babies," he said. "Nasty, smelly, upchucking babies."

"Who are?" I asked, having lost the thread. He shook his head mysteriously, patted his drink and tossed it down.

"Root of most evil," he said, swallowing. Then, affectionately, "Don't know where I'd be with it, don't know where I'd be without it."

He appeared to be talking about booze. "On your way home, without it?" I suggested.

He said obscurely, "Digging ditches, without it." Then he giggled. "Greatest business in the world! But oh! the worries! The competition! And when you come down to it it's all just aversion, right?"

"I can see you have a great aversion to liquor," I said politely.

"No, stupid! The *guests*."

Stiffly I signaled for Number Eight, but the bartender misunderstood and brought another for my friend, too. I said, "You have an aversion to the guests?"

He took firm hold on the bar and attempted to look squarely into my eyes, but wound up with his left eye four inches in front of my left eye and both our right eyes staring at respective ears. "The *guests* must be made to feel an aversion to *alcohol*," he said. "Secret of the whole thing. Works. Sometimes. But oh! it costs."

Like the striking fangs of Nag, the cobra, faster than the eye can follow, my trained reflexes swept the beer up to my lips. I drank furiously, scowling at him. "You mean to say you ran a drunk farm?" I shouted.

He was shocked. "My boy! No need to be vulgar. An 'institute', eh? Let's leave the aversion to the drunks."

"I have to tell you, sir," I declared, "that I have a personal reason for despising all proprietors of such institutions!"

He began to weep again. "You, too! Oh, the general scorn."

"In my case, there is nothing general—"

"—the hatred! The unthinking contempt. And for what?" I snarled, "For your blood-sucking ways."

"Blood, old boy?" he said, surprised. "No, nothing like that. We don't use blood. We use gold, yes, but the gold cure's old hat. Need new gimmick. Can't use silver, too cheap. Really doesn't matter what you say you use. All aversion—drying them out, keeping them comfy and aversion. But no blood."

He wiggled his fingers for Number Nine. Moodily I drank, glaring at him over my glass.

"In the wrong end of it, I sometimes think," he went on meditatively, staring with suspicious envy at the bartender. "*He* doesn't have to worry. Pour it out, pick up the money. No concern about expensive rooms standing idle, staff loafing around picking their noses, overhead going on, going on—you wouldn't be*lieve* how it goes on, whether the guests are there to pay for it or not—"

"Hah," I muttered.

"You've simply no idea what I go through," he sobbed. "And then they won't pay. No, really. Fellow beat me out of $14,752.03 just lately. I'm taking it out of the cosigner's hide, of course, but after you pay the collection agency, what's the profit?"

I choked on the beer, but he was too deep in sorrow to notice.

Strangling, I gasped, "Did you say fourteen thousand—?"

He nodded. "Seven hundred and fifty-two dollars, yes. And three cents. Astonishes you, doesn't it, the deadbeats in this world?"

I couldn't speak.

"You wouldn't think it," he mourned. "All those salaries. All those rooms. The hydrotherapy tubs. The *water* bill."

I shook my head.

"Probably you think my life's a bowl of roses, hey?"

I managed to pry my larynx open enough to wheeze, "Up to this minute, yes, I did. You've opened my eyes."

"Drink to that," he said promptly. "Hey, barman!"

But before the bartender got there with Number Ten the little man hiccoughed and slid melting to the floor, like a glacier calving into icebergs.

The bartender peered over at him. "Every *damn* night," he grumbled. "And who's going to get him home this time?"

My mind working as fast as *Ngo*, the dancing spider, spinning her web, I succeeded in saying, "Me. Glad to oblige. Never fear."

Garigolli

To Home Base

Chief, All right, I admit we haven't been exactly 144 p.g. on this project, but there's no reason for you to get loose. Reciting the penalties for violating the Triple Directive is uncalled for.

Let me point out that there has been no question at any time of compliance with One or Three. And even Directive Two, well, we've done what we could. "To repay sentients in medium suitable to them for information gained." These sentients are tricky, Chief. They don't seem to empathize, really. See our reports. They often take without giving in return among themselves, and it seems to me that under the circumstances a certain modification of Directive Two would have been quite proper.

But I am not protesting the ruling. Especially since you've pointed out it won't do any good. When I get old and skinny enough to retire to a sling in Home Base I guess I'll get that home-base mentality too, but way out here on the surface of the exploration volume it looks different, believe me.

And what is happening with the rest of our crew back at Host's domicile I can't even guess. They must be nearly frantic by now.

Garigolli.

There was some discussion with a policeman he wanted to hit (apparently under the impression that the cop was his night watchman playing hookey), but I finally got the little man to the Institute for Psychosomatic Adjustment.

The mausoleum that had graduated my brother in law turned out to be three stories high, with a sun porch and a slate roof and bars on the ground-floor bay windows. It was not all that far from my house. Shirl had been pleased about that, I remembered. She said we could visit her brother a lot there, and in fact she had gone over once or twice on Sundays, but me, I'd never set eyes on the place before.

Dagger-sharp fangs flecking white spume, none dared dispute me as I strode through the great green corridors of the rain forest. Corded thews rippling like pythons under my skin, it was child's play to carry the craven jackal to his lair. The cabbie helped me up the steps with him.

The little man, now revealed as that creature who in anticipation had seemed so much larger and hairier, revived slightly as we entered the reception hall. "Ooooh," he groaned. "Watch the bouncing, old boy. That door. My office. Leather couch. Much obliged."

I dumped him on the couch, lit a green-shaded lamp on his desk, closed the door and considered.

Mine enemy had delivered himself into my power. All I had to do was seize him by the forelock. I seemed to see the faces of my family—Shirl's smiling sweetly, Butchie's cocoa-over-laid-with-oatmeal—spurring me on.

There had to be a way.

I pondered. Life had not equipped me for this occasion. Raffles or Professor Moriarty would have known what to do at once, but, ponder as I would, I couldn't think of anything to do except to go through the drawers of his desk.

Well, it was a start. But it yielded very little. Miscellaneous paper clips and sheaves of letterheads, a carton of cigarettes of a brand apparently flavored with rice wine and extract of vanilla, part of a fifth of Old Rathole and five switchblade knives, presumably taken from the inmates. There was also

$6.15 in unused postage stamps. But I quickly computed that, even if I went to the trouble of cashing them in, that would leave me $14,745.88 short.

Of Papers to Burn there were none.

All in all, the venture was a bust. I wiped out a water glass with one of the letterheads (difficult, because they were of so high quality that they seemed likelier to shatter than to wad up), and forced down a couple of ounces of the whiskey (difficult, because it was of so low).

Obviously anything of value, like for instance co-signed agreements with brothers in law, would be in a safe, which itself would probably be in the offices of the Gudsell Medical Credit Bureau. Blackmail? But there seemed very little to work with, barring one or two curious photographs tucked in among the envelopes. Conceivably I could cause him some slight embarrassment, but nowhere near $14,752.03 worth. I had not noticed any evidence of Red espionage that might put the little man (whose name, I learned from his letterhead, was Bermingham) away for 10,104 and a quarter days, while I saved up the price of reclaiming our liberty.

There seemed to be only one possible thing to do.

Eyes glowing like red coals behind slitted lids, I walked lightly on velvet-soft pads to the *kraal* of the witch-man. He was snoring with his mouth opn. Totally vulnerable to his doom.

Only, how to inflict it?

It is not as easy as one might think to murder a person. Especially if one doesn't come prepared for it. Mr. Horgan doesn't like us to carry guns at the office, and heaven knows what Shirl would do with one if I left it around home. Anyway, I didn't have one.

Poison was a possibility. The Old Rathole suggested itself. But we'd already tried that, hadn't we?

I considered the switchblade knives. There was a technical problem. Would *you* know where the heart is? Granted, it had to be inside his chest somewhere, and sooner or later I could find it. But what would I say to Mr. Bermingham after the first three or four exploratory stabs woke him up?

The only reasonably efficient method I could think of to insure Mr. Bermingham's decease was to burn the place down with him in it. Which, I quickly perceived, meant with whatever cargo of drying-out drunks the Institute now possessed in it too, behind those barred windows.

At this point I came face to face with myself.

I wasn't going to kill anybody. I wasn't going to steal any papers.

What I was going to do was, I was going to let Mr. Klaw's lawyers go ahead and take our house, because I just didn't know how to do anything else. I hefted the switchblades in my hand, threw them against the wall and poured myself another slug of Mr. Bermingham's lousy whiskey, wishing it would kill me right there and be a lesson to him.

Garigolli

To Home Base

Now, don't get excited, Chief, But we have another problem.

Before I get into it, I would like to remind you of a couple of things. First, I was against exploring this planet in the first place, remember? I said it was going to be very difficult, on the grounds of the difference in mass between its dominant species and us. I mean, really. Here we are, fighting member to member against dangerous beasts all the time, and the beasts, to the Host and his race, are only microorganisms that live unnoticed in their circulatory systems, their tissues, their food and their environment. Anybody could tell that this was going to be a tough assignment, if not an impossible one.

Then there's the fact that this Host moves around so. I told you some of our crew got left in his domicile. Well, we've timed this before, and almost always he returns within 144 or 216 time-units—at most, half of one of his planet's days. It's pretty close to critical, but our crew is tough and they can survive empathy-deprival that long. Only this time he has been away, so far, nearly 432 time-units. It's bad enough for those of us who have been with him. The ones who were cut off back at his domicile must have been through the tortures of the damned.

Two of them homed in on us to report just a few time-units ago, and I'm afraid you're not going to like what's happened. They must have been pretty panicky. They decided to try meeting the Second Directive themselves. They modified some micro-organisms to provide some organic chemicals they thought the Host might like.

Unfortunately the organisms turned out to have an appetite for some of the Host's household artifacts, and they're pretty well demolished. So we not only haven't *given* him anything to comply with Directive Two, we've *taken* something from him. And in the process maybe we've called attention to ourselves.

"I'm giving it to you arced, Chief, because I know that's how you'd like it. I accept full reponsibility.

Because I don't have any choice, do I?

Garigolli.

"What the Hell," said the voice of Mr. Bermingham, from somewhere up there, "are you doing in my office?"

I opened my eyes, and he was quite right. I was in Mr. Bermingham's office. The sun was streaming through Mr. Bermingham's Venetian blinds, and Mr. Bermingham was standing over me with a selection of the switchblade knives in his hands.

I don't know how Everyman reacts to this sort of situation. I guess I ran about average. I pushed myself up on one elbow and blinked at him.

"Spastic," he muttered to himself. "Well?"

I cleared my throat. "I, uh, I think I can explain this."

He was hung over and shaking. "Go ahead! Who the devil are you?"

"Well, my name is Dupoir."

"I don't mean what's your name, I mean—Wait a minute. Dupoir?"

"Dupoir."

"As in $14,752.03?"

"That's right, Mr. Bermingham."

"You!" he gasped. "Say, you've got some nerve coming here this way. I ought to teach you a lesson."

I scrambled to my feet. Mighty thews rippling, I tossed back my head and bellowed the death-challenge of the giant anthropoids with whom I had been raised.

Bermingham misunderstood. It probably didn't sound like a death-challenge to him. He said anxiously, "If you're going to be sick, go in there and do it. Then we're going to straighten this thing out."

I followed his pointing finger. There on one side of the foyer was the door marked *Staff Washroom,* and on the other the door to the street through which I had carried him. It was only the work of a second to decide which to take. I was out the door, down the steps, around the corner and hailing a fortuitious cab before he could react.

By the time I got to the house that Mr. Klaw wanted so badly to take away from us it was 7:40 on my watch. There was no chance at all that Shirl would still be asleep. There was not any very big chance that she had got to sleep at all that night, not with her faithful husband for the first time in the four years of our marriage staying out all night without warning, but no chance at all that she would be still in bed. So there would be explaining to do. Nevertheless I insinuated my key into the lock of the back door, eased it open, slipped ghostlike though and gently closed it behind me.

I smelled like a distillery, I noticed, but my keen, jungle-trained senses brought me no other message. No one was in sight or sound. Not even Butchie was either chattering or weeping to disturb the silence.

I slid silently through the mudroom into the half-bath where I kept a spare razor. I spent five minutes trying to convert myself into the image of a prosperous young executive getting ready to be half an hour late at work, but it was no easy job. There was nothing but soap to shave with, and Butchie had knocked it into the sink. What was left was a blob of jelly, sculpted into a crescent where the dripping tap had eroded it away. Still, I got clean, more or less, and shaved, less.

I entered the kitchen, and then realized that my jungle-trained senses had failed to note the presence of a pot of fresh coffee perking on the stove. I could hear it plainly enough. Smelling it was more difficult; its scent was drowned by the aroma of cheap booze that hung in the air all around me.

So I turned around and yes, there was Shirl on the stairway, holding Butchie by one hand like Maureen O'Sullivan walking Cheeta. She wore an expression of unrelieved tragedy.

It was clearly necessary to give her an explanation at once, whether I had one or not. "Honey," I said, "I'm *sorry*. I met this fellow I hadn't seen in a long time, and we got to talking. I know we should have called. But by the time I realized the time it was so late I was afraid I'd wake you up."

"You can't wear that shirt to the office," she said woefully. "I ironed your blue and gray one with the white cuffs. It's in the closet."

I paused to analyze the situation. It appeared she wasn't angry at all, only upset—which, as any husband of our years knows, is 14,752.03 times worse. In spite of the fact that the reek of booze was making me giddy and fruit flies were buzzing around Shirl's normally immaculate kitchen, I knew what I had to do. "Shirl," I said, falling to one knee, "I apologize."

That seemed to divert her. "Apologize? For what?"

"For staying out all night."

"But you explained all that. You met this fellow you hadn't seen in a long time, and you got to talking. By the time you realized the time it was so late you were afraid you'd wake me up."

"Oh, Shirl," I cried, leaping to my feet and crushing her in my mighty thews. I would have kissed her, but the reek of stale liquor seemed even stronger. I was afraid of what close contact might do, not to mention its effect on Butchie, staring up at me with a thumb and two fingers in his mouth. We Dupoirs never do anything by halves.

But there was a tear in her eye. She said, "I watched Butchie, honestly I did. I always do. When he broke the studio lamp I was watching every minute, remember? He was just too fast for me."

I didn't have any idea what she was talking about. That is not an unfamiliar situation in our house, and I have developed a technique for dealing with it. "What?" I asked.

"He was too fast for me," Shirl said woefully. "When he dumped his vitamins into his raisins and oatmeal I was right there. I went to get some paper napkins, and that was when he did it. But how could I know it would ruin the plastics bin?"

I went into Phase Two. "What plastics bin?"

"*Our* plastics bin." She pointed. "Where Butchie threw the stuff."

At once I saw what she meant. There was a row of four plastic popup recycling bins in our kitchen, one for paper, one for plastics, one for glass and one for metals. They were a credit to us, and to Mr. Horgan and to the Fourteenth Floor. However, the one marked "plastics" was not a credit to anyone any more. It had sprung a leak. A colorless fluid was oozing out of the bottom of it and, whatever it was, it was deeply pitting the floor tiles.

I bent closer and realized where the reek of stale booze was coming from: out of the juices that were seeping from our plastics bin.

"What the devil?" I asked.

Shirl said thoughtfully, "If vitamins can do that to plastic, what do you suppose they do to Butchie's insides?"

"It isn't the vitamins. I know that much." I reached in and hooked the handle of what had been a milk jug, gallon size. It was high-density polythene and about four hundred per cent more indestructible than Mount Rushmore. It was exactly the kind of plastic jug that people who loved buzzards better than babies have been complaining about finding bobbing around the surf of their favorite bathing beaches, all the world over.

Indestructible or not, it was about ninety per cent destroyed. What I pulled out was a handle and part of a neck. The rest drizzled off into a substance very like the stuff I had shaved with. Only that was soap, which one expects to dissolve from time to time. High-density polythene one does not.

The fruit flies were buzzing around me, and everything was very confusing. I was hardly aware that the front doorbell had rung until I noticed that Shirl had gone to answer it.

What made me fully aware of this was Mr. Bermingham's

triumphant roar: "Thought I'd find you here, Dupoir! And who are these people—your confederates?"

Bermingham had no terrors for me. I was past that point. I said, "Hello, Mr. Bermingham. This confederate is my wife, the littler one here is my son. Shirl, Butchie—Mr. Bermingham. Mr. Bermingham's the one who is going to take away our house."

Shirl said politely, "You must be tired, Mr. Bermingham. I'll get you a cup of coffee."

Garigolli

To Home Base

Chief, I admit it, we've excreted this one out beyond redemption. Don't bother to reply to this. Just write us off.

I could say that it wasn't entirely the fault of the crew members who stayed behind in the Host's domicile. They thought they had figured out a way to meet Directive Two. They modified some organisms—didn't even use bacteria, just an enzyme that hydrated polythene into what they had every reason to believe was a standard food substance, since the Host had been observed to ingest it with some frequency. There is no wrongdoing there, Chief. Alcohols are standard foods for many organic beings, as you know. And a gift of food has been held to satisfy the second Directive. And add to that they were half out of their plexuses with empathy deprivation.

Nevertheless I admit the gift failed in a fairly basic way, since it seems to have damaged artifacts the Hosts hold valuable.

So I accept the responsibility, Chief. Wipe this expedition off the records. We've failed, and we'll never see our home breeding-slings again.

Please notify our descendants and former co-parents and, if you can, try to let them think we died heroically, won't you?

Garigolli.

Shirl has defeated the wrath of far more complex creatures than Mr. Bermingham by offering them coffee—me, for instance. While she got him the clean cup and the spoon and the milk out of the pitcher in the refrigerator, I had time to think.

Mr. Horgan would be interested in what had happened to our plastics eco-bin. Not only Mr. Horgan. The Fourteenth Floor would be interested. The ecology freaks themselves would be interested, and maybe would forget about liking buzzards better than babies long enough to say a good word for International Plastics Co.

I mean, this was *significant*. It was big, by which I mean it wasn't little. It was a sort of whole new horizon for plastics. The thing about plastics, as everyone knows, is that once you convert them into trash they *stay* trash. Bury a maple syrup jug in your back yard and five thousand years from now some descendant operating a radar-controlled peony-planter from his back porch will grub it up as shiny as new. But the gunk in our eco-bin was making these plastics, or at least the polythene parts of them, bio-degradable.

What was the gunk? I had no idea. Some random chemical combination between Butchie's oatmeal and his vitamins? I didn't care. It was there, and it worked. If we could isolate the stuff, I had no doubt that the world-famous scientists who gave us the plastic storm window and the popup eco-bin could duplicate it. And if we could duplicate it we could sell it to hard-pressed garbagemen all over the world. The Fourteenth Floor would be very pleased.

With me to think was ever to act. I rinsed out one of Butchie's babyfood jars in the sink, scraped some of the stickiest parts of the melting plastic into it and capped it tightly. I couldn't wait to get it to the office.

Mr. Bermingham was staring at me with his mouth open. "Good Lord," he muttered, "playing with filth at his age. What psychic damage we wreak with bad early toilet-training."

I had lost interest in Mr. Bermingham. I stood up and told him, "I've got to go to work. I'd be happy to walk you as far as the bus."

"You aren't going anywhere, Dupoir! Came here to talk to you. Going to do it, too. Behavior was absolutely inexcusable, and I demand—Say, Dupoir, you don't have a drink anywhere about the house, do you?"

"More coffee, Mr. Bermingham?" Shirl said politely. "I'm afraid we don't have anything stronger to offer you. We don't keep alcoholic beverages here, or at least not very long. Mr. Dupoir drinks them."

"Thought so," snarled Bermingham. "Recognize a drunk when I see one: shifty eyes, irrational behavior, duplicity—oh, the duplicity! Got all the signs."

"Oh, he's not like my brother, really," Shirl said thoughtfully. "My husband doesn't go out breaking into liquor stores when he runs out, you know. But I don't drink, and Butchie doesn't drink, and so about all we ever have in the house is some cans of beer, and there aren't any of those now."

Bermingham looked at her with angry disbelief. "You too! I *smell* it," he said. "You going to tell me I don't know what good old ethyl alcohol smells like?"

"That's the bin, Mr. Bermingham. It's a terrible mess, I know."

"Funny place to keep the creature," he muttered to himself, dropping to his knees. He dipped a finger into the drippings, smelled it, tasted it and nodded. "Alcohol, all right. Add a few congeners, couple drops of food coloring, and you've got the finest Chivas Regal a bellboy ever sold you out of a bottle with the tax stamp broken." He stood up and glared at me. "What's the matter with you, Dupoir? You not only don't pay your honest debts, you don't want to pay the bartenders either?"

I said, "It's more or less an accident."

"Accident?"

Then illumination struck. "Accident you should find us like this," I corrected. "You see, it's a secret new process. We're not ready to announce it yet. Making alcohol out of old plastic scraps."

He questioned Shirl with his eyes. Getting her consent, he poured some of Butchie's baby-food orange juice into a glass, scooped in some of the drippings from the bin, closed his eyes and tasted. "Mmm," he said judiciously. "Sell it for vodka just the way it stands."

"Glad to have an expert opinion," I said. "We think there's millions in it."

He took another taste. "Plastic scraps, you say? Listen, Dupoir. Think we can clear all this up in no time. That fool Klaw, I've told him over and over, ask politely, don't make trouble for people. But no, he's got that crazy lawyer's drive for revenge. Apologize for him, old boy, I really do apologize for him. Now look," he said, putting down the glass to rub his hands. "You'll need help in putting this process on the market. Business acumen, you know? Wise counsel from man of experience. Like me. And capital. Can help you there. I'm loaded."

Shirl put in, "Then what do you want our house for?"

"House? My dear Mrs. Dupoir," cried Mr. Bermingham, laughing heartily, "I'm not going to take your house! Your husband and I will work out the details in no time. Let me have a little more of that delightful orange juice and we can talk some business."

Garigolli

to Home Base

Joy, joy

Chief!

Cancel all I said. We've met Directive Two, the Host is happy, and we're on our way Home!

Warm up the breeding slings, there's going to be a hot time in the old hammocks tonight.

Garigolli.

Straight as the flight of Ung-Glitch, the soaring vulture, that is the code of the jungle. I was straight with Mr. Bermingham. I didn't cheat him. I made a handshake deal with him over the ruins of our Eco-Bin, and honored it when we got to his lawyers. I traded him 40% of the beverage rights to the stuff that came out of our bin, and he wrote off that little matter of $14,752.03.

Of course, the beverage rights turned out not to be worth all that much, because the stuff in the bin was organic and alive and capable of reproduction, and it did indeed reproduce itself enthusiastically. Six months later you could buy a starter drop of it for a quarter on any street corner, and what that has done to the vintners of the world you know as well as I do. But Bermingham came out ahead. He divided his 40% interest into forty parts and sold them for $500 each to the alumni of his drunk tank. And Mr. Horgan—

Ah, Mr. Horgan.

Mr. Horgan was perched on my doorframe like Ung-Glitch awaiting a delivery of cadavers for dinner when I arrived that morning, bearing my little glass jar before me like the waiting line in an obstetrician's office. "You're late, Dupoir," he pointed out. "Troubles me, that does. Do you remember Metcalf? Tall, blonde girl that used to work in Accounts Receivable? Never could get in on time, and—"

"Mr. Horgan," I said, "look." And I unscrewed my baby-food jar and dumped the contents on an unpopped pop-up Eco-Bin. It took him a while to see what was happening, but once he saw he was so impressed he forgot to roar.

And, yes, the Fourteenth Floor was very pleased.

There wasn't any big money in it. We couldn't sell the stuff, because it was so happy to give itself away to everyone in the world. But it meant a promotion and a raise. Not big. But not really little, either. And, as Mr. Horgan said, "I *like* the idea of helping to eliminate all the litter that devastates the landscape. It makes me feel, I don't know, like part of something clean and natural."

And so we got along happily as anything—happily, anyway, until the time Shirl bought the merry-go-round.

THE FOUR-HOUR FUGUE

Alfred Bester

The diamond-hard cynicism of a top-flight writer who knows for himself the ins and outs of the jungle of modern American publishing combined with a feel for science fiction and an ineradicable gleam of boyish humor makes Alfred Bester memorable. He doesn't write sf often, but when he does, it's news.

By now, of course, the Northeast Corridor was the Northeast slum, stretching from Canada to the Carolinas and as far west as Pittsburgh. It was a fantastic jungle of rancid violence inhabited by a steaming, restless population with no visible means of support and no fixed residence, so vast that census-takers, birth-control supervisors and the social services had given up all hope. It was a gigantic raree-show that everyone denounced and enjoyed. Even the privileged few who could afford to live highly-protected lives in highly-expensive Oases and could live anywhere else they pleased never thought of leaving. The jungle grabbed you.

There were thousands of everyday survival problems but one of the most exasperating was the shortage of fresh water. Most of the available potable water had long since been impounded by progressive industries for the sake of a better tomorrow and there was very little left to go around. Rainwater tanks on the roofs, of course. A black market, naturally. That was about all. So the jungle stank. It stank worse than the court of Queen Elizabeth, which could have bathed but didn't believe in it. The Corridor just couldn't bathe, wash clothes or clean house, and you could smell its noxious effluvium from ten miles out at sea. Welcome to the Fun Corridor.

Sufferers near the shore would have been happy to clean up in salt water, but the Corridor beaches had been polluted by so much crude oil seepage for so many generations that they were all owned by deserving oil reclamation companies. *Keep Out! No Trespassing!* And armed guards. The rivers and lakes were electrically fenced; no need for guards, just skull and crossbones signs and if you didn't know what they were telling you, tough.

Not to believe that everybody minded stinking as they skipped merrily over the rotting corpses in the streets, but a lot did and their only remedy was perfumery. There were dozens of competing companies producing perfumes but the leader, far and away, was the Continental Can Company, which hadn't manufactured cans in two centuries. They'd switched to plastics and had the good fortune about a hundred stockholders' meetings back to make the mistake of signing a sales contract with and delivering to some cockamamie perfume brewer an enormous quantity of glowing neon containers. The corporation went bust and CCC took it over in hopes of getting some of their money back. That take-over proved to be their salvation when the perfume explosion took place; it gave them entrée to the most profitable industry of the times.

But it was neck-and-neck with the rivals until Blaise Skiaki joined CCC; then it turned into a runaway. Blaise Skiaki. Origins: French, Japanese, Black African and Irish. Education: BA, Princeton; ME, MIT: PhD, Dow Chemical. (It was Dow that had secretly tipped CCC that Skiaki was a winner and lawsuits brought by the competition were still pending before the ethics board.) Blaise Skiaki: Age, thirty-one; unmarried, straight, genius.

His sense of scent was his genius, and he was privately referred to at CCC as "The Nose." He knew everything about perfumery: the animal products, ambergris, castor, civet, musk; the essential oils distilled from plants and flowers; the balsams extruded by tree and shrub wounds, benzoin, opopanax, Peru, Talu, storax, myrrh; the synthetics created from the combination of natural and chemical scents, the latter mostly the esters of fatty acids.

He had created for CCC their most successful sellers: "Vulva," "Assuage," "Oxter" (a much more attractive brand name than "Armpitto"), "Preparation F," "Tongue War," et cetera. He was treasured by CCC, paid a salary generous enough to enable him to live in an Oasis and, best of all, granted unlimited supplies of fresh water. No girl in the Corridor could resist the offer of taking a shower with him.

But he paid a high price for these advantages. He could never use scented soaps, shaving creams, pomades or depilatories. He could never eat seasoned foods. He could drink nothing but pure water. All this, you understand, to keep The Nose pure and uncontaminated so that he could smell around in his sterile laboratory and devise new creations. He was presently composing a rather promising unguent provisionally named "Correctum," but he'd been on it for six months without any positive results and CCC was alarmed by the delay. His genius had never before taken so long.

There was a meeting of the top level executives, names withheld on the grounds of corporate privilege.

"What's the matter with him anyway?"

"Has he lost his touch?"

"It hardly seems likely."

"Maybe he needs a rest."

"Why, he had a week's holiday last month."

"What did he do?"

"Ate up a storm, he told me."

"Could that be it?"

"No. He said he purged himself before he came back to work."

"Is he having trouble here at CCC? Difficulties with middle-management?"

"Absolutely not, Mr. Chairman. They wouldn't dare touch him."

"Maybe he wants a raise."

"No. He can't spend the money he makes now."

"Has our competition got to him?"

"They get to him all the time, General, and he laughs them off."

"Then it must be something personal."

"Agreed."

"Woman-trouble?"

"My God! We should have such trouble."

"Family-trouble?"

"He's an orphan, Mr. Chairman."

"Ambition? Incentive? Should we make him an officer of CCC?"

"I offered that to him the first of the year, sir, and he turned me down. He just wants to play in his laboratory."

"Then why isn't he playing?"

"Apparently he's got some kind of creative block."

"What the hell is the matter with him anyway?"

"Which is how you started this meeting."

"I did not."

"You did."

"Not."

"Governor, will you play back the bug."

"Gentlemen, gentlemen, please! Obviously Dr. Skiaki has

personal problems which are blocking his genius. We must solve that for him. Suggestions?"

"Psychiatry?"

"That won't work without voluntary cooperation. I doubt whether he'd cooperate. He's an obstinate gook."

"Senator, I beg you! Such expressions must not be used with reference to one of our most valuable assets."

"Mr. Chairman, the problem is to discover the source of Dr. Skiaki's block."

"Agreed. Suggestions?"

"Why, the first step should be to maintain twenty-four-hour surveillance. All of the gook's—excuse me—the good doctor's activities, associates, contacts."

"By CCC?"

"I would suggest not. There are bound to be leaks which would only antagonize the good gook—doctor!"

"Outside surveillance?"

"Yes, sir."

"Very good. Agreed. Meeting adjourned."

Skip-Tracer Associates were perfectly furious. After one month they threw the case back into CCC's lap, asking for nothing more than their expenses.

"Why in hell didn't you tell us that we were assigned to a pro, Mr. Chairman, sir? Our tracers aren't trained for that."

"Wait a minute, please. What d'you mean, 'pro'?"

"A professional Rip."

"A what?"

"Rip. Gorill. Gimpster. Crook."

"Dr. Skiaki a crook? Preposterous."

"Look, Mr. Chairman, I'll frame it for you and you draw your own conclusions. Yes?"

"Go ahead."

"It's all detailed in this report anyway. We put double tails on Skiaki every day to and from your shop. When he left they followed him home. He always went home. They staked in double shifts. He had dinner sent in from the Organic Nursery every night. They checked the messengers bringing the dinners. Legit. They checked the dinners; sometimes for one, sometimes for two. They traced some of the girls who left his penthouse. All clean. So far, all clean, yes?"

"And?"

"The crunch. Couple of nights a week he leaves the house and goes into the city. He leaves around midnight and doesn't come back until four, more or less."

"Where does he go?"

"We don't know because he shakes his tails like the pro that he is. He weaves through the Corridor like a whore or a fag cruising for trade—excuse me—and he always loses our men. I'm not taking anything away from him. He's smart, shifty, quick and a real pro. He has to be; and he's too much for Skip Tracers to handle."

"Then you have no idea of what he does or who he meets between midnight and four?"

"No, sir. We've got nothing and you've got a problem. Not ours any more."

"Thank you. Contrary to the popular impression, corporations are not altogether idiotic. CCC understands that negatives are also results. You'll receive your expenses and the agreed-upon fee"

"Mr. Chairman, I—"

"No, no, please. You've narrowed it down to those missing four hours. Now, as you say, they're our problem."

CCC summoned Salem Burne. Mr. Burne always insisted that he was neither a physician nor a psychiatrist; he did not care to be associated with what he considered to be the drek of the professions. Salem Burne was a witch doctor; more precisely, a warlock. He made the most remarkable and penetrating analyses of disturbed people, not so much through his coven rituals of pentagons, incantations, incense and the like as through his remarkable sensitivity to Body English and his acute interpretation of it. And this might be witchcraft after all.

Mr. Burne entered Blaise Skiaki's immaculate laboratory with a winning smile and Dr. Skiaki let out a rending howl of anguish.

"I told you to sterilize before you came."

"But I did, Doctor. Faithfully."

"You did not. You reek of anise, ilang-ilang and methyl anthranilate. You've polluted my day. Why?"

"Dr. Skiaki, I assure you that I—" Suddenly Salem Burne stopped. "Oh my God!" he groaned. "I used my wife's towel this morning."

Skiaki laughed and turned up the ventilators to full force. "I understand. No hard feelings. Now let's get your wife out of here. I have an office about half a mile down the hall. We can talk there."

They sat down in the vacant office and looked at each other. Mr. Burne saw a pleasant, youngish man with cropped black hair, small expressive ears, high telltale cheekbones, slitty eyes that would need careful watching and graceful hands that would be a dead giveaway.

"Now, Mr. Burne, how can I help you?" Skiaki said while his hands asked, "Why the hell have you come pestering me?"

"Dr. Skiaki, I'm a colleague in a sense; I'm a professional witch doctor. One crucial part of my ceremonies is the burning of various forms of incense, but they're all rather conventional. I was hoping that your expertise might suggest something different with which I could experiment."

"I see. Interesting. You've been burning stacte, onycha, galbanum, frankincense . . . that sort of thing?"

"Yes. All quite conventional."

"Most interesting. I could, of course, make many suggestions for new experiments, and yet—" Here Skiaki stopped and stared into space.

After a long pause the warlock asked, "Is anything wrong, Doctor?"

"Look here," Skiaki burst out. "You're on the wrong track. It's the burning of incense that's conventional and old-fashioned, and trying different scents won't solve your problem. Why not experiment with an altogether different approach?"

"And what would that be?"

"The Odophone principle."

"Odophone?"

"Yes. There's a scale that exists among scents as among sounds. Sharp smells correspond to high notes and heavy smells with low notes. For example, ambergris is in the treble clef while violet is in the bass. I could draw up a scent scale for you, running perhaps two octaves. Then it would be up to you to compose the music."

"This is positively brilliant, Dr. Skiaki."

"Isn't it?" Skiaki beamed. "But in all honesty I should point out that we're collaborators in brilliance. I could never have come up with the idea if you hadn't presented me with a most original challenge."

They made contact on this friendly note and talked shop enthusiastically, lunched together, told each other about themselves and made plans for the witchcraft experiments in which Skiaki volunteered to participate despite the fact that he was no believer in diabolism.

"And yet the irony lies in the fact that he is indeed devil-ridden," Salem Burne reported

The Chairman could make nothing of this.

"Psychiatry and diabolism use different terms for the same

phenomenon," Burne explained. "So perhaps I'd better translate. Those missing four hours are fugues."

The Chairman was not enlightened. "Do you mean the musical expression, Mr. Burne?"

"No, sir. A fugue is also the psychiatric description of a more advanced form of somnambulism . . . sleepwalking."

"Blaise Skiaki walks in his sleep?"

"Yes, sir, but it's more complicated than that. The sleepwalker is a comparatively simple case. He is never in touch with his surroundings. You can speak to him, shout at him, address him by name, and he remains totally oblivious"

"And the fugue?"

"In the fugue the subject is in touch with his surroundings. He can converse with you. He has awareness and memory for the events that take place within the fugue, but while he is within his fugue he is a totally different person from the man he is in real life. And—and this is most important, sir—after the fugue he remembers nothing of it."

"Then in your opinion Dr. Skiaki has these fugues two or three times a week."

"That is my diagnosis, sir."

"And he can tell us nothing of what transpires during the fugue?"

"Nothing."

"Can you?"

"I'm afraid not, sir. There's a limit to my powers."

"Have you any idea what is causing these fugues?"

"Only that he is driven by something. I would say that he is possessed by the devil, but that is the cant of my profession. Others may use different terms—compulsion or obsession. The terminology is unimportant. The basic fact is that something possessing him is compelling him to go out nights to do—what? I don't know. All I do know is that this diabolical drive most probably is what is blocking his creative work for you."

One does not summon Gretchen Nunn, not even if you're CCC whose common stock has split twenty-five times. You work your way up through the echelons of her staff until you are finally admitted to the Presence. This involves a good deal of backing and forthing between your staff and hers, and ignites a good deal of exasperation, so the Chairman was understandably put out when at last he was ushered into Miss Nunn's workshop, which was cluttered with the books and apparatus she used for her various investigations.

Gretchen Nunn's business was working miracles; not in the

sense of the extraordinary, anomalous or abnormal brought about by a superhuman agency, but rather in the sense of her extraordinary and/or abnormal perception and manipulation of reality. In any situation she could and did achieve the impossible begged by her desperate clients, and her fees were so enormous that she was thinking of going public.

Naturally the Chairman had anticipated Miss Nunn as looking like Merlin in drag. He was flabbergasted to discover that she was a Watusi princess with velvety black skin, aquiline features, great black eyes, tall, slender, twentyish, ravishing in red.

She dazzled him with a smile, indicated a chair, sat in one opposite and said, "My fee is one hundred thousand. Can you afford it?"

"I can. Agreed."

"And your difficulty—is it worth it?"

"It is."

"Then we understand each other so far. Yes, Alex?"

The young secretary who had bounced into the workshop said, "Excuse me. LeClerque insists on knowing how you made the positive identification of the mold as extraterrestrial."

Miss Nunn clicked her tongue impatiently. "He knows that I never give reasons. I only give results."

"Yes'N."

"Has he paid?"

"Yes'N."

"All right, I'll make an exception in his case. Tell him that it was based on the levo and dextro probability in amino acids and tell him to have a qualified exor-biologist carry on from there. He won't regret the cost."

"Yes'N. Thank you."

She turned to the Chairman as the secretary left. "You heard that. I only give results."

"Agreed, Miss Nunn."

"Now your difficulty. I'm not committed yet. Understood?"

"Yes, Miss Nunn."

"Go ahead. Everything. Stream of consciousness, if necessary."

An hour later she dazzled him with another smile and said, "Thank you. This one is really unique. A welcome change. It's a contract, if you're still willing."

"Agreed, Miss Nunn. Would you like a deposit or an advance?"

"Not from CCC."

"What about expenses? Should that be arranged?"

"No. My responsibility."

"But what if you have to—if you're required to—if—"

She laughed. "My responsibility. I never give reasons and I never reveal methods. How can I charge for them? Now don't forget; I want that Skip-Trace report."

A week later Gretchen Nunn took the ususual step of visiting the Chairman in his office at CCC. "I'm calling on you, sir, to give you the opportunity of withdrawing from our contract."

"Withdraw? But why?"

"Because I believe you're involved in something far more serious than you anticipated."

"But what?"

"You won't take my word for it?"

"I must know."

Miss Nunn compressed her lips. Afer a moment she sighed. "Since this is an unusual case I'll have to break my rules. Look at this, sir." She unrolled a large map of a segment of the Corridor and flattened it on the Chairman's desk. There was a star in the center of the map. "Skiaki's residence," Miss Nunn said. There was a large circle scribed around the star. "The limits to which a man can walk in two hours," Miss Nunn said. The circle was crisscrossed by twisting trails all emanating from the star. "I got this from the Skip-Trace report. This is how the tails traced Skiaki."

"Very ingenious, but I see nothing serious in this, Miss Nunn."

"Look closely at the trails. What do you see?"

"Why . . . each ends in a red cross."

"And what happens to each trail before it reaches the red cross?"

"Nothing. Nothing at all, except—except that the dots change to dashes."

"And that's what makes it serious."

"I don't understand, Miss Nunn."

"I'll explain. Each cross represents the scene of a murder. The dashes represent the backtracking of the actions and whereabouts of each murder victim just prior to death."

"Murder!"

"They could trace their actions just so far back and no further. Skip-Trace could tail Skiaki just so far forward and no further. Those are the dots. The dates join up. What's your conclusion?"

"It must be coincidence," the Chairman shouted. "This brilliant, charming young man. Murder? Impossible!"

"Do you want the factual data I've drawn up?"

"No, I don't. I want the truth. Proof-positive without any inferences from dots, dashes and dates."

"Very well, Mr. Chairman. You'll get it."

She rented the professional beggar's pitch alongside the entrance to Skiaki's Oasis for a week. No success. She hired a Revival Band and sang hymns with it before the Oasis. No success. She finally made the contact after she promoted a job with the Organic Nursery. The first three dinners she delivered to the penthouse she came and went unnoticed; Skiaki was entertaining a series of girls, all scrubbed and sparkling with gratitude. When she made the fourth delivery he was alone and noticed her for the first time.

"Hey," he grinned. "How long has this been going on?"

"Sir?"

"Since when has Organic been using girls for delivery boys?"

"I am a delivery person, sir," Miss Nunn answered with dignity. "I have been working for the Organic Nursery since the first of the month."

"Knock off the sir bit."

"Thank you, s—Dr. Skiaki."

"How the devil do you know that I've got a doctorate?"

She'd slipped. He was listed at the Oasis and the Nursery merely as B. Skiaki, and she should have remembered. As usual, she turned her mistake into an advantage. "I know all about you, sir. Dr. Blaise Skiaki, Princeton, MIT, Dow Chemical. Chief Scent Chemist at CCC."

"You sound like 'Who's Who.' "

"That's where I read it, Dr. Skiaki."

"You read me up in 'Who's Who'? Why on earth?"

"You're the first famous man I've ever met."

"Whatever gave you the idea that I'm famous, which I'm not."

She gestured around. "I knew you had to be famous to live like this."

"Very flattering. What's your name, love?"

"Gretchen, sir."

"What's your last name?"

"People from my class don't have last names, sir."

"Will you be the delivery b—person tomorrow, Gretchen?"

"Tomorrow is my day off, Doctor."

"Perfect. Bring dinner for two."

So the affair began and Gretchen discovered, much to her astonishment, that she was enjoying it very much. Blaise was indeed a brilliant, charming young man, always entertaining, always considerate, always generous. In gratitude he gave her (remember he believed she came from the lowest Corridor class) one of his most prized possessions, a five-carat diamond he had synthesized at Dow. She responded with equal style; she wore it in her navel and promised that it was for his eyes only.

Of course he always insisted on her scrubbing up each time she visited, which was a bit of a bore; in her income bracket she probably had more fresh water than he did. However, one convenience was that she could quit her job at the Organic Nursery and attend to other contracts while she was attending to Skiaki.

She always left his penthouse around eleven-thirty but stayed outside until one. She finally picked him up one night just as he was leaving the Oasis. She'd memorized the Salem Burne report and knew what to expect. She overtook him quickly and spoke in an agitated voice, "Mistuh. Mistuh."

He stopped and looked at her kindly without recognition. "Yes, my dear?"

"If yuh gone this way kin I come too. I scared."

"Certainly, my dear."

"Thanks, mistuh. I gone home. You gone home?"

"Well, not exactly."

"Where you gone? Y'ain't up to nothin' bad, is you? I don't want no part."

"Nothing bad, my dear. Don't worry."

"Then what you up to?"

He smiled secretly. "I'm following something."

"Somebody?"

"No, something."

"What kine something?"

"My, you're curious, aren't you. What's your name?"

"Gretchen. How 'bout you?"

"Me?"

"What's your name?"

"Wish. Call me Mr. Wish." He hesitated for a moment and then said, "I have to turn left here."

"Thas OK, Mistuh Wish. I go left, too."

She could see that all his senses were prickling, and reduced her prattle to a background of unobtrusive sound. She stayed with him as he twisted, turned, sometimes doubling back, through streets, alleys, lanes and lots, always assuring him that

this was her way home too. At a rather dangerous-looking refuse dump he gave her a fatherly pat and cautioned her to wait
while he explored its safety. He explored, disappeared and
never reappeared.

"I replicated this experience with Skiaki six times," Miss
Nunn reported to CCC. "They were all significant. Each time
he revealed a little more without realizing it and without recognizing me. Burne was right. It is fugue."

"And the cause, Miss Nunn?"

"Pheromone trails."

"What?"

"I thought you gentlemen would know the term, being in
the chemistry business. I see I'll have to explain. It will take
some time so I insist that you do not require me to describe
the induction and deduction that led me to my conclusion. Understood?"

"Agreed, Miss Nunn."

"Thank you, Mr. Chairman. Surely you all know hormones,
from the Greek *hormaein*, meaning 'to excite'. They're inter-
nal secretions which excite other parts of the body into action.
Pheromones are external secretions which excite other creatures into action. It's a mute chemical language.

"The best example of the pheromone language is the ant.
Put a lump of sugar somewhere outside an ant hill. A forager
will come across it, feed and return to the nest. Within an
hour the entire commune will be single-filing to and from the
sugar, following the pheromone trail first laid down quite un-
deliberately by the first discoverer. It's an unconscious but
compelling stimulant."

"Fascinating. And Dr. Skiaki?"

"He follows human pheromone trails. They compel him; he
goes into fugue and follows them."

"Ah! An outré aspect of The Nose. It makes sense, Miss
Nunn. It really does. But what trails is he compelled to follow?"

"The death-wish."

"Miss Nunn!"

"Surely you're aware of this aspect of the human psyche.
Many people suffer from an unconscious but powerful death-
wish, especially in these despairing times. Apparently this
leaves a pheromone trail which Dr. Skiaki senses, and he is
compelled to follow it."

"And then?"

"Apparently he grants the wish."

"Apparently! Apparently!" the Chairman shouted. "I ask you for proof-positive of this monstrous accusation."

"You'll get it, sir. I'm not finished with Blaise Skiaki yet. There are one or two things I have to wrap up with him, and in the course of that I'm afraid he's in for a shock. You'll have your proof-pos—"

That was a half-lie from a woman half in love. She knew she had to see Blaise again but her motives were confused. To find out whether she really loved him, despite what she knew? To find out whether he loved her? To tell him the truth about herself? To warn him or save him or run away with him? To fulfill her contract in a cool, professional style? She didn't know. Certainly she didn't know that she was in for a shock from Skiaki.

"Were you born blind?" he murmured that night.

She sat bolt upright in the bed. "What? Blind? What?"

"You heard me."

"I've had perfect sight all my life."

"Ah. Then you don't know, darling. I rather suspected that might be it."

"I certainly don't know what you're talking about, Blaise."

"Oh, you're blind all right," he said calmly. "But you've never known because you're blessed with a fantastic freak facility. You have extrasensory perception of other people's senses. You see through other people's eyes. For all I know you may be deaf and hear through their ears. You may feel with their skin. We must explore it some time."

"I never heard of anything more absurd in all my life," she said angrily.

"I can prove it to you, if you like, Gretchen."

"Go ahead, Blaise. Prove the impossible."

"Come into the lounge."

In the living room he pointed to a vase. "What color is that?"

"Brown, of course."

"What color is that?" A tapestry.

"Gray."

"And that lamp?"

"Black."

"QED," Skiaki said. "It has been demonstrated."

"What's been demonstrated?"

"That you're seeing through my eyes."

"How can you say that?"

"Because I'm color-blind. That's what gave me the clue in the first place."

"What?"

He took her in his arms to quiet her trembling. "Darling Gretchen, the vase is green. The tapestry is amber and gold. The lamp is crimson. I can't see the colors but the decorator told me and I remember. Now why the terror? You're blind, yes, but you're blessed with something far more miraculous than mere sight; you see through the eyes of the world. I'd change places with you any time."

"It can't be true," she cried.

"It's true, love."

"What about when I'm alone?"

"When are you alone? When is anybody in the Corridor ever alone?"

She snatched up a shift and ran out of the penthouse, sobbing hysterically. She ran back to her own Oasis nearly crazed with terror. And yet she kept looking around and there were all the colors: red, orange, yellow, green, indigo, blue, violet. But there were also people swarming through the labyrinths of the Corridor as they always were, twenty-four hours a day.

Back in her apartment she was determined to put the disaster to the test. She dismissed her entire staff with stern orders to get the hell out and spend the night somewhere else. She stood at the door and counted them out, all amazed and unhappy. She slammed the door and looked around. She could still see.

"The lying son-of-a-bitch," she muttered and began to pace furiously. She raged through the apartment, swearing venomously. It proved one thing: never get into personal relationships. They'll betray you, they'll try to destroy you, and she'd made a fool of herself. But why, in God's name, did Blaise use this sort of dirty trick to destroy her? Then she smashed into something and was thrown back. She recovered her balance and looked to see what she had blundered into. It was a harpsichord.

"But . . . but I don't own a harpsichord," she whispered in bewilderment. She started forward to touch it and assure herself of its reality. She smashed into the something again, grabbed it and felt it. It was the back of a couch. She looked around frantically. This was not one of her rooms. The harpsichord. Vivid Brueghels hanging on the walls. Jacobean furniture. Linenfold paneled doors. Crewel drapes.

"But . . . this is the . . . the Raxon apartment downstairs. I must be seeing though their eyes. I must . . . he was right. I . . ." She closed her eyes and looked. She saw a mélange of apartments, streets, crowds, people, events. She had always seen this sort of montage on occasion but had always thought it was merely the total visual recall which was a major factor in her extraordinary abilities and success. Now she knew the truth.

She began to sob again. She felt her way around the couch and sat down, despairing. When at last the convulsion spent itself she wiped her eyes courageously, determined to face reality. She was no coward. But when she opened her eyes she was shocked by another bombshell. She saw her familiar room in tones of gray. She saw Blaise Skiaki standing in the open door smiling at her.

"Blaise?" she whispered.

"The name is Wish, my dear. Mr. Wish. What's yours?"

"Blaise, for God's sake, not me! Not me. I left no death-wish trail."

"What's your name, my dear? We've met before?"

"Gretchen," she screamed. "I'm Gretchen Nunn and I have no death-wish."

"Nice meeting you again, Gretchen," he said in glassy tones, smiling the glassy smile of Mr. Wish. He took two steps toward her. She jumped up and ran behind the couch.

"Blaise, listen to me. You are not Mr. Wish. There is no Mr. Wish. You are Dr. Blaise Skiaki, a famous scientist. You are chief chemist at CCC and have created many wonderful perfumes."

He took another step toward her, unwinding the scarf he wore around his neck.

"Blaise, I'm Gretchen. We've been lovers for two months. You must remember. Try to remember. You told me about my eyes tonight . . . being blind. You must remember that."

He smiled and whirled the scarf into a cord.

"Blaise, you're suffering from fugue. A blackout. A change of psyche. This isn't the real you. It's another creature driven by a pheromone. But I left no pheromone trail. I couldn't. I've never wanted to die."

"Yes, you do, my dear. Only happy to grant your wish. That's why I'm called Mr. Wish."

She squealed like a trapped rat and began darting and dodging while he closed in on her. She feinted him to one side, twisted to the other with a clear chance of getting out the door ahead of him, only to crash into three grinning goons standing shoulder to shoulder. They grabbed and held her.

Mr. Wish did not know that he also left a pheromone trail. It was a pheromone trail of murder.

"Oh, it's you again," Mr. Wish sniffed.

"Hey, old buddy-boy, got a looker this time, huh?"

"And loaded. Dig this layout."

"Great. Makes up for the last three which was nothin'. Thanks, buddy-boy. You can go home now."

"Why don't I ever get to kill one?" Mr. Wish exclaimed petulantly.

"Now, now. No sulks. We got to protect our bird dog. You lead. We follow and do the rest."

"And if anything goes wrong, you're the setup," one of the goons giggled.

"Go home, buddy-boy. The rest is ours. No arguments. We already explained the standoff to you. We know who you are but you don't know who we are."

"I know who I am," Mr. Wish said with dignity. "I am Mr. Wish and I still think I have the right to kill at least one."

"All right, all right. Next time. That's a promise. Now blow."

As Mr. Wish exited resentfully, they ripped Gretchen naked and let out a huge wow when they saw the five-carat diamond in her navel. Mr. Wish turned and saw its scintillation too.

"But that's mine," he said in a confused voice. "That's only for my eyes. I—Gretchen said she would never—" Abruptly Dr. Blaise Skiaki spoke in a tone accustomed to command: "Gretchen, what the hell are you doing here? What's this place? Who are these creatures? What's going on?"

When the police arrived they found three dead bodies and a composed Gretchen Nunn sitting with a laser pistol in her lap. She told a perfectly coherent story of forcible entry, an attempt at armed rape and robbery, and how she was constrained to meet force with force. There were a few loopholes in her account. The bodies were not armed, but if the men had said they were armed Miss Nunn, of course, would have believed them. The three were somewhat battered, but goons were always fighting. Miss Nunn was commended for her courage and cooperation.

After her final report to the Chairman (which was not the truth, the whole truth and nothing but the truth) Miss Nunn received her check and went directly to the perfume laboratory, which she entered without warning. Dr. Skiaki was doing strange and mysterious things with pipettes, flasks and reagent bottles. Without turning he ordered, "Out. Out. Out."

"Good morning, Dr. Skiaki."

He turned, displaying a mauled face and black eyes, and smiled. "Well, well, well. The famous Gretchen Nunn, I presume. Voted Person of the Year three times in succession."

"No, sir. People from my class don't have last names."

"Knock off the sir bit."

"Yes s—Mr. Wish."

"Oi!" He winced. "Don't remind me of that incredible insanity. How did everything go with the Chairman?"

"I snowed him. You're off the hook."

"Maybe I'm off his hook but not my own. I was seriously thinking of having myself committed this morning."

"What stopped you?"

"Well, I got involved in this patchouli synthesis and sort of forgot."

She laughed. "You don't have to worry. You're saved."

"You mean cured?"

"No, Blaise. Not any more than I'm cured of my blindness. But we're both saved because we're aware. We can cope now."

He nodded slowly but not happily.

"So what are you going to do today?" she asked cheerfully. "Struggle with patchouli?"

"No," he said gloomily. "I'm still in one hell of a shock. I think I'll take the day off."

"Perfect. Bring two dinners."

TWIG

Gordon R. Dickson

Once more the question of the unity of an intelligent species is raised and once again answered in a different manner. We have had a lot of literature about plant sensitivity in the past year. Leave it to one of the most respected pros in the field to carry the theme to its logical conclusion.

For four hours Twig had been working up her courage to approach the supply post. Now in the pumpkin-colored afternoon light of the big, orange-yellow sun, she stood right beside one of the heavy rammed-earth walls. From the slice of dark interior seen through the partial opening of the door not two meters from her, came the sound of a raucous and drunken tenor—not a young tenor, but a tenor which cracked now and then on the dryness of a middle-aged throat—singing.

. . . 'As game as Ned Kelly,' the people would say;
'As game as Ned Kelly,' they say it today . . .

It would have been something, at least, if the accent of the singing voice had been as Australian as the ballad of the old down-under outlaw who, wearing his own version of armor, had finally shot it out with the police and been slain. But Hacker Illions had never seen the planet Earth, let alone Australia; and his only claims to that part of Sol III were an Australian-born mother and father, both over twenty years dead and buried here on Jinson's Planet. Even Twig knew that Hacker had no strong connection with Ned Kelly and Australia, only a thread of one. But she accepted his playing the Aussie, just as she accepted his foolishness when drunk, his bravery when sober and his wobbly but unceasing devotion to the Plant-Grandfather.

Hacker had been drinking for at least the four hours since Twig had arrived at the supply post. He would be in no shape to talk sense to now. Silent as a shadow, light as a flicker of sunlight between two clouds, Twig pressed against the coarse-grained earth wall, listening and trying to summon up the courage to go inside, into that dark, noisome, hutchlike trap her own kind called a building. There would be others in there beside Hacker—even if only the Factor of the supply post itself. There might even be others as drunk as Hacker, but worse-minded, men who might try to catch and hold her with their hands. She shivered. Not only at the feel in her imagination of the large, rough hands; but with the knowledge that if they did seize her, she would hurt them. She would not be able to help herself; she would have to hurt them to make them let her go.

Sinking down into a squatting position beside the earth wall, Twig rocked unhappily on her heels, silently mourning inside herself. If only Hacker would come out, so that she would not have to go in after him. But for four hours now, he had not left the building. There must be some place inside there where he could relieve himself; and that meant he would not have to leave the building until he ran out of money or was thrown out—and the posse must now be less than an hour from here.

"Hacker!" she called. *"Come out!"*

But the call was only a whisper. Even alone with Hacker, she had never been able to raise her voice above that whisper level. Normally, it did not matter. Before she had met Hacker, when she had only the Plant-Grandfather to talk to, she had not needed to make sounds at all. But now, if she could only shout, like other humans. Just once, shout like the human she actually was . . .

But her aching throat gave forth nothing but a hiss of air. The physical machinery for shouting was there, but something in her mind after all those years of growing up with only the Plant-Grandfather to talk to would not let it work. There was no time left and no choice. She pulled taut the threads that bound the suit of bark tightly about her body. Hacker had always wanted her to wear human clothes; they would give her more protection against ordinary men, he said. But anywhere except in a closed box like this building, no other human could catch her anyway; and she could not stand the dead feel of the materials with which other humans covered their bodies. She took a deep breath and darted in through the half-open door.

She was almost at Hacker's side before anyone noticed her, so light and swift had been her dash across the floor. None of them there saw her passage. Hacker stood, one of his elbows on a waist-high shelf called a bar. It was a long bar that ran along the inside wall of the room with space for the Factor to stand behind it and pass out glasses and bottles. The Factor was standing there now; almost, but not quite, opposite Hacker. Facing Hacker, on Hacker's side of the shelf, was a man as tall as Hacker, but much heavier, with a long, black beard.

This man saw her first, as she stole up beside Hacker and tugged at his jacket.

"Hey!" shouted the black-bearded man; and his voice was a deep and growling bass. "Hacker, look! Don't tell me it's that wild kid, the one the Plant raised! It is! I'll be damned, but it is! Where've you been keeping her hid all this time?"

And just as Twig had known he would, the black-bearded man reached out a thick hand for her. She ducked behind Hacker.

"Leave her alone!" said Hacker thickly. "Twig—Twig, you get out of here. Wait for me outside."

"Now, hold it a minute." The black-bearded man tried to come around Hacker to get to her. A miner's ion drill dragged heavily down on a holster fastened to the belt at his waist. Hacker, unarmed, got in the way. "Get out, Hacker! I just want to look at the kid!"

"Leave her, Berg," said Hacker. "I mean it."

"You?" Berg snorted. "Who're you but a bum I've been feeding drinks to all afternoon?"

"Hacker! Come!" whispered Twig in his ear.

"Right. All right!" said Hacker with drunken dignity. "That the way you feel, Berg . . . Let's go, Twig."

He turned and started toward the door. Berg caught him by the looseness of his leather jacket and hauled him to a stop. Beyond the black beard, Twig could see the Factor, a fat, white man, leaning on his elbows on the shelf of the bar and smiling, saying nothing, doing nothing.

"No, you don't," said Berg, grinning. "You're staying, Hack. So's the kid, if I've got to tie you both up. There's some people coming to see you."

"See me?" Hacker turned to face the black beard and stood, swaying a little, peering at the other, stupidly.

"Why, sure," said Berg. "Your term as Congressman from this district ran out yesterday, Hacker. You got no immunity now."

Twig's heart lurched. It was worse than she had thought. Hacker drunk was bad enough; but someone deliberately put here to feed him drinks and keep him until the posse caught up, was deadly.

"Hacker!" she whispered desperately in his ear. "Run now!" She ducked around him, under the arm with which Berg was still holding him, and came up between the two men, facing Berg. The big man stared at her stupidly for a moment and then her right hand whipped in a back-hand blow across his face, each finger like the end of a bending slender branch, each nail like a razor.

"What?" bellowed Berg jovially, for her nails were so sharp that he had not immediately felt the cuts. "You want to play too—"

Then the blood came pouring down into his eyes, and he roared wordlessly, letting go of Hacker and stumbling backward, wiping at his eyes.

"What are you trying to do? Blind me?" he shouted. He got his eyes clear, looked down at his hands and saw them running with his own blood. He roared again, a wild animal furious and in pain.

"Run, Hacker!" called Twig desperately. She ducked in under Berg's arms as he made another clutch on her, lifted his drill from its holster and shoved it into Hacker's belt. "Run!"

Berg was after her now, but even without the blood running into his eyes, he was like a bear chasing a hummingbird. Twig was all around him, within reach one moment, gone the next. He lumbered after her, a madman with a head of black and red.

Hacker, woken at last to his danger and sobered, was backing out the door, Berg's drill in his hand, now covering both the Factor and Berg.

"Leave off, Twig!" Hacker cried, his voice thin on the high note of the last word. "Come on!"

Twig ducked once more out of the grasping hands of Berg and flew to join Hacker in the doorway.

"Get back, Berg!" snarled Hacker, pointing the drill. "I'll hole you if you come any farther!"

Berg halted, swaying. His mouth gapped with a flicker of white teeth in his black and crimson mask.

"Kill you . . ." he grunted hoarsely. "Both. Kill you . . ."

"Don't try it," said Hacker. "Less you want to die yourself first—from now on. Now, stay, and that means both of you, Factor. Don't try to follow. —Twig!"

He slipped out the door. Twig followed. Together they ran for the forest.

Twig touched with her hands the first trees they came to, and the trunks and branches ahead of them leaned out of the way to let them pass, then swayed back together again behind them. They ran for perhaps a couple of kilometers before Hacker's breath began to labor hoarsely in his lungs and he slowed to a walk. Twig, who could have run all day at the speed they had been keeping, fell into a walk beside him. For a little while he only struggled to get his breath back as he went.

"What is it?" he asked at last, stopping so that he would be able to hear Twig's whispered reply.

"A posse, they call it," she said. "Ten men, three women, all with drills or lasers. They say they'll set up a citizen's court and hang you."

"Do they?" grunted Hacker. He stank mightily of alcohol and ugly anger. But he was most of the way back toward being reasonably sober now; and Twig, who loved him even more than she loved the Plant-Grandfather nowadays, had long since gotten used to his smells. He sat down with a thump, his back against a tree trunk, waving Twig down to sit also.

"Let's sit and think a bit," he said. "Plain running's not going to do any good. Where are they now?"

Twig, who was already sitting on her heels, got up and stepped forward to the tree against which Hacker was sitting. She put her arms around the trunk as far as they would reach, laid her cheek against its dear, rough bark, closed her eyes and put her mind into the tree. Her mind went into darkness and along many kilometers of root and by way of many children of the Plant-Grandfather, until she came to the littlest brothers, whom other humans said were like a plant called "grass" back on Earth. Less than forty minutes walk from where she and Hacker were, some of the littlest brothers were feeling the hard, grim metal treads of human vehicles, pressing down to tear and destroy them.

"Peace, littlest brothers, peace," soothed Twig's mind, trying to comfort them through the roots. The littlest brothers did not feel pain as the variform Earth animals and humans like Twig felt it; but in a different way they felt and suffered the terrible wrongness that was making them not to be in this useless, wasteful fashion. Those being destroyed wept that they had been born to no better purpose than this; and, down below all living plants on the surface of Jinson's Planet, the Plant-Grandfather echoed their despair in his own special way. He was weary of such destruction at the hands of alien men, women and beasts.

"Peace, Grandfather, peace," sent Twig. But the Plant-Grandfather did not answer her. She let go of the tree, stepped back from it and opened her eyes, returning to Hacker.

"They're riding in carriers," she told him. From the grass, the trees looking down on the passing carriers, she could now describe the open, tracked vehicles and the people in them as well as if her human eyes had actually seen them. "When they first started, there were eight of them, and they were only walking. Now there are five more who brought the carriers. They can catch up to us in half an hour if we stay here. And the carriers will kill many trees and other children of the Grandfather before they come to us."

"I'll head for the High Rocks district, then," said Hacker. The frown line was puckered deep between the blue eyes in his stubbled, bony face. "They'll have to leave their vehicles to follow me on foot; and there's little for them to tear up and hurt. Besides, there they'll chase me a month or weeks and never catch me. Actually, you're the one they really want to catch so they can make you tell where they can find the Grandfather; but they daren't try that while I'm alive to tell the law. We've still got some law here on Jinson's Planet; and supraplanetary law beyond that. That reminds me—"

He fished with two fingers in a shirt pocket under his jacket and came out with a small slip of writing cellulose. He passed it over to Twig.

"While I was still down at Capital City with the Legislature," he said, "I got the Governor-general to send for an ecology expert from the Paraplanetary Government, someone with full investigative powers, legal and all. That's his name."

Twig squatted down once more and unfolded the cellulose

strip which had been bent double to fit the small shirt pocket. She was proud of her reading ability and other schooling, which Hacker had gotten for her with a teaching machine he had carried upcountry himself: but the original printing on this sheet had been in blue marker and Hacker's sweat had dimmed it to near unreadability.

"John . . . Stone," she read off aloud finally.

"That's the man." Hacker said. "I had it fixed so the whole business of sending for him was secret. But he was supposed to land two days ago and be on his way upcountry here to meet me now. He shouldn't be more than a day's walk south of here on the downcountry trail. He's been told about you. You go meet him and show him that piece of paper. Bring him up to date about what's going on with the posse and all. Meanwhile I'll lead that crew around the High Rocks and down to Rusty Springs by late noon tomorrow. You and Stone meet me there, and we'll be waiting for the posse when they catch up."

"But there's only going to be two of you, even then," protested Twig.

"Don't you worry." Hacker reached out, patted the bark covering her shoulder and stood up. "I tell you he's a supra-planetary official—like someone from the police. They won't risk breaking the law with him there. Once they know he's around, none of these croppers that want to burn out new farming fields from the Grandfather's woods will dare try anything."

"But when he goes again—" Twig also rose to her feet.

"By the time he goes," said Hacker, "he'll have recommended a set of laws for the legislature that'll stop those forest-burners for all time. Go south now, Twig; and when you find him stay with him. If that posse's out after me, it's out after you, too, if it can just find you."

He patted her shoulder again, turned and went off through the trees, moving at a fast walk that was a good cross-country pace—for anyone but Twig.

Twig watched him go, wanting badly to go with him, to stay with him. But Hacker would be right, of course. If what was needed was this John Stone from another world, then he was the one she must go and find. But the unhappiness of everything—of everything all around here and to all the things she loved—was overwhelming. When Hacker was gone, she dropped face down on the ground, hiding her face against it, spreading her arms as if she could hold it.

"Plant-Grandfather!" she called, letting her mind only cry it forth, for it was not necessary to touch one of the plant children when she called the Granfather. But there was no answer.

"Plant-Grandfather!" she called again. "Plant-Grandfather, why don't you answer?" Fear shook her. "What's the matter? Where have you gone?"

"Peace, little running sister," came the heavy, slow thought of the Grandfather. "I have gone nowhere."

"I thought maybe people had found you there under the ground," said Twig. "I thought maybe they had hurt you—killed you—when you didn't answer."

"Peace, peace, little runner," said the Grandfather. "I am tired, very tired of these people of yours; and maybe sometime soon I may actually sleep. If so, whether I will wake again, I do not know. But do not believe I can be killed. I am not sure anything can be killed, only changed for a while, made silent until it is remembered by the universe and regrown to speak once more. I am not like your people who must be one form only. Whether I am root or branch or flower makes no difference to me. I am always here for you, little runner, whether I answer you or not."

Twig's tears ran down her nose and dampened the earth against her face.

"You don't understand!" she said. "You can die. You *can* be killed. You don't understand. You think it's all just sleeping!"

"But I do undertsand," said the Plant-Grandfather, "I understand much more than any little runner, who has lived only a moment or two, while I have lived long enough to see mountain ranges rise and fall again. How can I die when I am more than just the thing of woody roots these people would find and destroy? If that is gone, I am still part of every plant thing on this world, and of my little runner as well. And if these things should someday be gone, I am still part of the earth and stone that is this planet; and after that, part of its brother and sister planets, and after that even all worlds. Here, alone, I taught myself to speak to all my plant brothers and sisters from the largest to the smallest. And all the while, on a world so far away it is lost even to my view, your people were teaching themselves to speak. So that now I and you speak together. How could that happen if we were not all one, all part of each other?"

"But you'll still be dead as far as I'm concerned!" sobbed Twig. "And I can't stand it! I can't stand to have you dead!"

"What can I say to you, little running sister?" said the Grandfather. "If you will make it that I am dead, then I will be dead. But if you will let it be that I cannot be killed, then I cannot be killed. You will feel me with you forever, unless and only if you shut out the feeling of me."

"But you won't help yourself!" wept Twig. "You can do anything. You took care of me when I was a baby, alone. There was only you. I don't even remember my mother and father, what they looked like! You kept me alive and grew me up and took care of me. Now you want to take yourself away, and I'm not to care. And you don't have to give up, just like that. You could open the ground in front of these people and let the hot rock out. You could empty the rivers they drink from. You could send seeds against them with pollen to make them sick. But you won't do anything—nothing but lie there until they find and kill you!"

"Doing what you say is not the way," said the Plant-Grandfather. "It is hard to explain to a little runner who has only lived a moment, but the universe does not grow that way. Along that way of damage and destruction, all things fail and their growth is lost—and so would mine be. You would not want me to be sick and no longer growing, would you, little running one?"

"Better that than dead."

"Again, that thought which is no thought. I cannot make you unsad, small runner, if you insist on sadness. I have put to use many of our brothers and sisters, from the littlest to the largest, to keep and care for you as you grew, alone and away from your own people, because I wished that you should come to run through this world and be happy. But you are not happy; and I, who know so much more than a small runner, know so little of a greater knowledge which I have yet to learn, that I do not know what to do about this. Follow your own sadness, then, if you must. I am with you in any case, though you will not believe it—with you, now and forever."

Twig felt the Plant-Grandfather turning his attention away from her. She lay sobbing her loneliness to the earth under her for a little while; but in time her tears slowed and she remembered the errand on which Hacker had sent her. She got to her feet slowly and began to run toward the south, letting the wind of her passage dry the wetness upon her face.

It did not come at once, but slowly the poetry of her own motion began to warm the cold lump of fear and sorrow inside her. If Hacker was right about what the man John Stone could do, then everything could be all right after all. Suddenly remembering that it would be well to check on the posse, she turned sharply from her original route to angle back toward the supply post. She came right up to the edge of the trees surrounding the clearing in which the post stood, and sure enough, the vehicles and the men and women were there. She looked out at them without fear, for like most of her people they saw and heard poorly in comparison to herself; and, in addition, the trees and bushes had bent around her to screen her from any discovery.

She was close enough so that she could hear clearly what they were saying. Apparently one of the vehicles had broken a tread and needed fixing. Some of the men there were working on its left tread, now like a huge metal watchband come uncoiled from around the drive wheels on that side beneath the open box of the vehicle body. Meanwhile those not working stood about arguing in the now westering, late afternoon sunlight.

". . . bitch!" Berg was saying. He was talking about her. The blood from his facial cuts had stopped flowing some time since, and what had leaked out had been cleaned away. But he was flushed about the forehead and eyes where the cuts had parted the flesh. "I'll hang her in front of Hacker himself, first, before we hang him when we get them!"

"You'll not," said one of the women, a tall, middle-aged, bony female in a short, brown leather jacket and country leather pants showing a laser in a black holster over her right buttock. "First she's got to talk. It's that Grandfather plant-devil that really needs killing. But then she comes into a proper home somewhere."

"Proper home—" shouted Berg, who might have gone on if another woman—shorter and heavier, but wearing a dress under her once-white, knee-length weathercoat and boots—had not snapped him off short. This one wore no visible weapon, but her voice was harsher and more belligerent even than that of the taller woman.

"Shut it, right there, Berg!" said this woman. "Before you say something you'll be sorry you ever thought of. There's plans been made for that girl among the decent croppers' families. She's been let run wild all these years, but she's a child of man and she'll come to be a good grown woman with loving rules and proper training. And don't go getting ideas about getting your hands on her after we catch her, either. It's us wives along on this posse who'll be making her tell where that Grandfather devil hides, not none of you men."

"If you can . . ." growled Berg.

The heavier woman laughed, and Twig shivered through all her body at the kind of laughter it was.

"Think we couldn't make you talk?" the heavy woman said.
"And if you, why not a kid like her?"

Twig drew back until the leaves and the bushes before her
hid the vehicles and their passengers from sight. She had
learned all she needed to know anyway. The vehicles were
now held up; so there was no danger of their catching up with
Hacker before he reached the High Rocks—a hill region pep-
pered with rounded chunks and blocks of stone where the vehicles would not be useable. Not that there had been much
chance of their catching Hacker anyway—but now, at least,
she was sure.

She turned and began to run once more southward in search
of the man John Stone, as the sun lost itself among the trees
and began to descend into twilight.

Once more, she ran. And once more the intoxication of her
own running began to warm away the shivers that had come
on her from the overheard conversation. Now, running, no
one could catch and hold her, let alone do terrible things to
her to make her say where the rootbody of the Plant-Grandfather rested in the earth.

The sun was down now; and the big white moon of Jinson
was already in the sky. It was full, now, and seemed—once
her eyes were adjusted to it—to throw almost as much light as
the twilight sun; only this was a magic, two-tone light of white
and gray without color. In this light the trees and bushes
leaned aside to let her pass, and the littlest brothers underfoot
stretched like a soft gray carpet before her, making a corridor
of moonlight and shadow along which she fled so lightly it was
as if she went without touching the earth at all.

There was no effort to her going. She put on speed and
earth, bushes, trees and moonlight swam about her. Together,
they made up the great, silent music of her passage; and the
music swept her away with it. There was nothing but this—her
running, the forest and the moonlight. For a moment she was
again only a little runner—even the Grandfather and Hacker
were forgotten, as was the posse with its other humans. It was
as if they had never existed. She danced with her world in the
white-and-black dance of her limitless running; and it was she
and the world alone, alone and forever.

Twig had run the moon high up into the night sky, now,
and he rode there, made smaller by his isolation in the arch of
the star-cap that fitted over the world when the sun had gone;
and she began to hear through her mind, which was now fine-
tuned to the plant brothers and sisters whom she passed and
who made way for her, that the individual she ran to find was

close. The brothers and sisters turned the corridor they were making ahead of her to lead her to him. Shortly beyond the far moonlight and shadow she saw a different yellow light that brightened and dimmed. She smelled on the night wind the scent of dead branches burning, the odor of an animal and a human man.

So she came to him. He was camped in a small clearing, where a stream Twig could easily jump across curled around the base of a large moss-patched boulder before going off among the trees again. A small fire was on the far side of the stream; the man was seated on the other side of it, staring into the flames, so still and large with his dark outdoor clothing and clean-shaven face that he seemed for a moment only another mossy boulder. Beyond him was one of the large hooved riding beasts that her people called a horse. This smelled or heard Twig and lifted its head and snorted in her direction.

The man lifted his head then, looked at the horse and away from the animal toward Twig.

"Hello," he said. "Come in and sit down."

His gaze was right on her, but Twig was not fooled. In no way could he see her. She was among the trees, a good four meters from him; and his eyes would be blinded by the light of his fire. He was simply going on what his animal had told him.

"Are you John Stone?" she asked, forgetting that only Hacker could understand her whisper at this distance. But the man surprised her.

"Yes," he said. "Are you Twig?"

Astonished, now, she came forward into the light.

"How do you know?" she asked.

He laughed. His voice was deep-toned, and his laugh even deeper—but it was a soft, friendly laugh.

"There ought to be only two people know my name up here," he said. "One would be a man named Hacker Illions; and the other might be a girl named Twig. You sound more like a Twig than a Hacker Illions." He sobered. "And now that I see you, you look more like Twig."

She came closer, to the very edge of the stream, hardly a jump away from him, and peered down into his large, white, handsome face. His blond hair was not long, but thick and wavy upon his head, and under light eyebrows his eyes were as blue as a summer lake. He had not moved. Behind him, his horse snorted and stamped.

"Why do you just sit there?" Twig asked. "Are you hiding something?"

He shook his head.

"I didn't want to frighten you," he said. "Hacker Illions left word not to move suddenly or try to touch you. If I stand up, will that scare you?"

"Of course not," said Twig.

But she was wrong. He stood up then, slowly, and she took a step backwards instinctively; because he was by far the biggest man she had ever seen. Bigger than she had imagined a man could be, and wider. At his full height, he seemed to loom over everything—over her, and the fire and the boulder, even over the horse behind him that she had thought was so large. Her heart began to beat fast, as if she was still running. But then she saw that he was merely standing still, waiting; and there was no feel of menace or evil in him, as she had felt in Berg, in the Factor of the supply post, the women of the posse and others like them. Her heart slowed. She felt ashamed of herself and came forward to jump the stream and stand right before him.

"I'm not frightened," she said. "You can sit down again."

She sat down cross-legged herself on the ground facing him, and he settled back to earth like a mountain sinking into the sea. Even now that they were seated, he towered above her still; but it was a friendly towering, as a tree-brother might loom over her when she nestled against the trunk below his branches.

"Does my horse bother you?" John Stone asked.

She looked at the big beast and sniffed.

"He has metal on his feet, to cut and kill the little living things, just like vehicles do," she said.

"True," said John Stone, "but he did not put that metal on by his own choice. And he likes you."

It was true. The animal was lowering its huge hammer-shaped head in her direction and bobbing it as if to reach out and touch her, although it was far out of reach. Twig's feelings toward it softened. She held out an arm to it, thinking kind thoughts, and the beast quieted.

"Where is Hacker Illions?" John Stone asked.

All her anxiety came flooding back into Twig in a rush.

"At the High Rocks," she said. "There are people after him . . ."

She told John Stone about it, trying to do the telling in such a way that he would understand. So often when she talked to people other than Hacker they seemed to understand only the words as words, not the meaning behind them. But John Stone nodded as she talked, and he looked thoughtful and concerned, as if understanding was honestly growing in him.

"This Rusty Springs," John said at last when she was done. "How far is it? How long will it take us to reach it from here?"

"For an ordinary human walking, six hours," she said.

"Then if we leave just before sunrise, we should be there when Hacker gets there?"

"Yes," she said, "but we ought to start right now and wait there for him."

John looked up at the moon and down at the woods.

"In the dark," he said, "I'd have to travel slowly. Hacker left word for me you didn't like to travel slowly. Besides, there are many things you can tell me that are easier to hear sitting here than traveling. Don't worry. Nothing's going to stop us from getting to the Rusty Springs on time."

He said the last words in a calm, final way that reminded her of the Plant-Grandfather speaking. Twig sat back, somehow reassured without being convinced.

"Have you eaten?" John Stone asked. "Or don't you like the same sort of food as the rest of us?"

He was smiling a little. For a second Twig thought he might be laughing at her.

"Of course I eat people food," she said. "Hacker and I always eat together. I don't have to have it; but it's all right."

He nodded gravely. She wondered uneasily if he could tell what she was not saying. The truth was that for all his knowledge, the Plant-Grandfather had no real understanding of a human sense of taste. The fruits and nuts and green things on which he had nourished her as a child had been all right—and still were, she thought to herself—but the people foods to which Hacker had introduced her were much more interesting to the tongue.

John began opening some small packages and preparing food for them, asking questions as he worked. Twig tried to answer him as well as she could. But even for a person as special as John, she thought, it must be hard to understand what it had been like for her.

She could not even remember what her parents had looked like. She knew, because the Plant-Grandfather had told her, that they had both died of sickness in their cabin when she was barely old enough to walk. She herself had wandered out of the cabin and had been touched, mind-to-mind, by the Plant-Grandfather; and because she was young enough then that nothing was impossible, she had heard, understood and believed him.

He had directed her away from the cabin and the burned-over fields her parents had intended to plant, into the woods, where trees and branches wove themselves into a shelter for her from the rain and wind, and where she could always find something to eat growing within arm's reach. He had kept her away from the cabin until she was much older. When she had finally gone back there she had only glimpsed white bones on the cots in the cabin, hidden under a thick matting of growing green vine the Grandfather had advised her not to disturb. With those bones she had felt no kinship, and she had not been back to the cabin since.

Hacker was something else. By the time she had encountered Hacker, three years ago, she had already become the small runner the Grandfather had named her. Hacker had originally been a cropper like the ones now hunting him. A cropper—as opposed to a farmer who had homesteaded his acres of originally open land and had fertilized, ploughed and planted them year after year in a regular cycle—was someone who made a living by farming no more than two years in a row in any one place.

Most of the good land, the open land, on the world's one continent had been taken over by the first wave of emigrants to Jinson's Planet. Those who came after found that the soil covered by the plant-children of the Grandfather (the existence of whom they never suspected) was a thin layer over rock, and relatively unfertile—unless it was burned over. Then the ashes were rich in what was needed to make the soil bear. But two succeding years of planting sucked all those nutrients from what had been the bodies of plant sisters and brothers into produce, which was then carried downcountry and away from the wooded areas forever. To the cropper, however, this was no matter. He only moved on to burn out a new farm someplace else.

Just before the spring rains, three years ago, Hacker had moved into the territory where Twig ran. An ideal time for burning over an area, so that the coming showers would wash the nutrients from the ashes into the soil below. But Hacker came, pitched his camp and let the days go by. He did not burn, and he did not burn. Finally it was summer and too late to crop that year. Twig, who had watched him many times, unseen from a distance, drew closer and closer in her watching. Here was a cropper who was not a cropper. He helped himself to the fruits and nuts the Grandfather had made the plant-children put forth for Twig, but other than that he did not take from the woods. She could not understand him.

Later she came to understand. Hacker was a drunk. A crop-

per who might never have been any different from other croppers except that, following one fall's sale of produce, he got
into a card game and won heavily. Following which, in one
sober moment he was to appreciate all his life, he took the ad-
vice of a local banker and put his money away at interest,
drawing only enough for supplies to go upcountry and burn
out a new cropping area.

But when he had gone upcountry once more, he had taken
along a luxury of supplies in the way of drinkables. He had
pitched his camp; but instead of setting to work to burn land
clear immediately, he had delayed, enjoying his bottles and his
peace.

Here in the woods, alone, he did not need to pour the drink
down in the quantities he required in civilization. A nip now
and then to blur his surroundings pleasantly was all it took.
And besides, there was plenty of money still down there in the
bank, waiting for him, even if he did not bring in a cash crop
this year.

In the end, he did not.

In the end, he began to change. Among the woods, he needed alcohol less and less, for here there was none of the sharp
and brittle corners of the laws that normally poked and
pricked him, driving him into rebellion. He was not an observing man; but little by little, he began to notice how the seasons
came and went and how every day the woods responded to the
changes of those seasons in a thousand ways. He became
aware of leaf and bush and plant stem as individuals—not as
some large, green blur. And in the end, after two years without cropping brought him to the point where he had to get to
work, he could not bring himself to burn this place where he
had lived and been content. He blazed the trees there to claim
the area for himself and to keep other croppers away, and he
moved on.

But the next place he chose made him part of it also; and he
found he could not burn it either. He moved again, this time
to Twig's territory; and there, unconsciously fishing with a
hook baited with his own differentness, he caught Twig's curiosity and hauled her in.

The day came when she walked boldly into his camp and
stopped a few feet in front of him, no longer shy or fearful of
him after months of observation.

"Who are you?" she whispered.

He stared at her.

"My God, kid," he said. "Don't you know you aren't supposed to run around without any clothes on?"

The wearing of clothes was only the first of many things they found they needed to reach an understanding upon. Twig's point was not that she was unaware of clothes and the fact that other people wore them; rather she did not like the feel of them on her body. Twig, in fact, was not ignorant. The Grandfather had seen to it that as she grew she learned as much about her own people as her maturity allowed her to absorb. He had also seen to it that she visited the woods fringing nearby croppers' farms and had a chance to watch her own people at work and hear them talk. He had even decided that she must practice talking as much out loud as she could, in her own tongue; and Twig, who did what he suggested most of the time without thinking, had obeyed.

But along with the human knowledge she had picked up through the Grandfather's prodding, she had also picked up a great deal of other, wordless wisdom and many skills belonging more to the Grandfather's environment than to her own. Also, the human knowledge she acquired through the Grandfather had been affected in transmission by the fact that the Grandfather was not human and did not think in human terms.

For example, while other humans wore clothes and the Grandfather knew it, such coverings were an alien concept to him; and in any case he forced nothing and no one. When Twig did not want to wear clothes, he taught her how to control her skin temperatures for comfort; then he let the matter go. And there were other ways in which he let Twig be herself, and different from her own kind.

So when Twig and Hacker met at last, it was something like an encounter between two aliens having an only limited amount of language and experience in common. They found each other fascinating in their differences; and from that first meeting their partnership began.

"You wear clothes now," said John Stone at this point in Twig's story, glancing at the soft bark bound about her body.

"That was Hacker's idea. He's right, of course," said Twig. "I don't mind the bark. It was living once, and real. It rubbed a little at first when I wore it, but I taught my body not to be bothered where it touched me."

"Yes," said John Stone, nodding his great head with the wavy, light-colored hair glinting in the firelight. "But how did Hacker get involved in the planetary government here, so that he could arrange to have me called? And why are his own constituents out to murder him now?"

"Hacker got a teaching machine and taught me a lot of things," said Twig. "But he learned a lot too. About the

Grandfather and everything. He can't talk to the Grandfather, but Hacker knows he's there, now."

"Downcountry, your people seem to think the Plant-Grandfather is a superstition," said John.

"The Grandfather never paid much attention to them downcountry," said Twig. "But the other croppers up here know about him. That's why they want to find and kill him, just like they want to kill Hacker."

"Why?" asked John patiently.

"Hacker ran for the Legislature two years ago," said Twig. "And at first the other croppers thought it was a great thing, one of their own people trying for the delegate-at-large post. So they all voted for him. But then he stood up in the Legislature-House and talked about the Grandfather and why the woods-burning should be stopped. Then the other croppers hated him because the downcountry people laughed and because they didn't want to give up cropping and burning. But as long as he was a delegate, the eye of downcountry law was on him to protect him. But his two-year term ran out yesterday; and now they think no one cares."

"Easy. Be easy . . ." said John, for Twig was becoming frightened and unhappy again. "There are people on other worlds who care—for all Hackers, and for all beings like your Plant-Grandfather. I care. Nothing's going to happen to either of them. I promise you."

But Twig sat rocking on her heels, now that she had remembered, refusing to let herself be comforted for fear that in some strange way to do so would bring down disaster.

In the dark morning, after they both had slept for some four hours, they rose and John packed his things, then mounted his horse. With Twig leading the animal through the woods, they started off for Rusty Springs.

Dawn began to join them before they were more than halfway there. As they rode into the growing sunlight, the horse could see where to place his large hooves and they began to pick up speed. But by this time, Twig hardly noticed—though she had fretted at the slowness of their going earlier—because she was becoming more and more fascinated with John Stone. Just as he was big in body, he was big in mind as well—so big that Twig walked around and around the way he thought with questions. But in spite of the fact that he answered willingly enough, she could not seem to see all at one time what he was by his answers.

"What are you?" she kept asking.

"An ecologist," said John.

"But what are you really?"

"Something like an advisor," said John. "An advisor to the social authorities on new worlds."

"Hacker said you were something like a policeman."

"That, too, I suppose," said John.

"But I still don't know what you are!"

"What are you?" asked John.

She was surprised.

"I'm Twig," she said. "A small runner." Then she thought and added. "A human . . . a girl . . ." She fell silent.

"There; you see?" said John Stone. "Every one is many things. That is why we have to go cautiously about the universe, not moving and changing things until we know for sure what moving or changing will do to the universe as a result, and eventually, therefore, to ourselves."

"You sound like the Plant-Grandfather," Twig said. "Only he won't even fight back when things are done to him and his children, like the woods-burning of the croppers."

"Perhaps he's wise."

"Of course he's wise!" said Twig. "But he's wrong!"

John Stone looked from his big horse down at her where she ran alongside them. He was riding with his head a little cocked on one side to catch the faint sound of her whispered words.

"Are you sure?" asked John.

Twig opened her mouth and then closed it again. She ran along, looking straight ahead, saying nothing.

"All things that do not die, grow," said John. "All who grow, change. Your Plant-Grandfather is growing and changing—and so are you, Twig."

She tried to shut the sound of his voice out of her ears, telling herself he had nothing to say that she needed to hear.

They came to Rusty Springs just before noon. The place was named for a small waterfall that came directly out of a small cliff about a quarter of the way down from its top. The stream fell into a wide, shallow basin of rock streaked with reddish color, and the water had a strong taste of iron. When they got there, Hacker was sitting waiting for them on a boulder beside the pool.

"You just made it," he greeted them as they came up. "Another couple of minutes and I'd have had to move on without waiting for you any longer. Hear up a ways, there?"

He tilted his head toward the woods at the opposite side of the basin of spring water. Twig did not have to reach out to one of the Grandfather's children for information this time.

Like the others, in fact much more clearly than the two men with her, she could hear the distant smashing of undergrowth as a body of people moved toward them.

"Hacker!" whispered Twig. "Run!"

"No," said Hacker.

"No," said John Stone from high on his horse. "We'll wait here and have a word with them."

They stood together, silent and waiting, while the noise increased; and after a while it came right into the clearing along with the ten men and three women of the posse. They emerged from the woods, but stopped when they saw Hacker and Twig together with John Stone on his big horse.

"Looking for somebody?" said Hacker derisively.

"You know damn well we are," said Berg. He had gotten himself another ion drill, and he pulled it from his belt as he started toward Hacker. "We're going to take care of you now, Hacker—you and that kid and that friend of yours, whoever he is."

The other members of the posse started to move behind him, and they all flowed forward toward the three.

"No," said John Stone. His deep voice made them all look up at him. "No."

Slowly, he dismounted and stood on the ground beside his horse. There was something unstoppable in the way he first stood up in his stirrups, then swung one long leg over the hindquarters of the beast and finally stepped down to the ground. The posse halted again; and John spoke to the people.

"I'm a Paraplanetary Government ecologist," he said, "assigned to this planet to investigate a possibly dangerous misuse of natural resources. As such, I've got certain areas of authority; and one of them is to subpoena individuals for my official Hearing on the situation."

He lifted his left wrist to his lips, and something on that wrist glinted into the sunlight. He spoke to it.

"Hacker Illions, I charge you to appear as a witness at my Hearing, when called. Twig, I charge you to appear as a witness at my Hearing when called," he said. "The expenses of your appearance will be borne by my authority; and your duty to appear takes precedence over any other duty, obligation or restraint laid upon you by any other local law, source or individual."

John dropped his wrist gently on to the curved neck of the horse beside him; and it looked like nothing more than some large dog that he petted.

"These witnesses," he said to the posse, "must not be interfered with in any way. You understand?"

"Oh, we understand, all right," said the thick-bodied woman in the white raincoat.

"Understand? What do you mean, understand?" raged Berg. "He's not armed, this ecologist. There's only one of him. Are we going to let him stop us?"

Berg started forward toward John, who stood still. But as Berg got closer he began to look smaller, until at a few steps from John, who had not moved, it became plain that his head would not reach to John's shoulder and he was like a half-grown boy facing a full-grown man. He stopped and looked back, then, and saw none of the others in the posse had moved to follow him.

As his head turned around to look, the woman in the white raincoat burst into a jeering laugh.

"You, Berg!" she crowed. "Your guts always were in your muscles!"

She came forward herself, elbowing Berg aside, stepping in front of him and staring fiercely at John.

"You don't scare me, Mr. Ecologist!" she said. "I been looking up at people all my life. You don't scare me, your supraplanetary government doesn't scare me, nothing scares me! You want to know why we don't take and hang Hacker right now and carry this kid home to grow up decently, right now? It's not because of you—it's because we don't need to. Hacker isn't the only one who's got connections down at Capital City. It happens we heard on our belt phones just two hours ago you were on your way up here."

John nodded.

"I'm not surprised," he said. "But that doesn't change anything."

"Doesn't it?" the tone of her voice hit a high note of triumph. "All we wanted Hacker and the girl for was to find out where that plant-devil lives. Hacker sent for you, but we sent for equipment to help us find it. Two days ago, we put that equipment in an aircraft and began mapping the root systems in this area. We figured it was probably in this area because here was where it brought up the girl—"

"That's got nothing to do with it!" cried Twig in her loudest whisper. "The Grandfather reaches everywhere. All over the continent. All over the world."

But the woman did not hear her and probably would have paid no attention if she had.

"Yesterday, we found it. Protect Hacker and the girl all you want to, Mr. Ecologist. How're you going to stop us from digging in our own earth, and setting fire to what we find there?"

"Intelligent life, wantonly destroyed——" began John, but she cut him short.

"What life? How do you know it's intelligent until you find it? And if you find it, what can you do—subpoena some roots?"

She laughed.

"Hey," said Berg, turning to her. She went on laughing. "Hey," he said, "what's all this? Why didn't you tell me about it?"

"Tell you?" She leaned toward him as if she would spit into his black beard. "Tell you? Trust you? *You?*"

"I got the same rights——"

But she walked around him, leaving him with the protest half-made, and went back to the rest of the posse.

"Come on," she said. "Let's get out of here. We can pick up these two after that Hearing's over. They won't be going any place we can't find them."

The rest of the posse stirred like an animal awakening and put itself in motion. She led them past the basin and forward, right past Twig, Hacker and John Stone with his horse. She passed so close by Twig that she was able to lean out and pat the back of Twig's right shoulder in passing—or, rather, where Twig's right shoulder would have been, except for the covering bark that protected it. Twig shrank from the touch; but Lucy Arodet only grinned at her and went on, leading her posse off into the woods, headed back the way John Stone and Twig had just come. Berg ran after them; and in a few moments the sound of their going was silenced by distance.

"Is that right?" Hacker asked John into the new quiet. "Is there equipment that can find a root mass like the Grandfather's?"

John's blue eyes in his massive face were narrowed by a frown.

"Yes," he said. "It's a variety of heat-seeking equipment—capable of very delicate distinctions, because all it has to go on is the minimal heat changes from liquid flow in the root. I didn't think anyone out here on your planet would know about it, much less——" he broke off. "And I can't believe anything like that could be sent here by anyone without my hearing of it. But in the commercial area there are always some who'll take chances."

"Arrest them!" whispered Twig. "Make it illegal for them to use it!"

John shook his head.

"I've no sure evidence yet that your Grandfather is a sentient being," he said. "Until I do, I've got no legal power to protect him."

"You don't believe us?" Hacker's lean face was all bones under the beard stubble.

"Yes. I believe, personally," said John. "Before man even left the world he started on, it was discovered that if you thought of cutting or burning a plant it would show a reaction on a picoammeter. Mental reaction of and by plants has been established for a long time. A community intelligence evolving from this, like the Grandfather you talk about, is only logical. But I have to contact it myself to know, or have some hard evidence of its existence."

"In another day or two, according to what that Lucy Arodet said just now," Hacker added, "perhaps there will not be anything to contact."

"Yes," said John. He turned to Twig. "Do you know where the Grandfather-Plant is?"

"He's everywhere," said Twig.

"Twig, you know what he means," said Hacker. "Yes, Stone, she knows."

Twig glared at the stubble-faced man.

"You must tell me," said John Stone. "The sooner I can get to the Grandfather, the sooner I'll be able to protect him."

"No!" whispered Twig.

"Honey, be sensible!" said Hacker. "You heard Lucy Arodet say they'd found the Grandfather. If they know, why keep it a secret from John Stone, here?"

"I don't believe it!" said Twig. "She was lying. She doesn't know!"

"If she does," said John, "you're taking a very long chance. If they can dig down to your Grandfather-Plant and destroy him before I can get to him, won't you have lost what you most want to save?"

"None of the Grandfather's children would tell where he is, even if they could," Twig whispered, "and I won't."

"Don't tell me then," said John. "Just take me to him."

Twig shook her head.

"Twig," said Hacker, and she looked at him. "Twig, listen. You've got to do what Stone says."

She shook her head again.

"Then, ask the Grandfather himself," Hacker said. "Let him decide."

She started to shake her head a third time, then went over

to a tree and put her arms around it; not because she needed
the tree to help her talk with the Grandfather, but to be able
to hide her face from the two men.

"Grandfather!" she thought. "Grandfather, have you been
listening? What should I do?"

There was no answer.

"Grandfather!" she called with her mind.

Still no answer. For one panic-filled moment she thought
that she could not feel him there at all, that he had either been
killed or gone to sleep. Then, reaching out as far as she could,
she felt him, still there but not noticing her call.

"Grandfather!"

But it was no use. It was as if with her whisper-limited voice
she tried to shout to someone far off on the top of a high
mountain. The Grandfather had gone back into his own
thoughts. She could not reach him. She fought down the surge
of fear and hurt that leaped inside her. Once, the Grandfather
had always been there. Only in these last couple of years, since
the burnings by the croppers had been so widespread, had he
started to draw into himself and talk of going to sleep.

Slowly, she let go of the tree and turned back to face the
other two humans.

"He won't answer," she said.

There was a moment's silence.

"Then it's up to you to decide, isn't it?" Hacker said, gently.

She nodded, feeling all torn apart inside. Then an idea came
to her.

"I won't take you to him," she said, raising her eyes to
John Stone's face. "But I'll go by myself and see if it's true, if
the croppers have found him. You wait here."

"No," said John. "I came up here to see some of the
burned-over areas for myself; and I should look at those now
while I have time. If I have to make it a court matter without
waiting to protect your Plant-Grandfather, I need as much evidence as possible."

"I'll show you places," said Hacker to him.

"No," John said again. "You go straight south to the first
town or village you can get to and report yourself to the authorities there as being under my subpoena. That will make
your protection under law a matter of public record. Can you
go straight there without that gang that just left here catching
you?"

Hacker snorted in disgust.

"All right," said John. "I had to ask to make sure. You go
to the closest community center, then—what's its name?"

"Fireville," said Hacker. "About twelve klicks southwest."

"Fireville. I'll meet you there after I've run a couple of burned-over areas. I've got a map with a number of them marked. And Twig," Tolnil turned toward her, "you'll go check on the Plant Grandfather to see if there's any sign he's been located. Then you better find me again as soon as you can. Do you think you can do that?"

"Of course," said Twig contemptuously. "The plant brothers and sisters will always tell me where you are."

But instead of turning to leave, she hesitated, looking at Hacker with the sharp teeth of worry nibbling at her.

"Don't you drink, now," she said. "If you get drunk, they might find some way to do something to you."

"Not a drop," said Hacker. "I promise."

Still she hesitated, until it came to her that if she stood here much longer she would not go at all; so she turned and ran, the forest opening before her and the other two left swallowed up from sight behind.

She went swiftly. She was not about to lose herself in the pleasure of her running now; for worry, like an invisible posse, followed right at her heels. From time to time she called to the Grandfather with her mind; but he did not answer and she settled down to getting to his rootmass as soon as possible.

In the woods, growing and changing every day, she had never had any means of measuring how fast she could go when the need was really upon her. She was only human, after all; so probably her top speed was not really much faster than that of a winning marathon runner back in the years when man was just beginning to go forth into space, before the Earth had died. But the difference was that she could run at that speed —or at very nearly that speed—all day long if she had to. Now, she did not know her speed; but she went fast, fast, her legs flashing in and out of the early afternoon sunlight and shadow as she raced down the corridor among the trees and bushes that opened before her as she went.

It was midafternoon before she came to the edge of the place where the great root-mass belonging to the Grandfather lay fifteen to forty meters below the ground and the forest above it. All the way here, the plant sisters and brothers of this area had showed her an empty woods with no sign of croppers anywhere about. But none of them could tell her about an earlier moment until she could actually reach and touch them. Now, arrived, she put her arms around one tall tree-sister and held her, forcing the slow-thinking leaves to remember daylight and dark, dark and daylight, through the past week.

But, other than the wind, the leaves remembered only silence. No humans had passed by them, even at a distance. No mechanical sounds had sounded near them. In the sky over them, only the clouds and an occasional spurt of rain had mingled with the regular march of sun and moon and stars.

The woman Lucy Arodet had lied. The croppers either had no special equipment as claimed, or if they had it, they had not used it here where they could find the Grandfather. Sighing with relief, Twig fell face down on the ground, spreading out her arms amongst the littlest brothers to hug and hold her world.

The Grandfather was safe—still safe. For a little while Twig simply closed her eyes to let herself ride off on the wave of her relief. And so sleep took her without warning, for in fact she had done a great deal of running and worrying in past hours.

When she woke, it was night. The moon was already high in the sky and the Grandfather was thinking—not at her, but around her, as if he mused over her, under the impression she did not hear.

". . . I have never reached beyond the atmosphere that envelops this one world," he was thinking. "But now, my little runner will run to the ends of the universe. Beyond are the stars, and beyond them more stars, and beyond and beyond . . . to depths beyond depths, where the great galaxies float like clouds or scatter like a whole crowd of little runners, pushing against each other, scattering out from one common point to the ultimate edges of time and distance. And in all that distance there are many lives. My little runner will come to know them, and the beginning and the end, and all that goes between. She will know them in their birth and their growing and whether it is chance or purpose that makes a path for all life in all time and space. So out of destruction will have come creation, out of sleep an awakening, and out of defeat a conquest, just as even at the poles of this world warm summer succeeds the harsh winter. All they have done to destroy me will only bring about the birth of my little runner into a Great Runner between the stars—"

"Grandfather!" called Twig; and the thoughts flowing about her broke off suddenly.

"Are you awake, little sister?" asked the Grandfather. "If you are, it's time for you to go now."

"Go?" demanded Twig, still stupid with sleep. "Go . . . why? Where? What for?"

"Your old friend Hacker is dying now, and your friend-to-be John Stone rides toward him," said the thought of the

Plant-Grandfather. "Those who wished to destroy him and me have tricked Hacker to death, and soon they will be here to kill me also. It is time for you to go."

Twig was awake and on her feet in one reflexive movement. "What happened?" she demanded. "Where is Hacker?"

"In a gully north of Fireville, where he has been pushed to fall and die, as if he had drunkenly wandered there and slipped. Those who are our enemies made him drunk and brought him there to fall, and he has fallen."

"Why didn't you wake me and tell me before?" Twig cried.

"It would have made no difference," said the Grandfather. "Hacker's death was beyond the stopping, even as those who come now to destroy me are beyond stopping."

"Come?" raged Twig. "How can anyone be coming? They don't even know where you are!"

"They do now," said the Grandfather. "When you came to me this time, you carried pinned to the bark behind your shoulder something placed there by the woman called Lucy Arodet. A small thing which cried out in a voice only another such thing could hear to tell her where you were at any moment. When you reached me and stopped traveling in this place, they knew you had found me and they knew where I was."

Twig threw a hand around to feel behind her shoulder. Her fingers closed on something small, round and hard. She pulled it loose from the bark and brought it around where she could see it. In the moonlight, it looked like a dulled pearl with small, sharp points on its underside where it had clung to the bark of her clothing.

"I'll take it away!" she said. "I'll take it someplace else—"

"That would make no difference either," said the Grandfather. "Do not suffer. Before they come I will have gone to sleep in a sleep without waking, and they can only destroy roots that mean nothing."

"No!" said Twig. "Wait . . . no! I'll run and find John Stone. He can get here before they can do your roots much damage. Then you won't have to sleep—"

"Little runner, little runner," said the Grandfather. "Even if your John Stone could save me this coming day, he would only put off the inevitable for a little while. From the day your people set foot on this world, it was certain that sooner or later I would have to sleep forever. If you understand that I go now to sleep gladly, you would not mourn as you do. What is of value in me goes forward in you, and goes where I could not, further and deeper, beyond all distance and imagination."

"No!" cried Twig. "I won't let you die. I'll run to where Hacker is and meet John Stone. He'll come and save you. Wait for me, Grandfather! Wait . . ."

Even as she continued talking with her mind to the Grandfather, she had spun about and begun to run toward Fireville. The little brothers opened a path before her, marking the way, and the bushes and trees leaned aside. But she was scarcely conscious that they did so. All her mind was on the fact that the Grandfather must not die . . . must not die . . .

She ran faster than she had ever run before. But still it was nearly dawn when she came near to Fireville, to the dark gully where the path of the little brothers led her. On the far side of the gully, silhouetted blackly against the paling sky between the trees, was the figure of a gigantic man on a gigantic horse. But down in the blackness of the gully itself was a little patch of something light that was Hacker. At the sight of that patch even the Grandfather went out of Twig's mind for a moment. She plunged recklessly down the side of the gully. Anyone else would have tripped and fallen a dozen times, but she felt the uneven ground and the presence of bush and sapling with her mind and kept her feet. She reached the shape of Hacker and dropped on her knees beside it.

"Hacker!" she cried. The tears ran down her face.

There was a great noise of tearing and plunging—the descent of a heavy body down the far side of the gully—and then John Stone, on foot, appeared on the far side of Hacker. He squatted and reached out to touch his fingers gently to Hacker's throat, under the sharp, bony line of Hacker's jaw.

"He's gone, Twig," John said, looking from Hacker to her.

Grief burst inside her like a world exploding. She lifted Hacker's head to her lap and rocked with it, weeping.

"I told you not to drink, Hacker!" she choked. "You promised me! You promised you wouldn't drink . . ."

She was aware that John Stone had moved around to squat beside her. He loomed over her like some huge cliff in the darkness. He put a hand on her back and shoulder; and the hand was so big that it was like an arch around her.

"It had to happen, Twig," the deep voice rumbled and rolled in her ear. "Some things have to happen . . ."

It was so like what the Grandfather had said that she was suddenly reminded of him. She lifted her head sharply, listening, but there was nothing.

"*Grandfather!*" she cried, and for the first time in her life, it was not only her mind that called. Her voice rang clear and wild under the brightening sky.

But there was no answer. For the first time not even the echo came back that said the Grandfather was there but not listening. The unimaginable network of the plant-children still stood connected, listening, waiting, carrying her call to the furthest limits of the world. But there was no response. The voice of the planet had fallen silent.

"He's gone!" she cried. And the words flew among the leaves and the branches, from grass-blade to grass-blade and along the roots under hill and valley and plain and mountain. "Gone . . ."

She slumped where she sat, even the head of Hacker forgotten on her knees.

"The Plant-Grandfather?" Stone asked her. She nodded numbly.

"It's over," she said, aloud, her new voice dead and dull. "He's gone . . . gone. It's all finished, forever."

"No," said the deep voice of John Stone. "It's never finished."

He stood up beside her, looking at her.

"Twig," he said again, gently but insistently, "it's never finished."

"Yes it is. Listen . . ." she said, forgetting that he, like all the others, had never been able to hear the Grandfather. "The world's dead now. There is no one else."

"Yes, there is," said John Stone. "There's you. And for you, there's everything. Not only what's on this world but on many others that never knew a Plant-Grandfather. They're out there, waiting for you to speak to them."

"I can't speak to anyone," she said, still kneeling, slumped by the dead body of Hacker. "It's all over, I tell you. All over."

John Stone reached down and picked her up. Holding her, he walked up the dark side of the gully to his horse and mounted it. She struggled for a second, then gave up. His strength overpowered hers easily.

"Time moves," he said. She hid her face against the darkness of his broad chest and heard his voice rumbling through the wall of bone and flesh. "Things change, and there's no stopping them. Even if the Grandfather and Hacker had stayed alive here, even if Jinson's Planet had stayed just as it was—still you, by yourself, would have grown and changed. What doesn't die has to grow. What grows, changes. Our decisions get bigger and bigger, whether we want them to or not —our jobs get larger and larger, whether we plan them to or not—and in the end the choice has to be to love all or to love none. There may be others like Hacker on other worlds, and perhaps somewhere there may be another Jinson's world. But there's never been another Plant-Grandfather that we've been able to find, and not another Twig. That means you're going to have to love all the worlds and all the growing things on them as the Grandfather would have, if he could have gone to them the way you're going to be able to. That's your job, Twig."

She neither spoke nor stirred.

"Try," he said. "The Grandfather's left it all to you. Take up the duty he left to you. Speak to the growing things on Jinson's Planet and tell them that losing the Grandfather wasn't the end."

She shook her head slightly against his chest.

"I can't," she said. "It's no use. I can't."

"Speak to them," he said. "Don't leave them alone. Tell them they've got you now. Wasn't that what the Grandfather wanted?"

Again she shook her head.

"I can't . . ." she whimpered. "If I speak to them, then he will be gone, really gone, forever. I can't do that. I can't put him away forever. I can't!"

"Then everything the Grandfather counted on is lost," said John Stone. "Everything Hacker did is wasted. What about Hacker?"

She thought of Hacker then, what was left of Hacker, being left farther behind them with every stride of the horse's long legs. Hacker, going down now into forgottenness too.

"I can't, Hacker!" she said to the memory of him in her mind.

"Can't . . . ?" the image of Hacker looked back at her, cocked one eyebrow at her and began to sing:

> "As game as Ned Kelly," the people would say.
> "As game as Ned Kelly," they say it today . . .

The familiar words in his cracked, hoarse voice went through her like a sword-sharp shaft of sunlight, and through the dark, hard wall of grief that had swelled up within her at the loss of the Grandfather. All at once, she remembered all the flowers that also were alone now, left voiceless and in darkness of silence; and contrition overflowed within her. From now on, she would be gone, too!

"It's all right!" she called out to them, with her voice and her mind together. "It's all right, *I'm* still here. Me. Twig.

You'll never be alone, I promise! Even if I have to go some-place else, I'll always reach out and touch you from wherever I am . . ."

And from valley and hill, from plain and forest, from all over, the words of her mind were picked up and passed along, tossing joyously from smallest brother to largest sister, on and on to the ends of the world.

Twig closed her eyes and let herself lie at last against the wide chest of John Stone. Where he was taking her, she did not know. No doubt it would be very far away from Jinson's world. But no world was too far, she knew that now; and also, out there in the great distances of which the Grandfather had dreamed and to which he could never go, there were other brothers and sisters, waiting for the sound of a voice, waiting for her.

Grandfather was gone beyond returning, and so was Hack-er. But maybe it was not the end of things, after all; maybe it was only a beginning. Maybe . . . at least she had spoken to all the others who had lived through the Grandfather, and they now knew they would never be alone again. Letting go of her grief a little, just a little, Twig rocked off to sleep on the steady rhythm of the pacing horse.

CATHADONIAN ODYSSEY

Michael Bishop

And again, fitting in with the Martin, Van Scyoc, Stableford and Dickson stories, here is yet another approach to the problem of planetary Utopian hap-piness. Perhaps this is the bottom-line totalization of them all?

Cathay, Caledonia. Put the words together: Cathadonia. That was what the namer of the planet, a murderer with the sensitivity of a poet, had done. He had put the two exotic words together—Cathay and Caledonia—so that the place they designated might have a name worthy of its own bewitch-ing beauty. Cathadonia. Exotic, far-off, bewitching, incompre-hensible. A world of numberless pools. A world of bizarrely

constituted "orchards." a world with one great, gong-torment-
ed sea.

Cathadonia.

And the first thing that men had done there, down on the
surface, was kill as many of the exotic little tripodal natives as
their laser pistols could dispatch.

Squiddles, the men off the merchantship had called them.
They called them other fanciful names, too, perhaps inspired
by the sensitive murderer who had coined the planet's name.
*Treefish. Porpurls. Fintails. Willowpusses. Tridderlings. Devil
apes.*

The names didn't matter. The men killed the creatures wantonly, brutally, laughingly. For sport. For nothing but sport.
They were off the merchantship *Golden* heading homeward
from a colonized region of the galactic arm. They made planet-
fall because no one had really noticed Cathadonia before
and because they were ready for a rest. Down on the surface,
for relaxation's sake, they killed the ridiculous-looking squiddles. Or treefish. Or porpurls. Or willowpusses. Take your
choice of names. The names didn't matter.

Once home, the captain of the *Golden* reported a new planet to the authorities. He used the name Cathadonia, the murderer's coinage, and Cathadonia was the name that went into
the books. The captain said nothing about his crewmen's san-
guinary recreation on the planet. How could he? Instead, he
gave coordinates, reported that the air was breathable, and
volunteered the information that Cathadonia was beautiful.
"Just beautiful, really just beautiful."

The men of the *Golden,* after all, were not savages. Hadn't
one of them let the word Cathadonia roll off his lips in a moment of slaughterous ecstasy? Didn't the universe forgive its
poets, its name givers?

Later, Earth sent the survey probeship *Nobel,* on its way to
the virgin milkiness of the Magellanic Clouds, in the direction
of Cathadonia. The *Nobel,* in passing, dropped a descentcraft
toward the planet's great ocean. The three scientists aboard
that descentcraft were to establish a floating station whose purpose would be to determine the likelihood of encountering life
on Cathadonia. The captain of the *Golden* had not mentioned
life. The scientists did not know it existed there. Preliminary
sensor scans from the *Nobel* suggested the presence of botani-
cals and the possibility of some sort of inchoate aquatic life.
Nothing sentient, surely.

Whatever the situation down there, the scientists aboard the
floating station would unravel it.

Unfortunately, something happened to the descentcraft on its way down, something that never happened to survey descentcraft and therefore something the *Nobel's* crew had made no provision for. In fact, the *Nobel*, as was usual in these cases, went on without confirming touchdown; it went on toward the Magellanic Clouds. And some odd, anomalous force wrenched the controls of the descentcraft out of the hands of its pilots and hurled it planetward thousands of kilometers from the great ocean.

It fell to the surface beside a sentinel willow on the banks of one of Cathadonia's multitudinous pools. There it crumpled, sighed, ticked with alien heat.

This, then, becomes the story of a survivor—the story of Maria Jill Ian, a woman downed on an out-of-the-way world with no hope of immediate rescue, with no companions to share her agony, with no goal but the irrational desire to reach Cathadonia's ocean. A woman who did not wholly understand what had happened to her. A woman betrayed by her own kind and ambivalently championed by a creature carrying out a larger betrayal.

—For Cathadonia.

I am standing on Cathadonia, first planet from an ugly little star that Arthur called Ogre's Heart. I am writing in a logbook that is all I have left of the materials in our descentcraft. God knows why I am writing.

Arthur is dead. Fischelson is dead. The Nobel *is on its way to the Magellanic Clouds. It will be back in three months. Small comfort. I will be dead, too. Why am I not dead now?*

The "landscape" about me is dotted with a thousand small pools. Over each pool a single willowlike tree droops its head. The pools are clear, I have drunk from them. And the long, slender leaves of the willows—or at least of this willow—contain a kind of pulp that I have eaten. Trees at nearby pools appear to bear fruit.

But drinking and eating are painful exercises now, and I don't know why I do it. Arthur and Fischelson are dead.

The light from Ogre's Heart sits on the faces of the thousand pools as if they were mirrors. Mirrors. Mirrors wherein I might drown and rediscover the painlessness of who I was before. . . .

Maria Jill Ian did not die. She slept by the wreck of the descentcraft. She slept two of Cathadonia's days, then part of a third. The silver lacery of the pulpwillow shaded her during the day, kept off the rains at night.

When she finally woke and began to live again, she "buried" Arthur and Fischelson by tying pieces of the descentcraft's wreckage to their mangled bodies and dragging them to the edge of the pool. Then she waded into the mirror surface and felt the slick pool weeds insinuate themselves between her toes. A strong woman well into middle-age, she sank first Fischelson's body and then that of Arthur, her husband. She held the men under and maneuvered the weights on their corpses so that neither of them would float up again. She was oblivious to the smell of their decaying bodies; she knew only that it would be very easy to tie a weight about her own waist and then walk deeper into the pool.

The day after accomplishing these burials, Maria Jill Ian looked away to the western horizon and began walking toward the pools that glimmered there. Just as she had not known why she bothered to eat and drink, she did not now understand why the horizon should draw her implacably toward the twilight baths of Ogre's Heart.

Later she would rediscover her reasons, but now she simply did what she must.

Today I walked a distance I can't accurately determine. My feet fell on the pliant verges of at least a hundred ponds.

A small thing has happened to keep me going.

The trees over the pools have begun to change. Although their long branches still waterfall to the pools' surfaces, not all these trees are the pulpwillows that stand sentinel in the region where Arthur, Fischelson, and I crashed. Some have brilliant scarlet blossoms; some have trunks that grow in gnarled configurations right out of the pools' centers; some are heavy with globular fruit; some are naked of all adornment and trail their boughs in the water like skeletal hands.

But I've eaten of the trees that bear fruit, and this fruit has been sweet and bursting with flavor, invariably. It's strange that I don't really care for any of it. Still, it's nourishment.

The sky turns first blazing white at twilight, then yellow like lemons, then a brutal pink. And at night the trees stand in stark tableaux that hail me onward.

I still hurt. I still hurt terribly, from the crash, from my loss —but I'm beginning to heal. After sleeping, I'll continue to walk away from Arthur and Fischelson—in the direction of falling, ever-falling Ogre's Heart. . . .

One morning Maria Jill Ian came to a pond beside which grew a huge umbrellalike tree of gold and scarlet. The tree bore a kind of large thick-shelled, mahogany-colored nut rather than the commonplace varieties of fruit she had been living on for the past two or three days.

She decided to stop and eat.

The nuts, however, hung high in the branches of the tree. Its twisted bole looked as if it might allow her to climb to the higher entanglements where she could gather food as she liked. Her simple foil jumpsuit did not impede her climbing. Leaves rustled and flashed. She gained a place where she could rest, and stopped.

All about her the pools of Cathadonia lay brilliant and blinding beneath their long-fingered sentinel trees.

Ogre's Heart was moving up the sky.

Maria Jill Ian turned her head to follow the sun's squat ascent. In the whiteness cascading through the branches overhead, she saw a shape—a shape at least as large as a small man, a form swaying over her, eclipsing the falling light, a thing more frightening than the realization that she was light-years from Earth, stranded.

Not thinking, merely reacting, she stepped to the branch below her and then swung out from the willow. She landed on the marshy ground beside the pond, caught herself up, and scrabbled away.

Something vaguely tentacular plunged from the scarlet-and-gold umbrella of the tree and disappeared noiselessly into the pool.

Maria Jill Ian began to run. She ran westward, inevitably toward another pool, struggling in ground that squelched around her boots, looking back now and again in an effort to see the thing that had plunged.

She saw the silver water pearl up, part, and stream down the creature's narrow head. It was going to pursue her, she knew. Although it came on comically, it flailed with a deftness that demolished the impulse to laugh. Maria Jill Ian did not look back again.

All of Cathadonia breathed with her as, desperately, she ran.

I call him Bracero. It's a joke. He has no arms; he swims like the much-maligned "wetbacks" of another time. I don't know what sort of creature he is.

A description?

Very well. To begin: Bracero has no arms, but in other re-

spects he resembles a man-sized spider monkey—except his body is absolutely hairless, smooth as the hide of a porpoise, a whitish-blue like the surfaces of Cathadonia's pools.

To continue: He is arboreal and aquatic at once. He uses his feet and his sleek prehensile tail to climb to the uppermost branches of any poolside willow. Conversely, his armlessness has streamlined his upper torso to such an extent that he can slide through the water like a cephalopod. Indeed, he moves with the liquid grace of an octopus, although one who is five times over an amputee.

To conclude: What disarms even me is Bracero's face. It is small, expressive, curious, and winning. The eyes are an old man's (sometimes,) the mouth a baby's, the ears a young girl's. The trauma of our first meeting has slipped out of our memories, just as Ogre's Heart plunges deathward at twilight.

We are friends, Bracero and I.

The creature had caught up with her when she could run no more. Halfway between two of the planet's glimmering pools Maria Jill Ian collapsed and waited for the thing to fall upon her.

Instead, it stopped at a small distance and regarded her almost sympathetically, she thought. Its body put her in mind of a small boy sitting on a three-legged stool, his arms clasped behind his back as if desirous of looking penitent. She lay unmoving on the marshy earth, staring at the creature over one muddied forearm.

Blinking occasionally, it stared back.

Finally she got up and went on to the next pool, where she leaned against the trunk of an especially blasted-looking tree. The naked creature with two supple legs and a lithe tail—or another leg—followed her, almost casually. It made a wide arc away from Maria Jill Ian and came in behind the willow she was leaning upon. Stoic now, she didn't even look to see what it was doing.

To join Arthur, to join Fischelson, to join the centuries' countless dead, would not be unpleasant, she thought.

The eel-beast hoisted itself into the willow and climbed silently to the highest branches. Then it hung there, looking down at her like a suddenly sullen child swinging by his knees.

That evening, her fear gone, she named the creature Bracero. On the second day beside this pond she saw how it fed.

Ogre's Heart gave them a characteristically magnesium-bright dawn. Sentinel trees cast shadows like carefully penned lines of indigo ink. A thousand mirror pools turned from slate to silver. Lying on her back, Maria opened her eyes and witnessed something she didn't entirely believe.

Bracero was still high in the tree. He clutched a narrow branch with his "tail" and both "feet," his head and torso swaying gently, freely, like a live pendulum.

Clusters of mahogany-colored nuts swayed, too, in the dawn wind.

Then, looking up, Maria Jill Ian saw one of the oversized nuts snap away from the others and float directly up to the creature that had pursued her. Bracero took one foot away from the limb, grasped the willownut, expertly shelled it, and fed himself.

Several times he repeated this procedure, on each occasion the willownut floating within his reach seemingly of its own volition.

The Earth woman stood up and watched in astonishment. Bracero paid her no mind until she moved as if to obtain her own breakfast. Then he shifted in the uppermost branches, descended a little, and made *screeing* noises with his teeth. Maria decided not to go after the mahogany-colored shells that split, so easily it seemed, into meat-filled hemispheres. Did Bracero intend to deny her access to food? Would she have to fight?

Then a willownut fell toward her. But it broke its own fall in midair, bobbed sideways, and floated just beyond her startled hands—a miniature planet, brown and crustily wrinkled, halted in its orbit just at eye level. Bracero had stopped making *screeing* sounds.

Maria Jill Ian looked up. Then she gratefully took the gift and ate.

For the next several weeks she did not have to clamber into a tree again to obtain her food, nor search among the sodden grasses where the fruits and nuts sometimes fell. Bracero saw to her wants. When these were filled, he plunged out of the sentinel willows and rippled the mirror pools. Blithely he swam—until the woman made a move to continue her odyssey westward. Then he again followed.

Maria supposed that the only payment Bracero wanted for serving her was the pleasure of her company. She didn't mind, but she couldn't stay her urge to march relentlessly on Cathadonia's western horizon. Something there pulled her, compelled her onward.

Bracero has telekinetic abilities. He's been with me for almost twelve days now, as best as I'm able to reckon days—and I've been trying very hard to mark the successive risings and settings of Ogre's Heart since it is impossible to determine time by distances covered or landmarks passed.

But for slight variations in the willows, the terrain of Cathadonia is beautifully self-repeating. Looking at it, I can't understand why Bracero is the only native of the planet I have so far encountered; he is so meticulously adapted to this environment that there must be others like him. Can it be that the men of the Golden were unfortunate enough to miss seeing even one creature like Bracero?

A word about telekinesis, Bracero's uncanny skill at manipulating objects at a distance.

He does it for me every day, several times a day, and does so for himself as well; afterwards, he appears no worse for this not inconsiderable psychic strain than during times of simple physical activity. His mind is as sleek as his body.

Just today, for instance, I have seen him move the casabalike melons of an unusual willow that we passed this morning. He moved them, in fact, all the way to the pool where we're now loitering. This is no mean distance. It indicates that Bracero can extend his psychic aura to far locations, fix upon a specific object, and draw it toward him at will. Without noticeable aftereffects.

Ordinarily, though, he puts under his influence only those foodstuffs in the trees by which we stop. The casabas (if I can call them that) were a rare exception, a treat that he lovingly tendered to both of us. And although I seldom think about what I eat, I enjoyed these melons, and Bracero seemed to appreciate the delight I took in them.

He has an intelligence which is both animal and human. I have begun to talk to him as if he were a close friend, or a small child, or (I hesitate to write this) a new incarnation of Arthur. Bracero watches me when I talk, and listens—truly listens.

But I'm off the subject.

I'm still amazed at the placidity with which Bracero accomplishes his psychokinetic feats, the childish nonchalance of this supranormal juggling. Does it cost him nothing?

Aboard the Nobel, of course, we have two PK mediums: Langland Smart and Margaret Riva. Langland is the older, and his abilities are more fully developed than Margaret's. In free-fall he can maneuver an unresisting, hypnotized subject in any direction he wants, can make the subject raise an arm and scratch his nose, can settle him gently into a padded lift-seat.

But afterwards, and even during, Langland pays. He loses weight, suffers dizziness, has nightmares and insomnia later—

and his heartbeat does not fall back into a steady, safe rhythm for hours, sometimes two or three days, after such activity.

It's the same with Margaret, although she can move only small objects and these only across relatively smooth surfaces. She has no ability to levitate things, as do Langland and, more impressively, Bracero. And only Bracero does not pay for the mental forces which he so astonishingly commands over the inert.

The Nobel, meanwhile, expected us to find this watery orchard of a planet uninhabited. Did the men off that merchant-ship see only pools and trees when they set down here? Arthur and I talked to its captain before we left. He was a nervous ferret of a man. . . .

Ogre's Heart has set. I'm going to stop writing. In the morning we'll be off again. I wonder how much longer it will be before we're there. The willows to the west, the pools limning the horizon—these things call me.

But for tonight it would be nice if Cathadonia had a moon. . . .

For the next two days Maria Jill Ian kept up her compulsive journeying, through terrain that did not alter.

She began to suspect that Bracero was observing her for others of his own kind, that he followed her and fed her not merely to enjoy her company but to maintain a keen and critical surveillance of her movements. She was not an unintelligent woman, by any means, and she was as susceptible to doubts as any healthy paranoid human being.

She believed that she had evidence of Bracero's communicating telepathically with other members of his species. Her evidence consisted of the fact that she still hadn't stumbled across a single one of Bracero's brethren. Before the two of them approached each new willow, each new pool, her sleek friend undoubtedly "wired" ahead an imperative to stay out of sight. The recipient of this communication undoubtedly dove into the water and remained there, nearly insensate, until they departed. Undoubtedly.

That was what Maria Jill Ian believed, and once, as they approached, she saw rings on the surface of a pool. Bracero had been careless, she surmised, and wired his warning later than usual. The slowly fading rings on the surface of the pond corroborated her suspicions. But, of course, she saw nothing but the tree and the water when they had fully arrived. Little corroboration, very little indeed.

Her affection for Bracero did not dwindle because of these

suspicions; surely, he did only what he must. Also, none of his brethren had made any hostile move against her. There had been no assaults on her person, nor even any attempts to impede their trek westward.

Maybe Bracero's people had decided jointly to save both her and them the confusion, the upheaval, of further contact. Because he'd seen her first, Bracero had necessarily assumed the combined role of his people's roving watchman and Maria Jill Ian's solicitous escort. She was sure that he returned at least a small portion of the affection she felt for him. His attitude, his expressive face, conveyed as much.

One evening (the evening after she had written the last log entry) they stopped for the night, and Bracero moved as if to clamber up into the inevitable willow. Involuntarily, Maria held up her hand.

"Don't go up there," she said. "There'll be plenty of time to eat. Stay down here." She patted the ground beside her. "We'll talk."

Bracero responded as if he understood her.

His bluish porpoise's skin gleaming in the twilight, he faced her and assumed his comical tripod stance about two meters away. He appeared quite ready to converse—as clinically receptive, Maria thought, as a probeship psychiatrist. His smooth brow was slightly wrinkled, his eyes looked upon her with the estranging narrowness of a devilfish's eyes. Still, his posture suggested no hostility.

Maria Jill Ian talked:

"I'm not a dependent woman, Bracero. I know what I'm about. Even now I realize that what draws me on isn't entirely rational. Maybe not rational at all. I know that my loss of Arthur and my idea of home may not be redeemed by following Ogre's Heart to the horizon every day—but because I understand my irrationality, I know what I'm doing. Do you see that, Bracero? One day I'll explain myself to you with more certainty, much more."

Bracero shifted his position. His expression allowed her to think that he did see her point, intuitively.

"Arthur and I used to talk, Bracero. Sometimes without words. Neither of us was dependent on the other, though we were somehow wordlessly interdependent. I know. That sounds like a contradiction—but it's not, not really.

"We had an affinity—a love, you have to call it—that synchronized our feelings and moods in a way not at all mechanical, a spiritual meshing. This was our interdependence, Bracero.

"But we could function with the same rigorous smoothness while apart. He worked his work, I mine; and our shared independence only bound us that much more closely in our love. I miss him, Bracero, I wish he were here beside me now—so that we could talk again, even wordlessly. As before."

She paused. The far ponds twinkled with the day's last light.

"Did you know that I didn't even weep when I buried Fischelson and my husband, when I sank them to the bottom of the pool two weeks behind us? I still can't weep, Bracero. The memory of Arthur's total *aliveness* is still too powerful.

"So different from other men," she concluded. "So different from the cruel ones, the petty ones, the men with stupid hates and overbearing passions. Fischelson, too. Both of them so different."

Maria Jill Ian fell silent. It had done her good to talk, especially to a listener who seemed so congenial. She wished that Bracero could talk. Since he couldn't, she said, "I think Arthur would approve of what we're doing."

A moment later she said, "You don't have to sit there any more, Bracero. You can climb up into the willow if you like."

Bracero didn't move immediately. He waited as if refraining from the subtle rudeness of leaving too quickly. Then he gracefully swung himself aloft. He hung by his tail from a low limb.

More than on any other similar occasion, Maria Jill Ian was grateful for the Cathadonian's seemingly intentional courtesy. If he were deceiving her, she didn't care.

My hands are trembling almost too violently to write this.

The night before last, I engaged in a long monologue and made Bracero listen to me hold forth on independence, communication, spiritual meshing, love, et cetera.

We haven't moved from this pool, this willow, since that night. The reasons are astounding, they're out of the pale of credibility—but my heart, my head, my trembling hands all attest to their realness. I have to put it down here. I have to set it down as everything happened—even if my scrawl is ultimately illegible even to me.

On the morning after our "conversation," I awoke and looked up to find Bracero. He was there, his legs and tail wrapped around a branch. When I stood, I could almost look him squarely in his topsy-turvy eyes, eyes that were open but glazed over as if with cataracts.

"Wake up," I said.

He didn't move. His cephalopod's clouded eyes looked as removed from me as two useless, tarnished Earth coins.

"It's morning, it's time to get going again, Bracero."

He didn't move, still didn't move, and a kind of subdued panic gripped me. I thought that I would try a feint, a bluff, to see if that wouldn't set the good warm blood circulating through him again.

"I'm going," I said. "You can join me if you like."

That said, I set off briskly and had slogged through a good half a kilometer of unending marshland before I actually convinced myself that Bracero wasn't going to follow and that it was wrong to leave him there: a sort of Cathadonian possum who had never before put on the stiff, frightening mask of Death.

I went back.

Bracero wasn't dead. I could tell that by putting my hand against his gimlet-hole nostrils and feeling the rapid but quiet warmth of his breathing. He was in a trance, a coma, a state of suspended animation—but not really any of these things, though, because his breathing was hurried, his sleek body feverish, his pulse (which I found in his throat) telegraphically insistent. Only in his relation to the ground was Bracero suspended; otherwise, his stupor—though deep—was very animate.

I felt I had to stay by him even if it meant losing a day to our assault on the horizon; I was morally obligated. Morally obligated. Too, my affection for Bracero has deepened to a point that embarrasses me. Even the horrible manner in which he chose to demonstrate his feeling for me has not turned me against him—though my hands shake, my head swims.

All of yesterday I stayed by him. Bracero didn't improve; his condition altered not at all.

Occasionally I fetched water in a bag made of my overtunic and then moistened Bracero's face. I tried to put food in his mouth—pulp from the willow's leaves, some nut meat I had saved, a piece of fruit—but his mouth wouldn't accept these gifts; they dribbled from his lips.

I went to sleep when Ogre's Heart set. I had nightmares. Shapes moved, voices sang, eerie winds hissed. The awful clamminess of Cathadonia seeped into my bones.

Then, before this ugly little sun had come up again, in the haggard, predawn glimmering of the pool, I saw a shape of genuine substance. A shape that wasn't Bracero. A shape floating over the pool.

It was a medieval vision, a fever picture out of Dante.

I screamed into the haggard silence. Inside, I am still screaming; the horrible no-sound of this inward screaming deafens my mind to my heart. Otherwise I couldn't even write this down.

Over the pool, stretched out there as if asleep on his back, a piece of our mangled descentcraft pulling his left leg down into the water, floated Arthur's corpse—horrible, horrible, horrible.

Mercilessly, Ogre's Heart came up to light this fever picture. And nothing I could do would stay its coming.

Maria Jill Ian calmed herself. For the second time in two weeks she waded into one of Cathadonia's pools and laid her husband to rest.

She caught Arthur's beautiful, hideous body in her arms. The force that had been holding him in state above the water flicked off and shifted Arthur's melancholy weight entirely to her.

A strong woman, Maria Jill Ian accepted this weight. She lowered her no-longer-human, plundered-of-dignity husband gently into the pool. The anchor she had tied to him two weeks ago pulled him down, but she refused to let him sink away. She supported him. Strangely, it seemed that invisible hands in the water helped her steady Arthur's body and slide him with precision into the silt below.

But Bracero still hung from the branch where he had remained during the whole of his "illness." Weeping quietly, Maria waded toward him.

"You did that for me, didn't you, Bracero? You brought me my husband because I said I wanted him beside me again."

A bitter gift. Over an incredible distance, a distance that it had taken them fourteen of Cathadonia's days to walk, Bracero had exerted his will upon the dead Arthur Ian and reeled him in with his mind—in the space of two nights and one waking period.

The Earth woman could not bring herself to condemn the eel-beast, the agent of her horror. Although her heart still beat savagely, and her eyes were raw with the sting of salt, she couldn't condemn him.

"No matter what I wish about my husband now, Bracero, let him sleep in peace," she said. "But understand me now: I can respect you for this, I can respect you for your sacrifice."

And Bracero was looking at her again, she saw, with eyes more like a feeble old man's than a devilfish's. His breathing had slowed, too. His limbs and tail appeared less rigid. Three hours later he rippled out of the tree's golden umbrella and took up his expectant, tripod stance only a meter away from her.

The Earth woman pulled on her boots and looked back toward the east, at Ogre's Heart climbing the pale, yellow sky.

"You're right," she said. "It's time to go again. We've got to forget this place. Arthur wouldn't want us to linger here."

They ate—Bracero ravenously, she only a little—and set off again. Toward the horizon, the western horizon.

We were able to walk, to slog westward, only a half day today—because of Bracero's most recent telekinetic exploit and its aftermath. I've resolved never to think of Arthur as I saw him this morning, but to remember him as he was when I met him, and as he grew to be over the years of our marriage.

I don't know why, but I haven't written here how wearying it is to trek across Cathadonia. The ground sucks at your feet, the marshy soil betrays your sense of balance, the lack of firmness tortures your knees. The muscles in my calves have become extremely hard, my upper thighs like supple marble. Even so, it's sometimes difficult to keep going.

Today, amazingly, I kept going by talking to Bracero. (I still haven't learned my lesson.) I told him everything I could remember about Arthur. Even quotes.

"I'm as hardy as you are," I told Bracero. "Men are hardy creatures. Arthur used to say, 'Men are the ultimate vermin, Maria, as indefatigable as cockroaches, capable of outlasting the universe.' I guess that's why I can keep up with you—go beyond you even."

Even though I can't really go beyond Bracero.

He doesn't have the same trouble with Cathadonia's marshiness that I do. His body is less heavy; his slender limbs are capable of skimming the ground almost without touching it. Usually he swims each of the pools that we come to and reemerges at the western shore, where he lets me catch up with him. But this afternoon, seeing that I wanted to talk, he stayed beside me every step and listened to my schoolgirl's chatter, my woman's wisdom, with the diplomacy of a probeship captain.

Once of twice he immersed himself in a pond, but he always came back, his glistening face radiating a depth of awareness about me, Maria Jill Ian, that I've seen before only in Arthur's face. And so I talked to him of Arthur, fed on Bracero's sympathy, and didn't tire—even though so much talking ought to have made me short of breath.

Once, when we rested and ate, I told him how important it was that we continue pursuing the horizon. I even recited to him from Arthur's favorite poem. And Bracero seemed to respond to the lines as if he understood and even approved the sentiment.

Tho' much is taken, much abides; and though
We are not that strength which in old days
Moved earth and heaven, that which we are, we are:
One equal temper of heroic hearts,
Made weak by time and fate, but strong in will
To strive, to seek, to find, and not to yield.

More than I ever thought I could lose has been taken from me, but Bracero's companionship and my own strength remain. These things abide. They make it possible to go on with free hearts, free foreheads, toward the westering sun of Cathadonia.

So be it, Arthur, so be it . . .

And so they went on, day after day, seeing no one, encountering terrain that repeated itself over and over again—though the fact that they now and again came across a tree that bore different kinds of fruit, or blossoms, or nut capsules, convinced Maria Jill Ian that they were actually making progress.

At last Maria remembered that Cathadonia had an ocean, that eventually these endlessly recurring pools would send out tentacles, link arms, and spill into one another like countless telepathic beings sharing a single liquid mind.

Fischelson, Arthur, and she had made one complete orbit of the planet in their descentcraft before attempting to land, and, she remembered, they had seen the great ocean from the air. How had they fallen so short of their goal? Indeed, what force had so cruelly wrenched the descentcraft from them and sped it raging planetward?

Such things never happened.

Now all Maria Jill Ian had to live for was her march upon that ocean. The ocean. The Sea of Stagnation, Fischelson had suggested before something unprecedented wiped out the two men's lives and her own memory. But now, but now, it couldn't be far, that ocean.

Day-by-day, Bracero kept pace with her—loping, swimming, outdistancing her when he wished, sometimes lagging playfully behind.

Then he began to lag behind more often, and there was

nothing playful in it. Frequently Maria had to call him, almost scold, in order to summon him on.

He came, but he came reluctantly. At each new pool he plunged in and made her wait while he swam five or six more turns than he had taken in the early days of their journeying.

But Maria Jill Ian always waited for him. To leave Bracero now would be to default on a trust. The two of them, after all, still belonged together. Despite his now chronic straggling, even Bracero seemed to recognize this.

One evening, as they prepared for sleep, Maria looked out over their pond and was struck by its size. It was several times larger than the one beside which their descentcraft had crashed. In fact, it had the dimensions of a small lake.

The sentinel tree that bordered this pool trailed its long leaves only in the shallows of the pool's margin, not out over the center.

Why hadn't she noticed before? All of the pools they had passed recently were at least of this size, the trees all as proportionately dwindled in stature as the one she leaned against now. Looking westward, she saw the silhouettes of far fewer trees etched into the lavender sky, than she had seen at twilight only a few days past. The change had occurred so gradually, so imperceptibly, that it was only now apparent to her.

"Bracero!" she called.

The lithe Cathadonian, who had long since learned his name, dropped gracefully from the tree and sat inches away from her.

"We're approaching the ocean, aren't we? Is that why you've been lagging? Does that have something to do with it?"

Bracero looked at her. His stare attempted both to answer her and to comprehend whatever it was compelling her toward the sea. Maria Jill Ian could read these things in the creature's face.

"Let me try to explain," she said. "I'm going toward your great ocean because Arthur, Nathan Fischelson, and I were trying to reach it when something happened to us. Second, I'm going there because all life on Earth, my own planet, arose in the seas. Do you understand, Bracero? That cellular memory is all I have left of home, a little planet in this spiral arm, ninety light-years distant.

"To me, your ocean represents ours.

"That must be how it is. And our oceans whisper to me across the light-years—with the surf noises of Earth, the seething of our species' spawning place."

Maria Jill Ian put her hand to her face. What she had just spoken filled her with an indefinable fear of the cosmos—of its infinite capacity to awe, to stagger, to overwhelm.

"And third," she said finally, "your ocean draws me on because it lies there, to the west. . . ."

I'm afraid. This time is like the other, when I awoke and saw Arthur floating above the dawnlit pool.

But it isn't dawn, it's late afternoon, and in our slender willow Bracero hangs suspended with the glazed look and the catatonic rigidity of that last time. But this, this is the fifth day, and he hasn't eaten or drunk since this violent trance began. His body is incredibly hot.

I'm afraid because the planet seems to be in sympathy with Bracero's efforts, whatever they are.

Two days ago I deserted Bracero and began walking again, in hopes that he would come out of his trance and follow. Instead, when I reached the one semifirm passageway between the two lakes west of here, their surfaces were suddenly riven with roaring waterspouts that reared up taller than the sentinel willows on their banks. The waterspouts rained torrents on the isthmus where I hoped to pass.

I had to turn back. When I reached Bracero, he was swinging more violently than ever, rocking feverishly.

I'm afraid because even though he calmed a little after my departure-and-return, all of Cathadonia still seems a part of his effort.

Several times a day a waterspout forms on this lake and on all the lakes that I can see from here. These funnels snarl and pirouette, flashing light and color like giant prisms.

I think perhaps Bracero has enlisted, telepathically, the aid of all his people. From all their individual pools they strain with him in this new enterprise, working through Bracero as if he were the principal unit in their mind link.

I'm afraid because the skies have several times clouded over during the middle of the day, eclipsing Ogre's Heart and suffusing the world in indigo blackness.

Then the rains fall.

Then the clouds strip themselves away, as in time-lapse sequences, and shred themselves into thin wisps that let the glaring light of Ogre's Heart pour down again.

Even now I can feel the wind rising, the planet trembling. Bracero seems vexed to nightmare by his own rocking, metronomic ecstasy. I'm afraid, I'm afraid. . . .

On the sixth day the wind was of hurricane force, and Maria Jill Ian heard the voices of Cathadonia's great ocean calling to her through the gale. She could scarcely hear herself think, but she heard these phantom voices as if they were siren-crooning from the inside of her head.

Astonishingly, Bracero clung with uncanny strength to his branch. Although his head and torso lifted and fell with every gust, it seemed that nothing could shake him loose.

Maria held on to the bole of their willow and kept her eyes closed Was the world ending? At last she risked being blown to her death; she let go of the tree, pulled off her foil overtunic, stripped it into ragged pieces. With these, she lashed herself to the willow and waited for the storm to end, or for her life to go out of her.

All that day and all that night Cathadonia was riven by merciless tempests.

The great ocean to the west sang hauntingly. Maria Jill Ian had fever visions of gigantic creatures several times Bracero's size, but otherwise just like him, boiling the seas with their prodigious minds and feeding limitless power into the receptacle and conductor that Bracero had become.

A psychic umbilical from the seas fed the poor creature, kept him alive, channeled energy into his every brain cell.

And all through the sixth day and night the voices persisted.

The seventh day broke clear and cold. Ogre's Heart showed its wan, sickly crest on the eastern horizon and the lake surfaces twinkled with muted light.

Maria unlashed herself and slid down the tree to the wet ground. She slept. She awoke to find Bracero in her lap, the first time he had permitted her to touch him—although he had often come achingly close. His body was rubbery and frail. His eyes were narrow and strange. Nothing about him seemed familiar. Still, she stroked his dry flesh and spoke to him a string of soothing nonsense words.

Together they waited.

At last, far away to the west, she saw a rounded shape rising over the horizon, looming up as if to intercept Ogre's Heart on its afternoon descent. The shape, a planet, cleared Cathadonia's edge and floated up into the sky like a brown and crustily wrinkled balloon.

It was Earth.

She knew at once it was Earth. She knew despite the fact that its atmosphere had been heated up, boiled off, and ripped away in the colossal, psychokinetic furnace of Bracero's people's minds. It was a lifeless, battered shell that floated out there now, not an ocean upon it.

Maybe they had brought it to her in hopes that she would rest satisfied with the gift and leave off her assault on the great ocean. They had dislodged Earth from its orbit, hurled it into the continuum of probeships and nothingness, and drawn it through that surreal vacancy to Cathadonia.

Now, for the first time since the creation of its solar system, Cathadonia had a moon.

Bracero is dead. He brought me my planet out of love, I'm sure of it. How do I bear up under this guilt?

Tomorrow I walk west again. . . .

Love or vengeance. Which of these prompted Bracero to carry out the will of his people? Maria Jill Ian felt sure it was love. But we, you and I, aware of more substantive factors than this poor Earth woman had at hand, you and I may reach a different conclusion.

The answer, of course, is implicit in the story. Perhaps I ought to stop. Imprudently, I choose to add a sort of epilogue. All stories have sequels, written or unwritten, and I don't want you going away from this one believing it solely a love story with a monstrously ironic conclusion. I'm interested in human as well as alien motivation, and you don't want to believe that all of humankind died as the result of an incomprehensible force, a force superior in kind and in quality to our own technological achievements.

Very well. It wasn't so.

Although Earth was still officially the "home" world of our species, men had not lived there in great numbers for several centuries. The entire planet had become a sanctuary, a preserve seeded back into wilderness, and perhaps only a thousand human beings lived there as wardens, keepers, physicians, gardeners, biologists, ecological experts. Men and women of good will.

All of them died, every one of them. Nearly twice as many human beings as (if you'll pardon the expression) squiddles who were slaughtered by the crewmen of the *Golden*.

It didn't take men long to discover what had happened to their world, the home of the primeval oceans in which we had spawned. The probeship *Nobel* returned from the Magellanic Clouds and found a double planet where there had once been only Cathadonia. They attempted radio contact with Fischelson and the Ians. Nothing. Well away from this puzzling twin system they hovered, mulling over ludicrous stratagems. After a time, they left.

In other vessels men came back.

They bombarded Cathadonia with nukes of every variety, concentrating on "The Sea of Stagnation." Then they swept the atmosphere clean of radiation and permitted men to go down to the surface.

Of course, they never found Maria Jill Ian, nor the apocryphal log from which you have just read.

How could they? Cathadonia now had tides—colossal, remorseless tides—that swept back and forth across her watery surface with cruel, eroding regularity. To find Maria would have required a miracle. But a legend grew up around her and the two men aboard her descentcraft, the legend you have just read, and almost everyone believed this legend to be true.

Worldshapers came.

In a hundred years they turned our runaway Earth into a paradise; restored to it an atmosphere, mountains, streams, lakes, greenery, everything but oceans; stocked it with every manner of beautiful and awesome beast from the colony worlds. Cathadonia and Earth, the most breathtaking double planet in the universe. When visitors began coming, hotels were built amid the landscaped gardens of our erstwhile spawning place, and people rose early in the morning to watch Ogre's Heart turn the seas of Cathadonia—across 300,000 kilometers of space—into mother-of-pearl mirrors.

Eventually, on Cathadonia, the downed descentcraft was recovered.

Men speculated. The legend surrounding Fischelson and the Ians took on a mystical quality.

This could not last.

Someone, some enterprising soul, developed the idea of retracing the route Maria Jill Ian had traversed during her abortive "odyssey" and of flying tourists over it in a skimmercraft piloted by a glib well-briefed guide. The idea caught on. Recorded voices now detailed every step of Maria and her Cathadonian sidekick.

" 'Men are hardy creatures,' " the recordings mimicked in their never-varying commentary. " 'Men are the ultimate vermin, Maria, as indefatigable as cockroaches.' "

Everyone aboard the skimmercrafts nodded sagely at the profundity of these observations.

No one ever asked for his money back.

THE BLEEDING MAN

Craig Strete

*Though this was the last story in the last 1974
issue of* Galaxy, *it may well be the farthest out.
The author is the first American Indian to become
a successful science fiction writer. We mention this
not for any racist reason but because the particular
philosophy of this story is derived from that culture rather than from Western thinking and there's
a real intrinsic difference.*

*The medicine shaker, the bone breaker. I have seen and
been all these. It is nothing but trouble.*

*I have sat on the good side of the fire. I have cried over
young women. It is nothing but trouble.*

Miss Dow leaned against the observation window. Her
stomach revolted and she backed away. Unable to quell the
nausea rising within her she clamped a hand to her mouth.

Dr. Santell gently took her arm, led her away from the window and helped her to a couch facing away from the observation window.

Nausea passed; Miss Dow smiled weakly. "You did warn
me," she said.

Dr. Santell did not return the smile. "It takes getting used
to. I'm a doctor and immune to gore, but still I find it unset-
tling. He's a biological impossiblity."

"Not even human," Miss Dow suggested.

"That's what the government sent you here to decide," said
Dr. Santell. "Frankly, I'm glad he's no longer my responsibility."

"I want to look at him again."

Santell shrugged, lit a syntho. Together they walked back to
the observation window. He seemed amused at her discomfort.

Again, Miss Dow peered through the window. This time it
was easier.

A young man, tall and well-muscled, stood in the middle of

the room. He was naked. His uncut black hair fell to the small of his back.

His chest was slit with a gaping wound that bled profusely; his legs and stomach were soaked with blood.

"Why is he smiling? What is he staring at?" she asked, unable to take her eyes off the figure before her.

"I don't know," said Dr. Santell. "Why don't you ask him."

"Your sense of humor escapes me," said Miss Dow through tightly closed lips.

Dr. Santell grinned and shrugged. His synthetic cigarette reached the cut-off mark and winked out. The butt flashed briefly as he tossed it into the wall disposal.

"Doesn't everything?" suggested Dr. Santell, trying not to laugh at his little joke.

Miss Dow turned away from the window. Her look was sharp, withering. "Tell me about him," she snapped, each word like ice. "How did he get—that way?"

His amusement faded. He licked his lips nervously, nodded. "He has no name, at least no official name. We call him Joe. Sort of a nickname. We gave him that name about—"

"Fascinating," interrupted Miss Dow, "but I didn't come here to be entertained by some droll little tale about his nickname."

"Friendly, aren't you?" asked Santell, drily. A pity, he thought. If she knew how to smile she might have seemed attractive.

"The government doesn't pay me to be friendly. It pays me to do a job." Her voice was cold, dispassionate. But she turned to face Dr. Santell in such a way that she would not see the bleeding man. "How long has he been like this?"

"It's all in my report. If you'd like to read it I could—"

"I'd prefer a verbal outline first. I'll read your report later; I trust that it is a thorough one." She eyed him sharply.

"Yes, quite thorough," Dr. Santell replied, the polite edge in his voice wearing thin.

He turned away from Miss Dow, gazed in at the bleeding man. His words were clipped, impartial. "He is approximately twenty-three years old and has been as he is now since birth."

"Incredible!" said Miss Dow, fascinated in spite of herself. "All this is documented?"

"Completely. There is no possibility of fakery. Nor point either, for that matter."

"Just as you say," echoed Miss Dow, "what have you done to try to cure it? Is it some form of stigmata?"

Dr. Santell shook his head. "If this is stigmata, it is the most extreme case this world will ever see. Besides, it is inconceivable that a psychosomatic illness could cause such a drastic biological malfunction."

"But surely some sort of surgery?" began Miss Dow. "Some sort of chemical therapy would—"

Dr. Santell shook his head emphatically. "We've tried them all in the seven years he's been here. Psycho-chemistry, primal reconditioning, bio-feedback tried singly and together; none have had any effect. He's a biological impossibility."

"What is his rate of bleeding?" she asked.

"It varies," said Dr. Santell. "Somewhere between two and three pints an hour."

"But it's not possible!" exclaimed Miss Dow. "No one can—"

"He can and does," interrupted Dr. Santell. "He doesn't do anything normally. I can give you ten reasons why he should be dead. Don't ask me why he isn't."

Miss Dow turned her head around and stared at the silent figure standing in the center of the room. The bleeding man had not moved. The blood flowed evenly from the chest wound, gathering in a coagulating pool at his feet.

"I've had enough." She turned away from the window. "Show me to my office. I'm ready to read that report now."

Two hours later, the last page of Dr. Santell's report slipped from nerveless fingers. The bleeding man lay outside the parameters of human biology. By all rights he should have been dead, indeed, could never have lived. Her hands were a little unsteady as she punched in Dr. Santell's office on the videophone. His face appeared on the screen—and it was flushed.

"Report to me immediately," Miss Dow snapped.

"I doubt it, sweetheart," said Dr. Santell, grinning. "I'm off the case, remember?" He drank something out of a dark tumbler.

"You're drinking!" snapped Miss Dow.

"Now that you mention it," admitted Dr. Santell agreeably. He gave her a lopsided grin. "Perhaps you would care to join me?"

"You are a disgusting, undisciplined lout. And I should like to remind you that you are still responsible to me. You may be discharged from this case in your professional capacity, but your standing orders are to cooperate with me in any way possible."

"So I'm cooperating," muttered Dr. Santell. "I'll stay out of your way, you stay out of mine."

"I won't tolerate this!" she raged. "Do you realize to whom you are talking?"

Dr. Santell thought that over slowly. His face tightened. He did realize who she was. It sobered him a little. He took another drink from the tumbler to compensate.

"Are you sober enough to answer a few questions?"

He thought that over for a while too. "I'm drunk enough to answer any questions you have. I don't think I could answer them sober," he said.

"I am trying to be understanding," said Miss Dow, a note of conciliation in her voice. "I realize it is quite natural for you to resent me. After all, I am responsible for your termination at this installation."

Dr. Santell shrugged it off. He took another drink from the tumbler.

"We're both professionals, Dr. Santell," reasoned Miss Dow. "We can't let emotional considerations enter into this. There is no place for emotion here. Our goals must be—"

"Hell! That's easy for you to say!" growled Dr. Santell. "You don't have any!"

"That's quite enough, thank you," said Miss Dow, pressing her lips together in a tight, angry line.

"No, it's not enough—" started Dr. Santell. "You can't—"

"The subject is closed!" she shouted.

There was an uneasy silence.

Miss Dow broke it by changing the subject. "What about his parents?" she asked.

"Didn't you read my report?"

"It said they committed suicide. It did not specify or go into any details. I have to know more than that. Your report was supposed to be thorough. You didn't list your sources of information on his early life, for one thing. I need to know—"

"Ask Nahtari. He can tell you everything," he said. He shrugged as if to say it was out of his hands.

"Who?"

"Nahtari. His uncle. He comes every week to visit his nephew. Nahtari used to exhibit him at the carnival until we discovered him and brought him here. If you'll turn to the financial report near the back, you will see that we pay him a small gratuity for the privilege of studying his nephew. We pay him by the week and he stops in to pick up his check and talk to his relative."

"Did you say he talks to his relative?"

"Yeah. It's pretty strange. Nahtari talks to Joe every week for an hour. I don't know if Joe understands anything that is said to him or even if Nahtari cares if he understands. I've never heard Joe respond in any way, not in the seven years I've been here."

"When does this Nahtari make his weekly visit?"

"He's here now in my office. He brings me a pint of whiskey every week. Makes it himself. You'd never believe how good—"

Miss Dow hit the dial-out button viciously, cutting him off in mid-sentence.

She pushed the door open to Dr. Santell's office. She hadn't bothered to knock. Dr. Santell had his feet propped up on the edge of his desk. He held a drink in one hand and a deck of cards in the other. Across the desk from him sat a grey headed Indian dressed in faded blue jeans, cracked leather boots and a tattered flannel shirt.

"I'll see your dime and raise you a dime," said Dr. Santell, slamming a dime onto the pile of change on the desk between them.

"Are you Nahtari?" demanded Miss Dow, coming into the room. The two studiously ignored her.

"It depends," said the old Indian, not looking up from his cards. "I'll meet your dime and raise you a quarter."

Dr. Santell bit his lip. "You're bluffing! I know you don't have that other ace!"

Miss Dow marched up to the desk, snatched the cards out of Dr. Santell's hands.

Dr. Santell pounded his desk in anger. "Stupid bitch! I had him beat!" He tried to collect the torn cards in his lap.

"Is she some kind of nut?" asked Nahtari, holding his cards out of harm's way.

Dr. Santell dumped the torn pieces of cards on the top of the desk and sighed. "Yeah. A government nut. She's in charge of Joe now."

Nahtari scowled and laid his cards face up on the desk. "And that means she wants to ask me about my relative."

"It certainly does," said Miss Dow. "Would you like to come to my office?"

Nahtari shrugged. There seemed to be no way to avoid it.

"You are owing me twelve dollars," he said to Dr. Santell as he rose to leave the room.

"Don't I always," growled Dr. Santell, staring at the ace that Nahtari had had after all.

"Sit down, Nahtari. This may take a while. I have a great many questions I want to ask you." She put a new cartridge in her tape machine and turned it on.

"If Dr. Santell had taken down all facts from before when I tell him I would not having to be saying again," said Nahtari. "I get tired of telling the story and having no one taking down so I don't have to do all over again."

Miss Dow patted the tape machine. "Don't worry about it," she assured him. "This recorder will make a permanent record of everything you say. I guarantee you won't have to tell it again."

"You going to listen and take down no matter what?"

"Every word," she replied.

She started to ask a question but Nahtari held up his hand. "Let me tell whole story," said Nahtari. "It will be a saving of time and you can ask questions after if you have any. I want to get this over before too long. Got to catch Dr. Santell before he leave with my twelve dollar."

Nahtari scratched his chest over his right shirt pocket.

"That sounds all right to me," agreed Miss Dow. "Could you start with his parents? I'd like to know—"

"He killed them."

"What?" Miss Dow was stunned.

"He killed them," repeated Nahtari matter-of-factly. "I was there the day he was born. His father and mother died within an hour of his birthing. He killed them."

Miss Dow was confused. "But how did it happen? How could—"

"You was not going to ask questions until I finished," accused Nahtari, dragging the back of his hand insolently across his nose.

Miss Dow settled back into her seat with a tight-lipped smile. She motioned for him to continue.

"His parents were medicine people. They were people of great power. My brother was one of the strong ones. They had this child stronger than them."

Miss Dow made a face. "You don't expect me to believe in primitive super—"

"I am expecting of you to keep your stupid mouth shut so this telling can be done and over with. I want to tell this so you will no longer pester me when I come to see my relative. I know all of your kind of government people. You harass a person—"

"Tell the story!" rasped Miss Dow. "For Christ sakes, just tell the story!" She drummed her fingers impatiently on the desk.

"My brother and his woman were filled with the sickness of the world. I knew that my brother did not want to live. His wife knew this and was content to go with him. Then when they had decided the road, she became heavy with child. They had no expecting of this. They became uncertain and did not know the way. But they could not change their decision for the living of the child. They went into the mountains, looking for their road. It was in the fifth month of the child in her belly."

Miss Dow sighed impatiently and settled back in her chair. It looked to be a long story, unrestricted by the inclusion of anything factual. Already she regretted asking him for information.

"They were high in the mountains. They laid down for dying but something strange happened. The child began speaking to them. The child was angry. They ran to the high places, to throw themselves off before the power of the child got too strong for them. But the child stopped them at the edge of the cliff and turned them around. The child forced them back down the mountain. And for four months, they were prisoners of the child."

"Are you seriously telling me that—" began Miss Dow with disgust.

Nahtari snorted contemptuously and passed his hands in front of his eyes. His eyes seemed to be focused on some far horizon. His voice mocked hers. "I just had a vision. I saw you and Dr. Santell embraced upon the ground and then suddenly crushed by a falling outhouse."

"I'm not laughing," said Miss Dow. She wasn't laughing.

"Somebody is," said Nahtari with a straight face. "I knew you was going to not let me finish the story and take it all down so I don't have to tell it again. Nobody ever lets me finish my story," complained Nahtari.

"Christ! I don't blame them!" said Miss Dow. "I've never heard such an outrageous piece of trash." She turned the tape machine off. "You may have all the time in the world but I haven't got time to listen to this idiocy!" She stood up and marched around the desk. "When you leave, shut the door."

Nahtari came around the desk and sat down in her chair. He tilted the chair back and rested his bootheels on the desk. He turned the tape recorder microphone around so that it pointed at him. He pushed the recording button and began talking into the machine.

"You bet this time, record is made of all the facts," he said and went on with the story. "For four months, they were prisoners of the child. Five days before he was born, the child began to fear leaving the belly. The fear did not last long but it lasted long enough for his father to put poison in their food without the child's knowing. They ate this poison, the mother, the father and the child.

"The child felt the poison and changed it into water in his belly. He felt great sadness in his heart and an anger because they did not want him to live. They did not want him born into a world they had grown sick of. It was not their right to choose for him because his power was greater than theirs. He did not change the poison flowing through them to water. His hatred was at them for they had let the world beat them. They began the agony of poison dying but they could not die.

"I sat with them through this time. I sat with my brother and my sister by law and they told me these things through their agony. They screamed to die but the child was punishing them for letting the world beat them. I, Nahtari, did not want to see the child born into this world. I feared his coming. There was nothing I could do. He came to birth.

"It was not a child like expected. He bled. His chest was bleeding. I had expected hot roaring fires. I had expected a child of frightful appearance. It was but a small baby that bled and could not talk.

"The father pulled the baby up and beat him into breathing. He laid the baby on the bed and went outside the house. After a little while, my sister by law got to her feet, swaying on dizzy legs, and she staggered out after him. I tried to stop the bleeding of the baby chest but I was too scared about my brother and sister by law. I ran outside. They laid side by side in the black dirt of the garden. There were dead and five days decayed.

"I took the little one into my home but the bleeding sickened my old woman and she died. So I took the bleeding one to the traveling show. The white people there did not sicken and die at the sight of his bleeding.

"In lines all around the tent they would stand to pay good money to see the bleeding one. They all wanted to see him bleeding and they were not sickened by it and they did not die. But the government people came and took the bleeding man from me and made me sign little pieces of paper and gave me money so they could do what they do. I turned him over to the government ones and that is all there is to the story and it is the truth.

"Now I come every week to talk to him. I know he is too powerful to have a name. I am waiting for him. I am telling so I will not have to tell it again and so that this warning is given to all who would have dealings with him. He is not ready to do what he will one day do. Do not walk in his shadow. Leave him alone for he is not you. For twenty-three years he has been gathering power. That is all I have to say."

He switched off the tape machine, smiling to himself because there was no one to hear it. He closed the door carefully behind him and went looking for Dr. Santell and his twelve dollars.

Miss Dow pushed open the door cautiously. She was not sure if she had the stomach for what she was doing. But making up her mind, she stepped into the room. She kept telling herself that he was perfectly harmless.

The drain in the center of the floor was stopped up with clotted blood. He stood in a shallow pool of his own blood. His body was motionless, his breathing just barely perceptible by a slight rising and falling of his chest. The blood flowed steadily to the floor.

"Can you hear me?" she asked nervously. She shut the door behind her. She kept her eyes on his face. He stared at her but gave no sign that he had heard her. He seemed to be in no pain, despite the stream of blood flowing down his chest.

"I'm not going to hurt you." She approached him slowly with a small, glass lab beaker. Averting her eyes slightly, she placed the glass container below the wound. She felt a little foolish for having spoken to him. It was obvious to her now that he was little better than a cretin and that he could not understand a word she said.

She stood there awkwardly, the glass beaker filling with his blood. The naked man seemed unaware of her presence, yet still she felt an unreasonable fear. There was something frightening about the still figure. Something threatening, otherworldly in the steady flow of blood down his chest. He did not seem vulnerable. Rather it was as if the world were too insignificant for him to notice it.

She backed away with a full glass of his blood. She felt better with each step she took. He stared at her, no expression on his face, his eyes unusually bright. She had felt very uncomfortable under his stare.

Miss Dow had turned and started out the door, watching him all the while. Suddenly he moved. She turned quickly. Fear rose in her like a tide. The bleeding man cupped a hand beneath the wound in his chest.

Slowly, he brought his hands to his lips and drank. Miss Dow fainted.

Dr. Santell found her in the doorway. A tiny, red pool of fresh blood was beginning to blacken on the floor beside her head. The glass beaker she had brought into the room was gone. "What happened?" asked Dr. Santell, bending over the couch, his voice oddly gentle despite its gruffness. "Here—take a sip of this," he said, offering her a small glass of whiskey. "It'll steady your nerves."

She was too weak to refuse. The whiskey burned her throat and made her cough. He made her take another sip. It almost made her gag but it seemed to help. A touch of color reappeared in her face.

"He—he—he drank his own blood!" she whispered, tottering on the edge of hysteria.

Dr. Santell leaned forward eagerly. His features sharpened, his manner became intent and forceful. "Are you sure?" he demanded.

"Yes, I'm sure," she said with a trace of her normal sharpness.

"Are you sure—absolutely sure—he drank his own blood?" he asked again, impatiently. The answer seemed unusually important to him.

"Of course, I'm sure, damn it! It was absolutely disgusting!" She wrinkled up her nose. "That revolting animal did it on purpose! Just because I collected a beaker of—"

Dr. Santell suddenly became greatly agitated. "You collected a glass of blood?" he husked.

She nodded, bewildered by his strange behavior.

"God! It's happened again," he muttered. "It's happened again!" A look of dread passed over his face.

"What the devil are you talking about?" demanded Miss Dow.

"When I heard you scream, I started running. I was the first one to reach you. You were sprawled in the doorway. There was a big bloodstain beside your head on the floor. There was no glass on the floor of the room and it wasn't in the hallway."

"Don't be ridiculous! I had it with me. Isn't this an awfully big fuss to be making over a—"

Dr. Santell turned his back on her and dialed security.

"Hobeman? This is Santell. Have room 473 searched for a glass beaker. Delay his feeding time if you have to, but find that beaker!" He shut off the view screen.

He looked at Miss Dow. Her face was blank with bewilderment. Before she could ask a question he began, "Something strange has developed in the last few weeks. Our monitors have been picking up unusual activity levels. They aren't sophisticated enough to tell us exactly what's happening but his heartbeat and galvanic skin responses have been fluctuating wildly."

"But what does that have to do with the glass?" asked Miss Dow.

"I'm coming to that. A week ago, during one of his strange activity levels, the observation port on the wall of his room disappeared."

Miss Dow's face registered shock. "Disappeared? How is that possible?"

Dr. Santell was grim. "I have no idea. We found traces of melted glass on the floor of the room. But what disturbs me the most is that we could detect no coronary activity. For two hours his blood was circulating but his heart wasn't functioning."

"He's not human, is he?" said Miss Dow.

"I don't know," said Dr. Santell, staring off into space. "I just don't know."

He pushed the carts through the door. The bleeding man stared at him as he had stared for the seven years he had been there.

"Soup's on, Joe," said the man with the feeding carts.

Two men hidden from view by the door, were examining two streaks of melted glass on the floor.

"Hey, hold up there," said one of the men. "He's not to be fed until we've finished our search."

"I won't get in the way. What's disappeared this time?"

"Nothing important," grumbled one of the men. "Just a glass jar from the lab."

"Shame on you, Joe," said the cartman, waving a finger at the motionless figure in the center of the room. "You oughten to be stealing stuff like that." He opened the top of his cart and took out a pair of gloves.

"It won't hurt if I feed him will it? I don't have to hose him down until you guys have finished," he said, pulling the gloves over his hands.

"Go ahead. We aren't going to find anything anyway."

The cart man opened a panel on the side of the cart and brought out a bowl of raw meat. He sat it on the floor in front of the bleeding man. From the other cart he got a large bowl of uncooked vegetables and a large wooden ladle.

He detached a water hose from the wall and started backing toward the bleeding man, uncoiling the hose as he walked. When he got to the end of the hose, he turned around.

The bleeding man had overturned the feeding bowls with his feet. He was drinking his own blood from cupped hands.

"This is what you are looking for," said Dr. Santell, handing Miss Dow a clipboard. "His blood type is O lateral. We've run hundreds of tests on it and it seems to be perfectly normal blood, a little more resistant to some diseases than ordinary blood but otherwise normal. It's too bad the government won't let us use his blood. He's a universal donor and at the rate he produces blood, I'll bet he could supply Intercity all by himself."

"But that's just the point. We *are* going to use his blood," said Miss Dow. "We are going to use a lot more besides. That's why I was sent here."

"The government's changed its policy, then?" asked Dr. Santell. "Why?"

"We've given transfusions of his blood to prisoners and it seems to have no bad effects. Tell me, you've studied him for seven years. Do you have any idea how something like him is possible?"

Dr. Santell lit a synthetic cigarette slowly. He gave her a curious look.

"Did you listen to Nahtari's explanation?"

"That lunacy," sniffed Miss Dow. "I think we should pay a little more attention to a chromosomal mutation theory than some wild story from some primitive like Nahtari."

Dr. Santell shrugged. "It doesn't really matter what caused it. I couldn't even make an educated guess. His version is the only evidence we have."

"Confine yourself to specifics, please," said Miss Dow. "What biological evidence do we have?"

"There is biological evidence pointing to chromsomal differentiation. He has sixty-four paired chromosomes. I have been unable so far to determine their exact structure. He seems to have all the normal ones. Technically, that makes him a member of our species, I suppose. But it's those extra chromsomes that are so unusual. They seem to be entirely new structures unlike anything we are familiar with. It must be something outside our experience. I think I pointed this out in more detail in my report."

"But technically, he is human?" asked Miss Dow.

"I would say he is," said Dr. Santell.

"Very well. Then I am going to give the final go-ahead on this project," said Miss Dow.

"And what project is that?"

"We're going to transfer him to the military dome at Intercity where he will be dissected for tissue regeneration. Hopefully, his cellular matrix will reproduce like functioning biological constructs."

"What!" Dr. Santell jumped to his feet. "You're not serious! That would be murder! Matrix reconstruction from tissue cultures has never advanced beyond the experimental stage! We don't have the technology to stimulate the reproduction of brain and nerve tissue! Good lord, woman, you can't seriously—"

"I am quite aware of our shortcomings in the field of tissue regeneration," said Miss Dow coldly. "For years, our work in this area has been little better than a waste of time and materials. We have yet to produce a successful unit with a well-developed nervous system. Nor have we been able to successfully clone an individual. These matters, however, are not relevant to this case."

"Not relevant! You'll kill him! And to what purpose? A line of research that you yourself admitted has been a waste of time!" stormed Dr. Santell, his face flushed with anger.

"Be careful, Dr. Santell," she cautioned him. "I don't think I am happy with your choice of words. We are not going to kill him. Many of our first tissue regeneration experiments are still alive—alive after a fashion, that is. Their bodies still function, their cells still grow, it is only their minds that are dead." She smiled.

"It's still murder! You have no right!" Dr. Santell looked away from Miss Dow. He had suddenly realized that the things he was saying could be considered treason.

"When's the last time you had an attitude check, Dr. Santell?" asked Miss Dow. "I almost thought I heard you say something that was opposed to the wishes of our government. You did agree that my patient can be made ready for transport tomorrow morning, didn't you?"

"Of course," said Dr. Santell. "He will be ready."

"And did I hear you use the word *murder*, Dr. Santell? I *did* hear you use the word! I'm sure General Talbot will be most interested in your attitude."

Dr. Santell turned and began walking out of the room. He knew that he was in trouble and nothing he could say would make it any better.

"Dr. Santell!"

He turned to look at her.

"I'm really not hard to get along with," said Miss Dow. "You have the reputation of being a brilliant scientist. I've handled your type before. I am willing to overlook a small measure of eccentricity. But I draw the line at treason."

His expression remained blank.

"It's only natural that you're defensive about your patient after seven years," she soothed. "You have personalized him, lost your objectivity. But you must know as well as I do that the bleeding man is a brainless vegetable, hopelessly retarded since birth. You can see that, surely?"

Dr. Santell stared wordlessly.

"It would be a lot easier for me," she continued, "if I had your cooperation on this thing. You've had seven years experience on this project and you could help us smooth over any rough spots we might encounter. This isn't exactly a normal case. It will require special procedures. Procedures that your cooperation will make possible." She smiled at him. "My report could be a very positive one. It depends on you."

Dr. Santell forced himself to smile. "Believe me," he said, "I shall cooperate in any way I can. I apologize for my behavior."

Miss Dow nodded. "Good. Now, how much blood could, let's say, ten of his regenerations, produce in a forty-eight hour period?"

Dr. Santell began punching up figures on his desk calculator.

The bleeding man continued to drink. The men studying the glass streaks on the floor had fled.

A security guard unlocked the door and looked into the room. The bleeding man did not seem aware of the other's presence. A call went out for Dr. Santell.

Dr. Santell, followed by Miss Dow, arrived just in time to see the heavy door buckling outward.

"He's gone berserk!" screamed Miss Dow, as the door was battered off its hinges. The bleeding man walked through the wreckage of the door. He advanced upon them, a crimson trail of blood behind him on the floor.

Miss Dow fled, screaming. Dr. Santell stood his ground. The bleeding man brushed him lightly as he walked past. He looked neither to left or right. He strode down the corridor, moving quickly, relentlessly.

Dr. Santell ran in front of him and tried to push him to a halt. His hands slipped, coming away blood soaked. His efforts to stop him were futile. Through the plasti-glass corridor walls he could see the security guards gathering around Miss Dow at the corridor exit. Dr. Santell took hold of the bleeding man's arm and tried to drag him to a stop but found himself being dragged instead. The bleeding man did not even break stride.

Miss Dow stood within a cordon of security men. Dr. Santell knew what she would order them to do even before the bleeding man smashed through the exit door.

"Aim for his head!" she shouted.

A burst of stunner fire took the bleeding man full in the face. He walked several steps, then toppled.

Dr. Santell rushed to his side and put a hand on his chest. "He's still alive," he muttered to himself.

"Good shooting, men," congratulated Miss Dow. "A couple of you men carry the body down to the lab."

"Is there very much damage to his head?" she asked. "Is he still alive? Not that it matters. We can't risk another episode like this. We might as well do the dissection here. It'll make him easier to handle. We'd have to ship him frozen anyway now that we know more about his capabilities."

The security men carried the body away.

"He's still alive," Dr. Santell said, pronouncing each word slowly and distinctly. "He's very much alive."

Miss Dow had a surgical gown on and a mask. "Are you sure you can handle the dissection all by yourself, Dr. Santell? I could fly someone in to assist."

"Quite sure," said Dr. Santell, bending over the still form on the surgery table. "I'll begin soon. You'd better leave now."

"I'll be waiting at the military base in Intercity for the body," said Miss Dow. She came over to the table and stood beside him. Her voice was cold and emotionless as usual. "You realize I still must report your treasonable remarks to General Talbot."

Dr. Santell nodded, not looking in her direction.

"However, your behavior has shown marked improvement. That too will be noted in my report. Trying to stop this creature single-handedly in the corridor like you did was a very brave if somewhat foolish thing to do. You realize of course that the matter is out of my hands. General Talbot will be the one deciding, not I. Perhaps, after a short period of retraining, you may even be reassigned. A man of your reputation, I'm sure, will find it very easy to rejoin the fold. Only a fool—or a traitor—bucks the system."

Dr. Santell seemed not to be listening. He stuck a needle into the arm of the body on the dissection table.

"What a shame a body like that should have no mind," mused Miss Dow. "Just think of the power he must have in order to smash through those doors like he did."

"Yes," Dr. Santell replied tonelessly.

Miss Dow pulled her mask off and turned to leave.

"Wait," said Dr. Santell. "Before you go, could you hand me that box of clamps under the table here?"

She bent over and looked under the table. "I don't see any—"

His scalpel sliced through her right carotid artery. Her body jerked convulsively and she crashed heavily to the floor.

"Yes," said Dr. Santell with a strange look on his face. "It is always a shame to find a good body with a defective mind."

It took him a little over two hours to dissect her. By the time he finished, the stimulant he had injected into him had brought the bleeding man back to consciousness.

As he was putting her dismembered body into the liquid nitrogen packs for shipping, he kept his eyes on the body of the bleeding man. The body sat up slowly and opened its eyes. The head swiveled and the eyes regarded him. The eyes were alive with raw intelligence. The body slid off the table gracefully and stood up, the wound on his chest completely healed.

"I knew," said Dr. Santell. "I knew."

The medicine shaker, the bone breaker. I have seen and been all these. It is nothing but trouble.

I have sat on the good side of the fire. I have cried over young women. It is nothing but trouble.

These are the words I heard written in his skin. He made me kill her. I had to do it. I am not sorry. I knew. That is enough, knowing.

—Paul Santell

(This suicide note was found near the charred body of Dr. Paul Santell, who Intercity Police say, apparently soaked himself with an inflammable liquid and then set himself afire. Dr. Paul Santell, twice recipient of the Nobel Prize in psychochemistry, police report had been experiencing . . . —excerpt from Intercity Demographic Area Telepaper.)

The bleeding man cured of bleeding, walked without haste toward the door leading outside. He remembered the taste of blood, he who no longer had need of it. He pushed the door open and stepped outside. The sky pulled at him but he resisted for that last little moment. His feet touched the ground. His lungs filled with air. His eyes danced on the horizons of the world. Raising his hands into the air, he let the sky pull him away from the earth. He took the air in his lungs and thrust it out with a shout. Silently his lips formed words.

ly attracted his notice. Still it was time for one of his tedious trips to the creches and there was one likely possibility in West Virginia. He went there—and was disappointed into promising himself (for the fiftieth time) that he would thereafter make such visits by TV image. But then, having dragged himself to the general area, thought he might as well take a look at the Kentucky creche before returning home.

He expected nothing.

Yet he hadn't studied Randall's gene pattern for more than ten minutes before he was calling the Institute for a computer calculation. Then he sat back and perspired slightly at the thought that only a last-minute impulse had brought him, that without that impulse Randall would have been quietly cancelled. A drug would have soaked painlessly through his skin, into his bloodstream and he would have sunk into a peaceful sleep that gradually deepened into death. The drug had a twenty-three syllable official name, but William called it "nirvanamine"—as did everyone else.

William said, "What is his full name, matron?"

The creche-matron said, "Randall Nowan, scholar."

"No one!" said William, explosively.

"Nowan." The matron spelled it. "He chose it last year."

"And it meant nothing to you? It is pronounced *No one!* It didn't occur to you to report this young man last year?"

"It didn't seem—" began the matron, flustered.

William waved her to silence. What was the use? How was she to know? There was nothing in the gene-pattern to have given her warning. The usual textbook criteria was useless here. It was a subtle combination that William and his staff had worked out over a period of twenty years through experiments on autistic children—and a combination they had never actually seen in the flesh.

So close to cancelling!

Marco, the hard-head of the group, complained that the creches were too eager both to abort and to cancel. He maintained that all gene-patterns should be allowed to develop until initial screening, that there should be no cancellation without consultation with a homologist.

"There aren't enough homologists," William had told him.

"Well, we can at least run all gene patterns through the computer," said Marco.

"To save anything we can get for our own use?"

"For any homological use, here or elsewhere. We must study gene-patterns in action if we're to understand ourselves properly—and it is the abnormal and monstrous patterns that give us most information. Our experiments on autism have taught us more about homology than the sum total of existing knowledge on the day we began."

William, who still preferred the roll of the phrase 'the genetic physiology of man' to 'homology', shook his head. "Just the same, we've got to play it carefully. However useful we can claim our experiments to be, we exist on bare social permission, reluctantly given. We are playing with lives."

"Useless lives. Fit only for cancelling."

"A quick and pleasant cancelling is one thing. Our experiments, usually drawn-out and sometimes extremely unpleasant, are another."

"We help them sometimes," replied Marco.

"And we don't help them sometimes."

It was a pointless argument, really, for there was no way of settling it. What it came down to was that there were too few interesting abnormalities and no way of urging mankind to encourage a greater production. The trauma of the Catastrophe would never vanish in a dozen ways, including that one.

The hectic push toward space exploration could be traced back (and was, by some sociologists) to the knowledge of the fragility of the life-skein on the planet, thanks to the Catastrophe.

Well, never mind—that's another story.

There had never been anyone like Randall Nowan, not for William. The slow onset of autism characteristic only of that totally rare gene pattern meant that more was known about Randall than about any autistic patient before him. They even caught some last faint glimmers of his thought-processes in the laboratory—before he closed off altogether and finally shrank completely within the wall of his skin, unconcerned, unreachable.

Then they began the slow process whereby Randall, subjected for increasing lengths of time to artificial stimuli, yielded up the inner workings of his brain and gave clues thereby to the inner workings of all brains, those called normal as well as those similar to his own.

So vastly great was the data they were gathering that William began to feel his dream of reversing autism might be more than merely a dream. He felt a warm gladness at having chosen the name Anti-Aut.

He was almost at the height of the euphoria induced by the work on Randall when he received the call from Dallas, and the heavy pressure began—now, of all times—to abandon his work and take on a new problem.

Looking back on it later, he could never work out just what it was that finally led him to agree to visit Dallas. In the end, of course, he could see how fortunate it was—but what had persuaded him? Could he, even at the start, have had a dim, unrealized notion of the potential outcome? Surely, impossible.

Was it the unrealized memory of that printout-photograph of his brother? Surely, impossible.

But he let himself be argued into visiting the Project, and it was only when the micro-pile power unit changed the pitch of its soft hum and the agrav unit took over for the final descent that he remembered that photograph—at least consciously.

Anthony worked at Dallas and, William remembered now, at the Mercury Project. That was what the caption had referred to. He swallowed, as the soft jar told him the journey was over. This would be uncomfortable.

III

Anthony was waiting on the roof reception-area to greet the incoming expert. Not by himself, of course. He was part of a sizable delegation—the size itself was a grim indication of the desperation to which they had been reduced. Furthermore he was among the lower echelons; that he was there at all was only because it was he who had made the original suggestion.

He felt a slight but continuing uneasiness at the thought of that. He had put himself on the line. He had received considerable approval for it, but there had been the faint insistence always that it was *his* suggestion; if it turned out to be a fiasco, every one of them would move out of the line of fire, leaving him alone at point-zero.

There were occasions, later, when he brooded over the possibility that the dim memory of a brother in homology had suggested his thought. That might have been, but it didn't have to be. The suggestion was so sensible, so inevitable, that surely he would have had the same thought if his brother had been something as innocuous as a fantasy writer—or if he had had no brother at all, for that matter.

The problem was the inner planets—

The Moon and Mars were colonized. The larger asteroids and the satellites of Jupiter had been reached, and plans were in progress for a manned voyage to Titan, Saturn's large satellite. Yet even with plans underway for sending men to the outer Solar system there was still no chance of a manned approach to the inner planets, for fear of the Sun.

Venus was the less attractive of the two worlds within Earth's orbit. Mercury, on the other hand . . .

Anthony had not yet joined the team when Dmitri Large (he was quite short, actually) had given the talk that had moved the World Congress sufficiently to vote the appropriation that made the Mercury Project possible.

Anthony had listened to the tapes, and had heard Dmitri's presentation. Tradition was firm to the effect that it had been extemporaneous, and perhaps it was, but it had been perfectly constructed and held within it, in essence, every guideline followed by the Mercury Project since.

The chief point was that it would be wrong to hold inner-planet research in abeyance until technology had advanced to the point where a manned expedition through the rigors of Solar radiation would become feasible. Mercury was a unique environment that could teach much, and from Mercury's surface sustained observations could be made of the Sun that could not be made in any other way.

Provided a suitable man-substitute—a robot, in short— could be placed on the planet.

A robot with the required physical characteristics could be built. Soft-landings were as easy as kiss-my-hand. Yet once a robot landed, what next?

He could make his observations and guide his actions on the basis of those observations, but the Project wanted his actions to be intricate and subtle, at least potentially, and they were not at all sure what observations he might make.

To prepare for all reasonable possibilities and to allow for all the intricacy desired, the robot would need to contain a computer sufficiently complex and versatile to fall into the same asteroid with a mammalian brain.

Yet nothing like that could be miniaturized sufficiently to be used in the kind of robot they planned. Perhaps someday the positronic-path devices. that the roboticists were playing with might make it possible, but that someday was not yet.

The alternative was to have the robot send back to Earth every observation it made as it was made. A computer on Earth could then guide its every action on the basis of those observations. The robot's body, in short, was to be there, its brain here.

Once that decision was reached telemetrists became the key technicians. It was then that Anthony joined the Project as one of those who labored to devise methods for receiving and returning impulses over distances of from 50 to 140 million miles, toward, and sometimes past, a Solar disk that could interfere with those impulses in a most ferocious manner.

He took to his job with passion and (he firmly thought) with skill and success. It was he, more than anyone else, who had designed the three switching-stations that had been hurled into permanent orbit about Mercury. Each of them had the job of sending and receiving impulses from Mercury to Earth and from Earth to Mercury. Each was capable of resisting, more or less permanently, the radiation from the Sun, and more than that, each could filter out Solar interference.

Three equivalent Orbiters were placed at a distance of a little over a million miles from Earth, reaching north and south of the plane of the Ecliptic so that they could receive the impulses from Mercury and relay them to Earth—or vice versa —even when Mercury was behind the Sun and inaccessible to direct reception from any station on Earth's surface.

Which left the robot itself; a marvelous specimen of both the roboticists' and telemetrists' arts. The most complex of ten successive models, it was capable, with only a little over twice the volume and five times the mass of a man, of sensing and doing considerably more than a man—if it could be guided.

How complex a computer had to be to guide the robot made itself rapidly evident, however, as each response-step had to be modified to allow for possible variations in perception. And as each response-step itself enforced the certainty of greater complexity of possible variation in perceptions, the early steps had to be reinforced and made stronger. It built itself up endlessly, like a chess game, and the telemetrists began to use a computer to program the computer that designed the program for the computer that programed the robot-controlling computer.

There was nothing but confusion.

The robot was at a base in the Arizona desert and was working well. The computer in Dallas could not, however, handle him well enough; not even under perfectly known Earth conditions. How then—

Anthony remembered the day when he had made the suggestion. It was on 7-4-553. He remembered it, for one thing, because he remembered thinking that day that 7-4 had been an important holiday in the Dallas-region of the world among the pre-Cats half a millennium before—553 years before, to be exact.

It had been at dinner. (And a good dinner, too. There had been a careful adjustment of the ecology of the region and the Project personnel had high priority in collecting the food supplies that became available—so there was an unusual degree of choice on the menus, and Anthony had tried roast duck.)

The roast duck had made him somewhat more expansive than usual. Everyone was in a rather self-expressive mood, in fact, and Ricardo said, "We'll never do it. Let's admit it. We'll never do it."

There was no telling how many had thought such a thing how many times before, but it was a rule that no one said so openly. Open pessimism might be the final push needed for appropriations to stop (they had been coming with greater difficulty each year for five years now) and if there *were* a chance, it would be gone.

Anthony, ordinarily not given to extraordinary optimism, but now revelling over his duck, said, "Why can't we do it? Tell me why, and I'll refute it."

Ricardo's dark eyes narrowed at once to the challenge. "You want me to tell you why?"

"I sure do."

Ricardo swung his chair around, facing Anthony full. He said, "There's no mystery. Dmitri Large won't say so openly in any report but you know and I know that to run Mercury Project properly, we'll need a computer as complex as a human brain whether it's on Mercury or here, and we can't build one. So where does that leave us except to play games with the World Congress and get money for make-work and possible useful spinoffs?"

Anthony, a complacent smile on his face, said, "That's easy to refute. You've given us the answer yourself." (Was he playing games? Was it the warm feeling of duck in his stomach? The desire to tease Ricardo? Or did some unfelt thought of his brother touch him? There was no way, later, that he could tell.)

"What answer?" Ricardo rose. He was quite tall and unusually thin and he always wore his white coat unseamed. He folded his arms and seemed to be doing his best to tower over the seated Anthony like an unfolded meter-rule. "What answer?"

"You say we need a computer as complex as a human brain. All right, then, we'll build one."

"The point, you idiot, is that we can't—"

"*We* can't. But there are others."

"What others?"

"People who work on brains, of course. We're just solid-state mechanics. We have no idea in what way a human brain is complex, or where, or to what extent. Why don't we get in a homologist and have *him* design a computer?" With that Anthony took a huge helping of stuffing, savored it complacently. He could still remember, after all this time, the taste of the stuffing, though he couldn't remember in deatil what had happened afterward.

It seemed to him that no one had taken it seriously. There was laughter and a general feeling that Anthony had wriggled out of a hole by clever sophistry, so that the laughter was at Ricardo's expense. (Afterward, of course, *everyone* claimed to have taken the suggestion seriously.)

Ricardo blazed up, pointed a finger at Anthony and said, "Write that up. I *dare* you put that suggestion into writing." (At least, so Anthony's memory had it. Ricardo had, since then, stated his comment was an enthusiastic, "Good idea! Why don't you write it up formally, Anthony?")

Anthony put it in writing.

Dmitri Large had taken to it. In private conference, he had slapped Anthony on the back and had said that he had been speculating in that direction himself—though he did not offer to take any credit for it on the record. (Just in case it turned out to be a fiasco, Anthony thought.)

Dmitri Large conducted the search for the appropriate homologist. It did not occur to Anthony that he ought to be interested. He knew neither homology nor homologists—except, of course, his brother, and he had not thought of him. Not consciously.

So Anthony was up there waiting in the reception area, in a minor role, when the door of the aircraft opened and several men descended. In the course of the handshakes that began going around he found himself staring at his own face.

His cheeks burned and, with all his might, he wished himself a thousand miles away.

IV

More than ever William wished that the memory of his brother had come earlier. It should have—surely it should have.

But there had been the flattery of the request and the excitement that had begun to grow in him. Perhaps, he had deliberately avoided remembering.

To begin with there had been the exhilaration of Dmitri Large coming to see him—and in his own proper presence. He had come from Dallas to New York by plane and that had been very titillating for William, whose secret vice it was to read thrillers. In the thrillers men and women always traveled mass-wise when secrecy was desired. After all, electronic travel was public property—at least in the thrillers, where every beam of radiation that carried information was invariably bugged.

William had said so in a kind of morbid half-attempt at humor, but Dmitri hadn't seemed to be listening. He was staring at William's face and his thoughts seemed elsewhere. "I'm sorry," he said, finally. "You remind me of someone."

(Even that hadn't given it away to William. How was that possible?)

Dmitri Large was a small plump man who seemed to be in a perpetual twinkle even when he declared himself worried or annoyed. He had a round and bulbous nose, pronounced cheeks and softness everywhere. He emphasized his last name and said with a quickness that led William to suppose he said it often, "Size is not all the large there is, my friend."

In the talk that followed, William protested much. He knew nothing about computers. Nothing! He had not the faintest idea of how they worked or how they were programed.

"No matter, no matter," Dmitri said, shoving the point aside with an expressive gesture of the hand. *"We* know the computers; *we* can set up the programs. You just tell us what it is a computer must be made to do so that it will work like a brain and not like a computer."

"I'm not sure I know enough about how a brain works to be able to tell you that, Dmitri," said William.

"You are the foremost homologist in the world," said Dmitri. "I have checked that out carefully." That disposed of that.

William listened with gathering gloom. He supposed it was inevitable. Dip a person into one particular specialty deeply enough and long enough and he would automatically begin to assume that specialists in all other fields were magicians, judging the depth of their wisdom by the breadth of his own ignorance—and as time went on, William learned a great deal more of the Mercury Project than it seemed to him at the time that he would ever care to know.

He said at last, "Why use a computer at all, then? Why not have one of your own men, or relays of them, receive the material from the robot and send back instructions."

"Oh, oh, oh," said Dmitri, almost bouncing in his chair in his eagerness. "You see, you are not aware. Men are too slow to analyze quickly all the material the robot will send back—temperatures and gas pressures and cosmic ray fluxes and solar wind intensities and chemical compositions and soil textures and easily three dozen more items—and then try to decide on the next step. A human being would merely *guide* the robot, and ineffectively; a computer would *be* the robot.

"And then, too," he went on, "men are too fast, also. It takes radiation of any kind anywhere from ten to twenty-two minutes to make the round trip between Mercury and Earth, depending on where each is in its orbit. Nothing can be done about that. You get an observation, you give an order, but much has happened between the time the observation is made and the response returns. Men can't adapt to the slowness of the speed of light but a computer can take that into account. Come help us, William."

William said gloomily, "You are certainly welcome to consult me, for what good that might do you. My private TV beam is at your service."

"But it's not consultation I want. You must come with me."

"Mass-wise?" said William, shocked.

"Yes, of course. A project like this can't be carried out by sitting at opposite ends of a laser beam with a communications satellite in the middle. In the long run, it is too expensive, too inconvenient, and, of course, it lacks all privacy."

It *was* like a thriller, William decided.

"Come to Dallas," said Dmitri, "and let me show you what we have there. Let me show you the facilities. Talk to some of our computer men. Give them the benefit of your way of thought."

It was time, William thought, to be decisive. "Dmitri," he said. "I have work of my own here. Important work that I do not wish to leave. To do what you want me to do may take me away from my laboratory for months."

"Months!" said Dmitri, clearly taken aback. "My good William, it may well be years. But surely it will be your work."

"No, it will not. I know what my work is and guiding a robot on Mercury is not it."

"Why not? If you do it properly, you will learn more about the brain merely by trying to make a computer work like one, and you will come back here, finally, better equipped to do what you now consider your work. And while you're gone, will you have no associates to carry on? And can you not be in constant communication with them by laser beam and television? And can you not visit New York on occasion? Briefly."

William was moved. The thought of working on the brain from another direction did hit home. From that point on he found himself looking for exuses to go—at least to visit—at least to see what it was all like. He could always return.

Then there followed Dmitri's visit to the ruins of Old New York which he enjoyed with artless excitement (but then there was no more magnificent spectacle of the useless gigantism of the pre-Cats than Old New York.) William began to wonder if the trip might not give him an opportunity to see some sights as well.

He even began to think that for some time he had been considering the possiblity of finding a new bedmate, and it would be more convenient to find one in another geographical area where he would not stay permanently.

—Or was it that even then, when he knew nothing but the barest beginning of what was needed, there had already come to him, like the twinkle of a distant lightning-flash, an answer?

So he eventually went to Dallas and stepped out on the roof and there was Dmitri again, beaming. Then, with eyes narrowing, the little man turned and said, "I *knew*—what a remarkable resemblance!"

William's eyes opened wide and there, visibly shrinking backward, was enough of his own face to make him certain at once that Anthony was standing before him.

He read, very plainly, in Anthony's face a longing to bury the relationship. All William needed to say was, "How remarkable!" and let it go. The gene-patterns of mankind were complex enough, after all, to allow resemblances of any reasonable degree even without kinship.

But of course William was a homologist and no one can work with the intricacies of the human brain without growing insensitive as to its details, so he said, "I'm sure this is Anthony, my brother."

Dmitri said, "Your brother?"

"My father," said William, "had two boys by the same woman—my mother. They were eccentric people."

He then stepped forward, hand outstretched, and Anthony had no choice but to take it. The incident was the topic of conversation, the only topic, for the next several days.

V

It was small consolation to Anthony that William was contrite enough when he realized what he had done.

They sat together after dinner that night and William said, "My apologies. I thought that if we got the worst out at once that would end it. It doesn't seem to have done so. I've signed no papers, made no formal agreement. I will leave."

"What good would that do?" said Anthony ungraciously.

VI

William *had* tried, and as Anthony had predicted, the two had been left to work together. At first, they encountered others now and then and William had tried to use the shock value of the announcement that they were brothers since there was no use in denial. Eventually, that stopped and there came to be a purposeful non-interference. When William approached Anthony, or Anthony approached William, anyone else who might be present faded silently into the walls.

They even grew used to each other after a fashion, sometimes speaking to each other almost as though there were no resemblance at all, no childish memories in common.

Anthony made the computer-requirements plain in reasonably non-technical language and William, after long thought, explained how it seemed to him a computer might do the work, more or less, of a brain.

Anthony said, "Would that be possible?"

"I don't know," said William. "I am not eager to try. It may not work. But it may."

"We'd have to talk to Dmitri Large."

"Let's talk it over ourselves first and see what we've got. We can go to him with as reasonable a proposition as we can put together. Or else, not go to him."

Anthony hesitated. "We *both* go to him?"

William said, delicately, "You be my spokesman. There is no reason that we need be seen together."

"Thank you, William. If anything comes of this you will get full credit."

William said, "I have no worries about that. If there is anything to this, I will be the only one who can make it work, I suppose."

They thrashed it out through four or five meetings and if Anthony hadn't been kin and if there hadn't been that sticky, emotional situation between them, William would have been uncomplicatedly pleased with the younger—brother—for his quick understanding of an alien field.

There followed long conferences with Dmitri Large. Conferences with everyone, in fact. Anthony saw them through endless days and then they came to see William. Eventually, through an agonizing pregnancy, what came to be called the Mercury Computer, was born.

William then returned to New York with some relief. He did not plan to stay in New York (would he have thought that possible two months earlier?) but there was much to do at the Homological Institute.

More conferences were necessary, of course, to explain to his own laboratory group what was happening and why he had to take leave and how they were to continue their own projects without him. Then there was a much more elaborate arrival at Dallas with the essential equipment and with two young aides for what would have to be an open-ended stay.

Nor did William even look back, figuratively speaking. His own laboratory and its needs faded from his thoughts. He was thoroughly committed to his new task.

VII

It was the worst period for Anthony. The relief during William's absence had not penetrated deep and there began the nervous agony of wondering whether perhaps, hope against hope, he might not return. Might he not choose to send a deputy, someone else—anyone else? Anyone with a different face so that Anthony need not feel himself to be half of a two-bodied monster?

But it *was* William. Anthony had watched the freight-plane come silently through the air, watched it unload from a distance. But even at that distance he had recognized William.

That was that. Anthony left.

He went to see Dmitri that afternoon. "It's not necessary, Dmitri, for me to stay, surely. We've worked out the details and someone else can take over."

"No, No," said Dmitri. "The idea was yours in the first place. You must see it through. There is no point in needlessly dividing the credit."

Anthony thought: No one else will take the risk. There's still the chance of fiasco. I might have known.

He *had* known, but he said stolidly, "You understand I cannot work with William."

"But why not?" Dmitri pretended surprise. "You have been doing so well together."

"I have been straining my guts over it, Dmitri, and they won't take any more. Don't you suppose I know how it looks?"

"My good fellow! You make too much of it. Sure the men stare. They are human after all. But they'll get used to it. I'm used to it."

You are not, you fat liar, Anthony thought. He said. "I'm *not* used to it."

"You're not looking at it properly. Your parents were peculiar—but after all, what they did wasn't illegal, only peculiar, *only* peculiar. Anyway, it's not your fault, or William's. Neither of you is to blame."

"We carry the mark," said Anthony, making a quick curving gesture of his hand to his face.

"It's not the mark you think. I see differences. You are distinctly younger in appearance. Your hair is wavier. It's only at first glance that there is a . . . similarity. Come, Anthony, there will be all the time you want, all the help you need, all the equipment you can use. I'm sure it will work marvelously. Think of the satisfaction!"

Anthony weakened, of course, and agreed to at least help William set up the equipment. William, too, seemed sure it would work marvelously. Not as frenetically as did Dmitri, but with calm certitude.

"It's only a matter of the proper connections," he said. "Though I must admit that that's quite a huge 'only'. Your end of it will be to arrange sensory impressions on an independent screen so that we can exert—well, I can't say manual control, can I?—so that we can exert intellectual control to override, if necessary."

"That can be done," said Anthony.

"Then let's get going. I'll need a week at least to arrange the connections and make sure of the instructions—"

"Programing," said Anthony.

"Well, this is your place, so I'll use your terminology. My assistants and I will *program* the Mercury Computer, but not in your fashion."

"I should hope not. We would want a homologist to set up a much more subtle program than anything a mere telemetrist could do." He did not try to hide the self-hating irony in his words.

William let the tone go and accepted the words. He said, "We'll begin simply. We'll have the robot walk."

VIII

A week later, the robot walked in Arizona, a thousand miles away. He walked stiffly and sometimes he fell down. Sometimes he clanked his ankle against an obstruction, whirled on one foot and went off in a surprising new direction.

"He's a baby, learning to walk," said William.

Dmitri came occasionally, to learn of progress. "That's remarkable," he would say.

Anthony didn't think so. Weeks passed, then months. The robot had progressively done more and more, as the Mercury Computer had been placed, progressively, under a more and more complex programing. (William had a tendency to refer to the Mercury Computer as a brain, but Anthony wouldn't allow it.) And all the progress wasn't good enough.

"It's not good enough, William," he said, finally. He had not slept the night before.

"Isn't that strange?" said William, coolly. "I was going to say that I thought we had it about beaten."

Anthony held himself together with difficulty. The strain of working with William and of watching the robot fumble was more than he could bear. "I'm going to resign, William. The whole job. I'm sorry. It's not you—"

"But it *is* I, Anthony."

"It isn't *all* you, William. It's failure. We won't make it. You see how clumsily the robot handles himself, even though he's on Earth, only a thousand miles away, with the signal round-trip only a tiny fraction of a second in time. On Mercury, there will be minutes of delay, minutes for which the Mercury Computer will have to allow. It's madness to think it will work."

William said, "Don't resign, Anthony. You can't resign now. I suggest we have the robot sent to Mercury. I'm convinced he's ready."

Anthony laughed loudly and insultingly. "You're crazy, William."

"I'm not. You seem to think it will be harder on Mercury, but it won't be. It's harder on Earth. This robot is designed for 1/3 Earth-normal gravity, and he's working in Arizona at full gravity. He's designed for 400° C, and he's got 30° C. He's designed for vacuum and he's working in an atmospheric soup."

"That robot can take the difference."

"The metal structure can, I suppose, but what about the Computer right here? It doesn't work well with a robot that isn't in the environment he's designed for. Look, Anthony, if you want a computer that is as complex as a brain, you have to allow for idiosyncracies. Come, let's make a deal. If you will help me push to have the robot sent to Mercury, it will be six months en route and I will take a sabbatical for that period. You will be rid of me."

"Who'll take care of the Mercury Computer?"

"By now, you understand how it works well enough and I'll have my two men here to help you."

Anthony shook his head defiantly, "I can't take the responsibility for the Computer, and I won't take the responsibility for suggesting that the robot be sent to Mercury. It won't work."

"I'm *sure* it will."

"You can't be sure. And the responsibility is mine. I'm the one who'll bear the blame. It will be nothing to you."

Anthony later remembered this as a crucial moment. William might have let it go. Anthony would have resigned. All would have been lost.

But William said, "Nothing to me? Look, Dad had this thing about Mom. Alll right. I'm sorry, too. I'm sorry as anyone can be—but it's *done*, and something odd has resulted. When I speak of Dad, I mean your Dad, too, and there's lots of pairs of people who can say that: two brothers, two sisters, a brother-and-sister. And then when I say Mom, I mean *your* Mom, and there are lots of pairs who can say that, too. But I don't know any other pair, nor have I heard of any other pair, who share both Dad *and* Mom."

"I know that," said Anthony, grimly.

"Yes, but look at it from my standpoint," said William, hurriedly. "I'm a homologist. I work with gene patterns. Have you ever thought of our gene-patterns? We share both parents which means that our gene-patterns are closer than any other pair on this planet. Our very faces show it."

"I know that, too."

"So that if this project were to work, and if you were to gain glory from it; it would be your gene-pattern that would have been proven highly useful to mankind—and that would mean my gene-pattern as well. Don't you see, Anthony? I share your parents, your face, your gene-pattern and therefore your glory or your disgrace. It is mine almost as much as yours and if any credit or blame adheres it adheres to both of us. I've *got* to be interested in your success. I've a motive for that which no one else on Earth has—a purely selfish one, one so selfish you can be sure it's there. I'm on your side, Anthony, because you're very nearly me!"

They looked at each other for a long time. For the first time Anthony did so without noticing the face they shared.

William said, "So let us request that the robot be sent to Mercury."

And Anthony gave in. After Dmitri had approved the request—he had been waiting to, after all—Anthony spent much of the day in deep thought.

Then he sought out William and said, "Listen!"

There was a long pause which William did not break.

Anthony said again, "Listen!"

William waited patiently.

Anthony said, "There's really no need for you to leave. I'm sure you wouldn't like to have the Mercury Computer tended by anyone but yourself."

William said, "You mean *you* intend to leave?"

Anthony said, "No, I'll stay, too."

William said, "We needn't see much of each other."

All of this had been, for Anthony, like speaking with a pair of hands clenched about his windpipe. The pressure seemed to tighten now, but he managed the hardest statement of all.

"We don't have to avoid each other. We don't have to."

William smiled rather uncertainly. Anthony didn't smile at all; he left quickly.

IX

William looked up from his book. It was at least a month since he had ceased being vaguely surprised at having Anthony enter.

He said, "Anything wrong?"

"Who can say? They're coming in for the soft-landing. Is the Mercury Computer in action?"

"William was aware his brother knew the Computer status perfectly, but he said, "By tomorrow morning, Anthony."

"And there are no problems."

"None at all."

"Then we have to wait for the soft-landing."

"Yes."

Anthony said, "Something will go wrong."

"Nothing will go wrong."

"So much work wasted."

"It's not wasted yet. It won't be."

Anthony said, "Maybe you're right." Hands deep in his pockets he drifted away, stopped at the door. "Thanks!"

"For what, Anthony?"

"For being . . . comforting."

William smiled wryly and was relieved his own emotions didn't show.

X

Virtually the entire staff of the Mercury Project was on hand for the crucial moment. Anthony, who had no tasks to perform, remained well to the rear, eyes on the monitors. The robot had been activated and there were visual messages being returned.

At least, they came out as the equivalent of visual. As yet they showed nothing but a dim glow of light which was presumably Mercury's surface.

Shadows flitted across the screen, probably irregularities on that surface. Anthony couldn't tell by eye alone, but those at the controls, who were analyzing the data by methods more subtle than could be disposed of by unaided eye, seemed calm. None of the little red lights that might have betokened emergency were lighting. Anthony was watching the key observers rather than the screen.

He should be down with William and the others at the Computer. It was going to be thrown in only when the soft-landing was made. He *should* be. He *couldn't* be.

The shadows flitted across the screen more rapidly. The robot was descending—too quickly? Surely, too quickly!"

There was a last blur and a steadiness, a shift of focus in which the blur grew darker, then fainter. A sound was heard and there were perceptible seconds before Anthony realized that what he heard was, "Soft-landing achieved! Soft-landing achieved!"

The murmur arose and became an excited hum of self-congratulation until one more change took place on the screen and the sound of human words and laughter was stopped as though there had been a smash-collision against a wall of silence.

For the screen changed; changed and grew sharp. In the brilliant, brilliant sunlight, blazing through the carefully filtered screen, they could now see a boulder—clear, burning white on one side, ink-on-ink on the other. It shifted right, then back to left, as though a pair of eyes were looking left, then right. A metal hand appeared on the screen as though the robot was looking at a part of itself.

It was Anthony's voice that cried out at last, "The Computer's been thrown in."

He heard the words as though someone else had shouted it and he raced out and down the stairs and through a corridor, leaving the babble of voices to rise behind him.

"William," he cried, as he burst into the Computer room, "it's *perfect*, it's—"

But William's hand was upraised. "Shh. Please. I don't want any sensations entering except those from the robot."

"You mean we can be heard?" whispered Anthony.

"Maybe not, but I don't know." There was another screen, a

smaller one, in the room with the Mercury Computer. The scene on it was different, and changing; the robot was moving.

William said, "The robot is feeling its way. Those steps have got to be clumsy. There's a seven-minute delay between stimulus and response and that has to be allowed for."

"But already he's walking more surely than he ever did in Arizona. Don't you think so, William? Don't you think so?" Anthony was gripping William's shoulder, shaking it, eyes never leaving the screen.

William said, "I'm sure of it, Anthony."

*   *   *   *   *

The Sun burned down in a warm contrasting world of white and black, of white Sun against black sky and white rolling ground mottled with black shadow. The bright sweet smell of the Sun on every exposed square centimeter of metal contrasting with the creeping death-of-aroma on the other side.

He lifted his hand and stared at it, counting the fingers. Hot-hot-hot—turning, putting each finger, one by one, into the shadow of the others and the hot slowly dying in a change in tactility that made him feel the clean, comfortable vacuum.

Yet not entirely vacuum. He straightened and lifted both arms over his head, stretching them out, and the sensitive spots on either wrist felt the vapors—the thin, faint touch of tin and lead rolling through the cloy of mercury.

The thicker taste rose from his feet; the silicates of each variety, marked by the clear separate-and-together touch and tang of each metal ion. He moved one foot slowly through the crunchy, caked dust, felt the changes like a soft, not-quite-random symphony.

And overall, the Sun. He looked up at it, fat and bright and hot and he heard its joy. He watched the slow rise of prominences around its rim and listened to their crackling sound; and to the other happy noises over the broad face. When he dimmed the background light, the red of the rising wisps of hydrogen showed in bursts of mellow contralto, and the deep bass of the spots amid the muted whistling of the wispy, moving faculae, and the occasional thin keening of a flare, the ping-pong ticking of gamma rays and cosmic particles, and over all in every direction the soft, fainting, and ever-renewed sigh of the Sun's substance rising and retreating forever in a cosmic wind which reached out and bathed him in glory.

He jumped, rose slowly in the air with a freedom he had never felt, and jumped again when he landed, and ran, and jumped, and ran again, with a body that responded perfectly to this glorious world, this paradise in which he found himself.

A stranger so long and so lost—in paradise at last.

William said, "It's all right."

"But what's he *doing?*" cried out Anthony.

"It's all right. The programing is working. He has tested his senses. He has been making the various visual observations. He has dimmed the Sun and studied it. He has tested for atmosphere and for the chemical nature of the soil. It all works."

"But why is he running?"

"I rather think that's his own idea. If you want to program a computer as complicated as a brain, you've got to expect it to have ideas of its own."

"Running? Jumping?" Anthony turned an anxious face to William. "He'll hurt himself. You can handle the Computer. Override. Make him stop."

And William said sharply. "No. I won't. I'll take the chance of his hurting himself. Don't you understand? He's *happy*. He was on Earth, a world he was never equipped to handle. Now he's on Mercury with a body perfectly adapted to its environment, as perfectly adapted as a hundred specialized scientists could make it. It's paradise for him; let him enjoy it."

"Enjoy? He's a robot."

"I'm not talking about the robot. I'm talking about the brain —the *brain—here*." He pointed.

The Mercury Computer, enclosed in glass, carefully and delicately wired, its integrity most subtly preserved, breathed and lived.

"It's Randall who's in paradise," said William. "He's found the world for whose sake he autistically fled this one. He has a world his new body fits perfectly in exchange for the world his old body did not fit at all."

Anthony watched the screen in wonder. "He seems to be quieting."

"Of course," said William, "and he'll do his job all the better for his joy."

Anthony smiled and said, "We've done it, then, you and I? Shall we join the rest and let them fawn on us, William?"

William said, "Together?"

And Anthony linked arms. "Together, brother!"

☐ **THE 1974 ANNUAL WORLD'S BEST SF.** The authentic "World's Best" selection of the year, featuring **Sheckley, Ellison, Eklund, Pohl,** etc. (#UY1109—$1.25)

☐ **THE 1973 ANNUAL WORLD'S BEST SF.** This best of the year selection includes **Poul Anderson, Clifford Simak, Tiptree,** and many more. (#UQ1053—95¢)

☐ **THE CRYSTAL GRYPHON by Andre Norton.** The latest in the bestselling Witch World series, it is an outstanding other-world adventure. (#UY1187—$1.25)

☐ **HERE ABIDE MONSTERS by Andre Norton.** That parallel world was just off the map and out of legend. (#UY1134—$1.25)

☐ **GARAN THE ETERNAL by Andre Norton.** An epic adventure in lost worlds by the author of the Witch World series —never before in paperback. (#UY1186—$1.25)

DAW BOOKS are represented by the publishers of Signet and Mentor Books, **THE NEW AMERICAN LIBRARY, INC.**

THE NEW AMERICAN LIBRARY, INC.,
P.O. Box 999, Bergenfield, New Jersey 07621

Please send me the DAW BOOKS I have checked above. I am enclosing
$_____(check or money order—no currency or C.O.D.'s).
Please include the list price plus 25¢ a copy to cover mailing costs.

Name_____

Address_____

City_____State_____Zip Code_____
Please allow at least 3 weeks for delivery

The saga of Grainger of the Hooded Swan

☐ **THE HALCYON DRIFT by Brian M. Stableford.** A dozen worlds sought the secret of the Dark Nebula.
(#UQ1032—95¢)

☐ **RHAPSODY IN BLACK by Brian M. Stableford.** The light they sought could blind a hundred worlds.
(#UQ1059—95¢)

☐ **PROMISED LAND by Brian M. Stableford.** Where all is harmony and only man is vile. (#UQ1097—95¢)

☐ **THE PARADISE GAME by Brian M. Stableford.** If this world was Eden, in what guise was the snake?
(#UQ1121—95¢)

☐ **THE FENRIS DEVICE by Brian M. Stableford.** The Hooded Swan flies where no astronaut dare venture!
(#UQ1147—95¢)

☐ **SWAN SONG by Brian M. Stableford.** In a new universe is the first to arrive to be its God? (#UY1171—$1.25)

DAW BOOKS are represented by the publishers of Signet and Mentor Books, THE NEW AMERICAN LIBRARY, INC.

THE NEW AMERICAN LIBRARY, INC.,
P.O. Box 999, Bergenfield, New Jersey 07621

Please send me the DAW BOOKS I have checked above. I am enclosing
$_____(check or money order—no currency or C.O.D.'s).
Please include the list price plus 25¢ a copy to cover mailing costs.

Name_____

Address_____

City_____State_____Zip Code_____
Please allow at least 3 weeks for delivery

☐ **MARAUDERS OF GOR by John Norman.** The ninth book of the saga of Tarl Cabot. (#UW1160—$1.50)

☐ **THE BURROWERS BENEATH by Brian Lumley.** The Earth's original rulers are waking! A Lovecraftian epic. (#UQ1096—95¢)

☐ **THE WARRIORS OF DAWN by M. A. Foster.** A cosmic odyssey of man and superwoman. (#UY1152—$1.25)

☐ **FLOW MY TEARS, THE POLICEMAN SAID by Philip K. Dick.** Dick's first new novel in years—and one of his best! (#UW1166—$1.50)

☐ **2018 A.D. by Sam J. Lundwall.** The Seventies shocker in the tradition of **A Clockwork Orange** and **1984**. (#UY1161—$1.25)

☐ **THE R-MASTER by Gordon R. Dickson.** Russian roulette for the mind—with the winner taking the world. (#UY1155—$1.25)

DAW BOOKS are represented by the publishers of Signet and Mentor Books, **THE NEW AMERICAN LIBRARY, INC.**

THE NEW AMERICAN LIBRARY, INC.,
P.O. Box 999, Bergenfield, New Jersey 07621

Please send me the DAW BOOKS I have checked above. I am enclosing
$_____(check or money order—no currency or C.O.D.'s).
Please include the list price plus 25¢ a copy to cover mailing costs.

Name_____

Address_____

City_____State_____Zip Code_____
Please allow at least 3 weeks for delivery